Sisterhood of Jade

SAVING HIS HEART

BILLI JEAN

Saving His Heart
ISBN # 978-1-78686-077-4
©Copyright Billi Jean 2016
Cover Art by Posh Gosh ©Copyright September 2016
Interior text design by Claire Siemaszkiewicz
Totally Bound Publishing

Published in 2020 by Totally Bound Publishing, United Kingdom.

Totally Bound Publishing is an imprint of Totally Entwined Group Limited.

Totally Bound Publishing books by Billi Jean

Love's Command
Running Scared
Safe in His Arms
Catch Me If You Can
Trusting Love
Come a Little Closer If You Dare
The Promise of Love
Holding Fast
The Courage to Love

Sisterhood of Jade
Silver's Chance
A Spartan's Kiss
Midnight Star
Golden's Rule
Sorcha's Wolf
Eternal Embrace
Claiming a Demon's Heart
Gambling on Trouble
Hunter's Promise
Keeping his Heart
Saving his Heart
In her Dreams
A Siren's Song
Winds of Change

SAVING HIS HEART

Dedication

Sometimes we have to step outside the box to actually see clearly.

Chapter One

"The key to understanding is listening." Bryson settled his arms on the table once again to get the assembly of Vampires to listen to him. He might as well have been on the moon discussing cheese.

"Listen? Listen to what?" Aquinas, the second in command of the House, stood.

Gia, the true leader, watched him stand with a steadiness that spoke of allowing the Vampire more than perhaps she should. They were not bonded, but after centuries things didn't matter as much as they used to—*if* they were used to having their way in everything. Bryson was here to shake that authority, more precisely to take it from them.

"The Immortal Council is filled with witches and dogs, none of which listen to *us*." Aquinas touched his chest gracefully. His disdain was perfectly clear. "We have kept our House away from *connections* for centuries."

On Bryson's left, Warren snorted. Bryson hid his shock behind a mask of indifference, expecting

Aquinas to snap at the younger Vampire. *Rightly so, he's obviously not ready for dealing with ancients.*

Aquinas dipped his head slightly in acknowledgement. A condescending smile lifted his pale lips. "It may be true that at one time we strayed into dark dealings, but we have learned that these connections are of no benefit to us. Indeed, this *Immortal Council* is nothing more than warlocks attempting to rule all the other species. They will not listen to us mere Vampires—"

"Of course not, why would they?" Warren muttered again, drawing attention to himself.

Bryson steadied the younger Vampire with a hand on his arm. Now was not the time for the man to speak about his obvious hatred for ancients.

"The council is not run by one person. It is a *council* and all voices can be heard. Our degree of commitment to what the council deems important is, of course, limited by what Aidan thinks is best."

"And we should trust one man to decide this?" Gia spoke softly, but every one of the twelve Vampires present listened and turned to him to await his answer.

"Aidan is our king. He is our leader. This House has ignored that for far too long."

"Was it not Aidan who ignored *us* for centuries?" Aquinas peered up from his inspection of his nails with a sharpness to his otherwise lazy gaze. Bryson wasn't surprised as much as he was angered that now, at this meeting, the elder thought to question his lot in life. "Now that he wishes to take his father's role, we should bow to his wishes?"

Bryson's temper rose. "He turned his back for reasons you know well. But he is willing to guide us again." He steadied his anger and added, "I understand your misgivings, Aquinas, but, to gain his trust, you must trust him as well."

Aquinas sneered and turned to take his seat again, the noble with no time for the commoner sent to call him to heel. Little, if any, of the prejudices within the Vampire Houses had changed. Gia ruled this House much as she had for centuries. Her authority was given by her direct relation through blood to their forefathers. Such things still weighed heavily on all of the people in these Houses — even the lowest born would not stand against their royal leaders. Vampires like Aquinas and Gia fed off and scrutinized every single Vampire within their House so that they would never dream of attempting to change this sickening system.

That, among other even less savory traditions, was precisely why the Vampire Council was being formed. Aidan believed that, with more of a voice in their lives, Vampires would learn that royal authority meant nothing. The goal today was to take the authority from these two Vampires. Bryson wasn't fooled one bit into thinking they both weren't aware of that. They would fight this tooth and nail, but subtly, behind Aidan's back. But to that, Bryson had no answer. It was also the way Vampires had always acted. Serving their own desires above all others.

Gia stared pensively at him, then at her followers, and sighed. "He demands much from us."

"Such as?" Bryson held on to his temper with difficulty.

"Such as?" Aquinas repeated in a sarcastic sneer. He crossed his legs and tapped his long nails on his chair arms. The table was set up by the House, with Gia and Aquinas at the head, in chairs that resembled a bishop's cathedra. The seats were not quite thrones, but they were elegantly carved with crosses in the center high above their heads while the other plainer and less comfortable chairs were a blatant reminder that everyone else was not as blessed.

Christian, Warren and Jacob sat near him on his side of the table, while the Vampires of the House sat across from them. No one was seated at the opposite head from Gia and Aquinas because there were no chairs there. The lack was a direct slap in his face. As a captain of the king's guard, he should have been awarded a seat of honor. His lack of blood line was remembered, and would always be remembered, when dealing with the Houses.

"Aidan has left us, deserted us and we survived. Not only survived, but *flourished*. Our numbers are great. The age has provided us with freedoms we never possessed when his father, Aaron, ruled." Christian glanced at Gia who nodded to him.

"True," Bryson acceded. "Your rule has also led you to turn the name Vampire into a curse. More of our number side with the Death Stalkers than any other species. More death, more sickening horrors, have been done by Vampires and worse, sanctified by this *House*. Aidan has given you a choice." He paused and studied the disdain on Gia's porcelain face. He sat forward and rested his hands casually on the table. His king's guard signet ring was large and clearly visible in the glow from their extravagant chandelier. "If you do not wish his rule, then your choice is quite simple. Do not send an envoy to the council next week. Easy, you see?" He sat back and folded his arms. "You will be his enemy, but the choice is yours. I suggest you choose wisely, if you are able."

Gia stiffened, clearly offended. "You would dare to speak to me in this way?"

"I will always speak the truth, Gia. Take care how you address *me*." At her gasp of outrage, his anger rushed to the top. "Centuries of shit can't be brushed under the rug because you are high and mighty to be faced with your actions. That time is gone. Try to catch up before your entire House pays the price. Do you so easily forget what Aidan did to the House in Seattle? I think not." He slammed his fist down on the table hard enough to dent the wood. "Your response decides if your House will survive, or also become a public park for humans to enjoy summer strolls in the sunshine."

Silence, filled with the complete attention of everyone in the room, pinned on him. He narrowed his eyes in warning when Gia dared to open her mouth. She snapped it shut with a comical widening of her eyes.

"Nice one. Love your sense of diplomacy," Christian mumbled and sat forward. "What we're saying, is that there is still time for diplomacy, Gia. Bryson is allowing you that, but if you choose not to listen—"

"Then you will lose that chance. This is a wakeup call. Things have changed," Bryson bit out. "But perhaps Christian can explain it more…eloquently."

Christian laughed. "I doubt I will be more eloquent, Bryson. The time for that, I agree, has long since passed. But, my dear Gia, what Bryson is trying to explain is that after this House sided with Balrick and tried to annihilate not only Aidan, but also Alrick, King of the Lykae, Circerran, the head of the Jade Coven, and several top Vampire captains, not to mention aided in the creation of the changelings, it will take time to mend Aidan's trust in your ability to rule this House. Until then, we suggest you bide your time, say, for a few centuries, and let others make decisions for you."

Gia and Aquinas gasped almost as one and stiffened in their seats until they appeared more like statues of people rather than ancient Vampires. The Vampires across from them appeared to hold their breath.

"You call that smooth?" Bryson rubbed his mouth and sat straighter. "Two members of your House will sit on the Vampire Council. There will be two from each House, no more. You may choose, of course, but I would recommend you send ambassadors who can relay your concerns."

Aquinas lifted his nose higher. "Then we have nothing to gain."

"Your existence," Warren muttered. "Other than that, you're right, nothing."

Gia glared at Warren. "How dare you!"

"I'd dare a lot more."

Bryson steadied Warren with a hand on his arm. Again. The younger Vampire wouldn't have been his choice to bring along. He was a hothead, not ready to face ancients with their high opinions of themselves. He was also too new for Bryson to gauge where his alliances truly fell.

At Bryson's touch, Warren scowled. "Bryson, they'll never listen to—"

"Enough," Bryson snapped.

"Yes, listen to your elders, child." Aquinas laughed.

Warren's muscles flexed as he reached for his sword.

Bryson hardened his grip. "I said enough."

After a pause, the younger man nodded and relaxed his tense muscles. He would have to learn control, sooner rather than later, if he wanted to become a captain. Aidan needed to hear that the younger Vampire wasn't there yet. Not if he grew angry so easily. Not if he would go against Bryson's direct orders.

Bryson caught Jacob's eye and nodded to him. Jacob acknowledged him with a slow frown and sat forward, closer to Warren in case the young Vampire did something insane, such as attack the two ancients.

Bryson studied the pair at the head of the table as his men gained their feet as well.

"He is correct, Gia." Bryson stood. The meeting was done. "Aidan is firmly set on this council being a reality. I would not push where there is nothing to gain."

Gia sniffed. Aquinas narrowed his eyes.

Christian gave an exaggerated sigh. Jacob stayed silent, but he had enough age to know that dealing with the Houses was never going to go well. With a nod from Bryson, Jacob moved aside and gestured for Warren to precede him to the door.

Bryson turned back to the House, assured that even-tempered Jacob would keep Warren in line. "If you wish to continue, you will do as we demand. Next week we'll expect to have your ambassadors at the council or we will return, and you will be brought before Aidan to answer to him for your continued defiance of his authority."

"And you will lead this council of course, not Aidan." Aquinas also gained his feet. The words dripped with sarcasm, but Bryson was used to it.

"Yes, Aquinas, I will lead the council."

Aquinas took that like he'd swallowed sour lemon juice.

"Is there a problem?"

The Vampire bowed his head, hand over his chest. "Of course not, Bryson."

Gia rose to her feet, with Aquinas holding her hand. Graceful as a snake, she dipped her head ever so slightly. "We will send our envoys. It seems Aidan has left us little choice."

"I am pleased you were able to make a wise decision."

Bryson started walking, but Warren couldn't keep his mouth shut, "Other than facing the dawn."

Bryson narrowed his focus to the younger Vampire. Warren shook his sandy-blond hair out of his eyes. There was anger there, as well as something else. Jacob touched him on the arm and the two walked out ahead of Bryson down the hall.

"If I'd wanted a smart ass with me I would have brought Jaxon. In such situations, it is diplomacy that will win out, not throwing their mistakes in their faces."

Warren's shoulders stiffened, but he didn't acknowledge Bryson's dressing down otherwise.

Christian chuckled. "Jaxon wouldn't have come. He hates bullshit like this."

They walked on in silence, the Vampire sent to lead them out of the House ahead of them. Gia and Aquinas, of course, accompanied them, but were farther back, obviously more than ready to see the last of them.

"Are you really going to head this council?" Christian asked suddenly. "It sounds like hell to me. Give me a battle any day."

"Yes, well, we're trying to keep those to a minimum," Bryson snapped. His irritation was growing, not lessening. Dealing with the Houses was part of it, but he couldn't seem to find the cause of the deeper frustration he felt.

"Bloody hell we are. We still have plenty more of these to tame." Jacob snorted. He'd always been as bloodthirsty on the battlefield as he was calm off. His own dislike of the Houses was from his past, and the tortures he'd endured as a young Vampire. "If we even *can* tame them, that is."

Bryson agreed. This House was by far one of his least favorites. None pleased him, but Aquinas and Gia had a way of making his teeth ache. He'd feel better if every single ancient, save very few, were eradicated from the face of the earth. But he and Aidan were alone in that. And, at times, they did find decent, ancient Vampires. Christian was one of those rare ones.

A scent struck Bryson as he walked, stopping him in his tracks. *I know that scent.*

Christian barreled into him from behind. "Bryson? What the hell is it?"

"Wait." He took Christian's arm and scanned the corridor. Jacob was doing the same, Warren scowling at the walls now as well. The Vampires from the House halted, a sudden nervous presence at Bryson's back.

Jacob's dark brow furrowed. He shifted his silver eyes to the wall next to them and reached out as if to touch the stones. "There's something here."

Bryson couldn't move. He could barely draw his hand up to lay his palm against the tapestry. A heartbeat, small and barely making a sound, pulsed every few seconds against his hand. A rush of awareness, along with memories he'd suppressed for centuries, erupted and paralyzed him. *Isobel?*

"What is it?" Christian asked. "We should go. This House sickens me."

He didn't answer. He couldn't. *Isobel. She is…here.* With the realization, he switched his focus onto the ancients. Aquinas backed away from him. He grabbed the Vampire by his silk shirt and brought him in close to snarl, "Why do I suddenly want to rip your throat out, Aquinas? Do you know?"

The Vampire paled to a pastier white, but didn't fight back. His gaze landed on the wall then back on Bryson so quickly Bryson almost missed it. He didn't miss the faint, very faint heartbeat—*in* the walls.

Isobel.

She was here, entombed in the House. It was an old custom, one reserved for the most severe punishments.

"There is someone there." Jacob indicated the spot where Bryson sensed the same.

Bryson dropped Aquinas.

Aquinas stumbled back and raised his hands. "No, you are mistaken. It is nothing. Rats, I assume."

Jacob shook his head. "No. You have entombed a young Vampire here."

There was no need for more. Bryson drew his sword.

"Bryson!" Christian shouted and grabbed his sword arm. "What are you doing?"

"Let him go, Christian." Jacob dragged Christian backward.

"What's going on?" Warren yelled, drawing his own blade.

Bryson ignored them all. Urgency pulsed along his limbs. He ripped the tapestry off the wall. Behind it someone had placed newer, different colored stones from the flagstone floor to shoulder height. The texture was still ancient. *Six hundred, nearly seven hundred years ancient.*

He punched into the plaster with his sword hilt. Stones fell at his feet, but he kept pounding until he broke through to another wall, this one of round river stones mudded together into a hastily constructed wall.

"Stop at once! We demand you stop!" Aquinas shouted.

Jacob, Christian and Warren subdued the other Vampires. He ignored them. All his focus was centered on the faint heartbeat.

"Holy fuck. Is that... Is there really a *person* in there?" Christian cried.

There was more shuffling behind Bryson but he was unable to think past the rage choking him.

"Stop! I demand you stop. This is our House! We do what we feel is right to punish offenders of our rule!" Gia grabbed his arm, digging her nails in his flesh. "This is our business, not yours, Bryson!"

Bryson cocked a brow at the woman. There was no way she knew how close he was to ripping her head from her body. Something must have come through because she gasped and dropped her hand.

"This is your House, but these punishments are banned. And have been for centuries."

"Who is in there?" Christian muttered at his elbow.

"No one of importance. No one of..." Gia backed away from him.

It was spoken quickly, and was, he knew, untrue. The elder brushed her hair from her shoulders and straightened her pristine white gown. The high collar had her holding her head up, but Bryson believed she always had her nose in the air—the dress made no difference.

He seized her by her chin.

Her eyes flared wide, in outrage, he thought, not concern.

"Lie to me one more time, Gia, just once more, and I will end you and make it so your name is never uttered again. Not even in whispers."

She trembled under his hand—finally, she seemed to realize that he was the one to make or break her. The fall would be hard, and he'd warned Aidan of the rage and hatred Vampires like this would feed to others. For now, though, her existence hung on a thread.

He tightened his hold. "Who is it you have entombed?"

Gia's trembling increased. Her eyes widened so that he could see the telltale sign of her addiction to killing when she drank. The red glow was there, behind the contacts she wore to hide it, but the colored contacts slipped, revealing the bloodlust.

"Answer me. Name her. Now. Aloud."

Gia paused only a moment before she said, "Isobel Katrina Fernandez-Augustine."

A pin could have fallen and it would have shattered the silence. Gia's whispered words sounded louder than battle drums. Isobel Katrina Fernandez-Augustine, King Killer. Gia left off the epithet but it was there, hanging in the hallway.

Warren moved closer. "How long has she been entombed?"

"For six-hundred and seventy-five years," Bryson answered.

He dropped Gia. She staggered back, holding her neck. Aquinas wouldn't meet his eyes, neither would his men. Christian had eyes only for the bricks holding the woman who had killed Aaron, Aidan's father.

Jacob turned to him, frowning. "How did she get here? And how is it we were never told?"

"Does it matter?" he snarled past the pain slicing through the walls he'd built around his heart. "For her crimes, entombment isn't enough. Dig her out, Jacob. When you do, take her to Aidan. He will decide her fate. Anyone that plots against the king will follow." He faced the heads of the House. Both held themselves perfectly still. Gone was the arrogance of earlier, replaced with fear. "Do you understand me now?" he shouted.

He didn't wait for the replies that immediately fell from their lips as they went to their knees.

He shifted, escaping to his home, deep in the highest mountain peaks of the world. There, he released his rage, shouting to the heavens. It didn't ease the impotent fury. It rose to bury him underneath such renewed sorrow it even eclipsed the bitterness of what life had given him—a killer for a bride.

Isobel recognized the difference between living and dying. She knew the trap she was in, the long sleep that would keep her between these places—for an eternity if her tormentors so chose.

But she also knew that there, within the walls they'd built to hold her in, she was free. Free to dream and free to leave the world and its pain behind. Free to be someone she'd never been allowed to become. The ties of her obligations had been tight. The duty to her family, her lineage, had been far too heavy for her to shift even the slightest bit to gain a miniscule amount of independence. But here, in the in-between place, she spun dreams from the scattered memories of her life. She had once treasured the study of all that made the world beautiful—from the vast mountains, to the smallest flower sprouting up from the deserts' harsh, unforgiving landscapes. To live again, to have a choice, that was the biggest dream of all. *A family of my own…*

But she knew, even as she floated on the highest, most freezing air above the tallest peaks that she was merely dreaming. So, even as she did, she carried sorrow with her, coloring the fiber of each moment with its painful brush.

A sound entered the existence she'd built. The walls of her mind shivered. There had been no break in the constant sleep in so long. Not even mice ventured near her now. No insect crawled along her still form, nor sought to nest in her long hair. She couldn't recall the last infestation.

A sensation she'd nearly forgotten, air, touched her skin, prickling the long unused flesh with the shift of it along her bare arms before it disappeared. Tingles began again, so like the spiders that had crawled over her in those first few years. She tried to scream and yet no sound passed her dry, brittle lips.

Not again. Please, not again. I cannot stand the insects. Anything but not the insects, please. The vermin had nearly driven her madder than the constant struggle for freedom.

Ropes had once held her, woven in a pattern of spells she had been too weak to decipher. Over time those spells had wasted away, leaving only tattered bits of rope behind. But by then it had been too late. With no food, no blood, and drained to the point of near death, she had wasted away. When the time came for the ropes to fall, freeing her, she had no means of lifting her hands, even if she could have beaten the stone wall down to gain her freedom.

Another odd sound filled her existence.

After a time, she realized it might be…shouting. Men cursing, and the sounds of battle, not sharp with the ring of swords, but harsh with voices she heard deep within her being. A man's voice, rough with rage and loud with fury, drew her awake, fully, painfully awake.

No! Ignore it. Do not listen. Do not follow that path of madness.

No one will save you.

No one will hear you.

Even if you beg for release, no one cares.

Outside the warnings in her mind, the voice continued shouting. Other sounds intruded until it was too painful and loud to bear after so long with nothingness as her only companion. She raced for the deeper, blacker sleep that lay in wait under the third healing sleep and the fourth forgetful sleep. The fifth, it was named, and known only to a few of her kind.

It rose up like a lover to cradle her in its black arms. Dark, velvet dreams cocooned her, memories of walking through the woods at night, her brother a laughing, heavy shadow ahead of her as they raced over the lush, scented landscape.

Everything else fell away. Once again, she held her innocence without understanding how precious it was. Once again, she followed where her brother led. Once again, in her dreams, the world made sense.

When next she rose, sounds and sensations she'd gone centuries without assaulted her. *Wind. Air. Lights. Voices. People speaking in murmurs near me. Whispering things I should know.* Her skull ached. She dived down again, craving the soothing caress of her own mind, but was halted by a voice of command.

"Isobel. I order you to rise."

The words rushed along her skin and dug deep into her long-forgotten muscles to her bones. She refused, clutching the darkness to her. *I will not listen. I will not rise. I cannot. I am of no use. I can do nothing that I promised.*

"Isobel! I order you to rise."

Something warm, something rich, something *loathsome* was pressed to her lips. She struggled, fighting as hard to deny the offering of blood as she had the imprisonment. But it was not to be. Her heart beat faster, her body clenched, and she strained to gain more even as she refused the call. Her eyes flew open as blood saturated her parched lips.

As quickly as it was offered, she shoved it away and launched herself from it. *Never drink from another Vampire. Never allow connections!* The room was a bright, painful white. The floor was constructed of cold marble, too smooth against her long-unused bare feet. A man faced her, his terrible features set in rage, his eyes glowing silver-bright and filled with the authority she recognized on a cellular level. *My king. To him I owe my allegiance, my life.*

"Isobel. You will come to me. Now."

Obey. She stood, unable not to, and began putting one foot in front of the other. Her strength was gone. Her limbs were weak and, even with his blood coursing through her, she stumbled several times. Memories, filled with faces and people she had once known, rushed up from the past and crowded in her mind for purchase. She couldn't bear it. Each one wanted something from her. Each demanded she listen and obey. The inner torment continued as she walked to him, halting only when he raised his hand.

"Stop. Look at me."

Her head rose on its own at his command. She stared into the silver eyes of Aidan, the king of all Vampires. The memories solidified into faces shouting at her, mouths gaping, spittle flying. They made their demands, their curses, and when she denied them, once again she felt the burn of their whips and weight of their heavy chains.

Kill him. Kill him. Kill him. Kill every last one of his House. Kill them all and only then will our House be satisfied. Only then will we rise to where we should be. Only then will you be safe. Only then will your brother be returned to you!

She screamed silently even as she faced Aidan's heavy gaze. Within her mind, memories dragged her downward, clawing, grasping in a battle for leadership. *Brother! Aid me now! Aid me now so I may aid you.* There was no response. Just as there hadn't been all those nights before when she'd been caught and imprisoned. *He is lost to me. It's only my will that will save him. Is this my chance? Will he question me? I can save you, brother, if only they allow it!*

Aidan's gaze was strong, his mind as unbreakable as his control. No sound left his lips, no question was spoken, but she knew judgment had once again been passed. *'No one will ever ask you, Isobel, no one will care to ask. They will see a killer and nothing more. Take care, for what you choose will decide your fate for all eternity.'* As if those hated words were a prophecy, she stood, helpless to defend herself as her king passed judgment.

"You have been accused and found guilty of crimes against your people. You will burn, Isobel, and your ashes will be spread throughout this land so that you may never rise again."

Stillness settled in the room again. It spread, filling her with a sense of wonder. *Is it this simple? Were all the silent years simply a torture leading up to this? This fated ending?*

She lifted her hands, touching her mouth as a smile lifted her lips. *My lips feel the same and, yet, they are not mine. Nothing of me is mine. Not even my mind.* She laughed. All the years of suffering and hoping for a chance to save her brother disappeared, replaced by something so vast it overwhelmed everything else. The laughter built, spilling out, tripping and falling like the streams she used to play in as a child. *Surely, I am mad now.*

"Enough. Silence!"

His command was heard, but there was no stopping nature. She was a stream, flowing downhill to her death.

A sharp slap jerked her head to the side. Memories of more beatings surfaced, along with other, harsher punishments before her entombment. The laughter built, causing her pain, but spilled from her as all her dreams were crushed. What was left she didn't understand but couldn't control.

"Take her. She's clearly insane. Tie her to the post and leave her for the sun."

It's almost over. It's almost done. Soon, Jorge, soon, I, too, will be finished with this world. The pleasure at the thought diminished. *I have failed, then. You will never be free.*

Longings, hopes she'd once dreamed as a young Vampire sprang up like bright daisies in the fields she and Jorge used to run through. They had always pushed the limits placed on them from the night and waited, watching as the dawn had colored the sky. Jorge had always held her hand, smiling in joy at the colors of the sunrise.

The sunshine was always bright, but also deadly.

So too were the oaths she swore — oaths she would now be unable to fulfill.

'Kill them, Isobel, only then can I join her.'

'I will, Jorge. I vow it.'

And now, after all this time, I fail you, brother.

Pain, worse than any other, filled her mind, ripping into her chest and slicing deeply. Even as she allowed two Vampires to tie her in the Chamber of the Sun, it clawed at her.

It cannot end like this. Not after so many years. Not this way. More laughter bubbled up as she realized it could, in fact, end like this.

Chapter Two

Bryson paced his study. The wind whistled through the house, no doubt because he'd left the door to the outside open. He ignored the icy cold blast and focused on his steps. Twenty-seven to the window, twenty-seven back to the desk. Twenty-seven to the window, twenty-seven to the desk. To leave this room and walk back to shut the door would break the pattern, something he couldn't manage.

His phone buzzed, but it had several times already. He ignored it as he had every other time.

She will be gone soon.

She will be burned in the sun making this life as empty as it has always been.

Will always be.

Aidan and Allie, Jaxon and Joey, Circerran and Jack, Sorcha and Alex, Elsa and Jamie... All have bonded and created happiness where there was never more than a slice or two at the most during this existence some called life.

Twenty-seven. One. Two. Three. Four —

"Why are you upset, Bryson?"

He spun and nearly struck the small boy, Faolan, before he realized it *was* Faolan.

"How the hell did you get in here?" he shouted.

The boy only smiled then slowly frowned, and did the oddest thing the kid had done yet. He walked up to Bryson and hugged him. Not knowing what else to do, Bryson stood still, allowing the boy to tighten his small arms around his waist and press his face to his stomach. His warmth reminded him that he'd left the door open, allowing his home to turn frigid.

"Why are you here, Faolan?" He nudged the boy, needing to close the door and perhaps light a fire in the hearth. Such normal ideas felt alien against the pain of losing Isobel — again.

"You cannot let her burn. You will always be alone."

"Damn it," Bryson cursed, but only under his breath. He gently removed the child's arms from their death grip around his waist. If Faolan feared his size, he never showed it. From the first, the child had regarded him thoughtfully, with intelligence in his eyes that far outpaced his youth. Bryson felt protective toward the child, something that he couldn't quite understand, but chalked up to the boy's lack of fear in him. All his life, Bryson had been a warrior men feared, even the ancients. His strength alone was cause for some of this, but his rise to the top through his deeds on the battlefield had also caused it. He was also built like a warrior, not an elegant noble. Jaxon's jokes that he should have played rugby weren't far from what he'd heard all his existence. He would never be the thin, elegant Christian or Aquinas. He was built from common stock, solid, and thankfully, deadly. Faolan understood none of that. For some reason, Bryson found himself liking that about the odd little boy.

"Faolan, what have I told you about reading my thoughts?"

"Not to, but sometimes adults don't know when they're not being smart. Jamie didn't and I should have told him, but I didn't. I thought with you, I should. Aidan will burn her. I heard Jamie discussing it with Jaxon."

"Why was Jamie discussing it with Jaxon?"

"Jaxon got a call when he was at our house. Elsa heard some of it and was…not happy."

He could imagine that was an understatement. Elsa was new to the immortal world and, as of yet, hadn't officially met Aidan. She didn't understand their ways. Neither did Faolan. *Maybe that is why I enjoy their company.* Even Jamie, the Lykae who had bonded Elsa was better company, in his opinion, than most Vampires he now had to deal with.

"So I came to speak with you, Bryson. Before you made a mistake and Elsa grew angry with you."

Bryson sighed heavily. The boy was always doing something odd like this. "Elsa is too new to understand. If she grows angry with me, I will deal with her. So are you. These are adult matters. *Vampire* adult matters. Shouldn't you be at home?" He calculated quickly and realized it must be midnight in LA. "Why aren't you sleeping?"

"I wasn't tired. You should leave now. Before the sun rises and takes her from you."

"Faolan, enough."

"No." Faolan grabbed his arm and frowned fiercely. "You will not go to her?"

"I can't *go to* her. She killed Aidan's father," Bryson snarled. "You are too young to understand, but not too young to understand loyalty. Would you betray Jamie for someone else?"

Faolan frowned.

"My loyalty was given to Aidan, and, before him, his father, Aaron. I cannot forsake these vows simply because…" He shoved his hands through his short hair and turned away. *I want to save her. Because I want her. Isobel, why did you have to be a murderer?* "Enough. You should leave."

"I will free her, then—"

"Like fucking hell you will!"

Faolan's eyes rounded. Immediately Bryson drew back. *Calm down. Calm.*

Careful of the boy, he took Faolan by his hand and led him to one of the sofas near the hearth and had him sit. Sighing, Bryson crouched in front of Faolan so they were at eye level. The boy was unusual and unique in ways they were still learning. He met Faolan's gaze. Large, dark-brown eyes held knowledge and something else—pain, he supposed, but more was there, as if, inside Faolan, an older, wiser soul existed. He shook his head at the thought. "There is nothing you can do. Nothing. She killed Aaron, boy. That kind of crime isn't forgivable."

"Why did she do that?" Faolan asked, tipping his head to the side as if he'd been given an unusual puzzle. "*How* did she do it? Wasn't Aaron old and powerful?"

Bryson didn't answer. He had no answer. No one did. Isobel was a mystery to him. He had no knowledge of what made her do the things she'd done back then. He'd never even met the young, beautiful Vampire. *I should have. I should have gone to her and not worried what she would think of me, an uncouth common warrior, as her mate.*

"No one has ever asked her, have they? Why she did this," Faolan said, crossing his legs Indian-style. "Or how. Could *you* kill Aidan?"

"Faolan, sometimes there doesn't have to be an answer as to why, sometimes what is done is enough. Look at Samuel. We didn't want to hear his sick stories, did we?"

The boy seemed to consider that for a moment, then dismissed it. "She didn't torture anyone, did she?"

"No." He watched the boy shiver in the chill of the room and realized that nothing outside of shouting at the kid would make him leave. There was no reason to freeze him. Elsa would be angry with him if Faolan grew sick from a chill. He stood and filled the room with candles, lighting the hearth with a thought as well. "How did you find me here, Faolan?" *And why didn't my alarms sound?*

"You are easy to find. You didn't shut the door."

"So my alarms didn't know I was in or out."

"You *should* be out. It will be midday soon. I can go with you if you would like."

Bryson almost laughed but realized by Faolan's eager expression he was making a sincere offer. "Ah, you wish to read her mind? I doubt it's sane."

"No, probably not, but I could ask her why she killed Aidan's father. I would not accept she is guilty and not ask why."

Bryson turned back to the flames. He was exhausted, empty and, worse, knew the loss of Isobel would only increase his agony. Without her— "Faolan, it's best you go back to Elsa and Jamie."

Faolan watched the fire in the hearth. "I think you should go. It will be a mistake to let her die with so many unanswered questions. If I were you, I would go."

"Thankfully, you are not me." He set up barriers in his mind, ones he knew the boy couldn't see through. "It's not my place to go—"

"You are her mate. Isn't it your job to always watch over her? Shouldn't your loyalty be to her first, then to Aidan? Jamie says it is. Jamie says Elsa comes first, not Alrick. Derrick is clear on this as well. Is it not a Vampire way?"

"It is a Vampire way, but she—"

"How do you know she killed Aidan's father?"

"Enough, Faolan!"

He paced to the window and stared out at the expanse of mountains beneath him. The need to go to her was what was keeping him here. Six hundred and seventy-five years ago, he'd never known that misery came from longing for something that you knew you'd never have.

Now he knew. The past centuries had bricked him right alongside her. He'd been outside, but inside where he knew there could be happiness and more, he had only an incomplete feeling, an emptiness that never left him for long.

"If you don't go to her, you will always regret it."

Bryson sighed heavily. "If I go to her, Faolan, I will be going against my king, and my friend."

Faolan was studying him when he turned. The boy was young, but he had suffered much in his short life. "You are too close. You cannot see. But if you do not go to her, then you never will."

Bryson fisted his hands and steadied the need to leave, to rush to her side and save her.

Faolan got up and walked over, seemingly unconcerned that rage beat at Bryson harder than any other emotion he'd ever felt. Faolan wrapped his arms around him and hugged him as if Bryson was a good person.

"I love you, Bryson. I hope you don't let her burn."

Seconds later, Faolan was gone, his small cherubic face with the scars of his own torture vanished as if Bryson had dreamed the visit up. Bryson lifted his head and yelled at the ceiling, raging against something he didn't understand but couldn't stop wanting.

Isobel.

Before he could process what he was doing, he pulled free a cabinet by the window. It crashed to the floor, but what he needed was inside, buried where he'd put it over two hundred years before.

* * * *

The sounds around Isobel had grown dim, either from her awareness of her surroundings becoming clearer or her mind settling. Deep inside, where Isobel had buried any hope for her own survival, her own dreams, a wisp of sorrow, nothing more, tried to grow.

She buried it, ruthlessly extinguishing it. She would not beg for mercy.

Aidan had none.

Jorge, will I join you now? Will we forever roam this earth?

No answer came. This wasn't the same hall in which her brother had burned. This wasn't the small church set near the banks of a river that emptied into the sea. This wasn't the ground where he had been staked down, his murdered bride near him so the sun could erase his existence from this world.

His killers had made certain of it.

She knew, even in her dreams, that Jorge was unable to journey on.

Aidan did not choose the same death for me. Does that mean I will not see my brother again, or that I will?

She was held in a tower made of red bricks with a hole where the ceiling should have been. There were no stakes through her arms and legs, no whip marks on her back. No dead beloved at her side.

But there were chains. Heavy, painful chains on her arms that kept her bound to the wooden pole set in the middle of the room.

A shift in the air was her only warning that she was no longer alone. "So you will go meekly into death."

Aquinas.

At the whisper from the shadows, she kept her eyes closed. Revulsion, but also a sudden mad hope rose in her throat.

One of the council.

She didn't dare move as Aquinas walked closer. His footfalls crunched on the dirt and pebbles lining the cobblestones at her feet. Each step drew him closer. With each second her hatred burned brighter. She wondered how she hadn't gone up in flames even as she tensed her body in preparation. *This is a chance I cannot waste. There will be no other, I must not fail.*

Aquinas had been responsible for so much of her pain and anguish. Not all the council revealed itself to her, but him, she knew.

"A pity." He ran his foul hand along her upraised arm. "I had wondered if you wouldn't rise up and kill the son. After so long in your wall, I had expected more from you than simply going to your death like a lamb to slaughter."

His hand didn't stop at her arm, but traveled down to her breast, where he squeezed hard enough to have brought tears if tears were still open to her. "Indeed, Isobel, the sister of a betrayer, to come to this." His grip tightened even more painfully but she waited, until he either left or made a mistake.

He laughed harshly and released her.

"But you always were a self-righteous bitch, too high and mighty to obey your own blood-kin. That's why you were entombed, wasn't it? Because you wouldn't heel." He gripped her between her thighs. "I voted to breed you. Did you know? Perhaps after years of being fucked until you birthed us several babes, you wouldn't have been so high and mighty." He moved closer again, and she felt the brush of fabric on her legs as he circled her. "I can't tell you how many times I wanted to come to you, to see the mighty Dragon Guard brought to her knees. The mighty Isobel down on her knees sucking my cock like a good little bitch. Your brother was a useless whelp, unfit to wear the scarlet and black. It was no wonder he rutted with a base whore."

Another brush of his hand, this one indicating he was in front of her. The heat of his body hinted at a closeness he shouldn't have allowed. But, above all, Aquinas had always thought more of himself than anyone else ever would.

She didn't pause but swiftly drew herself upward with the chains, and just as fast, looped the metal links around his neck. He cried out but it was too late. She wrapped her legs around his hips. He fell hard against her, caught in her trap. She bit him. There was no mercy, no rush of accomplishment either as she sucked the life from him. His struggle was fruitless, but fitting as he grappled with a stronger, more intelligent foe than he had ever faced. Aquinas had fought in battles, but always behind the protection of his elite guard. Never had anyone ever caught him and proved that they were stronger.

She did. It devastated him more than if she had thrown him to the worst of the half-Vampires and let them have their way with him.

She drew hard, drinking deeply until his life was in the balance, until he was one sip away from death. Only then did she draw back. With the power of his ancient blood flowing through her starved body, she quickly gained her full strength. She jerked her arms and the chains holding them broke.

As soon as she dropped her legs, releasing him, the mighty Aquinas fell forward like a rag doll. His head slammed into the flagstones. She watched him struggle and crawl away on his stomach. He made mewling sounds, knowing there was no hope of escaping her but still attempting freedom. Intoxicating heat surged to life within her, drawing her power to the front even as she stepped away from the stake she'd thought she would die on. Walking barefoot over the rocky ground, she wound her way around his body until she stood at his head. Only then did she crouch down and grab his hair to pull his head up so he could meet her eyes as he fought to live.

His gray eyes were bloodshot, his expression one of terror and agony. "Isobel, mercy. I will give you anything, anything—"

"You have nothing I want, except your death."

"Isobel, have mercy, I never meant those things, I never wanted you harmed—"

"No? Well, Aquinas, I never wanted any of this, not you, not your *House*." She tightened her grip on his black hair, much as he had on her breast. "But you brought it to me, didn't you? To my brother, as well. Tell me, Aquinas, are you familiar with vengeance?" She dragged him back to the post. He sobbed and pathetically tried to pull away. She wrapped the chains around his arms to hold him to the post.

"Isobel," he gasped.

She tightened the chains on his throat and stopped his pleas.

"Vengeance can do more than provide a pitiful satisfaction. Your death, and that of your *council*," she spat the word and gained his full attention by drawing down the power of the heavens into her hand, "made one mistake, Aquinas."

His face was pale with ghastly splashes of blood marring his features. But she knew him. He would have done exactly what he'd said if *he* had been the one making the decisions. Thankfully, he hadn't been.

"You and your council let me live."

She pulled the lightning from where she'd held it, hitting him with every ounce of power she possessed. She would not allow the sun to burn him. He didn't deserve another second on this earth. As he burned, she watched his flesh crack and his blood bubble, then ooze through his skin, revealing his bones. With one more gasp, he burst into flames.

As his spirit lifted from him, she gathered it to her, drawing it in with her hand so she could swirl the mist of who he was into the air. When she knew she had every fiber of his essence, she flung her hands up and called the wind, scattering the ashes of his body along with the pieces of his soul.

"Accept this offering, brother. There will be more. Then you will be free."

Another presence drew nearer, one that startled her. The Vampire from where she'd been entombed. She knew the members of the council, all save one. But this man was not evil. As he drew nearer she misted, gaining strength to float above the ground and merge with the moss growing along the shelving high in the tower.

The trick had saved her more times than she could count, but this time, she sensed she may not fool the man who'd leapt from the hole in the ceiling. He landed perfectly without a sign of stress from having had to linger in the sun for seconds before dropping in. He stayed down on one knee, his head bowed, until, slowly, he stood.

At first she couldn't understand what he was doing here. She didn't know him – or from what she could see of him and sense of his aura, she didn't think she knew him. Suddenly, she realized, he was assessing the area. She hid deeper, aware that here was an opponent she may have difficulty besting.

As he walked toward the post, he turned his head, scanning the room as he drew a broadsword from the air. Many of the best warriors kept their blade at the ready, in a place only they knew, and thus could call to it with the simple power of their mind. This man was certainly a warrior, broad-shouldered and heavily muscled. He would have stood in defense of their people under even the most deadly attacks.

He walked slowly and carefully to where she had been chained. When he reached the post and empty chains he touched the wood and bowed his head. "Isobel?" As he whispered her name, anguish and disbelief colored his tone. She almost slipped from her hiding place. *Who is this warrior? Why would my death matter?*

"How is this possible? Who has...?" He knelt again and touched the ground where Aquinas had left a footprint in the dirt. It was odd, but she sensed something familiar about this ancient, though, even as she thought it, she wasn't certain if that were true. He had yet to turn and face her, but his profile was chiseled as if from the marble the Greeks adored.

He was also strong, with broad shoulders and long-fingered hands he slid over the cobblestones. All at once he cursed foully and stood, searching around him for something it appeared he thought should be there.

Me?

"Aquinas!"

If her name fell from his lips with pain, Aquinas' was growled in rage. *He is good. Very, very good if he can sense the tiniest partial of Aquinas remaining.*

"I will rip your heart out and feed it to you!"

He spun and punched the pole, cracking it in half so that it fell, revealing large sharp splinters of paler wood from the core as it dropped to the ground. More curses fell from his lips, ones she had never heard, but understood must be reflective of the rage he was experiencing.

At the idea of my death?

She thought he would race off, but instead he seemed to gather himself. His chest and shoulders rose and fell with each of his labored breaths. He clenched his hands into fists at his sides. She waited, uncertain what to think. He began studying the room again, slowly touching a stone or a bit of wood here, a rock there, tracking, she realized. *Can he sense what I did?*

"Did you kill him? Did you survive? But how?" he whispered.

He shook his head. The light had already gained entrance to the hole above them. She waited, anxious to see his face for the first time. He had neared where she hid, but with another curse, he glanced up at the sun drawing near.

No, not yet. Turn! Turn!

He didn't. He disappeared, leaving her alone, and oddly...worried.

Chapter Three

"Bryson! Why the hell can't you — Oh, fuck! Bryson, what the hell, man?" Jaxon shouted.

Bryson rolled his head to the side, seeing Jaxon rushing toward him. He lifted his hand to ward him off, but his arm felt dull and far off as if someone else had hold of it. He managed to wave it and groaned out, "Go away."

"Oh, fuck, man, what is this?" Jaxon picked up the black box his opium had safely been stored in for centuries and gave him a fuck-me look. A small whiff of the powder floated to him. The call of more was strong. It would keep him under for years if he were careful.

"Bryson?"

Isobel was gone, which meant he hadn't been in time to rescue her. He hadn't needed to. She'd saved herself and, if he had to guess, she'd done it by killing Aquinas.

Another death to lay at her feet.

His anguish was only slightly stronger than the righteousness he experienced at the thought of Aquinas gone from this world.

Already I side with her. Already I betray my king.

Bryson's mouth grew dry. The sudden, urgent need for more of opium's swift release from his pain rose, terrifying in its intensity. He shoved himself away from Jaxon and, more importantly, the opium.

"What…night is this?" he asked.

"I thought you gave this up years ago. Why would you start down this crazy street again? Have you lost your mind?"

"Fuck you." Bryson made it to his feet painfully and dug out his phone. "Go away. I'm not in the mood."

Tuesday. Last night she'd escaped. Only one day had passed.

Where are you? How did you escape so easily?

Jaxon didn't go away. "All right, so this is *not* what I expected to find. And can I just say, I am so fucking glad I didn't bring Joey on this fun trip to the fucking freezing lands. Did you even light the fire? You're lucky you didn't freeze into a Vampire Popsicle."

The room wouldn't stop spinning but he didn't sense it was any colder than his heart. He laughed at the miserable thought.

"I fail to see the humor, man. You need to get your shit together!"

"Fuck —"

"I know," Jaxon snapped and threw his arms out dramatically. "Fuck you. I got that, but you know what? You can't. So, here's the deal." Jaxon pointed his finger like a gun at him. "Aidan wants you. So you're going to have to grow a bigger set of balls and — "

"I already possess a big set of balls, Jaxon," Bryson muttered, trying to get his head to slow down and focus. The room buzzed in an unsteady kaleidoscope of dark and light. He found Jaxon's outraged face in the middle of it and latched onto his arm. "You know that."

"I do *not* know the size of your nuts, man." Jaxon's voice rose octaves with his denial. "And would you sit down before you fall down?"

He didn't dignify that with an answer. Instead he made his way, unsteadily, after dropping Jaxon's arm, to the mantel and held on for dear life. The room still spun, but at least his legs were solidly placed. A moment later he fell backward and crashed into the couch, falling to the side of it to land on his ass.

"Damn, you are in sorry, sorry shape. Here, drink before you embarrass me." Jaxon shoved his bleeding wrist under Bryson's nose, a foul, dirty trick. Blood, the rich, ancient blood only the ancient possessed, was all Bryson could comprehend. It roared at him through the dizzying array of prisms clouding his vision, hijacking his every cell and forcing his fangs down. The drop preceded the grip he took on Jaxon's arm. Instantly, he plunged into Jaxon's firm flesh and drank, pulling long drags until he was shoved off and away.

One breath, two, and the spell of the opium receded. He took another breath, then another, testing the air for a trace of her. She still lived, but...where? *Where are you? How did you survive?*

"Ah, damn, I forgot how hard you hit it." Jaxon licked his wrist closed then settled his fists on his hips. "Now, you want to tell me what the fuck is going on?"

"No. Why are you here?" He rose to his feet, a bit unsteady still, but managing to gain his balance more easily by the second. Still, he sat on the sofa, not entirely certain he wouldn't end up back on the floor. *I've got to go. Got to find her. She isn't safe.* "Better, don't tell me. Just get the fuck out," he said when Jaxon grumbled something about ungrateful friends.

"Man, you are cranky when you rise. Look, Aidan needs you. Didn't you hear me? And what is up with this?" Jaxon kicked the cabinet. More opium, in velvet bags, toppled out of one of the half-open drawers.

Bryson shoved Jaxon back before he'd even registered he'd stood. "It's not your business is what it is." He picked up the mess and placed the bags back in the cabinet and shut the doors. His head swam when he straightened, but he was gaining his feet again.

"Right. Not my business. Seriously, I actually don't *want* to know. Whatever gets your rocks off, man." Jaxon walked to the couch and paused in the process of sitting down. "Faolan's been here? Why was the boy here?"

Faolan. If not for Faolan I wouldn't have gone to her. Wouldn't have found her already gone. Why did Aquinas come to you?

Jaxon snapped his fingers loudly. "Earth to Bryson?"

Bryson focused back on Jaxon. The Vampire would not let up until he answered, Bryson knew from years of experience. He'd known the tall, black-haired smart ass for more centuries than he liked to remember. But through it all, Jaxon had stood by his side. *Will I betray him now, for you?*

"Why was the kid here?"

"Faolan likes me." Bryson lifted a shoulder. "He visits."

"Yeah? Well, I sure hope he didn't see this." Jaxon waved at the floor where Bryson had fallen after the dose of opium had hit. "Not sure how to explain to the kid his hero has a drug problem." Jaxon rested his feet out in front of him as if he were going to stay and crossed his arms over his stomach. "I mean, how do you begin that conversation? So, what did you do last night?" Jaxon mimicked a kid's voice. In a deeper tone he went on, "I drank some ancient opium I'd saved up for centuries and wound up on the floor, drool hanging out of my mouth."

"Fuck you, and would you get the hell out? It's not like I have a drug addiction."

Jaxon snorted.

"I also don't want company right now," Bryson snarled.

"Really? I wouldn't have guessed that. Man, I can't believe you still do that shit. It's like I suddenly walked in on you stroking off to midget porn. I just don't see that shit making sense to you."

Bryson turned away and walked to the windows. Jaxon was never going to leave until he'd dug down and tried to figure Bryson out. In his own way, Jaxon was as hard to deal with as Faolan. It might have saved his buddy the effort to know that he couldn't figure out what the hell he was doing either, but he kept that to himself. He could have saved his buddy the trouble. Bryson couldn't figure out what he was doing. How could Jaxon?

The moon was high, painting the snowy mountains in its silver light beneath him and somewhere—possibly—Isobel was looking up at the same moon.

Or murdering another Vampire under it.

"Why did you come here? You hate this place. It's one reason I chose it instead of my other homes." High mountains were most Vampires' favorite haunts, but Jaxon had never liked the cold or the snow. Bryson knew why and cut him slack over it, but not tonight. Tonight was different. "I had hoped you would avoid it like the plague."

Another snort. "I can see that. Well, sorry to disappoint, but we have an issue."

Bryson sighed, fogging the glass. "An issue?"

"Isobel has escaped."

Every muscle tightened until his bones ached from the strain. He relaxed his fingers, one by one, from the fists he'd clenched. *Now the lies begin.* "How is that possible? Wasn't she too weak to move, let alone escape?"

Jaxon sighed heavily. "Yes and yes. But that's just it. She's gone. She broke the chains, tied someone else down in her place, and is now who knows where."

So many times in his existence he'd been disappointed, given situations where tough calls and even harder decisions had to be made with less than a second of thought. Where sacrifices were demanded and had to be given. He'd never balked. But never before had he craved something for himself, someone, above all else, that he wanted and could have.

Her.

The trouble was, as much as he wanted her, he wanted to honor the bond that held this man, and Aidan, close. *Respect. Honesty. Integrity. Do these mean so little to me now?* These were the markers of a true warrior and friend. *Will I lie for you? Forsake everyone I once held as a companion to simply have you?*

"It seems impossible," Jaxon muttered. "She was weak, chained."

"It does seem impossible. When that occurs, perhaps it *is* impossible. Did you look over the place yourself?"

"Warren did. He was the one that reported her missing and someone else dying in her stead. Christian double-checked the kid's facts. She's free. And, worse, it appears she's more than willing to start killing again."

Bryson kept silent, damning himself with his own omission.

Warren. He latched on to what Jaxon was saying. *Why did Warren go there? Did he sense my presence? Or did he find Isobel's and follow her trail?*

Bryson fisted his hands again until his short nails bit into his palms. *He'll have to get through me first.*

So I've made my choice?

Confusion and anger were his only answers.

Chapter Four

Nothing made sense. Not the noise, not the people, not the world spread out below Isobel.

She gripped the ledge she'd crouched on and watched, unable to process what she saw. But at least she could make sense of things more than she had a week ago. Everything was so foreign she couldn't grasp that this was the same world and not some mysterious land that existed on another plane.

She tensed as two fast-moving cars nearly collided. The use of horses was no more. Even the people who walked didn't really walk as they had when she'd last been among them. She watched one young human on one wheel that took him down the street as if he hovered on the paving stones. The others, who did use their legs, did so with long, quick strides, their heads bent to something they held in their hands as they hurried to wherever it was they needed to go. The cars, the vehicles that were designed to hold many, held one. The metal cars screeched to a halt abruptly and fought to win a race she couldn't see an ending to.

There were women, there were men, there were even small children, but all of them seemed shiny, clean, yet dressed in clothing that mystified her. Men wore long trousers, women and children did as well, but some of the women wore gowns that seemed to reveal more than they covered. Some of the men wore their trousers so short they came to just below their knees and hung down low enough in the back for other garments they wore under the trousers to show against their bare flesh. Many men wore no upper garments at all, instead decorating their skin with a multitude of designs. Women wore such short skirts that the entire length of their legs was revealed, up to where the skirt hid the bare minimum required to conceal their sex. They too were covered in inked artwork, some so heavily that an entire arm, shoulder, or leg was lost under the designs. The more color they inked on their skin, the less clothing they wore.

The displays of flesh stunned her. It was as if these people had shed confinement, flying free like butterflies from the cocoon of clothing she had always worn. For her, it had been layer upon layer of elaborate silks and lace, piled on with warmer layers of the finest wool and softest spun fabrics of their times. All of that had then been covered by leather and finally a cape of darkest purple. As a young Vampire, she could recall not being able to sit properly because of the pinch of her clothing. When she'd grown into her proper age and rank, she'd been forced to stand for hours, weighed down by the clothes of her order.

Yet here, in this day and age, the children wore free-flowing, loose clothing that appeared to be made for comfort and little else. The soldiers — the warriors of this time — wore nothing more than shirts of odd colors and belts that held weapons.

In the days since her rising, she'd learned much, but the more she discovered the more alien the world became. She'd picked up quickly that her gown of dark-red silk drew more attention than she wished. She'd been forced to take what she thought was normal for this age from a large, indoor market with clothing of all styles and sizes.

Like many of these women, she'd chosen trousers. Yet their material was soft and stretched with her movements, conforming to her size so that she, too, could move freely. The long, flowing blouse she'd found reminded her of the ones her brother had worn. She had chosen a pale, almost white one. With it she'd found serviceable boots of the finest leather — in bright blood red. The footwear had been displayed in a window on an odd plastic creature with no face, yet had hair, arms and legs. She had found they fit to her size exactly. With them, she had discovered stockings so comfortable she wore two pairs. Over it all, she had chosen a soft jacket of dark green that hung loosely down past her thighs. She'd tied up her long black hair into a braid. Dressed this way, she had walked unseen through the hordes of humans, learning more about this age than she could process. Each day, she had returned to her hiding place, and there she had tried to understand the changes brought on by the passage of time.

Of the remaining Vampires she needed to kill, she'd had no sign.

Until tonight.

On this rising she sensed them, or one of them. Gia.

Her scent was on the air, as if she'd entered London while Isobel had slept during the daylight hours.

She had heard rumors. Long ago, when she'd been a child, the elders had told of ancient Vampires who could move in the day as long as the kiss of the sun did not touch their skin. Since her rising, she had stayed awake past dawn, sometimes lingering even longer than that. Jorge had always tested the dawn, but they had only been able to see the first blush of the sun as it had hit the fields and woke the world. Then, as if its rising brought on their rest, they had both always drifted off, back to their homes, to sleep the daylight hours away.

She studied the building below her, considering the idea that with age came more freedom. She was ancient—now. More than six hundred years had crept along while she'd slept.

Can I move during the day, as well? I have stayed awake, but I have always been at my home, or nearing it.

A door opened below her, and she scanned the man coming out.

Tall, broad-shouldered with brown hair. A Lykae. He paused, but the Vampire with him pulled his arm and they continued on down the street. A couple.

Shocked, she watched them as they walked, hand in hand, until they were out of sight.

It is good. The woman is...more. Their bond is strong, smelling of past pain, but of love. Was this coupling now common? A slice of pain came with the thought.

The sudden scent of her prey stopped the regrets. She stood, balancing on the ledge as the surety of Gia drawing near settled over her flesh. Gia hid, but she had to know that nothing and no one would save her.

Isobel stepped off the high-rise and landed softly on the pavement thirty-odd stories below.

The door was locked, spelled even, but she ripped it from the wall and tossed the metal behind her. Once inside, she encountered more spells, but she tore through them as she would spider webs. Just as easily as the entrance, they gave way as she passed. Doors faced her on either side of a long corridor, so many she didn't bother to count.

A spell? She shoved the illusion away and stepped through it as you would a window. A heavy, carved wooden door drew her attention. She pulled it off its hinges.

Gia.

Her face registered shock, then fear, but by that time it was too late. Gia tried to move back, to shift, to do anything, but there was nothing she could do. Her blonde hair flowed, free and straight as ever, past her hips. The gown she wore was a dark burgundy, revealing the soft curves of her bosom in a plunging neckline that only stopped at a point directly above her navel. The length of the fabric touched the floor, falling longer at her back so when she walked, the graceful folds would trail after her the way she preferred men to do.

Jorge never had.

"Isobel. Think what you do. I am of the —"

Isobel took her by the neck and shoved her down. Gia's eyes bulged and she grappled awkwardly with her hands, as if she were unsure how to defend herself.

"Isobel, please, you must understand. We thought only to spare you the king's fury."

"Do you believe lies will fall on my ears as truth?"

Gia gasped and shook her head, or attempted to.

"Enough. You will die, Gia. You thought to punish Jorge for not choosing you, but it is your death that will aid me in freeing him to once again be with his beloved."

"No! No, you cannot."

Isobel allowed her fangs to drop. "You are wrong. He will be freed." She pierced Gia's hated flesh. She didn't drink. She ripped the woman's throat out and, when she sobbed a desperate breath of her name, Isobel tore her head from her body.

Not satisfied, she called forth the power of lightning and brought it down through the building and into Gia's shuddering body.

Just like Aquinas, flames erupted along flesh. Through the smoke, Isobel watched Gia lift her hand, beseeching for mercy even on the cusp of death.

"There is no mercy for what you did, just as there was none for Jorge or his bride."

A flare from behind Isobel brought agony to her shoulders, then her side, but she held her power in her hand and flung wind at Gia's burnt remains. She swept them up and shoved them out into the chilly air of London. With another bolt of lightning she turned and struck the witch at her back, knocking her aside, but not killing her.

Killing was for her brother's murderers.

Satisfied that Gia would never rise from the ashes she blew across the land, Isobel shifted, leaving through a spell that sought to trap and keep her. She struck it hard, snapping it in two as she flew out and away. She didn't stop until her trail was invisible, hidden by too many paths. Only then did she drop to the ground and to her knees.

Pain, not satisfaction, ripped through her. Jorge was gone, forever beyond her reach, and nothing she did now would bring him back.

But it will free him.

She lifted her head and sought the source of her surety. The texts she'd left open on the stone bench caught her, aiding her in quenching the pain. *Every time I take one, will I relive your death?* The thought chilled her, for her brother hadn't died quickly and cleanly. Gia and the king's council had made certain of that.

* * * *

"How the hell did this happen?" Torque raged. He brought his fist down on the council table and the entire thing shuddered. Next to him, Beauty called him back with a hand on his arm. She'd suffered from the backlash Isobel had flung at her, but she was alive.

The thought that Isobel had enough sanity to hold back a killing blow should have soothed Bryson's fears, but it only made him even more anxious. *How many lies will I have to spin for you?* Already he had lied to Jaxon, Aidan, and even Jamie when he'd called, at Elsa's urging, to find out what was going on with the rumors the couple had been hearing. Thankfully, Faolan had been absent this last week. He feared that lies wouldn't work with the child. He *knew* lies wouldn't work with the child.

Even now, he barricaded his mind knowing that Beauty could sense his turmoil, perhaps more if he let his guard down. It hadn't been that long ago he'd aided

Torque and Beauty and saved the life of Sydney, a witch who'd been on the wrong track. Beauty had worried he'd bind Sydney to him. He nearly laughed at the memory. The witch was beautiful but didn't hold a candle to Isobel. Although Sydney had disappeared along with her brother, so perhaps she *was* as insane as Isobel.

But is Isobel insane? She hadn't killed when she could have. Everyone who had tried to stop her was alive. The only one who wasn't was even now merely a bit of ash on the wind Isobel had brought to London. The high gales were being discussed on the news as the strongest sudden storm in recorded history.

"It's a great question," Circerran muttered, dabbing at her bloody nose. She'd been struck harder than Torque and Beauty. "She's damn good." Circerran laughed and dropped the tissue she'd been using. "That kind of good isn't easy. That kind of…well, hell, I'll just say it, *determination* isn't found every day. Why do I sense there is more to her story than she killed Aaron, Aidan's father, and was entombed for six hundred and seventy years for it?"

"Six hundred and seventy-five," Jaxon muttered.

Circerran gave him the famous death stare.

Jaxon merely shrugged. "Facts are important to get straight."

"Well, give me this super important fact, would you? How was it that she was entombed without you guys knowing it? Why didn't Aidan do the entombing himself, or better, the die by sunlight himself, back then?"

Jaxon shot him a frown, but Bryson leaned forward anyway. Jaxon had brought him here after the attack, he could damn well let him tell these people what they were dealing with.

"Aidan was…out of sorts after his father's death. It also took us time to find him, and, by then, we had no idea where she was, or if she lived. We don't monitor the Houses. Or we didn't." He held up a hand and Circerran sat back, gesturing for him to continue. Torque was just as pissed off. Beauty waited, the only calm in the storm that Isobel had left behind. Isobel had entered the Immortal Council's stronghold as if the protective spells and barriers meant nothing. That kind of thing came with questions, hard questions he and Jaxon had avoided.

Jaxon was tense, Joey quiet, but watching them both closely. He had Aidan's approval to work with the Immortal Council, but even he knew that didn't include discussing their secrets.

"Go on. Explain because I *lent* you." Torque pointed a finger at him like a gun, something Bryson secretly thought he got from hanging out with Jaxon too often. "I lent *Aidan* a room to have your *Vampire Council,* and I end up with our protections down, the doors ripped open, and a dead—no scratch that—a *destroyed* Vampire, and people bloodied by her entrance *and* exit."

"But not dead." Joey sat forward and gave Jaxon a steady stare when he tried to stop her. "I think we are looking at this all wrong. Even if my lovely husband doesn't agree, I see this as one thing. A strike. She killed one person. Why? That's what I think is important, not that she broke through the protections or how Cir got a bloody nose, no offense, Cir. But come on, you've gotten worse in the practice ring. Right?"

"I don't appreciate a Vampire walking through my spells like they don't exist, Joey. That's not done."

"Only because we're too polite." Jaxon popped his gum.

Circerran paused with the tissue back at her nose. Bryson groaned and hung his head.

"We know that, but they hold for a *little* while," Torque stressed. "Look at Balrick. We're holding him."

"Balrick is a freak. He doesn't count." Jaxon dismissed the crazy half-Lykae, half-Vampire with a wave of his hand. "If a Vampire wants past spells, then eventually those spells won't hold. She might have been doing whatever, beating against them or whatever you call it for a while then just walked in."

"I thought you had to be invited." Beauty smiled and shrugged. "Right?"

Joey returned the grin. "I think what Jaxon means is this place isn't owned by one soul. This is a public, if secret, establishment. Can you imagine us having to ask to go inside at McDonalds?"

"Do you eat McDonalds?" Circerran asked, clearly getting side-tracked.

"Let's focus, shall we, ladies?" Jack could always be counted on to stay focused. If Circerran minded his redirection, she didn't show it. The couple were a solid match. *Something I will never know.* "So, if Isobel can walk in here and do damage, why did she only kill a visiting Vampire?"

"Right, see, Jack understands me." Joey relaxed back in her chair. "Why just the one?"

"I understand you," Jaxon growled jealously.

Joey gave him a frosty glare that Jaxon ignored and curled her up closer.

"Good point. Why was that?" Torque settled his gaze on him. In it Bryson knew that the time for coming clean was now.

Jaxon sighed heavily. "Be my guest, fill them in." Joey gave him a soft slap to his chest, but Jaxon took her hand so he could kiss her fingers. "It's not a tale without tragedy. Let Bryson tell it. He's the better man at this kind of thing."

The absolute lie in that was hard to swallow. Bryson had to fist his hand under the table and try to gather his thoughts before he could speak. Isobel's scent was strong, sweet to him, but filled with rage, and something that confused him — pain so deep it was truly the definition of sorrow.

Why sorrow? Why, when you again leave behind a bloodbath in your wake?

"Bryson?" Torque called. "This has touched us. We need to hear why so we can stop her from doing the same thing again."

"You all understand that she is the Vampire responsible for the murder of Aaron, Aidan's father. But what you don't understand is that she didn't merely kill Gia. Killing a Vampire is difficult. Any immortal, as you know. What you aren't aware of, perhaps, is that to truly kill a Vampire, you must first drain them of blood, burn them with fire, and spread their ashes so that not one iota of them remains."

Joey glanced at Jaxon and Bryson could sense her unease. Jaxon had not told her this.

"Why would she want to kill Gia, then?" Beauty asked.

"Her reasons are simple. Her brother was put to death for crimes against his people by Aaron and a council of Vampires. Gia was heading that council."

It made sense. He'd been told all he knew of what happened to Aaron from Gia. She had also told him she was head of Aaron's appointed council. Now, none of what happened back then was making sense. He'd also been told Isobel had disappeared — something few Vampires could accomplish with Hunters after their trail. But she hadn't died. He would have known that, and so, as the years passed, he had begun to believe she had disappeared — for good. *Why did I never question Gia on this? Why did I never consider she was imprisoned?*

"So you believe she will come after the remaining members, until all suffer the same fate?" Beauty asked quietly.

Jaxon shifted in his chair. "Unless the ash we found in the Chamber of the Sun is one of those council members."

"The Chamber of the Sun where she was supposedly chained and too weak to save herself?" Circerran clarified.

"That's the place." Jaxon cracked his knuckles.

Circerran's gaze sharpened.

Jack cut off whatever Circerran was going to say by leaning forward. "If she was there, left chained to a post so the sun would kill her, then there is little she could have done to free herself. Not if she was entombed as long as you say and only given enough blood to wake her." Jack waited until Bryson nodded then went on. "Another person — Vampire — came into that room. Now why is that, I wonder? I can't help thinking that having her helpless, about to die, but no longer entombed in a wall for centuries, was too good an opportunity to pass up. Someone wanted to gloat. What better way to do it than when your enemy is chained and helplessly has to face you?"

"So you think whoever burned in her stead came to *gloat* over her being trussed up like a Thanksgiving turkey and she served them a plateful of death instead?" Jaxon asked.

Jack shrugged.

Jaxon laughed and shook his head. "Could be."

"If so, she's one badass." Circerran touched her nose once more. "Wait, we already know that. What I want to know, *Bryson*, since you were around when she was, correct…?"

Bryson hesitated but nodded when Circerran lifted a delicate eyebrow at him.

"Well, then why have you not mentioned her brother's bride? She was killed as well, was she not?"

The room went still, as if Circerran had set down a bomb in the center of the table.

"What is she talking about, Bryson?" Jaxon frowned over at him. "No mention of this was told to me."

"No." Bryson shook his head and gazed steadily at Circerran. No one ever mentioned Jorge. Never had there been any whisper of a bride. For the first time, he felt uncomfortable with the facts he'd been given. *What else did I miss?* "What did Isobel say?"

"Well, let's see, I think her exact words were, '*There is no mercy for what you did, just as there was none for Jorge and his bride.*'"

Chapter Five

Isobel studied the boy below her. This location shouldn't be safe for a young one. It certainly wasn't guarded — by anyone other than her. He seemed to be searching for something, or perhaps someone. Each tombstone he passed got a glance from him, some a brush of his hand over the snow-covered script so he could read a name. He kept on, though, never stopping for long as he steadily made his way through the rows. She couldn't imagine what would be his goal here.

He was a mystery. He was different. Not Vampire, but not completely *not* a Vampire. But something about him was...familiar.

He reached a small rectangle with two inches of snow on top of it. After standing there for a little while, he crouched and brushed away the snow, revealing a fallen grave marker. The stone was black, with deep etchings spelling out a name in flowing careful script. It was a small tombstone, perhaps that of a child, she thought.

The breeze carried his scent. She stepped off the roof of the burial chamber and walked over to him. He didn't turn, but she sensed he knew of her approach. It was unique enough for her to pause and study him again. Many traps were lined with mysteries. The boy drew her attention from her hunt.

"Who are you?" she asked.

He rose to his feet, steady and graceful as only an immortal could be. "I am Faolan."

She smiled, revealing her fangs. If the sight bothered him, he didn't show it. "You are not merely a *little wolf*. You are more."

"Yes." He nodded. "Who are you?"

He asked the question as if he should know her, as if he were surprised he *didn't* know her.

"I have never met you before. You do not know me," she assured him, suddenly worried that perhaps he was not right in his head. Trauma could take away a person's memories and distort their view of the world — and its dangers. There were faint white lines on his cheeks, as if someone had drawn their nails there to mark him.

"You are ancient?"

She considered the question. She had been but one hundred and twenty-five winters when she'd suffered entombment, but the centuries since made her very ancient indeed. "Some may say so. I feel ancient. But you do as well, do you not?"

Another nod, then the flash of an enchanting smile that oddly seemed to hide the telltale scars on his face.

"Do not think that will work on me, boy. Why are you here, and at this grave?"

His smile faded and he frowned at her, again as if he thought something of her and it hadn't happened.

She narrowed her vision and sought his soul. He was pure, but there was something there, something shielding him in a power she could not understand.

"You are Isobel."

The vision of his inner being vanished, replaced with the boy's curious face as he waited on her answer.

"Yes."

"You killed Aidan's father. And Aquinas. And Gia."

"Did I?" She watched him tilt his head. It was oddly enchanting as well, as if he found her curious. "Why are you here?"

He scratched his head then dropped his hand and shoved it into his small jacket pocket. "I was searching for someone."

"And this child is that someone?"

"Yes, but she was not a child."

Isobel studied the grave marker again, but there was no mention of birth or the year of her death. "Then you found what you sought." She turned to go and heard him follow. "Do not."

"But I must tell you something."

She regarded his earnest face and felt a shift of unease. "I am dangerous. You should not be here. You should be with your mother and father."

"I don't have those, but I have good friends, they watch over me."

"Where are these good friends now? You are alone in a cemetery after the moon has set. How is this watching over you?"

He shrugged and smiled. "I snuck out. They were busy."

There was something in his tone that spoke of him lying. "Why are you lying?"

"I wanted to find you, too. Not just Shelby. You are in danger, much danger."

Interesting and even odder considering he was in more danger here than her. "Shelby is the name on the tombstone."

"Yes."

She glanced down at the grave to read the name. Shelby Lynn Lafayette. "You found her, now what will you do?"

"Nothing, I suppose. I just wanted to…find her." He shuffled his feet, rubbing a line of snow free at the bottom of the grave.

"Ah, I see. She is not here. She has gone beyond this place."

He glanced up at her through his hair, shifting it aside with a toss of his head. "I know. But here is where they placed her…you know, body."

"Ah." She had no words to aid him in his sorrow. Losing someone was never easy. This child's short life was tragic and unfair, but nothing she could do would return Shelby to her friend. "You should be in your home."

"I wanted to speak to you. You are in danger —"

"I *am* danger. I am not *in* danger. You should go to your friends." She walked away, disbelieving when he followed her again. He caught up, and surprising her even more, he took her hand. His was warm and sent a shock through her body, as if he'd burned her.

"Bryson is your mate. He will be lost without you."

It took her several seconds to make sense of his words. "You believe there is a Vampire who is my mate? And he knows of me?"

"Yes. He found you."

He found me. The voice from when she'd still been locked away behind mortar and centuries of starvation. *Was he the Vampire in the chamber?* His voice... The cursing... He had been familiar to her. Was that because she had heard him before, upon waking?

She shook her head to banish her thoughts. He was not her mate. He could not be. He had handed her over to die. He was not a man who cared for her above all others, who would rather *die* than see her come to harm.

"Do not grow angry. Do not be upset. I can explain—"

"You are wrong, boy." She pushed his hand off hers. "Do not come here again."

"But, can't I visit you at least? I won't bring the others—"

"No." She studied his odd features and decided that he needed to know that danger lurked everywhere. "You should go. Go now, and when you arrive with your friends, you will not speak of this, or me, to them. Understood, *little wolf?*"

His eyes grew hazy with her command, then surprising her, they cleared and his impish grin returned. "They will not know I spoke to you. Do not be too quick to judge Bryson. May I come visit you?"

She had no answer for him because she was too shocked by how easily he threw her commands off. But for some reason her silence seemed to satisfy. He crouched and, as if going to launch himself into flight, burst into mist, disappearing on the wind.

A Vampire then? Or perhaps something much stronger.

Either way, he was gone, taking with him his odd scent and the truth in his eyes.

Do not judge him – do not judge him as I was, is what the child meant. No, she realized, she would not, neither would she think on such a bizarre revelation.

Tonight she hunted.

Samuel, you have been busy over the centuries. Tonight you will find your time on Earth has come to a much-deserved end.

Chapter Six

Jorge had a bride.

The fact changed everything but nothing. Jorge had had a wife. If he'd had a wife, perhaps he'd had a child as well. *Why did he hide this? Who was his bride?* She couldn't have been a Vampire. There were fewer, much fewer females then male Vampires. It was one reason the bloodlines mattered so much. But when Vampires married Vampires there was always cause for celebration. No wedding had occurred for Jorge.

"Bryson." Jaxon caught his arm as he headed out of the room. "Did you know?"

Bryson didn't have to ask what, he knew. "No. I didn't."

Jaxon dropped his arm and shook his head. "How —? Scratch that. What the fuck is going on? Why do I feel like we're only being fed part of the problem, and by the ones that we don't fucking trust?"

"Christian? We trust him."

"Christian, yeah, I trust him, sure, about as far as I can throw him. Look," Jaxon snapped, "all I'm saying is if this girl rose, after almost seven hundred fucking years in a wall in Gia's House, then managed to escape, killing Aquinas, perhaps, but definitely Gia, then we have something here we need to step back from and study. It isn't fitting together. Even Aidan admitted that he never knew who held him prisoner. He also admitted, when he did rise, he was *told* Isobel killed his father. He thought her mad when she rose, she was laughing, crazy laughing, and he was pissed... You know how he can be."

"What are you getting at?"

Joey ducked under Jaxon's arm and hugged her mate around his waist. Bryson held back the curses he wanted to throw at Jaxon. He couldn't now, not with Joey's eyes on him.

"What Jaxon is getting at is what if she *didn't* kill Aaron?" Joey asked quietly, probably because he would have snapped Jaxon's head off for asking it. Just like Faolan, Joey wasn't someone he could punch in the face, unlike Jaxon.

"It's worth asking." Jaxon shrugged.

"It's worth asking," he agreed and marched off. "I've got things to do. I think that meeting has to be postponed. But I'll let you know."

"Wait," Joey called. "We can help you —"

"Joey, hotshot, let's let Bryson dig his own grave, shall we?"

"Jaxon —"

"Is right." Bryson shoved his hair off his forehead. "I'm off. I'll call if you're needed. You won't be," he added when Jaxon frowned at the suggestion.

Joey grimaced and bit her lip but nodded.

He shifted to his home in Seattle, something drawing him there, his gut he realized. It was something he had begun to trust more and more.

Immediately, he exhaled in relief. *Isobel.* She is here. But... He shifted to where he'd taken Samuel's body and burned his ashes. The trees here were thick, but he still could see the burned remains of a few saplings that had caught in the fire. Had *Samuel* been on the council?

There was only one way to find out. He broke into mist and flew toward the house he'd hoped to never step foot in — ever again.

* * * *

Bryson.

Isobel had known a man, once, named Bryson, or had *heard* of a warrior named Bryson MacAfee. He was a fiercely loyal captain in the king's guard, directly under Aaron himself, but not of royal blood. He was unusual. Instead of being born by birth into that honor, he'd risen through the ranks of Vampires on his own merit. His parents had been mixed — one royal blood, one commoner.

However he had been spawned, Bryson was a man to fear. And not on her list of those who would die. Nor was he her mate. If he was the man from the Chamber, then he was nothing more than someone she should avoid. Even in her mist form, she had been intrigued by him, curious in ways she had never been for another.

The chill of night grew wetter as dawn approached, reminding her she shouldn't be thinking about a Vampire she had no desire to meet.

She studied the night sky and tested the wind. Her hunt had brought her here. This town wasn't old, but parts of it were infected with so much sin she felt dirty standing in the shadows.

But the answers she sought were here, buried underground.

Christian. At one time, he'd been Aaron's closest confidant. Now he was...sick. Filled with greed and an insane desire for power she couldn't understand. She'd found Christian by following a trail of dead. The aphrodisiac of drinking until death was heavy in the air. Drenching the ground she walked on. Closely linked to Christian's trail, she found another of those she sought.

Samuel.

Both had saturated themselves in the blood of their conquests. But Samuel had celebrated his bloodlust with another, much more powerful being she didn't know and didn't wish to ever encounter.

She stepped deeper into the catacombs. Madness dripped along the corridors, leaving behind a sickness she sensed everywhere. She kept on, passing empty branching side tunnels and vast, open underground areas that smelled of waste and water. Farther in, she found what had drawn her. A hidden sanctuary for the ultimate of their hideous acts lay before her, the stench of evil so thick she was surprised it hadn't drawn someone, anyone to cleanse it. She threw her hand up and let light shine down upon the room.

There, at the entrance, she paused, struck by the horror facing her from every angle. Many innocents had died here, but not until they had been subjected to the most horrifying and inhuman tortures. There were no limits here, except those of their shallow, perverted minds. Sickness and insanity dripped from the tools they had used to torture their victims, before killing them gruesomely.

It was here that Samuel and Christian and this other had brought their victims and here they had hidden the bodies — what was left of them. She walked to the far wall, over an uneven, slick floor, and pushed aside a hanging of the devil eating a virgin. There, in the dark behind the fabric lay what remained. The bodies were piled up, burned, but not completely. No, whoever had orchestrated this had wanted to keep something of them behind. Something to savor when he chose, she thought. A flash of gold caught her eye and she bent and turned over a small locket. *Forever* was scrolled along the back of it. She stood and walked toward the altar.

The being who had done this wasn't Christian. It hadn't been Samuel. This was someone far more dangerous and far more evil. The scratching on the altar indicated the victim's struggles, but beneath the claw marks were other, deeper lines. Words she recognized, but only from the most ancient texts she had ever studied. They spelled evil words that no man or woman should ever write.

Frowning, she backed away from the stone and drew her sword from the air. Lifting it high in both hands she spoke the words to cleanse this place, pushing against a force that was deeply entrenched. She swam through it, forcing herself upward even as she drew her power, pulling a storm from the heavens to bring light to the vile darkness. As her voice rose, she brought the lightning to strike right through the soil above her head. It connected with the earth. She slashed her blade down, breaking the altar in two.

A flood of black, angry spirits rose screaming from the thing, but she held on. Eyes clenched tightly closed, she whispered her guarding words. The blackness disappeared and moonlight filtered down on the filth left behind. Peace settled over the ground, growing as the silver light of the moon cleansed the lingering evil.

She lowered her sword, exhausted, but exhilarated at the same time. Breathlessly, she let her blade hold her weight so she could regain her balance.

This place was just one of the reasons Samuel had to die. Christian would follow. *Does this mean that our kind has sunk to nothing more than monsters? Is even Aidan guilty of this madness?*

There were no answers, only the night air blowing gently on her face. With it came a scent she knew. She tensed, nothing more.

"Don't move."

The rush of cooler air, brought on by a shift, should have alerted her, but the words were enough of a warning. A warning she wouldn't have given if their roles had been reversed.

She spun and struck, encountering the cave wall where a man had stood. *Bryson*. He had found her.

Not waiting for him to return, she threw herself into mist, realizing, as she did, that he followed. *No! This is my only chance. I cannot end it now, before I am finished.*

He was good. But she was better.

She lost him but for a moment, then he appeared again, much closer this time. Lightning struck inches from her, impacting the forest floor and throwing her backward.

"I said don't move."

"Why do you chase me?" *When he could kill me?* It was there, in his moves, in his strength and speed. An ancient. But one that had lived long before she had ever drawn breath.

"What were you doing there in that chamber? How did you break the altar and the roof?"

The way he asked seemed to imply that she would leave evil behind. *Because I am evil?* Anger swelled in her breast. *He thinks to judge me.*

"With my sword." His scent. It had been in the chamber...but not a part of the horror. He had discovered the place, though. "Which is more than you did. You left that evil there to stain the earth."

"I fought the men who created that place!"

She looked for him, but he didn't step into the moonlight. She knew such maneuvers, had been taught them since she could first transfer her body from its solid state to the droplets of mist that hung low in the air.

Hiding would do him no good. Not when he spoke. She spun a circle, and with it the wind, knocking the trees down at their roots. Timber went flying and, through it, she sought escape trying to outsmart an enemy stronger than herself. *On his terms. Take the battle away from him. Move. Move to low ground, he will expect high.*

She ducked closer to the ground until she was moisture among the heavy fog. Keeping her speed slow, she eased along, hoping he believed she had already shot skyward to hide within the heavy clouds. Shifting again would draw him to her. Until he left, she would have to remain.

Another crash landed from the heavens, but she dodged it, and instead of rising to the bait of going to higher ground, she stayed down, melting into the shadows. He had struck to see if she still remained. His techniques were common among the king's captains. She would not fall for tricks.

She concentrated on nothingness at the surface of her mind while her inner mind worked on what she could do. Nothing for now. She could not choose another form, not the wolf, nor bat, nor eagle. He would expect that and worse, give chase and more than likely catch her. The captains were feared as much as the king's hunters, for when they were called to action, nothing stopped them.

Until me.

Time went by, the clouds flew quickly over the moon, letting shadows play a cat and mouse game over the countryside. She sensed he lingered, and fear crept up to strangle her. He was better than she'd believed.

I cannot be entombed again. Why is he not throwing down a killing strike? I cannot be taken. Not again. Why does he remain, remain and not chase after the shadows?

No answers came to her. If the boy were to be believed, if this man was the same from her waking, the same from the chamber, and was the same Bryson she remembered from the stories of her youth, then he was strong. But was he her mate?

And if he is…why does he come now, and not once during the centuries while I suffered in silence?

Anger burned her fear, but she changed tactics. Taking to the air, she rose above the forest she'd sheltered in and toward the houses lining it. The humans were rising, just as the sun was, but it didn't matter. She spilled into their garden, covering the shaded growth of clover with her essence. Seconds crawled by, but he did not appear. The longer she waited assured her that the rising dawn would bind him. Only when the light threatened to touch her did she shift.

He stood across from her, a shadow in the eaves of the house. At her appearance, he turned to face her.

Bryson.

It *was* him. The warrior from her past. The warrior from the chamber she had been sentenced to die in.

She had glimpsed him once, when she had been but a young apprentice. Now, seeing his face clearly, she knew him. He stood with his head held high. The wind picked up and tugged his light brown hair, daring to play with the short strands. His strong, proud brow was furrowed, his dark eyebrows veered downward over his nose in aggression. Power radiated from every inch of him. Yet it still wasn't as much as filled the space between them. The air *crackled* with it.

A certainty, as if she'd slid a key into an ancient lock and discovered that the fit was perfect, settled over her.

The boy spoke the truth.

"Do not run again."

The tenor of his voice stroked along her flesh, but, instead of soothing her, the sound roused an emotion she didn't understand. The last time she had heard his voice it had been rough from shouting. This time it was soft and lingered on her bare flesh in an unwanted caress.

Her brother's face was dear to her, and that of his chosen bride, but this man caused her heart to clench.

Was it fear? Was it dread? Or was it rage, white-hot and so powerful it eclipsed all else?

This man was hers. *This man is meant to be mine.*

Only he wasn't. This was the voice that had called her out of her endless sleep, but instead of welcoming her as he should have, he had sent her to her death.

'Trust no one, Isobel. They are all liars, scheming for something so evil we have no chance of defeating it.' Jorge's passionate words came back to her as strong now as they had been all those centuries before. *'Trust no one for they will only hurt you.'*

Chapter Seven

Isobel's blow was powerful, striking Bryson perfectly. At the same time, she blasted the house, destroying it so that it covered him. Her abilities were staggering. Her training must have been from the time of her birth. Even as he thought it, Bryson surged upward, rising above the devastation to seek her out.

She fled, but he chased. There was no other way. He *had* to have answers. She had survived the Chamber of the Sun. She had survived her entombment. Apparently, she was unharmed in body and mind. She had destroyed the underground lair used by Samuel and his friends. She'd even broken their altar and cleansed the evil.

The winds blew the flavor of her shift, along with the breath of air from her new location. He followed, bursting into being above mountains. Long ago, she had lived here, near this place. He wondered at her choice, then knew she had left again.

He followed, shifting five more times before he found her in Istanbul. She seemed to prefer churches, ancient ones that he avoided. There, in the parapet of one, he spotted her. He waited, letting her gain her confidence. When enough time had passed that she eased her stiff posture and leaned on the low wall overlooking the bustling city below, he moved.

She spun, too late, much too late for him. He had her. Her eyes widened. She raised her hand to ward him off, but he showed no more mercy than she had by burying him in rubble. She crumpled to the ground, giving him just enough time to catch her head before she suffered injury from the rough flagstones. He held her close to his chest.

Mine. This woman is mine.

The reality stunned him. Instead of joy at finally holding her, dread crept up his spine. *I've made a mistake.* There had been something in her expression back in Seattle. Recognition followed with fury. He had known when she struck, she would do so hard.

He'd been right.

He stared down at the perfection of her face in slumber. Gone was the frown that drew her delicate, winged brows down into a slashed furrow. What remained was a small, delicate woman. Just a woman.

But she wasn't. She was an oath-breaker. A king-killer.

Seemingly of their own will, his fingers stroked along her cheek. The satin smoothness boggled his mind. He knew evil could take many forms, but this... It was sinful how much he wanted, *needed* to excuse her crimes. Any reason, just as long as she had one...but there were no reasons to place herself above the laws of their kind.

The long strands of her midnight hair feathered over his fingers, so soft he watched it slide through his hand, falling in long waves to the ground. It'd been tightly braided but had unraveled during their battle. Satisfaction ached along his bones as he stared down at her, eclipsing the dread trying to take over this moment.

No woman in his long existence had ever been so dear to him and yet so hated. They had no future because she had destroyed their past.

She will hate me now. Unless she already does...

Had it been hatred in her eyes in Seattle? For a moment that had left him unable to move, he'd thought he'd sensed recognition. Was he right about this awful suspicion? Did she know he was hers? If so...

She'll know that I didn't attempt to save her. She'll know I was the one who sent her to her death.

The thought crystallized into painful shards. The fleeting pleasure of moments before vanished. Still, he dared to crush her to him. Once again he experienced the contentment, followed quickly by hopelessness. Just this once, he let the contentment win. He bowed his head and brushed his cheek against hers, drawing deeply of her perfect scent. Her skin was cool but so ultra-smooth his throat grew tight.

There would never be a time when he could dare to do the same with her awake and aware.

If I do, I will truly be damned.

* * * *

"You stupid woman," Christian snarled. He backhanded Agatha on her perfect porcelain face. Her head twisted to the side, but she didn't fall. Pity that, but the royal was much too strong. The blow released his temper, though, which counted for a lot. "You've come to me to tell me that Aquinas has fallen? Do you realize you could have brought *her* here?"

Agatha brushed at her lip. A drop of crimson colored her fingers. She studied it as if she'd never seen the like before.

"Aquinas was a fool. Will you be, as well?"

Christian ground his teeth but knew a threat when he heard one. Agatha was not only extremely spoiled. She carried royal blood directly from their forefathers.

And I struck her.

He stiffened but asked, "What do you mean?"

"It was not *I* that led Bryson by her crypt. It was not *I* that sentenced her to death. Nor was it *I* that went to her, thinking to gain something before she kissed the sun. But…" She locked gazes with him.

Belatedly he understood that he'd been outsmarted by her quiet acceptance these past centuries. He'd deemed her merely a pretty face. A bobble to gleam and shine for him to gaze upon in his leisure.

The power she held made that assumption ridiculous. And yet, she rarely let her full strength shine. She did now. His flesh shivered at it. To have that kind of power — at his side — would gain him much that he sought.

She lifted her finger, just the one, and studied the drop of blood. It traveled downward slowly. As it did he swallowed and loosened his tie. There would be more blood lost tonight, but not hers. She licked out and quickly caught the drop, sucking the blood free from her finger with her gaze firmly locked on his. He only wished she meant do the same to the arousal swelling his flesh.

"I have bloodied you." He unbuttoned the first two buttons on his shirt. At her nod, he made room for her to sit on the arm of his chair.

"Your temper always was your biggest obstacle, Christian." She glided over, prepared to accept his offering—no doubt *after* she punished him. "I will *not* be next on her list."

"Why did you come here today? After all these years, you have never come to me, never shown me more attention than any other man."

She bent over, revealing the lush expanse of her weighty bosom as she smoothed the hair from his eyes. Above all else, he was a man. Still guided by the power a desirable woman wielded. Agatha was the *most* suitable choice for his plans. She possessed not only the elegance and refinement of royalty, but also the seductive aphrodisiac of a voluptuous woman. She aroused him every time he neared her. To have her by his side *and* in his bed would be well worth the centuries of waiting for his chance to rule.

"Perhaps the time has come, my fierce darling, for more direct measures."

At the endearment his cock stiffened against his dress slacks. He caught her hand. Forced her to meet his gaze. He read the truth in her amber eyes.

"And those measures would be what? You cannot be discovered. Not at this point." He caressed her ivory cheek. She allowed it. He attempted to draw her into his arms.

She stopped him with a hand to his chest. Her bewitching smile snagged his attention from her lush bosom. She straightened to cross her legs. The sound of her stockings sliding along her silky flesh provoked him further. But he relaxed in his chair. He knew the game she played. He watched the burgundy satin slip along her thigh, revealing the top of her charcoal stocking and the porcelain of her skin.

No woman had ever dared to tease him as Agatha did by breathing. Agatha wasn't some weakling that would fall to the ground and sob if he struck her. She would punish him in her own way — then demand her due.

"She does not know I even exist. She has nothing to connect me to anything." She tipped his head up from the sight of her coveted flesh. "But you, on the other hand, believed bringing her forth would cause a stir. You believed the idea of this council would be dropped. That the focus will return to cleaning the Houses. Thus, cause more distrust with Aidan."

"I am not letting Aidan ruin what has taken me years to create. Bryson was supposed to sense her, and, when he did, attack. He showed more restraint than I believed he possessed. I will not make that mistake again." Ever again. Bryson proved harder to read than he'd believed. No self-righteous, ignorant commoner should never have been given a position of power. Any other ancient would have struck her down. Then and there.

"I believe this is not your first mistake when it comes to Bryson MacAfee."

"He is a serf," he sneered. "He should have never been given a rank."

"True."

He studied Agatha, surprised by her agreement.

"I do not feel the lower class should be given the same rise to power as those of us born with royal blood." She ran the tip of her long, scarlet nail along his throat. A delicious tingle stirred along his cock. If she used that nail there, he would come until his balls cried mercy. "They will never be what we are, just as a dog is not the same as its noble cousin the wolf."

Agatha was a mystery, a seductive siren he had dreamed of possessing for longer than he had sought to rule. She was much closer to the royal line than he was, which made her perfect for what he desired. Both in his bed *and* by his side. *To sate myself on her prized flesh.*

"I always wondered why you sided with our plans." His voice had dropped several octaves. She barely noticed. Or if she did, she didn't appear interested.

She waved her hand as if shooing a pesky fly. "My reasons are my own, but in this, we must be clear, Christian, for it will not be my blood that spills forth should you fail. It will not be my body burned to ash, will it?" Her gaze turned razor-sharp as she lingered her fingers on the line of his jaw.

"Never."

"Will you succeed, Christian? This is the question we will have to answer first, before you gain what you truly desire."

She settled a hand on his cheek and turned his head to the side. Her hot breath tormented him. The chair groaned as he tightened his hands on the wood. He anticipated her bite almost as much as bedding her.

"I would kill anyone you wish to have you by my side," he grated. "And in my bed. For that, I would kill Aidan himself."

Her amber eyes flew wide then narrowed. "I hope you are correct, my darling," she whispered, licking along his neck. The hot, wet stroke was even better than her sharp nail. "But for now, I will take it."

Blood for blood.

"Christian." She whispered his name, then bit him with a suddenness that made his grip on the chair arms crack the wood. Her bite was deep. Her drinking strong, so strong his vision grew dim. He allowed it. The room began to disappear around him. She released him with a breathy sigh. The hot glide of her tongue along the wound sent him near to coming. She closed the mark. Seconds later she was across from his desk, sitting in a chair.

Her face came into focus. The amber of her eyes glowed hotly from the blood he'd provided. Desires reflected in those eyes. For along with sharing blood came the lust for more. She blinked and the heat diminished but still lingered, reassuring him that it was him she wanted.

"There now, all is forgiven. Your blood is strong, my darling. Perhaps soon, we will show everyone how strong."

"For you?"

A laugh, then she walked over and stroked along his cheek.

He snatched it. "I am not a man to be played with, Agatha."

"Of course not, darling."

"I will want you. Often."

She dared to laugh again. "If you gain the throne, you get more than merely me in your bed, Christian. You will earn a right to rule no one will refute."

"With you by my side and in my bed." He would insist on it. On her. To open those thighs and know they were his alone. After so long, to walk beside her and understand the envy other males experienced at his prize.

She lowered her lashes demurely. "Is that your desire?"

"Yes."

"Then, by all means, I will join you in both, my darling."

Again he studied her eyes. The heat was there, lingering, not extinguished. He reached out and traced the line of her throat. She didn't protest. Better she didn't stop him. He watched her as much as his finger gliding down the gold chain she wore. Without blinking, she managed to fire his loins as if she'd given him a come-hither smile. He swallowed audibly. His fingers sank deeper between her bosoms.

"I want you now."

She leaned closer, enveloping his fingers in her ultra-soft cleavage. "And you shall have me, but only once you take care of Isobel." She caressed a hand down his chest, stopping right at his belt. "Then we shall see if you have the strength for what *I* will want."

Chapter Eight

The bars of the cell Bryson placed Isobel in were welded with the thickest of metals. They'd been spelled by witches. Traps of spirals, acting as puzzles that would hold a Vampire for years, hung over every inch of the open space. Invisible to the eye — until a Vampire tried to breach the cell. Each bar was also drenched in toxins. They would burn like acid on the skin.

He'd built it during a darker time. For much more brutal prisoners than the woman who now lay on the cold slab of stone. *Isobel.*

It was designed to keep most Vampires for years.

For her, he worried they would not hold past dawn.

And so, instead of resting upstairs, in comfort on his couch reading, he stayed in the dimly lit corridor outside her cell. He was glued there as if he were welded there more firmly than the bars.

I hit her too hard.

The purple bruise on her cheek disturbed him to the point it was like nails on a chalkboard. He rubbed his chest. The center of it felt odd. His entire body felt alien.

It should not bother me that she suffered.

It should not concern me that she sleeps so still.

It should not *matter* if she had fallen into the deepest and darkest of sleeps.

But it does. It matters. She matters.

He punched the wall. One of the rocks cracked. Mortar dusted the bench. The pain wasn't punishment enough.

I struck her. If she is mine, how is it that I feel rage, yet confusion when it comes to her? Protect her. Punish her. Which will win out?

"Why are you holding me here?"

He spun, startled to see her sitting up. The worrisome bruise was all but gone. Her pale skin flushed as he watched, even glowed with health.

Isobel.

She was beautiful beyond words. Most of his kind, when they reached maturity, paled and lost their coloring. Not so with her. She had the soft blush to her cheeks, as if sun-kissed. Her every feature captivated him. Delicate and small, with the longest, thickest black hair a woman could possess, she caught and easily held his complete attention. The essence of her sparkled with light. Just like the dark wells of her eyes.

How can an ethereal beauty hide evil?

Dressed in leggings and a simple, overlarge blouse she was more beautiful than any Vampire who had once graced the most noble of Vampire Houses in formal silks and satins.

"You are Bryson."

He nodded, suddenly recalling that not only was that his name, but that this woman was his. Swiftly with that thought, his worry returned. He adjusted his long coat, glad of the layers hiding his reaction to her.

Does she know? Does she realize I failed her? More than failed her, I sent her to her death.

She arched her delicate eyebrow at his lack of verbal response but made no other move. It fascinated him. If she was bothered by silences she didn't show it. He could barely keep his questions at bay. He cleared his throat. Understanding dawned on him. If he was to find out more about her, he would have to be the one speaking.

"I am."

He hoped she'd speak again, but her small face grew cold. Her eyes were the darkest, deepest pools framed by thick, black lashes. She would never need to apply cosmetics. Artifice would only distill her natural beauty. If she were free he could see how beautiful her eyes were up close, not with bars between —

He blinked. Realized he was walking toward her as if to free her and froze.

"Don't," he grated harshly. Her power stunned. Or the draw of his mate was indescribably strong. *My mate.* His erection weighed heavily from his hips. The tip drove him mad, rubbing along the fabric of his jeans.

"Why did you put me in here? Why am I not there?" she asked, lifting her hand gracefully to indicate something above them he wasn't catching. "With them."

Them? Did she mean Christian and his Hunters? Or Aidan? He had sensed the Hunters closing in on her in Seattle. "You fear the Hunters?"

Again her expression gave nothing away, but he sensed her unease. The Hunters were called when death was the only objective. They spared no one. They were given complete authority, something that chilled his soul.

"Christian leads the Hunters?"

"Yes."

She appeared amazed by that.

Did she fear Christian harming her? His fangs tingled. His fists tightened. *I would kill him for touching you* –

"It will do him no good."

Her disdain made him smile. It also dispelled any worry over her fearing Christian. There was pride in her tone. There was also an understanding of her power.

When he had first learned that she was his, she had been a shy, insecure young Vampire, always in the shadow of her twin brother. Then she had killed their king. Disappeared. Only she hadn't, had she? She'd been entombed for over six hundred years. The years of captivity hadn't broken her. They had made her stronger. But he worried they'd also made her insane.

He settled on the bench across from her cell. She studied him then stared at the bars. "These will not hold me."

She would learn that pride would do her no good. *Eventually.*

"They are for now."

That seemed to stump her.

"What have you been doing since you rose?" he asked, trying for conversational. Inside he was frantic to learn more of her. She had broken a three-foot thick slab of evil by drawing a storm to the area. A storm she had wielded as if she were a weather witch, not a Vampire.

How did she break that altar? And why?

"Killing."

He ignored that for it wasn't exactly correct. She had killed, true, but only the one Vampire, possibly two. He would have known if she had taken the life of another. Had she sought someone in Seattle? But there were no ancients there—any longer. Could Samuel have been her target? She wouldn't have known Samuel was gone, ashes on the wind these past months. He considered another tactic.

"How have you survived?"

Again she made him wait until he had to concentrate on standing in place to keep from opening up the cell and shaking her. Finally, he heard her quietly say, "By killing."

He would have thought she'd have had trouble adjusting to life in this age. If she did, she wasn't showing it. The way she had worn her hair back from her face to hide the length in a long, intricate braid intrigued him. It spoke of her understanding this age's culture. In this day and age, long, lush hair would draw attention.

Above all, no Vampire sought human notice. That alone spoke of her sanity. She hadn't risen, wild and untamed to rush among humans to feed in frenzy.

"I find that hard to believe." He watched her fold her hands in her lap, neatly and calmly as if his attention meant nothing to her.

"You have adjusted well to this time."

She had, nothing about her would stand out. Nothing, except a pair of candy-apple-red combat boots.

Is red her favorite color? He could easily imagine her in all red—the bonding color for Vampires.

Did she take the boots because she likes the color, or is the fit comfortable?

He wanted to know, but he wanted to know everything about her—now, immediately. His neck ached. His shoulders were continually tensing. Even his thighs were tight, as hard at least as his shaft. He studied her neck. If he bonded her, he would gain access to all he wanted—her mind, her reasons for killing...her body.

No. I might betray my king by keeping her alive, but I will never force our bond. Never force *her.*

Sin like that would take him down a path he wouldn't return from. He had already sinned enough. To force her would send him straight to Hell. If she were a killer, if she were insane, it would be his duty to take her life. *But Isobel appeared sane, human even, until you met her gaze. Only then did you realize she was more beautiful than any other creature –*

He halted, again almost rising to his feet to go to her. That kind of power stunned him into shouting, "Stop it! I will leave you down here, alone, with no blood for decades—"

She smiled, catching him off guard. The pinkness of her fuller bottom lip, the dip in the upper one, both...so close he could lean in and suck, lick and know they were his. Angered again, he fisted his hands until his knuckles protested.

"Do not think I jest with you. My threats are real, Isobel."

She appeared to consider that, then said in a wondering tone, "Do you believe your threats will somehow cause me to *do* something?"

He laughed, enchanted with her when he knew better. "Behaving would be a start."

She squinted at him as if he'd suddenly sprouted another head.

"If you wish to survive, you will have to do as I say, understood?"

"No."

No? He considered her response but still had to clarify. "No, you don't understand?"

"I understand." She lifted her feet and scooted back on the bed, drawing her knees up and rested her wrists on them.

See? It wasn't so hard, he wanted to say. The trick was listening.

"Good. The first thing —"

"I understand, *Bryson*, that no matter what, I will not survive. So I will not do as you say, nor do what anyone else says. You may leave. I will rest now." She matched words to leaning her head on the wall and closing her eyes. *She thought to test my resolve?* "Later, I will leave this place."

"I hope you try, Isobel. It would be amusing to watch, since I know, and you have to realize, that I can easily stop you. It would be all too simple to take you to Aidan."

"If you had wanted to do this, you would have. Instead, I am here." She opened her eyes again. Deep, dark pools he wanted to drown in stared at him unblinking. "Why is that?"

He stood and stepped close to the bars. They would have no impact on him, for he had designed the cage that held her. "Isobel, if I wanted you dead you would be. For now, I want answers. Tell me why you murdered Aaron."

She grimaced and stared at him as if that extra head had grown back. Slowly she closed her eyes and sank back against the wall of the cell with a heavy sigh.

He had the oddest sensation she thought him…an idiot.

He watched her intently. She didn't move. Anyone else would have been unable to sit there. If his gaze bothered her she didn't show it.

His tolerance unraveled. Control slipped. "Why were you after Samuel? Was he on the council with Gia?"

She tensed her fingers. He only noticed because every nuance of her was burned into his brain. Her reaction seemed to indicate he had guessed correctly.

What had Aaron been thinking? Gia, he could see, with her blood line, but Samuel had always been weak and pathetic.

"He is dead."

This time she didn't tense, but he noticed her complete attention was on him. *So, it was Samuel she sought?*

"How are you finding the members?"

No response. The members were secret. He had never known for certain who was on the king's council. He'd guessed. Perhaps she did as well.

"Was it Aquinas in the Chamber? Did he come to…gloat over your captivity?"

No response.

He exhaled. His patience would be tested. He knew that. But he'd never dreamed she'd be this unreasonable. Her opposition was childish. He wanted to open the cage and shake her.

Then test her lips. Taste her slim neck. Smell the silk of her hair.

No!

He stretched his neck, tipping it left then right. The kink in his shoulder remained.

I will not open the cell.

Instead, he studied her beauty, looking for a flaw. Evil could not completely hide. If it could, more would suffer. But she had no artifice. She was without the usual Porn Star make-up and low cut, short-skirted dresses so many of this time favored. She was...

She was either like a Venus Fly Trap or... She wasn't evil.

He couldn't say. The fact that he couldn't infuriated him. She should be sobbing. Crying. Begging him for mercy. She should be telling him *her* side. He got none of that. Just as he found nothing, saw nothing but perfection when he sought to find a flaw.

That was because she had none.

Even her small nose was graceful and swept down in a beautiful line. Her lips pale pink, the bottom ever so slightly puffy as if it were made for him to kiss —

He stopped his hand from reaching for the lock.

"You will never leave this cell. I will ensure you stay here, locked away forever if I feel it will be safer — "

She didn't raise a hand, but she brought a snap of air down on his head, slicing along his cheek. Shocked, and now more pissed off than frustrated, he retaliated. He hated himself even as he struck. She was knocked backward — hard — against the cell wall. She erupted into movement, landing on her feet like a cat, hands up, fangs exposed. No doubt ready to rip him to shreds.

"Enough!" he shouted. "You will — "

"Enough?" she mocked. "You bring me here, and you think to make demands of me? You can't keep me here. No one can and most certainly not you! Do you believe so? Do you?" she screamed.

"Yes," he bellowed back at her. "I will keep you here. And in time you will see, I have the power to do whatever I wish to you."

Shit. Had he just shouted at her? Shouted *that* at her?

Her eyes flew wide. Her tiny nostrils flared. Instead of screaming at him, she slowly walked up until she was a scant inch from the harmful potion on the bars. Meeting his gaze, hers turned icy black.

"You will never have power over me. You forfeited that right."

His anger melted. Dread took its place. She knew. *Didn't matter*. Nothing mattered but finding out what he needed from her.

"I have all the power. The sooner you understand that the better. I will keep you in here until you answer my questions. Until I know you are no longer a threat. Until—"

"Until I am longer a threat?" she cried, fisting her hands at her hips. She leaned closer. Too close. The poison. Her smooth skin. *Protect*.

I fucking put her there!

"Tell me, Bryson, would you have slept through it? Would you have remained here, secure in your mountain home while I *burned* until nothing remained?" Her icy gaze roamed his face. What she saw he couldn't imagine. *A monster*.

"Or maybe not slept..." Her attention lifted to the cell's ceiling as if she could see through the five feet of solid stone. "Perhaps you didn't choose sleep, but this, instead." She held up her hand. With a soft sound, his opium landed in it. The burgundy velvet bag overflowed her small palm.

Every dream he'd ever tried to conjure with this woman had ended in horror. Always. Because, basically, she was a killer and there wasn't a happy ever after when you fucked up shit like that. She'd not merely killed but murdered his friend *and* his king.

There had never been a happy ending for him and Isobel. *There never will be.*

But nothing prepared him for this, his darkest, vilest weakness laid bare before a woman who appeared unsurprised to find him so deficient.

"Mates were created for one thing. To be to each other what no one else in the world can *ever* be." Her eyes were hypnotic. Even as her words sliced him deep, he couldn't look away. "Their protectors. If your life could have been given for mine, it should have been! But you had this." She threw the sack to the ground. The opium exploded in a black dust cloud that blossomed between them. "And this is all you will ever have!"

The silence that followed should have been followed by her disappearing in that cloud of dust. Instead, something almost as bad happened.

His alarms tingled a warning.

Someone approached. His fangs lengthened and dropped at this new threat. Few knew of this home. *Protect her.*

It wasn't Jaxon. He wouldn't have set the alarm off.

It wasn't the boy—he'd come in before and not set them off.

He tried to harness his thoughts. No one, not even Jaxon, had ever been below to this barricaded, dungeon level. There was no hint of its existence. Thus he should not fear someone had discovered Isobel. But tension tightened his stomach to the point of pain. He battled his instincts down. His fangs retracted.

He sensed her alertness. She also felt the alarm.

How is that possible? How is this nightmare even possible?

"I will return, Isobel. I want answers. Do not think to test me in this."

The threat fell between them. Amazing him, she lifted her lip in a sneer. Clearly she was not impressed. Or the least bit fearful of him. With the residue of opium powder still floating on the air, he could understand why.

"You will stay here, in this cell, until I have those answers. Trust me, you will *never* break free. I am the one in power now. When you accept this, then you *will* talk."

"Then I will never speak."

Amazed, he studied her mulish expression. She might not. Did it matter?

Yes.

No.

He left, leaving her intoxicating scent before he opened the door to her cage and dragged her out to claim her.

Chapter Nine

Throughout the dark centuries Isobel had regained consciousness enough to know that the walls still held her captive. The claustrophobic awareness that nothing she did would free her had nearly driven her mad. It had only been made worse by knowing that no one in the universe would come. Her brother had been taken. With him, anyone who might have aided her had also been annihilated.

And yet, there *had been* someone.

She had sensed it the way a wild creature knew that danger lurked under the deception of the traps laid by hunters.

It was him. *Bryson.*

I sensed him. In all those years, he never came to me. Never ventured to her hiding place, nor sought to release her from the endless torture. Not until he'd taken her from the darkness and cast her to burn in the light.

Rage and more pain threatened to choke her. Yet this wasn't directed at the Vampires responsible for her brother's plight. This was directed at the one being on this planet who should have laid down his life, if it saved her from one ounce of pain.

The anger built. It grew dangerous as she worked her mind around the bars holding her. Spells were there as well as punishing toxins. She knew both would cause her pain. Worse than pain, possibly leave her scarred. *I am already scarred. I will seek the sun when this is finished. Scars will not matter, nothing will.*

Above her she could not sense Bryson. She could feel things, possessions of his, but not him — or whoever had triggered his alarms. *Cloaking.* She had heard of it. Assassins used something similar. But for a Vampire to cloak one level of his home from another... His dungeon? From the upper, living area... Impressive.

The walls of her cell were primitive, cut out of the stone bedrock of the mountains he called home. Always it was this way with Vampires. They went to high ground. At least among those who *could*. Their homes were isolated, protected more by nature and its forces rather than spells they drew around themselves.

Not so with Bryson. This home was a fortress not only high in the clouds, but swirling with enough protections to thwart even the most cunning.

Especially on this level.

"He has several libraries."

Isobel started. *Faolan?* She took several steps backward before she could stop herself. The boy walked out of the gloom of the corridor, smiling sadly. His short brown hair had fallen in his eyes, but he didn't remove it or smile at her. The expression he wore... Worried?

"He's hurt you. I didn't think he would do that. I don't think he knows what to do with you."

"How…?" Her throat was dry. She swallowed. Studied him. Underneath the warm glow of his skin, there was power. Something she'd caught before but couldn't understand. "How did you get here?"

"I've been here before." He glanced over his shoulder then frowned back at her.

Her brain couldn't seem to match what he'd said with meaning. "You were in these *cells*?"

"No." Faolan laughed merrily. The somberness vanished. He tossed the hair out of his brown eyes. "It was upstairs. It's nicer up there. It's also nicer out here. Can I let you out?"

She tilted her head. "I am not certain. Can you?"

"Will you harm Bryson?"

Stunned. The audacity…

Harm him? I will kill him. She considered *not* murdering Bryson for what he'd done to her while gnawing a nail. He deserved to be *harmed*. He'd known of her. He had been older. She had known him by name only. But he had come. Once. He had come to the Dragon Blooding. *He would have seen me. Was I not to his liking? Was I not strong enough?* Realizing what she did when she bit down on another nail, she ceased.

'Show weakness – any weakness – and it will be used against you.' Why hadn't her brother heeded his own advice?

"Why do you ask me this?" Perhaps the boy cared for Bryson. But why would a warrior allow a boy here? He cared for the boy? *Highly unlikely.* But predicting the unpredictable was always part of war.

"He harmed you."

She touched her cheek. It had been a warning, nothing more. Why? Why not more? *I was bound by the cell, otherwise my strike would have toppled the ceiling on him.* But he'd retaliated with a small strike. The pain was not even remembered. Not compared to what else he had done to her.

For some reason, she couldn't regain the rage she'd felt moments before.

She grudgingly admitted to herself she wouldn't harm Bryson. Unless he attacked again. He might. The buzz of the anger neared but drew back. Bonding? She had heard, everyone had, that emotions ran high for a couple when they first discovered each other. Just as other things did. The thought of him harming her brought the rage closer. Imagining him keeping her in here…haze.

Useful.

The drug still filled the air with its heavy scent. A weakness like that stunned her. What would drive a strong warrior to take such a release from reality? She bent and picked up the half-empty bag, tipping it so the powder shifted to the floor of the cell. The scent was pleasing. But the draw lost to her. He would have to ingest an entire bag to bring on the effects.

"Why would he seek to use this?"

"To escape."

She hadn't expected an answer, especially from a boy. She lifted her attention to his cherubic face. He had taken a seat near the bars of her cell. Legs crossed, elbows on his knees, he'd been staring at her. *Fascinated by me?*

"What would he have to escape from? He was free."

"Your death."

My death? Was that why he sought the darkness?

She considered that. Bryson clearly thought her a killer. *Why bring me here, and not back to Aidan?* It was clear he was honorable. *He is misled by his beliefs.* One of the masses unable to think for himself, or was he more?

He should have been more.

Haze.

He keeps me from my duty. Confines me. Strikes at me — *if somewhat gently. He cannot keep me here!*

The cell was designed to hold a Vampire. The spells were lined with intricate designs, knotting the eye and trapping a person as firmly as the bars. Vampires loved puzzles. The more intricate the pattern, the better. She knew this and avoided them. They would not keep her.

The barriers lining his property, though. His mind was solid, a firm, harsh wall that expanded outward, enclosing his house within it. That would be harder to break through.

"The cell is not the only barrier. But if you release me from this, and the house, I will not harm Bryson. Unless he attempts to harm me."

"What will you do if I release you?"

"I will go."

Faolan sighed, as if disappointed in her. He reminded her of her old mentor, Rowan. A sad smile lifted her lips. *Rowan, if you had but been there...but you, too, are gone from me.*

"Then I can't let you out. If you go, he might hurt himself looking for you again. Already he has broken trust with his friends. Already he has chosen you over others who have earned his loyalty."

"Why do you speak to me of these things? They are not true. He gave me over to *die.*" Anger seethed. *Haze returning.*

Faolan frowned as if she'd given him a riddle he couldn't figure out...yet. "He would never allow you to die."

She blinked and sat on the cold stone. Bryson had come to her. It had been before the sun would have burned her. Well before. Confused, she buried her head in her hands.

Focus. Revenge. Kill. Return Jorge to his Tessa. Meet the sun.

"He did let them take you to Aidan, but he also went to free you. Only you had freed yourself, much like my friend Elsa. She was the one that killed Samuel. You will like her. She will teach you many things, even though she is young."

Isobel considered that and the boy. So Samuel was gone. The knowledge settled over her, creating a new reality. Three are gone. *Three more, Jorge. Only three more.*

"So you see, he is not so terribly bad, is he?"

She wasn't about to agree to that. "You seek normalcy. You wish for your family to be happy. Bryson is your family, as well, is he not?"

"Yes. Bryson is my family. Elsa and Jamie are my family. I have more, too, but they would not want to meet you, yet. Not until you find what you seek. But Elsa would. She is brave. She would understand."

She shook her head. "Understand what?"

"You."

The solemn tone, matched with his smile, was something she had never encountered before. She laughed, caught off guard by him. "No one can understand me, Faolan."

"I do. You are not evil. You do not need to kill these Vampires, but you will because you care about what is right and wrong. Like Bryson. If you tell him —"

"I will tell him nothing!" She bared her fangs.

"He will listen to you —"

"I will not *guide* him to the truth because I do not care if he *knows* the truth." The dangerous anger returned, and with it the pain. She needed gone from this boy. From this man. From this place. Here she faced a danger she had never considered.

"You do care, I can tell."

"Boy. There is no one left to care about. Leave me."

"Of course there is. There are a —"

"I care for nothing and no one!"

Faolan stood and reached out as if to touch the bars.

"No! Do not touch them like that!"

Faolan nodded and his smile returned. "See? You do care."

Chapter Ten

Fucked. I'm fucked.

Bryson had to *pretend* to give a shit about an ancient scroll Christian had brought. Ancient texts were valuable. They usually mesmerized him. This was one... *Who gives a fuck? I'm fucked.*

She knows. Hates me.

If that wasn't enough, a Vampire stood not five feet away from him who would like nothing better than to rip Isobel's throat out.

Christian.

Long ago, Bryson had let the Vampire into this stronghold. Now, he regretted that confidence more than anything else in his existence.

Christian's being was determined to find—and annihilate—Isobel. More than any Hunter Bryson had ever encountered, Christian behaved like a man who was doing more than following orders. It almost seemed personal.

Before she explained why she killed Aaron?

She killed Aaron because he had her brother executed.

"This appears straightforward." Bryson rolled the parchment and returned it to the FedEx tube. "Why bring it here?"

Christian gave him a floored look. "I thought you would want to see it. Longer."

"It's from Gia's library?"

"Yes, and if this is authentic, then we're dealing with more than a temporary pact with the Salem coven."

"Why wouldn't it be authentic?" Bryson asked. "Who would forge it?" Even touching the parchment had been distasteful. The signatures had been in blood. All of them, including the witches. He didn't want it near him. The blood was not theirs. It had been taken from a virgin. She, or he, would have been killed after they'd secured enough for the oaths. "It is hard to read the signatures, nearly impossible in some cases. We know Gia's House to be evil, this only provides more proof. Aidan has seen it?"

"He has."

"Then this could have waited. At least until the meeting." Coming to his home uninvited was only done when no other means of communicating existed. For Christian to come here, now, after so many centuries, right when he had Isobel mere feet below them was impossible to credit to chance.

Nothing is ever chance.

Then how was it that after centuries I happened upon the entombment of my bonded?

He handed the container back. Christian hesitated over accepting it. *Maybe I'm seeing enemies everywhere because I am now the enemy.* Still, he couldn't shake his unease.

"Why did you come here, Christian?"

Face tense, the Vampire bounced the tube against his thigh. "I didn't want to come to you with this, what with all your work on the council, but we've had no luck getting closer to finding Isobel."

The sense of relief he experienced was quickly followed by a bigger dose of suspicion. "I see. And what is it you want from me?"

"I assumed, since you were the one to detect Isobel in the walls, you might have more of a sense of her than we do."

Bryson laughed at the understatement. At the moment he could point to exactly where Isobel was—but he wasn't about to share that with *this* Vampire.

"I can't help you, Christian. I'm certain you will find her. She cannot hide forever."

I'm damned. Surely lightning will strike me for my lies.

Christian blew out a breath and nodded. "We thought we had her in Seattle, but something scared her off. Her going there was odd, don't you think? Why would she go to the States?" Christian mused.

Either Bryson was now seeing ghosts where none existed, or the Vampire was testing him.

"I was in Seattle. When was it you thought you sensed her?"

"Ah, you were? We were closing in on her, just this past night, but she vanished."

Bryson frowned and considered that. *If they were there, it was after I found her. Christian is many things, but he isn't capable of hiding.* Bryson's gut felt as if someone was wringing it dry. He fought the need that rose suddenly in his mind—the need to kill Christian.

No. I will not add the sin of murder onto the sins of my deceptions. He steeled himself and spun one more lie, hoping it would be the last.

"I was there checking that all had been cleared. Did she enter Samuel's home, or merely go to the city?"

Christian grinned and suddenly *patted* him on the back. "I see. So she fooled you as well, did she? She is good, what with all her years in that wall, I'm shocked she can shift, let alone recall how to become mist. But she's tricky. Always was, eh?" Christian seemed enormously pleased. As if Bryson's lack of sensing Isobel meant much more to him than Bryson could decipher.

Does he guess I am Isobel's bonded?

Kill him. Rip his throat open, drink him dry.

Bryson fisted his hands.

Control. Gain control.

Christian surveyed him with a penetrating stare. "She was part of the elite. A Dragon Guard. Such promise, but a disappointment in the end."

Bryson ground his teeth. Disdain his bonded? *I'll rip his throat out—*

My bonded who is…a Dragon Guard. Lucid thoughts resurfaced. He didn't have to *pretend* shock at Christian's words. He was stunned speechless.

Dragon Guards were legendary. And no more. Their secret sect had disappeared, concealed in their mystic home centuries before. Some thought murdered by Isobel, after she'd killed Aaron. Darker whispers said she had also killed Rowan, the head of their order.

But for frail-*looking* Isobel to be a Dragon Guard was astounding. *I thought her shy and weak.* Dragon Guards were the most mystic of the Vampire sects. They were taken at birth. She would have never known her parents. Never bonded with them or been shown love. They were bred to be strong—but also detached and ruthless. Each one had to be, for the training was begun as soon as the child could walk. Each one also had to be of noble blood. If she had been chosen, then her twin brother would have been as well. It explained why he'd never encountered her before — only the once and only from a distance.

The ramifications of this new reality made his head spin. It was no wonder she'd lost her mind when her brother had been sentenced to death. He would have been all she had, all she had ever known.

"Shocking, isn't it? You see now why we will have a difficult time locating her."

Difficult? How about impossible? But that still didn't explain Christian being here. In his home.

"True, but still, not impossible. She has been centuries away from the world, how much could she possibly learn in so short a time? Look where she would find comfort, familiarity." *If there was such a place.*

"Ah, yes," Christian's gaze grew intense, watchful. "That is…helpful."

It would be if she were free to roam.

"I must go now if I am to prepare for the council." Another lie, but not so damning since he *should* prepare for the meeting, but knew he wouldn't. Not with Isobel downstairs. Even now, she was probably attempting to break free. He needed to call Jaxon. He needed to cancel the meeting. Or have Jaxon head it. But, more, he needed to see her again. Check that the bars still held her.

"I have business back in London, myself." Christian strolled over to the mantel to pick up a small cross. Bryson barely held in a growl. "Your home is well suited, Bryson. A good find, and far enough from everything to give you peace, I assume." Christian set the cross down and walked over to the small library, smiling at the ancient clock nestled between the rows of books. He ran a finger over the glass containing three Greek Orthodox icons and tilted his head at Bryson.

"A religious man, are you, Bryson? The Greeks really were better at icons than the Russians, were they not? The use of color, the deep blues and golds are truly amazing." He sighed and turned, clearly not in a rush to leave. Or not in as much of a hurry as Bryson was to get rid of him. "Beautiful. I shall give some thought to something like this for the future. There will be less need for me to be tied to a House if we succeed, eh?"

"Very good." Bryson kept the snarl from his tone, but barely. "I'm surprised you don't already have your own place, away from the House. But now, perhaps you can find one to your liking."

"True, absolutely true. I shall give it some thought. Good luck with the council, I have a feeling you will need it."

Bryson nodded. *And you will need more than luck to find what you seek.*

Christian winked and, thankfully, disappeared. The scent of evergreens settled in the room from his passage. Assured he was gone, and gone far, Bryson dropped his security harder and faster than before. Relief brought with it a load of guilt so heavy he sat, resting his head in his hands.

What am I doing?

He considered his phone and calling... He couldn't ask Aidan for help in this. Aidan was furious. No one could make him listen, not when he was like that. Jaxon couldn't be brought into this—even if he would help, Bryson couldn't damn his friend with his troubles.

I'm a traitor, a liar and, worse, none of that matters as much as the woman in my dungeon. All he wanted to do was squeeze her tightly to his chest again. Hold her. *It felt so right... If I can get her to explain, to give me a reason for what she did, then I can speak for her. Win her release from this death sentence. Have her. Claim her.*

He jumped to his feet and punched a hole in the wall.

What kind of man am I that I will let a woman have control over me?

A sudden suspicion of someone else in his house settled over him. He woke the dogs, reassured by their howls. *No one is near.* Just then, his skin prickled in awareness. A moment later, he heard Isobel's feet touch the hardwood floor behind him.

"Drop your barrier, Bryson. I will leave this place now."

The complete conviction in that tone pissed him off. Here he was wrangling with his conscience over what to do with her and she had no doubts at all about her path.

He laughed. "You will never leave this place. I will not allow—"

The strike hit his shield hard, much harder than he imagined it would. He barely reinforced them. He should have known after Seattle when she'd felled a forest. Still, he was amazed. Quickly, he added more layers so that she couldn't break past, even if he were to lose this fight.

Another hit followed the first. She hissed when she shoved at his shields and couldn't break free. Blood dripped from her nose, a telltale sign of how hard she fought to push herself free. The evidence of how she struggled enraged him. She sought to break from him. His bonded. *Mine!*

"Desist from this," he commanded harshly. "You will only hurt yourself. You will stay here, with me, as long as I wish it."

Immediately he was struck by a blast. His body hurtled through the room. Another punch hit him as he slammed into the mantel. Stones fractured on impact. His ribs cracked.

She attempted to break through his wards again. Panic surged. He reinforced the barrier even as he struggled to rise. She wiped her wrist under her nose, eyes narrowed at him, then turned. Raising her hand, she then shoved it forward. The glass windows exploded. His hounds howled. Icy claws of fear tore into his gut.

When the barriers still held, she turned to him. Her onyx eyes shimmered. "You would keep me prisoner? Again?"

Is that hatred in her eyes or...fear?

In that instant, clarity came. Six hundred and seventy-five years she'd been held, trapped, and he would do the same. *I can't lose her. I can't. But I can't keep her here.*

She raised her hands again, and this time rage blackened her irises.

Just about to drop his wards, Bryson froze.

Faolan walked out from behind Isobel and held up his hands, facing her. "You promised not to harm Bryson if I released you!"

"I won't harm him, Faolan. I will *kill* him."

Hell. I am in hell.

The boy raised both hands higher as if that would stop her. Amazingly, it did. She stared at the child and threw her own hands up. "Faolan, he —"

"He went to *save* you. He didn't kill *you*. You should hear him out. Elsa and Jamie talk, Jamie says that's how he learns what she wants. Maybe if Bryson talks, you will know what he wants."

"I *know* what he wants."

Bryson doubted that. *Do I know?*

"I don't believe you do," Faolan answered for him. "He wants to save you. But for good, not so you can always hide from Aidan."

She widened her eyes and stared at Faolan then raised her head to glare at him. "Have you sent this boy to talk to me?"

"What? Of course not. I didn't know he was here. Faolan, how the hell did you get in my damn home, again?"

She stiffened at his words. Her eyes narrowed. Belatedly, he recalled how Elsa felt about him swearing around the boy.

Faolan laughed.

"You don't ward your home well enough, that's how he got in," Isobel snapped.

He let that insult go, then couldn't seem to keep his lips sealed. "I don't see you breaking free."

She crossed her arms and the glare deepened.

What has happened to my diplomacy? My sanity?

"Bryson, aren't you supposed to be leaving? I can stay with —"

Stunned, he glared at the boy. "You have lost your brain cells somewhere along the way to break into my home — again — and if you think I'm leaving *you* with *her.*" He pointed at Isobel, who appeared offended. "She's not safe."

Her delicate brows drew down to indicate that he wasn't safe either. His back throbbed from where she must have crushed his vertebrae. His ribs were mending already, but they reminded him of her power. No doubt she'd do worse if the boy left. Although, he studied her eyes and perceived she was calmer, perhaps keeping Faolan around just for a while—until he could get her back in the cell—would be a good idea.

"She will not harm me," Faolan insisted. "We are friends."

Isobel snorted and looked away. She didn't deny it.

He'd been about to do the same. "Either way, you can't stay with her while I'm gone. I'm already damned in hell for lying for her—"

"You did not lie for *me*," she muttered. "You lied for yourself."

"I lied and hid you so you wouldn't be killed!"

At his shout, she again gave him the look as if he had grown another head. Her chin went up. Expression mulish she gazed at him steadily. As if daring him to go on? *The little—*

Faolan sighed and flopped onto the couch. "I'm hungry. Maybe we should eat. Jamie always says—"

"Faolan, I want you to leave." Bryson kept his voice firm, hoping if he did the boy would realize this wasn't the time or place to hang out. It was better if he left. There wasn't a doubt in his mind that he and Isobel would come to blows. The boy couldn't be here for that. Bryson didn't want to be here for that. But, short of forcing her, he didn't see how he'd get her back downstairs in a cell. *Keeping her.*

"But, Bryson—"

"It's for your own safety."

"I'm safe here, Bryson. I think you're safer too. Can you make us something to eat? I think Isobel might be hungry, as well." The boy grinned, playing with the strings of his hoodie. Did Elsa even realize what this kid got up to when she and Jamie were…busy?

Just thinking on what the couple were probably doing caused his heart to speed up. *Sex. Sex without end. Blood drinking, meshing of lips, pumping of hips, sweat, tight heat…*

"Uh, Bryson?"

He blinked. *Bank the desire. No sex. Not even thinking of sex.* He concentrated on ice and the freezing temperatures outside his home and managed to control his instincts. *She's turned me into a base animal.* He glanced at her. She stood with her back to them, no doubt trying to free herself still.

"You want me to go make you *dinner*?"

Faolan smiled. "Yes, that would be nice. Dinner would be good. Have you eaten yet, Isobel? Bryson makes good pasta."

The boy is crazy.

Isobel didn't respond, but neither did she attack. *Can't make her dinner! What the hell kind of inquisition is this if I sit across from her? Watching her eat what I've made?*

Provide. Protect. Claim. He battled the instincts back down. How long before he couldn't? She needed to be back in that cell. He swallowed. Not to keep her there, but to keep her away from him.

"I have a meeting, and she needs back in her cell."

"In the dungeon?" Faolan asked, eyes wide. "Why? She cannot escape this house."

She snorted.

Before Bryson could snap at her, Faolan added, "Why would you put her down there? There aren't any pillows or blankets down there, Bryson."

"Where's Jamie? I'm calling him to pick you up." He pulled out his phone, realized it was dead, threw it on the couch and glared at the ceiling. He considered Isobel, who couldn't leave, then the boy who wouldn't leave, and the empty pit in his stomach. *When was the last time I ate?* He remembered a quick burger and fries, but that had been some time ago. Nights ago. "Where are Jamie and Elsa?"

Faolan's eyes grew distant, then he smiled. "Jamie and Elsa are...busy."

He bet they were. Newly mated couples were often *busy* for years. He swallowed past a suddenly dry throat. His body surged to life – again. He battled it back down. Again. *Can't keep her here. Can't let her sit across from me. Can't –*

She sighed and wiped her sleeve under her nose again. Still attempting to leave? Why not? *What have I done to make her want to stay?*

Want to stay?

He angled his head, his mind running through the new thought. *This is a battle. Treat it like one.* Getting her to talk would not come from threats. Neither would it come from forcing her into a dungeon. But what about allowing her to talk? On her own?

His heart raced. The possibilities were there – she had been alone for so long. She clearly enjoyed Faolan. Had formed a bond of sorts with the boy. Of course Faolan had let her out...but she'd not attacked him again. *Was* she a killer?

I want to know. I need to know.

Then change your strategy.

"I can make something. Only if you stop attempting to break my barrier." Both of them gave him identical frowns. He ignored that and nodded to the crimson drop under her nose. "If you continue, I *will* put you back in the dungeon." For some reason, his mouth had decided threats were far better than staying quiet.

After an agonizing silence, she gave one miniscule dip of her regal chin.

He took that as a yes. Wanted to press for more, but held off by some miracle of god. He turned and stalked to the kitchen, ready to strangle someone, just not sure who.

Isobel watched Faolan move his hands as he described getting on something he called a subway. She had seen the tunnels underground, the large metal tubes people rode in, but hadn't followed the humans inside.

"I think you need to watch movies. You kinda speak funny. Like me. Elsa says I don't fit in with kids my age. She says it's because I didn't watch television."

She rubbed her nose, not wanting to interrupt the child, but unsure what he meant.

"TV."

"Ah, the large screen? With the pictures. I have seen this. It is useless." She dismissed the bizarre mesmerizing tool humans were so attached to. "This thing, the computer, this is much better." She had seen one and used it in a store filled with white light and odd, simple outlines of apples. Such art was truly loved by this century. She found it childlike. The computers in that place, though, had been enlightening. So was this thing called Chrome, and Google. Through both, the shopkeeper had shown her the world. More of it than she cared to see. It had been revealing of this century. She had left with something called a notebook made of an odd, smooth material but no paper.

"Yes, a computer is like a library." He gestured to the books along the walls of Bryson's study.

The room was warm and comforting, surprisingly so. The books in here were well-taken-care-of leather tomes. Some dated back to the earliest of times. They were not all he owned.

The icons he had on display were beautiful. He'd set them up with Christ in the middle on his cross, the Holy Virgin and child on Christ's right, and on the Virgin's left, St. John the theologian. The screens holding them were intricately carved marble and a deep, rich wood. Clearly the display was a masterpiece among his collection.

He also possessed other crosses she was not familiar with. Each was set on a shelf, as if casually placed. She thought each was arranged according to some system only Bryson would know.

Bryson. Something had changed with him. Something she couldn't pinpoint. When he had cracked the mantel stones she thought he would retaliate. His eyes had gone from light gray to darkest black—rage, she assumed. At her. His bonded.

But I hurt him and I am his mate. It had felt…wrong.

This concerned her. So did the oddest sense that he wanted to believe her, wanted answers, but feared them. *He thinks me a killer and seeks reassurances that I am not.*

I should hate him. I should go now, before this…dinner. I did not give my word.

But she had. Sighing, she worried her lip. *Why? What is this feeling? This anxiety?* She studied the hall leading to where he had stomped off. The smells indicated he was doing what the boy had asked of him. Making *dinner*.

He baffled her.

"Does Bryson cook for you often?"

"Yes. He used to give me candy, but Elsa asked him to stop. She is worried over my teeth. She thinks I will get too many cavities. Now Bryson makes me meals. I have never had one that smells so good. I think he is cooking for you."

She dismissed that because the idea caused a strange tightening in her chest.

"What is a cavity?" She peered at the boy's mouth, not seeing any defects in the size or shape of his fangs. They were perhaps a bit larger, but taking into account that he was at least part-Lykae, he appeared normal.

"Cavities. Holes, in my teeth," he explained, pulling his lip down and indicating a tooth.

She leaned forward and saw nothing that would indicate a problem. His teeth were...childlike and adorable.

"I told her it was a baby tooth. You won't get cavities," Bryson muttered from the doorway. "Dinner is almost ready. Come set the table, Faolan."

Faolan jumped up and tugged on her hand. "You can help. I always get the forks and knives reversed."

She followed him, unsure what he meant by that until they walked into a smaller room, filled with the scents of garlic, basil, and fresh rosemary.

"This is Bryson's kitchen, but we eat in here, not the dining room."

"The dining room is too cold." Bryson stood with his back to her, but she could tell he was uncomfortable, still angry, no doubt. His warrior's body was tense. His broad swordsman shoulders tight under his black shirt. Even his jaw flexed. *Grinding his teeth?* She took in the width of his shoulders, the packed muscles of his back, and could admit he was a stunning male. His light hair fascinated her. A multitude of colors shimmered in it. And along his jaw she could see the lightest shadow of more. If they had met before, if she had seen him and known him for hers she would have been stunned. He could have stood by her side, protected her from any and all.

But he had not. And she had not. Those chances were gone. Fate had never had him walk close enough for her to recognize him. But he had her. And had not come to her.

Cold. Fierce. Dragon Guard. These were not qualities a man found appealing. Vampire warriors wanted lithesome, large-breasted maidens with simpering smiles and pouty lips. They wanted to keep their women in a silken bower and await their every need. They did not desire some fierce warrior who would get blood on her hands. Obviously he had found —

"Here, you do the silverware, I will do the glasses." Faolan sounded cheerful.

Her hands were immediately filled with silver spoons, forks, and knives so she had to clutch them to her chest. She focused on Faolan and swallowed her anger.

"Do you know how to set a table?" Bryson asked.

She didn't glance at him. *Would a warrior maiden know how to do domestic tasks?* He thought her incapable of being…feminine?

"Of course." She walked to the rectangular table covered in a green and white checkered tablecloth. He watched her. She wondered if he even found her desirable. Her hands grew unsteady. She could wield a sword and never lose her confidence, but having Bryson watch her set a table made her insides clench. He didn't speak but when she was finished setting the last spoon down, he brought over a basket that smelled of fresh bread. The warm scent mingled with his, intoxicating her. He took the lid off a smaller plate, revealing a cut of yellow butter. Did he glance at her chest? She couldn't be certain, but she thought he hesitated by her. Taking a deep breath only made his tension rise.

"You can clean up down there. First door on your left."

Did she smell…offensive to him? Heat burned her cheeks.

"I will show you," Faolan offered, tugging her hand again. "This will be your first meal? With…people?"

Focused back on the boy, she managed to say, "This will be my first meal with people. Yes."

That seemed to please him. Amazing her, she liked that he seemed to like her.

"Some people now believe Vampires don't eat. And that garlic will kill you. They also think Vampires hate crosses," Faolan said, laughter in his tone.

"Who are these people?"

He shrugged. "Movie writers, stuff like that. Authors, people, human people, maybe some witches, too. They have stories about Count Dracula."

"Who is Count Dracula?"

"He's supposed to be the first Vampire. He killed a bunch of Turks and stuck them on stakes. Jamie let me watch a movie about it, but Elsa wasn't happy. She doesn't want me to think all Vampires are bad."

"Very nearly all Vampires *are* bad," she reminded him. She could recall the name of every noble in the

Augustine's line. None were thus named. "But this count is not familiar to me, nor is he the *first* Vampire."

Faolan blinked. "Oh, I didn't think he was, but not all Vampires are bad. Elsa is good. You are good. Bryson is good. Aidan is…good. Sometimes strict, but he is fair. I think Jaxon is good, so is—"

"These are your friends?" she interrupted his flood of names.

"Yes."

"Ah, I see. We always want those we care for to be good. But often just because we want someone to be good, it isn't enough for them to *be* good."

"Dinner's ready," Bryson called. He sounded harsh again, as if he were getting ready to throw more threats out. "Faolan, wash up."

Faolan covered his mouth to hide a smile. They were in the hallway so Bryson couldn't see him, but for some reason the child still covered his mouth. It was…endearing, as if he were sharing something with her. Something naughty but amusing.

She found herself smiling in return. It *was* humorous to hear gruffness from a man who was making them a meal and instructing a boy to wash. The room held two sinks in a large, marble-topped cabinet. Faolan switched on the light. She blinked.

"Whoa! This is bigger than my bedroom," Foalan exclaimed.

She scanned the small room. It was quite spacious. A full-sized, sunken tub and a large, glassed-in area with several knobs and odd ledges. There was another door to the other side of the room. Towels lay on a shelf, so soft and fluffy she traced her fingers over them. This century had luxuries she had never dreamed existed.

"Here." Faolan turned on the faucet of one sink and squirted sweet, clean-scented soap into her hands. She quietly lathered. The boy did as well, with an odd song.

"Elsa says I must sing the ABCs while I wash. She said I didn't wash long enough to remove the dirt."

Ducking her head, she cleaned her face and neck, too, not because she had affronted Bryson with her scent, but because she hadn't that night. "Elsa sounds wise." She dried her hands and face.

"I am hungry! Aren't you? Bryson makes a lot of food. He eats a great deal, but he will save some for us. Hurry." The boy dashed off.

Suddenly alone, she considered breaking her oath for the first time in her life. It had been a nod. A *slight* nod. Not an oath. She felt ill, as if she were facing an enemy worse than Satan himself, instead of Bryson MacAfee at a dinner table.

Faolan's innocent words repeated in her head. *'Give him time. You will like him, I think. I do. I love him. I think you will, as well.'*

The boy was naïve, too young to understand what he was saying. Issues of love were far more complex.

He knew me. Knew and recognized me but never approached me for his claim. She gripped the marble counter top until the stone cracked under her fingers. Memories of her capture surfaced. *Enemies all around me. Can't break free. Betrayed.*

'Cold, scrawny bitch! You think you're a warrior? You couldn't even save your brother, oh mighty Dragon Guard.'

Laughter from all around.

'You wish you could please a warrior, but you can't even do that. Who would want you?' More laughter rose at the woman's snide questions.

'No one. And no one will ever come for you. You will rot in this wall for an eternity wishing you'd never left your bower.' Christian's voice had haunted her for centuries, not because of what she'd sensed he'd wanted, but because *I never had a bower.*

A laugh broke free. Pain filled her chest. *The river isn't happy, but it is fierce and free. Or will be soon. It was a nod. Not an oath.*

Chapter Eleven

Christian shifted to his House, still bothered by Bryson. The Vampire had always been difficult to read. He'd actually thought for a moment he was hiding Isobel. In Seattle when he'd caught Isobel's trail, Bryson's had crossed it.

But the anger in Bryson's eyes hadn't been faked. Bryson had been close to Aaron. The king had made him his personal pet. Aaron's death had taken away Bryson's rank, along with his authority. Only when Aidan had returned had Bryson been given his position back. If he'd had his way, Bryson would have followed Jorge to Hell.

He pushed open the door to his House and walked through the foyer ignoring Benson, his manservant.

"My lord, you have a message, from—"

"Leave it. I will see to it later. I am not to be disturbed."

"But, my lord—"

Christian snarled and the other Vampire bowed and shut up. Satisfied, Christian took the stairs two at a time, hearing the dull murmur of Vampires carrying on their night below. He pulled his phone free as he shoved his bedroom door open and entered his inner sanctuary. The moon lit the elegant room with its silver glow and revealed the man he had wanted to call sitting on his couch.

"Warren."

"What took you so long?" Warren set down his glass of wine. "I was about to wonder if Bryson hadn't killed you."

"*I* should have killed *him*."

Warren lifted his brow. "Then he has her?"

"No. But he will have to be disposed of sooner or later. He and Jaxon both. If we can locate Rhys and his bitch, they will have to be dealt with as well."

"My, my, your list is long, isn't it?" Warren laughed when Christian growled a curse at him. "Settle yourself. All will come in time. Did you show him the missive?"

Christian set the scroll down. "Of course. He barely studied it."

"But if asked, he would say he saw it, yes?" The sharpness of the question got Christian's attention.

"Why?"

"It is important, Christian," Warren stressed as if Christian were a child. "If asked, will he say he has been shown the missive?"

"Yes. He studied it. Now, why is this so critical? And why are you here, waiting for me, when you are supposed to be finding that bitch?"

Warren reclined his head on the couch cushions, completely at ease in his presence. From the satisfied expression on his face, and the residue of pink lipstick on his jaw, Christian had no doubt he'd been enjoying the luxuries a Vampire House offered.

"You're uptight. The *bitch*, as you call her, is trained by the best. She'll be difficult to locate, but not impossible."

Christian barely held in the growl at Warren feeding him the same lines as Bryson.

"And your training was the same. I expected more from you. Don't let me down in this, *Warren*," he said scornfully. "We're both in this too far, and too deep."

"Such dire warnings." Warren snorted. "I take it your hopes were high this would be easy? And now, when it proves difficult, will you go back to sulking?" Warren lifted his hand and gestured to the room. "Not that the splendor and life you have here isn't filled with enjoyable diversions."

By the Vampire's tousled brown hair and the flush on his otherwise pale completion, those enjoyable diversions were enough to sidetrack *him*.

"Let me make this clear to you." Christian poured himself a glass of brandy to steady his nerves. "I will be king. I will rule with Agatha by my side, and you will get all you ever wanted, as well. Revenge on the House of Augustine. But *only* if you kill Isobel!"

"My dear Christian, it will be so. Already we lay the trap. Soon, when she begins to realize how desperate her situation is, she will go there. Then we will have all we both ever wanted."

Christian downed his brandy in a long swallow, letting the burn soothe him as much as what was being said. "Where? Where will you accomplish this?"

"Why, where her brother was staked down and killed, of course."

Halfway to pouring another glass, Christian paused and turned his head to see if the man was being funny. "You think she will go there? Why there, of all places? It holds no special meaning, no significance at all. It was merely where we caught him."

Warren motioned with his empty goblet and Christian walked over to pour him a drink. The clink of the decanter on the crystal was loud in the silence. "You are wrong. It is not merely where Jorge was found. It is where his soul was bound so that he would never rise again, and with it, that of his precious *Tessa*. That place holds meaning, Christian. Believe me, to her, these places are sacred."

Christian swallowed another sip of brandy and savored it on his tongue. "Then we are nearly there. She will be caught and killed. When she is, Aidan will come to see if it was done. It is then we will strike."

"Yes. But until then, you need to begin to sow the seeds of his downfall. The scroll will need to be given to the Immortal Council, but casually, as if you are merely conveying a favor you just considered might be of use."

Christian took his seat opposite Warren.

"When they scrutinize it, they will discover names on it that will call certain people into question. If Aidan is busy dealing with the Houses, Isobel on the loose, and the Immortal Council demanding answers, he will be unprepared for you and your claim."

"You see, killing Aidan is not your only option, Christian. In fact, I would advise against it. Remove him from power — that is the key to ruling the Houses. They will follow you, and the Immortal Council will, as well, if you rise to the occasion."

"What is on that scroll?" Christian glanced at the tube.

"Why, Aidan's signature, along with Bryson's and five other of his top captains', which if you recall makes six, a necessary number to make a ruling over the Houses."

"But that would mean —"

"They are forged, of course." Warren waved away the implications of that as if it were some pesky fly. "But only by a master. No one, not even Aidan himself, could detect it wasn't his hand that signed the pact with the covens to destroy the Immortal Council and rule in their stead by any means necessary."

The glass of brandy nearly slipped from Christian's hand. "With this we can take him down now, we don't need to wait for —"

Warren snapped his teeth together, revealing his fangs as his eyes glowed red. "Patience. She will have to die first. Then we can strike. Isobel has the ability to see past this document, Christian. For that, she will die, just as her brother did."

Christian hid his alarm, he hoped well enough from the man sitting across from him. There was more going on, much more than regicide. For Warren, a young Vampire, to possess knowledge and power was impossible if he was, in fact, merely a *young* Vampire.

"But for now, we will wait. Soon she will come to us, and then we will have all we've been waiting for." Warren smiled.

Chapter Twelve

If Bryson had to conjure up a more bizarre situation than sitting at a dinner table with Isobel while she was wanted by every single one of the people he called friends, he couldn't imagine it. Added to that, he struggled with an erection that was growing more and more painful.

This is more like a horror movie than a meal.

"This is delicious, thank you," Isobel said suddenly, not glancing up from her forkful of pasta, but still saying it loud enough that he couldn't pretend not to hear her. She'd been quiet, much quieter than before. Not *quieter*, more…distant. Was that possible? She sat a few inches from him, but it felt as if she were miles away in a different place. And not in a good place either.

He cleared his throat. There was nothing he could do. Politeness was more ingrained than the damn need to reach across the table and touch her skin. Smooth the delicate frown on her brow. He kept his hands on his side of the table. "It's nothing. I'm glad you like it."

Faolan slurped up a long line of spaghetti and gave him the thumbs up.

"He eats a great deal," Bryson said, by way of apology for the boy's lack of manners.

Isobel seemed to shake off her trance. Her dark gaze focused back on the boy and turned from cold marble to warm flesh once again. The tightness in his chest eased. For some reason he wanted her to be happy. Or at least not clearly miserable.

"He is growing. He will need large meals four or five times a day, if he is to grow properly."

Bryson halted with the fork halfway to his mouth at that. "Don't most children need two or three meals?"

"Yes, of course, but a Vampire child needs more."

The fork almost fell.

Faolan choked on his mouthful.

Isobel stared from him to the boy, then back to him for answers.

Bryson set his fork down and picked up his wine and sipped it slowly. Tried to grapple with his thoughts. All he could think was that her irises sparkled like onyx. His growing obsession over every facet of her was disturbing. "It is a nice vintage. Do you drink wine?"

Expression confused, she asked, "What have I said that has alarmed you both?"

He set the wine down. "Well, what makes you believe that Faolan is a Vampire?"

She pressed her napkin to her lips then folded it into a precise rectangle on her lap. Her manners were exquisite. The way she ate, mesmerizing. How she smelled, intoxicating. He wanted to rub his hands all over her and remove the distasteful soap smell from her so it was just her — sweet, pure, warm Isobel smell.

"He has the scent. He has the ability to shift. He is Vampire, something else, Lykae, of course, but... Something else as well. An old soul, perhaps."

"Something else?" Bryson questioned.

"I'm a Vampire?" Faolan exclaimed. "I don't drink blood."

She smiled when Faolan covered his throat as if she might drink from him. It was a warm, purely happy smile on her lips, but it was gone too fast. Bryson felt it, deep inside where he could sense something between them, where tenderness wanted to blossom. He clenched his hand under the table.

Isobel didn't see his reaction since she only had eyes for Faolan. It was obvious the charm Faolan used on all adults worked as well on her as it did on everyone else. For some insane reason, that caused his heart to feel as if it had tightened painfully.

"No, you *are* a Vampire." She squeezed Faolan's hand.

"What did you mean by old soul?" Bryson asked when she released Faolan and both took to their meal again.

By the look she gave him, he had the feeling he was stepping into that unspoken area they had not discussed — her. The color of her eyes turned with her emotions. Now they were shimmering lighter, the irises revealing shards of amber.

When Faolan didn't speak, and he didn't either, she politely sat straighter. "Do you know what occurs when a Vampire is killed? Not with fire, but killed, say by breaking a neck, or removing a head, or — "

"I get the picture." He held up his hand. Dinner was not the time to discuss maiming and killings, at least not with the boy here. "Yes. He or she can return to their body."

"Yes. But if, for example, you were to kill a Vampire, then burn him or her, then spread his or her ashes, then what would happen?"

"They cannot return to their bodies." Faolan grinned when Isobel nodded.

"How did you know that?" Bryson asked.

Faolan chewed an enormous piece of bread. "I guessed."

Isobel smiled and nodded. "Good guess, although perhaps you were using logic. If a Vampire were to be killed in such a way..." She paused and played with her glass of wine. She had killed in such a way, twice if he was correct about Aquinas. "Then their soul cannot move on. Sometimes, *sometimes*," she stressed, "that soul finds another home. Perhaps in a recently deceased. Or sometimes overtaking and occupying another, weaker host."

Bryson blinked a few times to get his brain working. It had been so long since he'd had company. And even those times had been limited to quick outlines of battle plans. He'd almost forgotten what it was like to theorize with someone who was obviously well learned in ancient lore and intelligent.

My perfect match in so many ways. Strong. Brave. Sexy. Beautiful. Enchanting. Clear headed – when not angered beyond reason. Logical – even after being angered beyond reason. Loves food. Appears to like children. Everything about her was ideal – except regicide.

"You mean a Vampire can be killed, burned, spread over the land and still survive to latch onto someone so they can suck their life out and exist in their body?" Faolan asked, wide-eyed.

Isobel was silent but finally winced. "Well, I wouldn't have put it in that context, but basically, yes." Before Bryson could demand more, she turned to him. The speculation in her eyes intrigued him. *What would she say next?*

"With Faolan, I don't sense another soul within his body. Nor do I believe him evil enough to have done something as vile as take over someone's body and force them to be nothing more than a passenger."

Faolan choked on his mouthful again. He grabbed his milk and drank a large swallow.

"But, at times, especially with babes that do not survive birth, a soul leaves unable to live on after the trauma, and that is when another can."

Stunned silent, he grappled with the idea. He stared at Faolan as if he'd never seen him before. But he couldn't help it. His big, brown eyes were innocent, but the shade would deepen and lighten depending on his moods. Vampires did such things. But so did Lykae. His hair was shot through with sandy shades, similar to the wolf clan.

Still, Faolan was different.

Faolan, *little wolf*, wasn't even his name, not really. Jamie had given him the name, and no one had discovered another. He was different. He read thoughts. Not minds, thoughts. Elsa had shared that he read the thoughts of ancient Vampires.

"You believe Faolan is such a creature? He is not evil," he repeated. It needed repeating. "He's a boy, albeit with special gifts, but he's not evil."

Isobel seemed to mull over that with a great deal more consideration than he thought necessary. Her expression thoughtful, she ran her finger over the top of her wine glass.

He glanced at Faolan, but the boy was watching Isobel as if she would spell his doom.

"Faolan, do you feel any of this is right?"

"Right?" he stuttered. "I don't know if it's right or wrong, Bryson. Maybe Elsa would know. I should call her." He stuffed his hand into his pocket.

Bryson stopped him. If Elsa showed up, Jamie would, as well. He didn't need to deal with the newly mated couple clouding his already murky ability to process his thoughts. "No, no phone calls. The mountains interfere." *The lies become so easy.*

"I am not saying that Faolan is such a creature. I think he is an old soul, perhaps a reincarnate, or else simply wiser than his years from his trauma."

Faolan seemed to think that was the answer. "I am wise."

"You are wise," she agreed. After sipping her wine, she added firmly, "And a Vampire."

Faolan made a face at that, which made Bryson laugh, even though the situation was extremely tense. He felt as if he were having dinner with the enemy, while a young innocent boy sat and watched. At the same time, he felt as if it were only natural that Isobel should sit and eat what he'd prepared for her. She should enjoy discussing philosophy or the weighty matters of what powers Vampires held.

"It is difficult," she went on, smiling warmly at the boy again. "You should start to require blood when you reach ten and three. It is then you will begin to—"

"Wait, he might not be a Vampire at all. I sense something, true, but I am not convinced. What makes you so certain? Even Aidan was unsure."

She gave him the expression he'd already grown used to—the mixture of surprise and embarrassment for him as if he'd spoken silliness. He'd never been silly in his life.

"I have no idea why you do not recognize him."

Is there a bite to her words?

He sought her eyes, but she avoided his. "How could I know?" She sighed heavily, sounding tired. "And as for Aidan, I also cannot say one way or the other what his abilities are on such things. I have never met Aidan. Nor do I wish to under the current circumstances." She trailed her fingers along the wine glass again, but he saw tension in her delicate body. "I do know that Faolan is a Vampire. It is as apparent to me as we have two hours and twenty-six minutes and thirty seconds until the sun rises."

Bryson grumbled under his breath at that. It was clear his question had offended her. But like a good guest, she had not snapped at him. Merely set him down through her logic.

"Be that as it may, I still feel he could be something else altogether."

She finally resigned herself to look at him. "Such as?"

"A demon. He could be a demon, or a Faye," he tacked on when his first suggestion seemed to amaze her.

An elegant eyebrow arched upward. "A demon? He is not evil."

"No, I am not evil. I am good. But we know demons that are also good. Jamie invited Fire and Moon over."

"Bethany and her demon mate, a Fire Demon, Agni. I see Jamie is determined to expand Elsa's limit on friends."

Faolan nodded. "Yes, he wants her to branch out."

"Branch out?" Isobel lifted her elegant eyebrows.

"Expand her limits," he explained. "Do things which make her uncomfortable or move away from what she's comfortable with."

"Ah, I see. But a Fire Demon does not count. He is a Guardian."

He was shocked she knew of such things then recalled what Christian had said about her being a Dragon Guard. Both were elite mystic warriors.

"Yes and no. Agni freed the Fire Kingdom from Lucifer's rule. He is aiding his bonded in the Faye Realm with the darkness spreading into that land."

She studied him, then her wine. He couldn't read her. *What is she thinking?*

"Why do you question that Faolan is a Vampire? Do you despise your own kind?"

Bryson pushed his chair back from the table and settled his wine closer. It had been a long time since he'd had discussions of this kind with anyone — far too long. He wanted to hate her, and should, but she fascinated him. Not only fascinated him. If not for the boy, he might have spread her out on the table tonight and feasted on her. Her neck, her...

He tensed and took control of his fantasies. The erection pulsed, making it difficult, but he mastered himself.

"Faolan, there is ice cream down the hall in my freezer in the laundry room. Can you find what you want and bring us each some as well?"

The words had barely left his mouth and Faolan was off in search of dessert.

"He has a sweet tooth." He explained the sudden departure.

"Ah, I see. He is a child."

He nodded and sat forward, studying his wine, but really thinking about what she had asked. It was a valid question. There were reasons to hate his kind. *She is one reason.* He ignored the whisper. "I do not hate my kind. Vampires have not done well since you last walked this earth. You must have seen this in the past few weeks since your rising."

She inclined her head only a fraction.

"Aidan was lost," he reminded her, noting that she didn't shy away from his gaze but met it steadily. She had claimed not to know Aidan, not to have met him. But if that was so, then how could she have trapped him and killed his father?

Listen to her. Wait. Discover why she did it. Then you will know.

He organized his thoughts, wanting to explain the world to her, what she had slept through, not merely his own beliefs.

"For a long time, he turned his back on us all. We who were closest to Aaron fell from power and drifted, some of us for centuries. New Vampires were born, more died. Some created strong Houses on the foundation of the slaves they collected. There were more Vampire-Lykae wars." He rubbed his chest, remembering a wound he'd taken in the last battle. It still bothered him when the seasons changed. "There were wars with the covens that linger in the deep resentments of the eldest of our race. There were human wars, world wars that impacted us. With the passage of time, the Death Stalkers rose in number. Splintered into fractions, each with seemingly no end to the horror they live by."

Sipping his wine, he considered what else to say. All. Everything. "Changelings were discovered, immortals and humans that are even now little more than wild beasts. Such is the way of the world, though. One group of evil is stamped out and twenty more rise up to take its place."

He shook his head and caught her gaze. "But no, I do not hate our kind. Aidan has returned, taken up his role and is attempting to bring the Houses to heel through a council, *and* his will. I have done what I can, where I can, but perhaps it is all too little, too late. The world is becoming smaller, and the terrible things that occur in it are not solely laid at our feet any longer. Humans have grown bolder, disregarding every sense of morality they once may have felt in their desires to feed even the darkest of their dreams."

She didn't speak. She was good at meeting his eyes and not shying away from his inspection. Eyes still lighter, not showing the rage from before, but not showing him anything else either, she pursed her lips.

"Now I am faced with this, with you. What is it I should do, Isobel? Tell me, as we sit here and enjoy a meal and conversation in the most civilized manner. What shall I do with you? Turn you over to my king? Again?" He shook his head. "I could not bear it the first time. I cannot do it again. Shall I kill you? End your life and take your lifeless body to Aidan to show my loyalty to a man long since dead? By your hand? What do you believe I should do?"

All the color drained from her face as his words spilled out. The lack was shocking. Her eyes bled black, shimmering with such emotion he wondered how he'd found her cold and unreadable moments before. She stood, shoving her chair back and leaned forward boldly, both hands on the table. Above him. The dominant position. He kept himself seated by sheer willpower.

"You ask me?" she rasped. "Why do you ask me? Are you not set on your path?"

"Obviously not," he growled, indicating the table between them. "Did I not just make you a meal? Are we not here, discussing this?"

She searched his expression, irises going from black to warmer amber.

Bryson broke her gaze to see Faolan had his arms filled with overflowing bowls of ice cream. Isobel sat back down.

"Maybe you could wait and do nothing," Faolan suggested, setting the bowls on the table without dropping one. "Just wait, and don't make a decision yet."

He frowned at Faolan. The boy smiled and put a spoon in a bowl and scooted it over the table at him.

"Boy, doing nothing *is* making a decision." He turned back to Isobel. "Tell me. Explain to me now, why would you kill Aaron?"

For a moment, he thought she would answer. Her expression wasn't cold, wasn't back to that marble mask. She appeared lost. Would the truth finally fall from her lips? Would he have his answers? And their doom?

There was nothing she could say to explain, nothing at all to justify the life she'd taken. She, above all else, knew her brother had been evil, a killer turned mad enough to destroy an entire village. Instead of accepting that Jorge's punishment was just, she had killed her king.

There was no explanation she could give, and therefore, no way out of what he had to do.

Kill her.

Chapter Thirteen

The food Isobel had eaten turned to a ball of misery in her stomach.

Bryson. He wanted things from her she couldn't give.

The truth.

Her death was in his eyes. She could sense it. And she knew, no matter what she said, no matter how she explained those terrible times, he would not see the truth.

Because he did not want to.

No one had.

Why would he be different?

'Frigid ice bitch, you thought yourself above us? That someone would come to save you? There isn't a man in the realm that would want a woman like you.' Gia's spiteful voice had ripped into her, harsher than the whips the witches had wielded.

Bryson, I thought, for a moment, you were different.

She gathered her strength and tested the boundaries of his estate and found only one outlet — his dogs. The hounds were bred for the cold, wintery environment. Their master had chosen wisely. Not so wisely, since he'd let her roam his house.

Without giving warning, she shifted to them, still within his protection, but now outside and not sitting across from him at his table and his accusations.

She thought she heard Faolan call her name. The sadness within grew. She did hear Bryson bellow something after her. She was already a female hound, similar enough to the pack of dogs to fit in amongst them.

The alpha immediately rose to its feet. She bared her fangs. Two more rose, tensing to attack. They were bred for battle. Large with brown and gray fur, they were wolf-like creatures with the keen instincts of killers. Their jaws would hold her, let alone their teeth. She prepared herself.

The dogs howled. In a frenzy, they charged. Baying as they raced toward her. She leapt over the fence, the pack all around her, and landed safely on the other side.

The trick to breaking free from spells, and from other Vampires, was to have nothing to lose. Rowan had taught her that the more she believed she had to lose the greater the difficulty of the task. If she shed everything but the essential need to survive nothing was too great a price.

I have nothing — just my oath to you, Jorge.

She reached the barrier and broke free, with the pack after her. The magic sliced agony, ripping down to the bone. She felt as if she'd torn out her own spine. *Ignore it. Fly. Fly.* She forced a shift to a hawk. Barely gaining her shape before she was forced to fight the currents and rise through the forest canopy. Each stoke of her wings was unbearable. *Go. Go. Or leave your oath to Jorge behind.*

Suddenly, above her she sensed Bryson. *Already? Need time.*

Focus.

The classical, superior Vampire move meant to take her out.

No! Be strong!

She tucked her painful wings in and dived, speeding back to the snow-capped trees. Wind in her face, clearing her mind. *Think! What won't he expect?*

She shifted in midflight to Paris. As soon as her feet landed, she shifted to London, and on to Berlin. Each jump drew directly from her power. Weakness made her stumble. Blood loss had her head spinning. Pain rippled down every nerve ending.

Finally, she regained her form on the banks of a familiar river. Sobbing with exhaustion, she gripped the earth with her claws. *Calm. Calm. Must gain strength.*

She waited. Certain he would burst into the air above her any second.

The river swirled beside her, and with it, memories from long past. There was a time when she would have visited the church that had once stood where she crouched.

She stayed still, counting slowly to a hundred. There was no sign of Bryson. No sign of anyone on the breeze. But there would be. Still, she remained motionless. Her hands anchored her to the tough grass. Memories rose as fresh this night as they had been centuries before.

Jorge. Broken, bloody. His bride by his side. Their babe — gone. Agony filling my body.

"You must aid me, sister."

"Anything." She sobbed and cradled his head in her lap. She reached down and pressed his dark hair off his brow.

"You must go. They will come. They will destroy me. I will need you alive. I will need you to avenge me, or else I will never be reunited with my Tessa."

Tears blurred his battered face. She touched Tessa's cold hand, anguish swelling through her like nothing she'd experienced before. Tessa had suffered much before death had taken her away.

"I can't lose you. Come with me. Together we will – "

"No! I cannot. They have her soul, as well, sister. Only if they are given me will they release her."

She shook her head. "They will not. I know them. They are – "

"Evil. I know." He reached up and touched his knuckles to her cheek and more tears flowed, hot and painful down her face. "I need you now, sister. We need you."

She knew what he asked. What it would mean. "But what if she is…damaged? And lost to you because of what they did?"

He grimaced and a tear fell from his eye, traveling down his proud features. "I cocooned her from that, sister. She was unconscious, not aware of them."

"Oh, Jorge!" Such a thing meant he had known, he had known what evil they did to her body and been unable to aid her. Such love he had for her, such joy they had once shared. She bowed her head. "I give you my oath. I will see your souls freed."

His eyes closed and ease spread over his taut expression. "I will love you forever, as well, my sister."

"Jorge." She sobbed once, unable to hold in the sound.

"Don't. Don't cry for me. I had her, I had her for a short while. I will have her after. You must believe this."

"Must I?"

"You must, sister. For it will strengthen you. I swear this to you. If you do not lose faith, you will not lose us. Nor will I lose her."

She nodded as he gripped her hand. "I will give myself to them freely, but after you must kill them. All of them. Only then will we be avenged. Only then will you purge our people of their evil. Give me your oath you will not try to stop what they do this night. That you will go and not return for a sennight."

Gasping, she shook her head. "I cannot!"

"You must."

Knees aching, cold blowing over her heated face, heart aching with agony, she bowed her head, defeated. "What if I fail?"

"You will not fail. You are my sister. They may win for a time, but you will not fail."

Such strength in his tone, such belief. She lifted her head and gave him what he wanted.

He smiled, a painful twist of his lips, and took Tessa closer in his arms. His grip on her hand loosened.

"I will not fail you, Jorge. I will crucify them for this."

The memory snapped closed. She gasped in a lungful of salt-scented air. Tears once again blurred her vision, but she wiped them away.

Jorge, I will not fail you. I will not. They will come, and, when they do, I will kill them.

The marshes were still, heavy with a night fog so familiar to her. What wasn't familiar was the absence of the church. The landscape was dreary, missing the quiet splendor it once possessed. In her mind, this place hadn't changed. But in reality everything had changed.

Has it been so long, brother?

The church's tower no longer cut through the night sky, tall and proud as it rose to Heaven. The lovely stained-glass windows depicting Chapters from its beloved bible were gone, along with the merry bells that would ring the martyrdom of the saints.

The sea was not far, nibbling at the land like a hungry child biting at a biscuit—that hadn't changed. The scent of salt called to her, reminding her of long gone times when she had swam beneath the rough surf and let the water buffer her from the world.

She stood and walked to where the small church had once stood. There, in the center of where the Christians had knelt in worship, she went to one knee and bent to touch the ground. *Here is where my brother died.*

Even after all this time, she felt his presence. The agony and utter helplessness he'd experienced reached up and struck her. Much as it had when she'd discovered what the council had done to him. He was here, but not here. Trapped within the blood they had let soak into the ground and locked into his misery as if he had just discovered his wife's broken body.

You want answers, Bryson. You would not be able to comprehend the lengths some would go to to gain that which they want above all else – I couldn't. But I do now.

A disturbance on the air alerted her to the arrival of the Hunters, but she didn't move. They had come strong, as she knew they would. But Christian led them, the fool. She would kill him, here, where he had helped destroy her brother.

"I see you are still filled with sentiment."

At the words, she didn't turn. She didn't need to.

The Hunters always attack first. But she would be the winner here, no matter how many of them Christian threw at her.

"I always wondered why he didn't leave. Why let us destroy him? He could find another woman." Christian's boots drew nearer. "My guess? With a cold-hearted bitch like you as a sister, he couldn't wait to get away."

She flashed a smile. "Such flattery won't save you."

He stopped, laughed as if she amused him. She heard the fear, though, under his bravado. More footsteps indicated more Vampires.

A stab of pain barreled through her palm as a stake rose between her knuckles. *Witchery?* He *did* fear her. Another appeared by her leg, missing her but touching the side of her knee.

She tore her hand upward and flung herself at the first Vampire, a young, untrained *boy*. They collided hard and she gained his neck, almost before he realized his danger. She bit him and drew from his blood even as she lifted him high into the clouds. The blood gave her strength. The wounds she'd received from Bryson's barrier began to heal.

He struggled, fruitlessly, in her arms. When she was satisfied he would not rise again to fight her, she tossed him aside. He plummeted, unable to stop his fall. He would survive. He was not the prey. The wound on her hand closed, leaving behind an ache, but nothing more. She needed more blood.

To her left, she sensed another. He dropped at an angle to capture her. She twisted and evaded him easily and misted to the clouds. Two Vampires still pursued her. Both were strong, but not the one wanted. But she would drink from them, gain her strength again.

She caught one in the chest with a bolt. He fell with a surprised shout and disappeared in the clouds. *Two down.*

The other one reached her. His eyes flared wide as he drew near. *This one will do.* He grinned, thinking her an easy catch. She spied the red of blood lust around his irises. A death drinker. *Not a source to drink from.*

She ducked under his arm and kicked him hard enough to drive him head first into the marsh. He made a desperate attempt to rise to his feet and away from her. She caught his long trench coat and tossed him face down and under the water. He thrashed, wetting them both, until within minutes, he weakened and ceased struggling.

Christian.

He hovered close. This one, she would drink until almost dry.

The coward stayed back. Hunters traveled in packs of six. Always six. Vampires believed such a number was lucky, but it wasn't luck, it was something much more sacred.

But where are the others?

Suddenly, she sensed someone coming closer. She launched herself away from her hiding spot. Lightning hit so close it burned her arm. The bolt buried itself in the spot she had been. It would have killed her. At least for a while.

Not Christian. The strike was too good. Even as she thought it, Christian appeared in the clouds. His silver eyes were bright with the need to kill her. She beckoned him with two fingers. *Come, try.*

His eyes flared wide, but he didn't attack.

She threw herself at him. At the last moment, she broke into a swarm of crows, pecking and stabbing him with her sharp beaks and tough claws. Just as fast, she shifted to herself and hit him hard enough to knock him back to earth. His impact was rewarding. She landed softly next to him. He was groaning, holding his head.

She kicked him savagely in the stomach before he could rise. He shouted and rolled away, gaining his feet.

Someone grabbed her from behind, attempting to bite into her neck. She tossed the man off. The death eater. She brought her boot down on his ribs then picked him up by his jacket and tossed him into the sea.

Just as she turned, Christian hit her hard in the face, knocking her back a step. Before she could recover, he grabbed her shirt. It ripped as she was thrown to the ground. He followed through with a kick that broke her ribs. *Focus! Can't lose.* She twisted her legs and captured him. At the same time, she hit him with a quick snap of power.

"Bitch!" He wiped at his bloodied lip.

Drawing a dagger from his waist he hunched over, then launched himself at her. She let him. He dove low, she twisted and kicked out. Her boot contacted with his head. Toying with him? She wasn't certain. He was enraged. His irises blackened, his face flushed. He charged, managing to slice her arm from elbow to wrist before she could dodge him.

"Fucking whore."

The words stabilized her need for his death. She ignored the pain, the blood loss, and brought down another strike of lightning, then another and another. He screamed and burst to mist, avoiding her only for a second. She launched skyward and only too late sensed…danger. A blast of pure white crackled by her head, missing her by a hair's-breadth. The tingle of electricity left behind traveled up and down her body. She searched the skies. Saw no one. Only *someone* was there. *Ancient. Powerful. A male.*

Suddenly she spotted Christian.

"Isobel!"

Bryson. He flew at her, grabbing her arms even as she tried to reach Christian and whoever the other was. She sensed him back off, as if Bryson being here caused him to pause. Bryson lifted her to the clouds, hiding them in the misty cover.

"Release me!"

"God damn it, you're hurt!" He bit into his arm and suddenly, before she knew what he was doing, shoved the wound up against her mouth. "Drink. You are wounded! Drink now!"

Her fangs dropped. Rich, spicy-scented blood intoxicated her. Never before had she smelled something that caught and held her like Bryson's blood. Against her will, she bit down. Warm, salty — perfect flesh surrounded her fangs. It felt as if lightning had struck — but on the inside. Awash in such warmth, she moaned, clung to firm, strong shoulders with one hand and clutched her prize closer to her chest with her other.

"Drink!"

She obeyed. The first sip was — life-changing. Heady, powerful blood soaked into her as she savored him. Bryson groaned raggedly. Sounding pained, but...not. He crushed her to him, proving he was as strong as he looked.

"Yes! Take what you need."

She drank, not deeply, not the way she did when she killed, but slowly, enjoying the rich vintage. She wanted more, wanted more of *him*. She pressed into him and wrapped her leg around his, drawing him even closer. Rigid muscles flexed beneath her nails. He bound her to him with his arm around her waist. She tightened her grip, moaning at the feel of his erection between them. Warm, suddenly moist flesh trembled as she ground against his manhood. The delicious stimulation made pleasure erupt throughout her body.

She gasped and pulled free. His eyes were dark, shimmering with such heated passion she shivered. His gaze flickered over her face, then focused on her eyes, mesmerizing her. Her mind blanked. Until, with a rush, the scents of the sea reminded her where she was. She pulled back the tiniest bit and he released her, his expression going hard.

"Why..." She swallowed and started again. "Why did you do that?" Had her voice ever been so breathless?

"You were poisoned. You were weak. You should never have—"

"Bryson! Grab her!" Christian shouted, sweeping toward them from above.

Bryson caught her arm, not to hold her but to growl at her, "Go. Damn it, Isobel, will you just listen to me and go?"

"Hold her!" Christian bellowed, materializing right in front of them, his sword lifted to take her head. Bryson shocked her by hitting Christian with enough power that the other man flew backward into a milestone far, far below them. Even from where they hovered it sounded as if it had cracked under him. Christian stayed down, unmoving in the grass.

"What are you doing?" she cried, scanning the area for the other. "There is danger here. Someone else has come with him. Someone dangerous—"

"Hell, don't you think I know that? They want you dead, Isobel. Every single one of them is dangerous!" Bryson hauled her closer, until their faces were inches apart. Rage filled his expression. "This is the hell you've put me in."

She wrenched free. "I haven't put you in hell, Bryson. You've put yourself there."

He grimaced and caught her again. His grip was like steel—covered with velvet because he took care not to hurt her, but this time, his hold was unbreakable. His handsome face tightened and the intensity in his gaze deepened. She couldn't look away from him. His eyes were hypnotic. She could sense his soul, the dark, powerful force that was Bryson. So brave, so honorable, but also so foolishly holding onto his beliefs. Why had he given her blood? She would be able to read him now, reach him now, find him. More important than that, why had he grown hard? *For me? Or was it blood sharing…?*

"If we are going to die, I want one thing before we do."

"*I* am not dying." She gave him an icy glare. "You might if you do not—"

He silenced her with the sudden shock of his mouth pressed to hers.

The feel of his lips, the heat of his kiss seared into her so she thought he touched her soul. For a brief, utterly unbelievable second, the world and every horrible thing in it ceased to exist. There was only this man—holding her as if she might disappear—and his kiss. He thrust his tongue past her lips, claiming her mouth with such urgency that she gasped. When she did, he stroked his tongue along hers, coaxing hers back along his. It was amazing. Even more so because he gripped her backside with one splayed hand and forcefully shoved her up against him. His solid—very large—erection pulsed between them, making it clear what that one thing was he wanted.

Me.

He couldn't possibly want to claim me? Now? Just the idea made her lightheaded and weaker than she'd ever been in her life.

With the same abruptness as he'd kissed her, he pulled free. She staggered, lost still in his kiss. If her world seemed turned upside down, the changes in Bryson were profound. She noted the color tingeing his high cheekbones, the swelling of his muscles, *all* his muscles. His handsome brow was furrowed with such concentration she wondered what he was thinking. He looked like a Greek god.

"Do not die this night, Isobel. Go, now, while you can."

She pulled free and hit him with her fist—lightly, she realized with a shock. "I'm not going anywhere! You should. Go!" Inside, she knew that now she was the one speaking lies. She desperately—and unexpectedly—wanted him to stay, to stand by her side, and prove that someone, him most especially, cared about her. *Believe* in *me*.

Lightning crashed down and the two Vampires she'd thrown earlier appeared, racing for them. More followed. Christian was one.

"Isobel, for God's sake, go!" Bryson caught one man around the waist and tossed him down so hard she thought his skull cracked. The power was stunning. "Isobel!"

She barely turned in time to defend herself. Bryson growled something under his breath that carried as another meaningless threat on the wind. She caught and held her opponent by his throat.

"You are hunting for the wrong Vampire. Now, stay down!" She tightened her hand and flew upward until the air was so thin it was brittle cold. Then she dropped the unconscious Vampire.

"Now. Now we go," Bryson called, breathless and bloody from where he had followed her into the clouds.

"I will *not* go. I came here, knowing they would be here!" He was no different. Even if he kissed her. Even if he grew hard for her. "I do not need your help, nor should you offer it if you believe such things of me!"

His eyes flashed lighter. "Then tell me what to believe, damn it!"

She sensed the ancient leaving the area, but Christian remained. Meeting Bryson's tormented gaze, she relented. "I am my brother's only salvation, Bryson. Do not get in the way of my oath again."

She dropped down, feeling the power of the wind as she spiraled through the clouds. *I will not allow him to distract me. Not now.*

She hit Christian hard in the chest with both hands. His eyes widened even as he struggled to dislodge her. But she knew him. Knew the coward he kept hidden from the world. She didn't try for a killing blow. This time, she twisted and caught him around the neck and shifted him in her arms.

Chapter Fourteen

The cavern Isobel settled in was ancient. Far more ancient than humans, who'd found only the merest percentage of it, far, far above this sacred place.

Christian fought, immediately attempting to throw her. She kept hold of him and let him beat at her sides. It wasn't his death she craved yet. It was his blood. He had the knowledge she needed. He knew who all the members of the council were — and who this *other* was.

She sank her teeth in and drank greedily, nearly ending his life as his fight weakened. On the cusp she released him but left the wounds open. He fell to the floor, gasping and attempting to crawl away from her. She broke his mind and found what she wanted in the selfish, manipulating mechanics of his thoughts. There, in the forefront was what he craved.

He'd been glad she had killed Gia. Thrilled to think she'd taken Aquinas' life, as well. Without them he had no one to stand in his way of claiming the throne. With Agatha by his side, he would win a regime. Everyone else who would ever know and possibly betray his involvement in Aaron's death — except one.

A man.

She didn't know him, didn't recognize Christian's memories of him, nor understand what part he could have possibly played in her brother's death. He was young. Merely of this century and yet...this was also the ancient she'd sensed.

She laid Christian's mind bare, and once he was groaning and begging for mercy, she threw his deeds at Bryson — forcing them through the bond Bryson had forged by giving her his blood. She felt Bryson stagger and fall to the ground, his head in his hands as the painful thoughts attacked him.

She struck Christian hard in the head with her boot.

The chamber filled with light as a thousand candles blinked into existence. Hands above her head, she called to the fire and drew it, building the flames brighter and brighter. When she could hold no more, she crouched and lowered her hand down on the still-thrashing body. Flames caught and erupted as Christian screamed. When he was no more, she called the wind and let it blow his black ashes to the surface, cleansing the sacred space of his evil.

Agatha. She will be next. Then I will have to find this other.

A sudden shout, inside her head, and she nearly lost her footing. *Bryson?*

But that was impossible. She had not shared *her* blood with *him*. There should be no bond. She spun, not seeing him, then realized why.

He is in trouble?

She waited, not sensing more, and unwilling to open the line. Except the longer she stood, the more she wanted to check. He had saved her from the Hunters. He had stayed, while she'd left, battling the last so she could escape with Christian.

She shifted, not materializing but hovering as he had, in the air, to scan the surroundings. Below her she found him. He was held by two Vampires. He could have easily thrown them off and killed them. Instead, he allowed them to bind him painfully and shove him to his feet. She breathed in and scented more. He was hurt. Somehow, he'd been stabbed. She remembered him shoving Christian off. He'd grunted. *Had he been wounded?* She had taken hold of Christian and left. She had assumed Bryson would do the same.

She came behind both men and slammed their heads together, but not hard enough to kill them. She could tell Bryson didn't want that, so she used enough force to stun them. Once down, she broke the tight cords on his arms. Bryson fell forward, barely catching himself from landing on his face by placing an unsteady hand to the grass.

"What ails you?"

He coughed then groaned. "Why did you come back?" he asked then quickly demanded, "Did you kill those men?"

"I came back because you were in trouble and I didn't think you should die." At her words, Bryson stared at her blankly. "And no, I did not kill them. Do you have enough strength to return to your home?"

Another cough that she realized was a laugh.

"I can't go home, Isobel. I just aided you in killing... You killed Christian?"

"Yes."

He groaned louder, much louder than she thought necessary.

"I...know why now. Although, for the future, if you wish to share someone's goddamn memories, do it..." He stared at her throat. Was he imagining sinking his fangs in her? Tasting her and gathering her memories? "With some warning." He hung his head and rubbed his temples.

She crouched in front of him. Now was not the time to discuss his foolishness. Or be preoccupied with thoughts of how his bite would feel. She pushed against his shoulder. "Can you rise?"

"I can rise." He didn't. He lifted his head and sat up but stayed on his knees.

He was weak, the loss of blood substantial. But still the width of his shoulders drew her eye. She'd felt how hard he was. Knew his body was corded with strength. He'd held them in the clouds without a sign of difficulty. Such brawn was exciting.

"Why did you kill the others?" The command in his voice angered her, but she waited and he grimaced — finally. "They were on the council that killed your brother," he guessed.

"You saw Christian's deeds."

He avoided her eyes at that, scanning, unnecessarily, the bodies of the two unconscious Vampires.

"Can you go to a safe place?"

He laughed then groaned and grabbed his side. She pushed his coat aside to see the dark stain of blood coming from two wounds on his stomach.

"You should heal by now."

"Help me up."

She shook her head. "I cannot help you up. You are too large."

"You just bashed their heads in with enough power to crack their skulls, you can bloody well — "

She helped him up, easing next to his unwounded side to get him on his feet. He stumbled and his weight nearly unbalanced her. She caught him with both arms, holding him around the chest so as not to press on his wounds. He dropped to one knee, bringing her with him. Before she could comprehend what he'd do next, he fell forward only catching them with a hand on the grass like before. She was stunned silent because when he landed, his thick thigh pressed right between her legs.

She thought he might fall all the way on top of her, especially when his hand slipped, but he straightened himself with a painful groan.

"Damn it, if I pass out, do not leave me here."

She laughed, caught off guard by the idea. "It would serve you right. You left me to the sun."

"I didn't leave you—"

He slipped and his hips pressed into her stomach. The weight of him was thrilling, or would have been, if he were not nearly passing out. She detected that either he was a well-endowed male, or erect all the time.

"If you pass out on top of me, I may have to shift home without you, because you will be too heavy for me to lift."

A groan answered her, but along with that came a puff of hot breath along her temple. She shivered, suddenly aware of how solid Bryson was, and how well he was made. His scent was spicy, an intoxicating reminder of the taste of his blood.

Bondings were different for each couple. Some knew immediately and could not resist the call, while others slowly eased into the need. The idea of Bryson, so stern and filled with conflicts over her caressing her body, knowing her more intimately than any other man ever had, or would, sent a shock of awareness down her flesh. It wasn't distasteful, she discovered, even if she still had lingering anger toward him.

But this is not the time. Not even to sample his lips again.

He managed to lift his head and gain a little distance between them by putting more of his weight on his knee. That also tensed his thigh, which rested against her sex.

"Bryson, I suggest you roll off me before I have to remove you." She was surprised at how breathy her voice sounded.

He jerked upward to his knees, wavering on them, but stayed upright. If she had to guess by his lowered brow and grimace, she thought he was worried he'd harmed her.

"Now, let me up." She scooted carefully free from between his legs, cautious of his groin now that she had felt the press of that particular part of him. "You will have to leave this place, quickly, and drink."

After struggling with almost all his weight, she got him upright and on his feet.

"I can drink from you."

"No, you cannot."

He laughed painfully. "Fine, take me where you hide, then."

"I will not." She could not do that, for if she did, she wasn't sure she could keep this desire to a level he wouldn't notice. Vampires had a good sense of emotions. She was certain her sudden and growing fascination with his muscles would eventually rise to his attention.

"Then leave me here because there is nowhere else for me to go. I might as well face the sun, because I prefer that to—"

"Fine." She couldn't think of another solution. He was a traitor now. His people—his friends—would discover what he had done and come for him. *I can't leave him to face that alone.* "Just hold on and do not pass out. You are too heavy." She shouldered more of his bulk. "We go now."

She shifted again, taking another man to the most private and sacred of places. Only this one was much more dangerous than the first.

Chapter Fifteen

The cavern's warm glow welcomed Isobel as she settled next to one of the low beds. She eased Bryson down, noticing again that his hair was shot through with gold. He wore it short, but he appeared more like a warrior from old with it like that. In fact, Bryson was the model of all she thought of when she recalled the brave men from her past. He was strong and capable of caring for a family. He was courageous and honorable, no matter what the task. Except, she worried, when it came to her, then he was blind.

"Here. You will be safe here for now. No more attempts at binding me."

With a grimace, he grumbled, "Damn it, Isobel. I will need blood to survive. What—"

"Yes. I will fetch you something, but you will *not* drink from me." She pushed his shoulder to get him to lie back.

He cast her a dubious glance but rested on the bed after another painful groan. "You aren't safe going out alone. If you shared your blood—"

"I am not sharing my blood so you can try and pick my mind for the truth you cannot see otherwise."

He lowered his hands over his face and shook his head. She wasn't certain what it meant, but she left him before she got lost in how his trousers pulled tightly over a bulge on the left side of his hip much more than the right.

Is he aroused, or merely relaxed and shaped so well that even flaccid his member fills in the loose fabric with its bulk?

She had never seen a naked man. Statues, paintings and such things, but she had never witnessed a male unclothed. Would Bryson's skin be as smooth as his forearm? Supple and silky-smooth? Or would he have hair on his chest? She knew from her own body that she had no hair under her arms or genitals like humans. But did Vampire men also not have this hair?

The urges within her were growing. Even though he'd not wanted her, he'd kissed her as if he might die without her.

'I want one thing before we both die...'

A kiss? Why now? Why when he thought me a monster, and not before when I was seen as honorable? And cold.

If I had more experience, I would know. I don't even have a person to ask...

She sighed heavily as she walked through the back of the hospital and right to the glass cabinet that held unusable blood. Inside, shelf after shelf of red, delicious and apparently unwanted blood was packed and waiting—for her it would seem. She took out several plastic containers. Debating Bryson's size, she finally added more until her bag was overflowing. Bryson was a truly strong warrior. He would need a lot of blood.

A few minutes after she'd left, she returned. Bryson was sitting up, clutching his side and from the look of it, trying to rise to his feet or perhaps falling back down after gaining them.

"Where the hell did you go?" he barked, getting to his feet unsteadily.

She gave him less than two minutes. She set down the heavy bag on the bed and pulled out a pint of blood. "You should trust me."

He sat back down as if he'd fallen. Of course he cursed in Latin, like she wouldn't know? *Does he always curse or is it the pain? Or me?* His stomach should have already begun healing, but she shifted the tattered remains of his shirt aside to check. The flesh was still covered in blood. But the wound was not as large. The trickle of crimson had all but stopped.

His strength was impressive. She moved away from the tempting sight.

"I will rest now. There." She pointed to the other pile of blankets she'd made into a bed against the far wall.

Bryson squinted at her, then the pallet. She took a bag off the top and walked away. There was no need to talk to him. But she wanted to. After so long alone, she wasn't sure what to say, how to create that ease he'd given her over his meal. Even aching inside, she'd grown comfortable.

Her mentor had once loved to discuss anything and everything with her. But with Bryson, if she hoped to have another stimulating conversation, it would be a disappointment. She could feel his questions, could feel the need to demand answers, but weariness began to creep through her body. He had all he wanted — the why of what she did now, if he would only search through Christian's memories.

She wasn't certain he was prepared for what *she* was beginning to want. *Am I?*

"You stole blood from the American Red Cross?"

At his outraged cry, she put her hand over her mouth, hiding her smile. "Yes."

"This saves lives!"

She held in the laugh, but only just. He truly thought the worst of her. Instead of angering her, she realized she was amused.

"Read the label, Bryson. I assume you learned to read as you grew older."

The reference to his humble roots had him grunting, or from the pain as he picked the bag up and set it on the floor next to the bed. He muttered something, but she turned on her side and curled her hands under her cheek, choosing to ignore him.

"It's unusable. You took blood marked for disposal. I see."

She sighed and closed her eyes. Her humor of moments before dwindled.

He didn't see because he didn't want to.

Bryson finished the last bag of blood and knew the wounds he'd suffered were healed.

Christian. Christian had been a part of the council. *I should have known when he came to the house. Or when I first found Isobel.*

Christian, the royal who never would gain what he'd always wanted. *Rule.*

When they had been unable to find Aidan after Aaron's death, it had been Christian and with him, Agatha and Aquinas, who had settled disputes among the Houses as if they would rule now that Aaron was no more. There had even been councils to decide on the matter.

Agatha. That would be Isobel's next victim. Then there would be one more.

Back then there had been several nobles all tracing their blood back to the beginning of time. Aaron and his brother Gregory were sons of Augustine, who was the eldest. Aaron had two sons, Aidan and Alec, and one daughter, Abigail. Gregory had Gia and her sister, Giselle, along with Gideon and Rowan.

Alec had died long ago, leaving Agatha behind as his only remaining heir.

Gregory was nowhere to be found. Lost in the ages, or gone from this world.

Gia was now dead.

Giselle had perished years before in the Lykae-Vampire wars.

Gideon and Rowan remained, but Gideon had chosen the long sleep, while Rowan was…unaccounted for. Some whispered he was deep in the mountain ranges of Eastern Europe, others that he, too, had died at Isobel's hand.

Aquinas had been the son of Abigail.

Christian had been the son of Giselle's great grand-niece, Gwendolyn.

That left Agatha as the only remaining direct descendant.

If Christian had wanted the throne, he would have needed Agatha by his side.

Gia, Aquinas, Christian, and Agatha were members of the council. They had to be. But who was the last, remaining member? Rowan?

Rowan was the only male left in Gregory's line, other than Aidan.

Bryson stood and walked to where Isobel slept. Unlike myths about Vampires that were so prevalent, his kind didn't sleep in crypts. Neither did they sleep on their backs, arms crossed over their chests like the dead. Isobel slept curled up on her side, her head pillowed on her hands.

The flickering light from the candles illuminated all the perfections of her beauty, giving her skin a warm glow. She had survived the ages but hadn't gained the ease most of his kind had through living near humans. She still spoke with care and only when necessary. Her complete lack of the colloquialisms he'd grown accustomed to from Jaxon and other immortals reminded him of another age, a simpler time. Sarcasm was missing from Isobel. So, too, was anything other than whatever she'd planned for the remaining members of the council.

Now he knew why. They had not just killed her brother. They had damned him. He would never journey on. He would never reach whatever waited for them after this existence. The council had done this, and worse, he sensed from the facts she'd shoved down his mind link with Christian that they had done this at Aaron's orders.

Aaron had ordered Jorge's death. But he'd punished him for slaying an entire village. *Had Jorge been accused and not guilty?*

He rubbed his shoulder, fighting the building ache. He couldn't recall the last time he'd slept, or the last time he'd slept *well*.

What to do? Sleep? Or get answers? There was something missing from this, something far worse than the horrifying death the council had brought down on Jorge. He turned away and exhaled. *I need to process Christian's mind, but it is filth.*

There had been another Vampire in the battle. Christian had come prepared, but he'd been no match for Isobel. Whoever the other Vampire had been, lurking in the shadows, he'd been powerful. He'd also been cautious. Near, but never close enough to make him out.

The candles caught his attention. He knew this place, or thought he did. They were somewhere underground in what was now modern Turkey. The cavern was enormous, far below where the humans had located a much smaller chamber, miles from where this one was hidden. This one dated back to well before the fall of the Roman Empire. As far as he could see, candles lined every nook and crevice, spilling dark purple wax in pools that alone were testament to its age.

Scroll upon scroll had been stuffed into the white sandstone shelves. In other areas, tables and desks, as well as the bed Isobel rested upon, had all been created from the existing rock. The blankets and sheets, along with the mattresses, were new, which intrigued him, but everything else was ancient.

Designs and decorative art gave a hint of the earliest days of Christianity, but most were so faded and worn by the ages they were difficult to read. Other forms of deities and ancient symbols were scattered through the cavern.

None of it was evil. Not an inch spoke of death, other than the spot by a broad slab of darker stone near to the back of the cavern's deepest wall. There he believed she'd killed Christian and burned his body, sending his

Billi Jean

ashes far up to the surface and away from this place. An enormous dragon rose up along the back, carved out of the stone with its wide wingspan taking up the entire wall. Its head was angled downward, its jaw open as it blew flames outward in a pattern of jewels. Even its claws held beautiful symbols of power. One a long, bright sword, the other a chalice radiating golden lines of light. Below it stood robed and hooded figures with their heads bowed, swords held with both hands so that the tips rested near their feet, crossed hilts at their chests. The Dragon Guard. This was their ancient location.

Isobel brought me here, an outsider, to her most sacred place.

He surveyed her again and couldn't believe he'd ever thought her evil. Isobel had unwittingly opened a window to her mind when she had taken his blood or perhaps when she'd shoved Christian's mind at him. She was not evil. She did not kill for revenge or madness, she killed for something else.

He dared to reach down and run his hand along her silky hair. He'd kissed her, tasted the flavor of her mouth and nearly drowned in her. Sharing his blood had been the most satisfying thing he'd ever done in his life. He'd given to her, the necessary blood for her to survive. Along the way, he'd gotten a glimpse of how blazing hot claiming her would be. She'd turned soft and needy in his arms. It had startled him so badly he'd been unable to comprehend the speed of her—and his—reversal from suspicion and distrust to an absolute staggering level of arousal.

Swallowing painfully, he rose and walked away. Just thinking of how right she'd felt in his arms— awake—still blindsided him. He found a desk, spying

166

money in several currencies, an iMac notebook, and a dozen scrolls held down by whatever she could find, on the large smooth surface.

Not willing to wake her to ask what he needed to know, nor to sit and wait, he wrote a quick note to her that he would return soon, and left it, propped up on her notebook so she would see it upon waking.

Without another glance, he sent himself far afield, seeking Rowan, where he knew once there had been a place, high in the mountains, that the Vampire had sought solace.

Chapter Sixteen

It was nearly dawn by the time Bryson experienced a shock and realized that, below him, he felt the presence of another Vampire. He ventured closer, letting his being become clear as he materialized near the side of the mountain's highest peak. He settled on an icy ledge. He breathed deeply, sensing awareness, but no barrier to his entering the other Vampire's home.

"Rowan. I come in time of great need. It is important I speak with you."

Silence, then, when he considered saying more, the wall in front of him cracked. A slit grew wider as the cliff slid backward to reveal an entrance.

"Come unharmed into my home, Captain MacAfee."

A man stepped partially out of the gloom. If Bryson hadn't known Aidan was nowhere near this place, he would have assumed his king had beaten him here. The man walked closer and revealed a jaw covered with a short beard shot through with gray. His hair was tied back at his nape away from a classical Roman face.

Bryson went to one knee and crossed his arm over his chest in the formal greeting to his king's uncle. "Rowan, I have need of your wisdom."

"Wisdom." Rowan laughed softly but reached out and gripped Bryson's hand, helping him to his feet. "There is no bowing to me, Bryson. I am no better, nor, I hope, worse than you. Come, though, it is not often I receive guests, and I am curious after all this time, why two have come to seek my council."

Bryson followed him as he spoke, only pausing when his words registered. The entrance led to a spacious room that was cut with light from the high slits in the mountain above them. The room was much like his own study in all of his homes. Bookcases lined the walls past twenty feet and higher in places. Between the books were items tucked away from centuries past. There was no evidence of anything from this century, no computer, no wires, no electricity at all, just a giant hearth and candles, oddly enough of purple wax, spaced throughout the room.

"May I ask who your other visitor was, Rowan?"

Rowan smiled and poured two glasses of dark red wine. After handing him one goblet, he then lifted his own glass. "A young boy. Remarkable lad, really. He brought me this." Rowan picked up a cell phone, an Apple iPhone 6. "Not much use, since I don't have the means to run it. He advised me that I would be helping a friend if I had it."

"A boy?" Bryson sat down, heavily unaware he'd done so until it registered he was looking up at Rowan. "A boy named Faolan."

"Aye, Faolan." Rowan sat and rested his arms on the back of the well-worn velvet couch. "He is an unusual boy. You are this friend, I assume, he spoke of?"

"I am *a* friend. He has quite a few, so I could be the one, but…"

"Ah, I can see that about him. He makes friends easily. He promised he would come back to see me. Said I needed to return to this century. Can you imagine that?" He laughed. "What does my cousin think of him?"

"Aidan thinks him unusual. But he believes the boy can walk on water."

"We all can. It's the lightness of our bodies if we were to lose the connection with this form and simply allow the earthly confinement to go… Oh, I see, you are merely saying he can do no wrong."

Bryson sipped his wine. It was good, an aged vintage that spoke of oak barrels and fields ripe with grapes drenched in the scents of wild rosemary and subtle bursts of mint. Rowan had been someone he'd rarely seen, let alone spoken to back before the troubles. Sitting with him now, he was reminded of a festival where he'd once shared a table with an elder. He had been the same as he was now, slightly long-winded and lost in thought, or else his own thoughts far more than he was present in the conversation. He'd chalked it up to being ancient, now he wondered if it wasn't part of Rowan's personality.

"It's good, is it not?"

"It is."

"Ah, but you have weighty matters on your mind. Much I sense is troubling you."

"Why did you come here and leave our world, our people behind?"

Rowan lifted his brow again but studied his wine glass pensively. "It is difficult to accept the animals too many of our kind have become. Worse than animals, rather, for animals seek only to kill to survive, while our kind often kill for nothing more than the pleasure. We were worse than the Romans with their bloodthirsty masses watching the gladiators. At least those brave warriors were granted their freedom after they had survived many battles. We, too, often piled on our kills, one upon the other."

Bryson sighed and closed his eyes. He agreed. Too many times he agreed. "Aidan is stopping that now."

"Now. But he will struggle and struggle, for what? The world is becoming increasingly smaller. Vampires are mixing with other species now and not just in children, but in pacts. Such children are glorious, are they not? The pacts between one evil creature and another are not. But such alliances exist. Such children exist. There is nothing I can do, nor Aidan, to stop it."

"Children of mixed heritage are not evil."

Rowan waved his hand in the air dismissively. "I never said they were, Bryson. But at one time they were forbidden, as were alliances with other species."

"Aidan makes alliances, and they are not evil. They are strengthening us."

Rowan exhaled heavily. "He sees it this way. You see it this way, but not all will. Have you studied the split in the wolf pack?"

"Yes." Bryson knew where this was going. He had heard the rumors of how the Houses would be better off without Aidan. How Aidan was dragging them into battles they had no business fighting. The whispers that no alliances should be allowed, good or evil, was louder than a whisper now. If he scratched the surface he would find the men and women who Isobel had killed at the heart of it all. "Alrick is having a difficult time. Aidan is as well. Change is not always welcome, nor is it wanted. But change has to come otherwise our kind will become so blackened by evil there will be no more of us left who understand we are not."

Rowan set the goblet down next to him and picked up a tome, at least five inches thick made of ancient parchment with a burgundy leather cover scrolled in gold. "Are you familiar with the *Book of Ages*, Bryson?"

He was about to laugh and respond such a thing was merely myth, but Rowan studied him carefully, as if expecting such a response.

"The *Book of Ages* was given to our forefathers to guide us through the changes that would occur in us as the centuries past. It is said to hold the key to our existence, as well as the truth of why we were created."

"Ah, you are a scholar. I thought you were, what with your manners and intelligent eye, but one never knows what can hide behind etiquette. Yes," he went on crisply. "This is that book. And some of what you have learned is true... Unfortunately most is merely myth. The book *does* foretell some of the changes that will occur within our people. That is what I find curious. While I might have sought solitude, I did not forsake our people. On the contrary, I have watched and witnessed recent events, and measured them to the foretelling in this book. I fear that now, this age, our existence is swinging on a pendulum, Bryson. And that pendulum will either slice our line across the throat or it will cut from us those cancerous growths that would rot us from the inside out."

Bryson didn't know what to say.

"*She*. She will do this." He opened the book and flipped through the pages, stopping at one and turned the book to face Bryson.

In front of him was Isobel, her hair blowing in an unseen wind, her face frozen in beauty, while behind her a cape flowed outward, and at her back a man stood, his shoulders bunched as if prepared to attack.

"Isobel?"

"Yes. Study it. What do you see?"

He turned back to the page, running a hand over the parchment. Above Isobel's head hung a moon, bright white, with dark clouds masking its beauty. In her left hand she held a bloody heart. In her right hand, on a beaded chain, she held a key. At her feet the artist had drawn a body of a man, his arms crossed in death, but holding a sword and knife. Alongside the warrior a woman, also dead, clung to him as if she had crawled to him in her time of need. A small, barely noticeable babe's hand reached out from where she cradled it, and touched the fingertips of some spiritual being.

"What do you see, Bryson?"

"I have no idea, Rowan." He shook his head, unsure what to say. "Have you shown this to Aidan?"

"Aidan has forgotten me." Rowan tapped the top of the page. "This is Isobel. This is her bonded, you. You are at the center. Her brother is at her feet, his bride at his side with his child in her arms. Above her left shoulder is my uncle, held down by a group of six, and on her right shoulder —"

"I stand."

"Yes. You stand."

"Why is Aaron held down by these others? Did they hold him down while she tortured him? Then killed him?" It made sense. She had been too young and much too weak to have killed an ancient.

"Have you asked her this question?"

He lifted his gaze to Rowan's. There was no anger there, no horror that Bryson had hidden her from his cousin, the woman responsible for killing a member of their family.

"I do not judge you, Bryson. Above all, you loved my uncle. And for his part, I believed you taught him much, but even you realize that Aaron was set in his ways. His thinking was that any muddying of the blood line had to be stopped. You know that he sentenced Jorge to death for bonding and fathering a child with a witch."

Bryson sat away from him. "That is not why Jorge died. He killed humans. He murdered an entire village!"

Rowan shook his head. "That is not true, Bryson. You were away. A campaign against the Wolves, I believe. You were not there when he passed judgment, but you must have heard the truth from Aaron."

"I did hear the truth from him." He had gone to Aaron straight away. Isobel, he had waited to go to, unsure of his welcome after such a thing had been done by her brother and by his king. But then it was too late. She had killed Aaron and set into motion the events he was even now living through.

"No, Bryson." Rowan sighed and sat back, searching the room for something, Bryson didn't know what. Eyes back on him, Rowan shook his head. "No, that was not what occurred."

"I went to that village. I saw —"

"Oh, that village was burned. That was true. But it was not *Jorge* that went mad and killed those helpless people. That was rumor only, made up by members of the royal family to hide their guilt."

Bryson's mind blanked. "What? What are you saying?"

"It has been so long, but it is fitting that she has been found, that she has risen. It was not her brother that murdered every man, woman and child in that village, it was *my* brother. It was Gideon."

Chapter Seventeen

Bryson felt as if he'd taken a mortal hit to his heart. *She is innocent.* Innocent.

Goosebumps shivered along his arms. *She should hate me.* Instead…his heart sped up. *She came back for me. She kissed me. She… I thought the worst of her. I did not break her free and demand to know if she did this thing, instead I judged her guilty without hearing her side. We all did.*

As they wanted. She wouldn't have killed Aaron. She couldn't have. She was strong but she could not have killed Aaron. She judged him correctly. *It was right there in front of me, and I did not see it.* "This means…" Bryson caught his breath, scenting the sweetness of Isobel. He turned and there she was.

"Rowan…" Isobel stood in an arched doorway, face white as a sheet, staring at Rowan. Her eyes were too big in her small face, the dark color catching and reflecting the candlelight. "You are…alive?"

Bryson could clearly hear what else she had *not* said *'You did not save me? Come to my aid? Protect me?'*

At Isobel's question, Bryson watched Rowan grimace and rise to his feet. Bowing his head slowly, he pressed his arm over his chest, hand over his heart. "I was...delayed. If I had but been there, I might have stopped him. If I could have truly read the future, I *would* have stopped him, and the events that followed. This I swear."

"I trusted you! I went to you, but you were not there. You were gone. As was everyone that could have saved Jorge! Gone! And then..." She gasped and clutched her stomach, as if hurt. "Then it was done. So quickly, done." Tears, large, wet paths of pain etched down her face. The outward display of such pain hurt him to watch. "They were so happy, then just like that, it was ripped from them."

Rowan moved before Bryson could think what to do. At Isobel's side, Rowan touched her shoulder and she leaned into him. The elder embraced her as a father would his daughter. "I know. I was..." He ducked his head, pressing it to her hair. "Detained."

She pulled away from him and clutched the front of his shirt to stare up at him. Desperation reflected on her face, slowly it eased and more tears fell. "You were taken?" She reached up and touched a thicker white streak of hair by his left temple. "Where?"

Rowan exhaled. "It was long ago. I found my way out and discovered I was in Jerusalem, of all places."

A laugh from her, then more tears. "He did this to you. Gideon."

"Yes. He did this. He beckoned to me, calling me in on a false need. I fell in his trap as nicely as he could want. But it is not I that suffered, is it? Not alone. But now, now you must heal. Did I rise from my desolation and seek out death from Gideon?"

"Did you?" Bryson asked.

Isobel glanced at him then Rowan.

"I tried," Rowan admitted with a laugh. "I couldn't find him. I had no idea of the loss of Jorge, not until it had passed into ancient history. I came here, unsure where to go in a world that had left me behind."

"But Aidan, he would have welcomed you," Bryson argued.

"Would he? He was gone himself, hidden away, not far, but still, alone but for a few. I was old, alone, and had lost all those that mattered to me. I was a Dragon Master, Bryson, and had lost everyone one of my order when Isobel was taken."

"They killed them," she whispered. "They came during the day and staked them down and drained them, much like they did to Jorge."

Bryson sat again, feeling like his whole world had been ripped to shreds. "I knew you were not evil. I knew you had not killed Aaron for no reason."

"You did not. You thought I was evil, a monster," she argued.

"I was told you were, but here, where such things matter little, I knew," he shouted and jabbed at his chest. He'd jumped to his feet without realizing it. "Why else did I go to the chamber, if not take you *from* that death?"

"You sent me *to* that death!" She fisted her hands on her hips, apparently ready to tear his head off otherwise with the tiny things.

"Children, should we—"

"Quiet, Rowan," he snarled, moving until he was right in front of her. "This time you will listen to me!"

"I have always listened to *you*," she whispered in an angry tone. "Yours was the first voice I heard upon waking. It was you that sent me to my death, Bryson. You."

"Now, now, Isobel, if I could lend some advice here, perhaps he was struck by —"

"No, Rowan!" She snapped her attention immediately back to Bryson once the elder held his hands up, much as Faolan had, and moved to the other side of the room, only then murmuring about getting more wine.

Suddenly alone, nearly, with her, Bryson didn't know what to say. She was right.

I sent her to her death.

But I also went to her, to take her away from that painful death.

He had planned it out, several times, what he would say to her if he could, but each time everything he came up with was useless in the face of what he'd done — what *she* had done.

Only she hadn't done half of what he thought.

"I went to you, forsaking my king, my oaths, to save you, not to have you argue with me and split hairs over my deeds. I am not perfect. I am far from it, but I am *not* your enemy, Isobel!" He dared to reach out and grip her arms and hold her in place, even though she hadn't moved. "I have never been your enemy. If anything I have made mistakes, but I have not done those thinking you were anything other than a woman who did something terrible in reaction to something equally terrible."

He ducked his head and tried to speak clearer. "I did not think when I found you. I had to get you away. I had to. Would you rather I had torn down that wall and bonded to you right then and there?" he asked. "I would have. I could have. You were weak, and nothing you could have done would have stopped me. So," he exhaled, not believing the words that were pouring from him, "I left. I saved you, for a time, and left so I could come back and save you for a bit longer." He laughed then at her incredulous expression and at the situation. The laughter was proof he was insane, he was certain, but once he started he couldn't stop. He threw his head back and covered his face with his hands and laughed even harder. "Why God has done this to us, I don't know. Maybe the book does."

A low laugh, feminine and warm, brought his head down to see her smiling at him.

Do I finally make sense to her? She should hate him. Instead she didn't seem to think him even worse for his admissions, she looked pleased. Her dark eyes sparkled, not with tears any longer, but with something else.

"Well, you are honorable at least. Your lies are growing less and less, but you are still narrow-minded and at best, only mediocre in building barriers, but you are the strongest warrior I have ever seen."

He opened his mouth then snapped it closed on her compliment. *She thinks me strong. My bonded looks to me and there is appreciation in her eyes.* He threw his shoulders back.

"But you yell entirely too often."

He was about to say that if he didn't she would never listen to him, but by some grace of God, the words stayed where they should be — unspoken.

"He is strong or he would not have survived. I believe you are wrong about his mind. He is open-minded for one so old. In fact, I would say he is more so than you, my dear." A glimpse of a smile tipped her pretty lips.

"Just tell me you believe me." He carefully took hold of her upper arms. "Is it that hard?"

She sighed as if it were impossible. "It is difficult to trust you, Bryson. But yes." She nodded. "I believe you." His relief was short-lived because her next sentence stole the joy right out of him. "I also believe I know the identity of the last, and final, member of the council."

"I thought there were two more," Bryson replied.

"There are. Agatha, and one I never knew the identity of. Until now."

Rowan sighed heavily and took his seat on the couch.

Isobel arched an eyebrow at Bryson's continued hold. He dropped his hands and watched her walk over and perch on the arm of the couch. He sat near her but not too close. Close enough to grab her in case she took flight again.

"Well?" Rowan prompted when all she did was study the book.

She tossed her heavy braid over her shoulder and sat away from the book. "Gideon. He is in possession of, or *is*, another Vampire. One called Warren."

"Ah, fuck." Bryson dropped his hands back over his face.

Chapter Eighteen

"What is it, Esmeralda?"

The younger Vampire hovered by the doorway to Agatha's suite of rooms, wringing her hands. Agatha motioned to her to come forward, not pleased to be disturbed. Christian was late. He had requested to come to her this night, upon rising, but now, when the moon was nearly set, she considered refusing him entrance. Such tardiness was unacceptable. Worse than rude, it was thoughtless.

"There is a...man here to see you, Agatha."

Agatha set down her book. At last. She considered Esmeralda's pale face and the intricate weave of her evening gown. The fit was perfect on the woman, but her modest upbringing made her appear to be wearing someone else's clothing. Even the hang of the silk over her small breasts was wrong. Agatha sighed, displeased by the simple lack of understanding of how to dress appropriately. Still, the girl would do for now.

Until she and Christian took their places such utterly oblivious individuals would have to do.

"A man? I see." She feathered her fingertips over her own substantial bosom revealed with artistry against the blood-red silk of her gown. "Well, by all means, who is this man who comes to call, pray tell?"

"A stranger, my lady."

A stranger? Esmeralda knew Christian. She had served with Agatha for centuries. At her serious, worried nod, Agatha glanced at her guards. All five of them wore the signets of her House, along with the weapons to protect her. In such times, precautions were necessary. There was no news that Isobel had been found, nor any that Christian had done as promised.

She smoothed her hand over the velvet couch and sent her mind out to discover who would call upon her. She encountered a man, but who the Vampire was proved impossible to decipher. His mind was closed, a still pond of knowledge and power she was unable to slip past.

"Does he have a name?"

"Warren, my lady."

"I know no one named Warren. Send him away." She dismissed Esmeralda with a wave and picked her book back up.

The door behind Esmeralda crashed inward, breaking upon impact with the wall. Her guards moved in to attack, but they were centuries too late.

* * * *

Bryson attempted to control his reaction to Isobel moving closer to him on the couch, but with no success. For hours they had pored over text after text, trying to discover if Gideon could have accomplished such a thing as she'd suggested. Rowan had long since retired, claiming much-needed rest, when Bryson knew such a thing was impossible.

The man had left him on purpose.

Bryson inhaled Isobel's scent. He suffered another pulse through his body, particularly the long, hard evidence he was trying desperately to conceal with the book on his lap. For some insane reason he had thought placing the enormous tome there, across his knees, was a wonderful solution. The erection wasn't something he could control. The stiff flesh had lengthened, swelling to a powerful distraction. The heavy tome pressed firmly down against his shaft, which pulsed maddeningly, no doubt happy for any amount of attention.

It didn't help that Isobel was next to him, her face inches from his tormented groin. It was worse each time she pushed down on the book to turn the pages. Unaccountably, the pressure sent a rush of pleasure rippling through him. He had to clench his jaw to stop the forces battling inside him to pull her to him and claim her mouth, then every inch of her.

No, not yet, not even close to yet. *She trusts me, is beginning to trust me, I can't force such a thing.*

But when she was ready...

"I still think there is something here." She tapped the page Rowan had shown him. "The babe...what is it reaching for?"

She would have silky skin, like the finest fabric ever spun. He had once touched such a fine silk, had wondered then, centuries before, if she had such flesh. She did. Her lips had been hot and ultra-soft. Her thighs would— He blinked, attempting to stop the fantasies.

"It worries me."

He thought she spoke more to herself than to him, he knew. She did that often, and each time he experienced a painful crush to his chest. She'd been alone for centuries, suffering…

"Everything on the page is important. So what does this mean?" Her gaze rose to his. "I see you there, I see my brother, and Aaron, even Rowan if you look closely."

He tried to process thoughts, but his brain was circling around sex. Long, hot hours, nights of sex and blood sharing, not deliberating over ancient meanings of tomes. "Perhaps it means what it shows. The babe did not die."

She stiffened, appearing alarmed.

"I mean, if souls can travel from their bodies to the air, then back to a body, why not a babe's?" As he spoke, he caught her hand and brushed his thumb along her wrist. The more he thought on it the more it made sense. "The child would have been half-Vampire."

"True." Her dark eyes flickered over his face. She frowned and tilted her head. "Are you well? Is it your wound?" She reached out as if to take the book from him. He gripped it hard enough to dent the leather binding and quickly shook his head.

"My wounds are healed."

She didn't shy away at the gruffness in his tone but she did arch an eyebrow. "Ah, I see. Perhaps you, too, need rest."

What he needed was her under him. He bit that reply back, glad that the impossible need to speak freely to her was limited by some of his willpower.

"Bryson?" She hadn't let go of the book, he realized, when she tugged it ever so gently. He held on tighter. "Why is it I feel you are hiding something from me?"

The answer to that speculation in her tone was even now begging to be revealed. Sweat dripped down his sideburns, marking his face as it slid down past his jaw and over his throat, but he held himself in check—for now. The need to shove the book aside and draw her into his arms was unbelievably strong. The future lay ahead of him, and right now, whatever he did would shape that. He held onto the book.

"Did you know that Warren was more?"

"What? No, of course not," he snapped and shoved a hand over his short hair, relieved that was her biggest suspicion and not that he was slowly unraveling under the pressure to make her his, secure her, mark her, take her...

She removed the book, taking it before he knew what she was about.

The small indrawn breath told him all he needed to know. He tried to stand, to move so she wouldn't fear he would use what was so obviously begging to be utilized, but she stopped him with a hand on his chest. He held his breath as she stared at his groin. She didn't stop staring either, even when the attention made him tense and his cock lifted at the pull of his muscles, to press against the dark fabric of his slacks. Every inch was outlined for her. Even the thick crown showed up as if he'd auditioned for a part in the hottest porn flick ever made.

Instead of drawing back in shock, she met his eyes. Hers were bright with amber. She was aroused. The thought dropped like a stone in a still pond, rippling and growing as he sat there realizing that he wasn't alone in the bonding urges.

"May I touch you, Bryson?"

"God, yes, anything you want, Isobel." He relaxed as much as he was able and widened his thighs for her, hoping it was his urgent cock she wanted to touch. *More than touch?* She reached for his chest tentatively and watched her hands as she stroked down. The feel of her hand shot adrenaline straight to his heart. He inhaled sharply at how *right* her caress felt. She lingered over his muscles, clearly pleased by his strength. More of his worries slipped away as she explored his shoulders then back to his chest, even his ribs.

"You are so well made. Big. Strong." She dug her nails into his pectorals, testing them.

"I will never harm you."

She smiled. "I know you will never harm me. Why do you say this now?"

"I don't want to frighten you." He took possession of her hand and slowly brought it to his erection. "With this. Or with my strength." Her eyes flared with emotions, darkening as if he'd said something right. "This is for you. All of me is for you."

He released her hand and waited. Instead of pulling away, she curled her fingers around the head of his shaft and gently squeezed.

"Holy fuck." He swore his eyes crossed. He knew his cock surged hotter, spilling pre-cum in a warm, wet surge past the narrow slit. If she so much as moved her hand, she would see the evidence of that rush to climax. He dug his hands into the couch cushions to keep from dragging her onto his lap. "Isobel."

"This is for me. All of this?" She smoothed her hand along the wedge of his erection then back down. He was either in Heaven, or in Hell, depending on what she did next.

He glanced at the stairs leading to Rowan's quarters. "Rowan—"

"Rowan didn't leave to rest, Bryson." She began massaging her hand up and down, measuring every inch. "He left because he knows what you seem to know, but not to understand." At the word understand, she whispered against his neck, "Do you know what that is?"

He bit back a groan as she, once again, squeezed the head of his cock then worked her fingers under the flared hood, managing to find that spot that drove him insane. He clenched his fingers in the couch cushions, ripping the fabric. She stroked every inch of him, but he wanted her hands on his bare flesh.

"Isobel."

"You want me. Take me, fill my emptiness with this," she beckoned, as if she'd fallen from Heaven and appeared out of his deepest fantasies.

"Bond with you," he managed, grabbing her hand to still her before he embarrassed himself. "Share our blood and begin our lives together? Here? Now?"

She hesitated then boldly shook her head. "First we can share our bodies, then when I can trust you, our blood, and yes, more."

If he had been told he would someday have to choose between the absolute surety of orgasms like he had never dreamed possible and the woman that would be his above all others, he wouldn't have known what to do. He didn't know, faced with such a choice now. "I want you."

She slid closer on the couch. "Then take me, but perhaps carefully, with this." She squeezed his cock again.

"I want *you*," he stressed, holding her still.

Her eyes widened. The dark cores of her pupils were only a shade darker than her amazing irises. This close he could distinguish the difference, but only barely. Her skin, her hair, her scent, all of her, tore at his control. He wanted her until his bones ached with the want. But deep down, where he had always held on to some desperate hope that she could be his, he knew with absolute surety that unless he bonded her, he would not bed her.

"I want you as *mine*."

"Do you think we can stop that?" she whispered with a smile he swore he felt.

"No, nothing will." He was certain of that, just as he was sure that the sun would rise soon. "But until you are ready for that, we will..." He swallowed and managed to say, "Wait." He gave the room a glance. "Besides, when I finally make you mine, it's not going to be on Rowan's couch."

She leaned closer and he thought for a moment she might laugh. Instead, she moved closer so that there wasn't a hair's-breadth between them.

"What if I do not wish to wait?" Then she did the last thing he could have anticipated.

She took hold of his head by his hair and kissed him.

Isobel slid her tongue along Bryson's lips, tracing them lightly, then bit his fuller bottom lip when he didn't respond.

This wasn't the time or the place for what she wanted — part of her, the logical part, knew that — but there was nothing she could do to stop the building feeling of *need*. It was stronger than the pull of the moon on the tides. Stronger than her, she knew. Bryson relaxed against her and groaned heavily in her mouth, proving it was stronger than him as well.

He stole her breath by suddenly tossing her to her back with his warm weight on top of her.

"You need," he growled.

"*We* need," she corrected.

With a stunning flash of his smile, he settled more comfortably on top of her. "Then I will see to giving us some relief."

The first feel of his body on hers, outside of almost passing out from blood loss, stole her breath. Her mind spun, lights flashed behind her eyelids and her body roared to such a level of alertness she could feel the fabric of her panties biting into her ass as he pulled her firmly against his hips. His erection was enormous. The heat of it both soothing and exciting. The pain he must be in… *As much as I am.*

He cupped her bottom and ground his hips to hers. Shocks of pleasure ripped up from her sex to every inch of her flesh then back down.

"Bryson!"

A heavy groan from him registered past the pleasuring, oddly making hers grow. She caught her breath when he breathed in her ear, doing that thing with his hips again. She caught at his muscled ass, clenching her fingers into the strong muscles.

"God, I want you, but not going to take you yet, Isobel," he grated. Sweat stood out on his brow, a drop sliding down his cheek and on along his stubborn jaw.

"I…need…"

His expression softened and just like that, he tightened his grip on her bottom and pressed his lips to hers. "I know, angel. I will give you something to ease the ache."

"Yes. For us both." She nodded, eager, anxious for the build up to stop. "It is so…"

"Powerful. I will be a good male to you, Isobel. I will make up for this." He ducked his head and kissed her jaw even as he rotated his hips and found that spot that made her gasp again. "I will, you will see."

She lifted her hips and held on tightly to his ass as he began moving again. The heat and tension in his muscles matched the heavy, firm weight of his erection rubbing her sex. The room disappeared. Everything centered on him, on his body waking hers. His breath against her neck — amazed her. The feel of his hot body, along hers — stunned her. He lifted his head, but only enough to find her mouth. This time his kiss was ownership. He possessed every ounce of her attention. He held her there, pressed tightly to him with a grip on her bottom. The steel column of his erect flesh burned a path along her sex and up to her navel. The sheer size of him thrilled her so much that she felt unable to breathe properly.

She wrapped her arms around his neck, and her legs around his hips. With a heavy shove of his firm manhood he had that something exciting drawing desperately nearer. He tensed and held himself there, the thick steel of his shaft bearing down on her clitoris perfectly as he kissed her desperately. He shoved a hand between them, did something and groaned into her mouth in relief. Seconds later she felt the first velvet touch of his flesh slide along her stomach. *He's freed his erection.*

She squirmed under him, wanting to feel it, but he held her in place, not allowing her access as he possessed her mouth. All the while he rocked his hips, marking her with the sizzling heat of his bare manhood. If that wasn't enough, he caressed her, waking her to a level of arousal that made her gasp in shock.

"Bryson!"

He took hold of her hands, threading their fingers together as he slowly softened his kiss. It made no difference. The careful stroke of his tongue ignited her with a deeper, more thorough burn as he pressed down, trapping her on the cusp of something she had to have.

"Bryson," she cried when he left her mouth to trail hot kisses along her throat. "I need, I need—"

He lifted his head and scanned her face, his flushed with hectic color. The outward sign of his passion triggered a deeper rush of tingles that had the muscles of her inner thighs tensing.

"I need—"

"I know what you need." His voice had deepened. But in his tone she found surety that he would help her, not leave her like this, almost experiencing something wonderful only to have it go away before she reached fulfillment.

He slowly lowered his head and took her mouth again in a firm, deep kiss while he drove his hips upward. The clothes stopped him from filling her, but it didn't matter. Not when he began to move his hips so every firm inch of his manhood rubbed along her sex.

She cried out in his mouth and tightened her hands on his hair.

His gentle first glide tested her, she realized because his second was stronger, firmer. She raised her hips, wanting more. He continued to surge up and down on top of her, kissing her with such passion she couldn't hold back the cries as he roused her until she trembled.

Within seconds, she exploded. Pleasure overwhelmed her and expanded to go deep into her empty body to spread down her thighs and onward to her toes. She dove into the climax the way she dropped from the clouds, but with open arms, letting the exquisite eruption take her where it would, where Bryson would.

The spasms seemed to please him, if the way he shuddered and groaned into her neck meant anything. As her body eased into a blissful afterglow, Bryson tensed and groaned and shocked her as hot wetness hit her bare stomach. The scent of his release tinged the air. She caressed his warm, muscled back, blinking as her own pleasure lingered in tiny tingles deep within her womb. Bryson went on for so long, his release spurting on her repeatedly that she arched under him, growing near that tightening spasm again.

When she could breathe, she doubted he would maintain his stance to wait until he could bond her before he possessed her completely. The thought made her smile and kiss his jaw. When she did he groaned louder and his muscles bunched to harder steel.

She knew she wouldn't last much longer before she took him as hers. Already she shivered under him, wanting him inside her. Her body felt alien. Her breasts were larger, heavier, the tips sensitive to a degree that the silk of her undergarments was too rough.

Bryson slowly raised his head. His face was still flushed, perhaps because his manhood jutted up so heavy and hard against her stomach. She could feel the wet tip along her flesh and knew he'd spilled copious amounts of seed on her—marking her? The idea pleased her. Everything about him pleased her. The contrast to how she'd felt before—the haze of anger—

to now was extraordinary. Even the way his lips were kiss-stung and his hair tousled from her hands pleased her.

Can I go from hate to love so quickly? She brushed his short hair away from his face, the sweaty ends silkier than ever. Her heart felt too full, too large with emotion to speak. *I can love him now. I don't need to be alone.*

The moment seemed to last longer than any in her life.

How had she never known him? Never sensed his soul? Now it seemed as if he had always been there, a dire warning on the wind, but also a deep rightness where she'd never known something could be so good.

"You are precious to me, Isobel. Even when I wanted to hate you, I could not. I will never fail you again. On this, you have my word."

Tears threatened at the emotion she heard in his tone. Instead of letting them fall, she pulled his head down and kissed his lips, needing the connection more than the words.

Chapter Nineteen

Have I fallen in love with this woman?

Bryson held his breath at the thought. This was not the time to discover such an emotion. *But when is the right time for such things? In the midst of battle? Or in the arms of a woman who will be my bonded for as long as we both live?*

Before Bryson could speak, Isobel touched his lips with her finger.

"We have forgotten something."

He frowned and licked his lips. He tasted her. The scent of their passion filled the air, mesmerizing him, but also soothing his need to take more from her. *I already took too much.* His seed marked her smooth stomach, a clear indication that even if he hadn't bitten her, or exchanged the bonding vows, she was his.

The primitive thought made him cringe. He cleared his throat and lifted up and lowered her blouse to cover her stomach. He immediately shifted his shirt to cover himself and readjusted his trousers so his manhood was hidden from view. He also cleaned her with a thought, then did the same to himself, erasing all evidence of their passion. With another thought he soothed her skin with sweet-scented lotion. She lifted a brow, the expression familiar to him now. So much so he leaned down and kissed her forehead. "I want you comfortable," he explained. "But what have we forgotten?"

She sat up quickly then touched her head.

"Isobel?" Worried, he caught her hand and steadied her. She frowned as if confused by something. "Isobel?"

"I'm fine, perhaps passion lingers." She rubbed her forehead. Bryson tipped her head up so he could see her face. "It's not normal?" she whispered.

"I have no idea." A smile broke free at the thought he'd given her such pleasure she was lightheaded. He'd heard rumors of women passing out from pleasure. Would Isobel? He pulled her gently but firmly closer, unable to tolerate the distance of even a few inches. She rested her head against his shoulder with a soft sigh and laid her hand on his chest. "Now, what mistake? Because if you regret what we just shared I assure you it's going to happen again, and each time it's going to be harder to stop when I did."

"Finally, you make a threat I actually believe," she muttered, shocking him with a merry laugh. Before he could reply, she went on. "Yes, we have made a mistake, but no, not this. I am not sure it's possible for you to make *more* mistakes—"

"I believe I wasn't the only one—"

"Perhaps, but I was referring to Warren."

He blinked at the sudden change from outrageous accusations to what they battled outside of their bonding. Warren. *How did I miss so much?* If he is Gideon... "He will go after Agatha."

She nodded, appearing pleased. "You are truly gifted, are you not?" She trailed a hand down his chest.

He stopped her at his belt, astonished to sense she meant the size of his cock. Just to be certain he asked, "Are you implying—?"

"I don't imply. You are well made." She spoke as if stating facts.

He shook his head. "I can't think straight around you," he muttered, recalling far too easily how Jamie had fought Elsa being by his side when the couple had first met. Perhaps all males lost the ability to think clearly when confronted with such things. He stood, pulling her up with him so she faced him with a suddenness that left her a bit breathless. "If Warren truly is Gideon, he will go after Agatha. He will kill her, won't he?"

"Yes." She straightened her clothing. He got the impression she was worried. But at what he couldn't say. *If we were bonded...* "Tell me, did you scatter Samuel's ashes to the wind after you burned him?"

He captured her hand from where she was nervously playing with her braid.

"Yes. Why do you ask?" She reached up and smoothed her fingers between his eyebrows.

"Isobel? What are you doing?"

"You frown entirely too often."

A burst of laughter escaped him. He took her hand, now holding both hostage. "If you do not stop, I will take us to my home and there, keep you until you cannot lift—"

"I do like these threats better, but" — she tugged gently and he released his grip — "I suppose we must focus. Perhaps you should sit over there."

She pointed to the opposite couch.

He laughed again then cut off abruptly. "Are you serious?"

When she nodded, he shook his head. There wasn't a chance of that — besides, he knew even if she was unaware, that they would need to be close, touching each other often in order to feel secure. He kissed her fingertips. "Samuel was one of the council."

"Yes, if you had not spread his ashes, then I could not free my brother. Warren, or Gideon, will try to stop me. He will possibly kill Agatha, but if he does, he will not send her ashes to the wind. He will not allow that, nor will he allow us to kill him and do the same to him."

Bryson trailed the back of his fingers along her cheek. Her worry showed in her paleness and in the depth of darkness in her eyes. "I doubt you will ask for permission. So whether he allows it or not, if he has done these things, *we* will kill him."

"If? You still doubt me?"

A smile lifted his lips. "Isobel." He drew closer to her, "I will never doubt you again. Nor will I deny you anything you wish."

"That is not true. I wanted —"

He pulled her closer with a hand behind her head and an arm around her waist. It was an intimate embrace that spoke of possession and right. She softened against him. The emotion that rose up in his chest at her sign of acceptance stole his breath.

"Did I not give you passion?"

"Yes, you know you did." She lifted a leg to stroke along the outside of his.

His body hardened to steel. In response, she rubbed her lips over his jaw.

How am I to keep from tossing her down when she does that? Control. Think of the goal. Her. Our lives. Forever.

He settled for brushing a kiss to her lips. "I also took, when I told myself I would not."

"You would not, what? Experience pleasure with me?"

"Yes, imagine that."

She appeared baffled. "But why? Do you not even now want me?" She boldly took hold of his erection.

God, yes! Take her. She is aroused again. She wants. No. Not here, not now. "I want you until there is little room for anything else. But I want all of you —your blood, your promise, your life, your body. I want to give you everything until you want the same from me. Until then" —he removed her hand and brushed a kiss to her knuckles and held her hand in his —"I suppose I will have to court you and earn what I want."

The idea seemed to thrill her. She scanned his face as if attempting to read the truth. But she held her breath as well. "Do you mean this?" she finally whispered in an awed tone.

"Yes."

At the simple answer, she smiled and stood on tiptoe to reach his lips with hers. "Then I hope your courting will include more of what we just shared." She ducked her head shyly.

He stopped her by tipping her head up. "Much more, but not claim you —"

"Yes, I know. Until then, we need to decide what to do. Shall we go save Agatha, or go kill her?"

"We can do both."

From above them, he heard Rowan clear his throat. "Then you two had better hurry. I sense the time draws short for my cousin."

"Then you had better be prepared to join us." Bryson stared up at where her mentor stood at the landing at the top of the stairs.

Rowan was dressed for battle. He'd put on his Dragon Lord robe and cinched it with the belt of their order. The hilt of his broad sword rose above his left shoulder, and at his hip he had belted on his ceremonial dagger.

Isobel stilled in Bryson's arms.

He tipped her head so he could see the pain in her eyes. "What is it?"

"Nothing, Bryson." She stepped away.

Rowan walked down the curved stairs. "I have been ready for some time. I thought perhaps now, though, would be a better time than later, when you would both be unavoidably unable to join me."

Bryson bristled, until she took his hand.

"It is true. Soon we will be unavoidably delayed by other matters," Isobel said.

"Such things are also private," Bryson said for her ears alone.

"From whom?" Rowan asked. "Who does not understand the wild mating our kind experience? I say it is only fools who pretend to—ah, I see. You were speaking to Isobel. Well, still, such things are understood." Rowan made it sound like they were discussing the downside of heavy rainfall. "Best we go now, though, don't you agree?"

"If Gideon is Warren, then we need to worry what his goal is with this. Why take a new body? Why hide all this time?" Bryson asked, still worried over his inability to see beyond the young façade Warren presented to the world.

"Well, he wishes to rise again, my boy. That is why. With Isobel doing all the work, of course."

"What do you mean?" Isobel asked, stopping Rowan when he walked past.

"Why, my dear, I thought you knew. When you kill the council, the six, you will unleash a powerful force, either setting your brother free at last to join his bride or…setting Gideon free to once again regain his bodily form."

"And you just now thought to tell us this?" Bryson growled.

Rowan straightened indignantly. Isobel stopped them by stepping between them. At her fierce frown, Bryson relented and took a step away from Rowan.

"Rowan, I have only killed four. I need to end Agatha's life and…oh, God have mercy on our souls." She stared from Rowan to Bryson and tightened her fist on his shirt. "Perhaps *Gideon* was part of the council. *He* was killed. If so, that means the council did to him what they did to Jorge."

"He has only to kill Agatha and say the words and he is once again given his body," Rowan confirmed.

"Then there is no hope?" Isobel hugged her arms around her middle, sorrow filling the space between them as she bowed her head.

"There is always hope. If we can stop him, we will." Bryson took her hand.

Her gaze was firm as she held his. He saw the moment she regained her hope. It was there, in the depths of her beautiful eyes. With a squeeze to his hand, she turned to face Rowan.

"Will you aid us?" Isobel asked.

Bryson's chest bowed. *Us. She is mine.*

Rowan nodded. "I will. I've lived too long in the shadows. It is time to join my cousin in support of his rule. And perhaps it is time to put right what was once done so wrong by you, Isobel."

"We have to save Agatha." She met Bryson's gaze bravely.

He brushed a wisp of dark hair from her cheek. "We will find another means of freeing your brother, Isobel. Trust me."

At his words, something glimmered in her eyes. Trust. For the first time in his life, hope burned brightly. *Aid her in saving her brother, destroy Gideon, build our lives. How difficult can it be?*

Chapter Twenty

"Release me! You cannot possibly think that this will bring you anything! I have riches beyond your wildest dreams. I can give you anything you desire —"

"You dead is what I desire, Agatha. Nothing more, and I will settle for nothing less." Gideon tugged the rope on her arm tighter than actually necessary, but enjoying the way she sobbed in pain too much not to. He walked around to her other side and drew her other pale arm up and looped the rope over, then around her slim wrist.

She gasped and shivered. "You cannot mean that. You cannot. You have only to tell me what you desire. Simply tell me," she begged.

Even pleading for her life she retained the beauty she was so well-known for. His cousin, Alec, would have been proud of the evil, self-absorbed woman she had become. A Vampire after his own heart, except for him to succeed, he needed her soul scattered to the winds.

The younger, weaker body he possessed still rose to arousal as he studied the way her slight, womanly struggles merely outlined the perfection of her body. Even the silk gown loved her form, slipping gracefully to showcase the mound of her womanhood as he pulled her arm higher. She sucked in a sharp breath and the gown slipped along the swell of her bosoms' generous curves. As he tightened the rope, the edge of her pink areole came into view.

His cock hardened, pressing painfully to the zipper of his slacks. Warren was a well-endowed Vampire, but he was still simply a means to an end. His body was the last in a long line of men Gideon had possessed throughout the ages. Gideon's body had been burned and left to the forces of nature, but he was a god compared to them. Still, the hard, heavy weight of Warren's cock was impressive. It had served him well over the last few years. Samuel, the Vampire who had served Gideon for centuries, had found what remained of him and, knowing Gideon's particular tastes, had made the transfer of his soul from much less pleasing specimen to this one.

Samuel. The loss of his long-time servant was grievous. Without him, finding release for the particular sport he enjoyed would be tiresome. Hopefully the last exchange, into his own form, would be much easier than moving his soul into another's shell.

Soul stealing some called it. It was more. He knew Warren remained, but the younger, much younger Vampire could do nothing to free himself or those Gideon chose to enjoy. In some ways it increased Gideon's pleasure to know that the Vampire was a prisoner, unable to stop him from his debauchery.

He'd hoped, at one time, that more of him—Gideon—would emerge. Some theories suggested it, but every time he looked in the mirror it was not his jet black hair and classical Romanesque features that graced the glass. Now he had to stare at this uncouth, brown-haired Vampire, who, although handsome and well-endowed, was not half the man Gideon had been. Still his features were striking, for, since taking over his body, Gideon had never had a lack of bedmates, nor had to work hard at gaining access to any woman he wanted.

Not that an easy mating had ever been what turned him on the most. He ignored the way the other Vampire kept attempting to gain control. He allowed it a few times, enjoying being a passenger when he hit the cusp of coming, and knowing Warren was unable to stop the climax he experienced even if it horrified him.

Agatha cried out, calling him back to the present. With possession, his mind wandered. More often than he liked, Warren rose when he slept, and he'd awaken, in a new place, unable to recall how he'd arrived there. Each time he punished the boy by killing an innocent in the most debased way possible. Even now, he could feel Warren fighting him to aid Agatha. The younger Vampire had no idea how alike Agatha was to Gideon. She was as arrogant as he was, as prideful and as cunning. He considered her perfection, and ideas on how to rip her pride right from her began to form in delicious detail.

He contemplated the idea. Agatha was lush, with a wealth of womanly attributes he normally found himself downright unable to resist. The idea of binding her, then fucking her while she couldn't do more than allow it, gave him something to consider. It would serve the arrogant bitch right. He bet she'd never been given a thorough fucking by a man who was able to go on until even the most seasoned whores begged him to stop. He could do *anything* to her—even the more bloody enjoyments—and she would endure. His other vessels had all died before he'd squeezed every ounce of enjoyment from the session.

A tingle along his spine made the idea even more appealing. He'd sampled the choicest offerings at Christian's House, but that was nights ago and he'd been forced to be tame with them. To not only try out, but humiliate the woman that arrogant prick Christian had wanted for his bonded was doubly enticing.

"There, now. We shall soon have this complete." He watched her, anticipating her trying to break free.

She squirmed and wiggled, giving him more of a show than he knew she realized. Even her breathing had turned erratic, indicating she was close to hyperventilating. He knew other methods of making it hard for her to catch her breath. He considered each but settled for something more…degrading.

He had once been a god among Vampires. He'd had women fawning over him, lining up to even have a chance of him gracing them with his attention. Agatha and her council had taken that away from him.

They could have helped him rise again. All those years ago, they could have easily called him back with blood sacrifices. They had not. He had suffered for decades until Samuel had found him. Even Samuel had been unable to find the perfect host from time to time. Such agony he'd suffered.

Agatha became more desperate the longer he stood near her. She was blindfolded. He considered gagging her as her pleas became more demanding, but enjoyed the sound of her hopelessness growing. When it reached a level he felt appropriate, he removed a necklace from his pocket. The pendant hung in a sweet oval from his fist, twirling gently as he held it above her. The word *forever* was scrolled in the gold. He could never have forever. Not any longer. His bonded had thrown herself onto the rocks below his keep, ending her life after he'd made her his — in all ways. A bonded should have allowed all he'd wanted from her. Instead, his had fought him, crying and sobbing as he'd fucked her for days, releasing the necessary sperm and blood to make her his. Her rejection had stung. But she had paid. Her body had been claimed by the sea, taken forever from him. With it, she'd freed him to grow more powerful than he'd ever dreamed. No one denied him. No one cried and sobbed unless he wanted them to, and when they did, by all that was holy, they had reasons to.

Like this woman. He slid the chain over her neck and the gold caught between her bosoms, much as it had nestled between his Catherine's breasts so long ago.

He moved to Agatha's left side and untied her hand, leaving the rope looped on her wrist, still in a tight, hard knot. She sobbed and nodded, clearly thinking he was freeing her. He didn't break the illusion. Instead he untied the other. Then when she was gasping for breath, trying to calm herself, he slowly drew both behind her back. He'd done the same to Catherine, introducing her to his needs gently, but still she had sobbed and fought him.

"What — ?"

With a savage tug, he tied Agatha's arms together. He made sure to use enough force to pop both of her large tits out of her gown. Only then did he remove the blindfold.

He settled on a chair, enjoying the way she sobbed and trembled. A smile tugged at his lips as his erection jutted up in a raunchy display of maleness. She seemed to realize exactly—or thought she did—what he wanted. Sex. It was never merely sex—not any longer. The soft games he'd wanted to play with Catherine, the gentle spankings and tender tie-ups, were long gone. Dust in the wind. Now, he craved much, much more. With Samuel no longer around to supply him with his pleasurable toys, and the bastard wolf in possession of Elsa, a female who he'd wanted for years, he was forced to play nice when he fucked.

Now, like a gift from the gods, he had a Vampire to whom he could do anything and everything he could think of. The first thing would be painful. His heavy sac tingled as he watched her tits tremble with each sobbing breath.

"Ah, yes, you are going to pay, but it's not your jewels I want." He reached up and smacked her breast. "Other than these." He twisted both nipples, watching her face flush with color. "Yes, that's it." Realization clouded her eyes even as he shoved her over and between his knees. He ripped her gown, exposing the ripe perfection of her rounded ass.

"I have changed my mind. First, for you, I think a punishment is in order. One you will feel even after I spread your ashes to the wind." The first smack of the paddle on her ass was so sharp and clear he had to breathe through his nose as his pulse skyrocketed. "Yes, a nice, hard spanking on your big ass, Agatha. That's what you need. Then a lesson on how to service a man when his cock is hard."

"How dare you! Stop this!" She struggled, screaming in outrage, jiggling and wiggling like he'd hoped. "I am demanding you let me go!"

He caught her face and squeezed her cheeks so her mouth was forced into a pout. Forcing her to angle her head like that, he brought the paddle down harder and harder, and by the time he had given her a dozen strokes she was sobbing.

"You're going to suck my cock, aren't you?"

She nodded eagerly.

"Yes, sir. Say it." He gave her more spankings until she screamed every word perfectly past her tears. It didn't help her but he released her face and let her fall forward for the rest of her spanking.

He got off more than once in the process of giving her what she needed. He made sure she was humiliated each and every time he spilled his abundant seed.

By the time he had fed his anger to satisfaction, she hung loosely over his knees, crying and shaking uncontrollably. Her rounded bottom was fiery red from the top of her curvy ass to the underside of each cheek and on down to her thighs. Agatha shivered like a horse that had been ridden hard.

He dropped her onto the floor and brought her up by gripping her hair, walking backward to force her to crawl on her knees, her face pressed to his cock. "Now you'll suck my cock like a good whore, won't you?"

She nodded eagerly, attempting to do just that. He let her, then he took her in every way imaginable by men or gods, he was certain. By the time there wasn't an ounce of sperm left in him, he was too sated to move and she was nearly unconscious. He barely had the energy to tie her back up, naked and covered in blood, sex, and tears, so he could rest.

She had the nerve to whisper, "Will you let me go now?"

"When I tire of you, you will die. But this day, you will linger, I hope, remembering that my revenge has only begun."

At her whimper he laughed, gladdened to know she knew he spoke the truth. He shut the doors on her, locking her in a cabinet, much like she had once locked Isobel.

Isobel.

You will be my first fuck when I gain my body again. And you, like Agatha, will crawl to me, begging me for your life. Shall I give it?

He considered the dark-eyed beauty and decided regretfully, she had to die. Along with Bryson, her guilt-ridden and conflicted bonded. *I will take Elsa instead. After I kill that runt boy and the wolf, I will possess the little dancer for as long as I wish.* A vampire-wolf. Such a being will endure for centuries, just as my bonded should have.

He had just enough energy to clean the residue of sex and sweat from his borrowed body before he sank onto his silken bedding. *Always it comes down to sex.* He laughed even as he closed his eyes, preparing for a much-deserved rest. *It always comes down to sex and power. Always the two go hand in hand.*

For some, it became their downfall. But not for him, for he was born to wield both his body and his power. Life would again be as it should have been since the day his father, Gregory, had died.

Aidan, you too will know of my coming. Soon, you will also understand that I was always the one meant to rule.

Chapter Twenty-One

Bryson broke out of his shift at the door to Agatha's House, only to find it open and silence coming from the interior.

"He has beaten us here," he warned as soon as Isobel settled gracefully on his left.

"Yes, but I can sense him, the same man from before."

"Warren," Bryson agreed. *How did I miss this?* Warren had been under his command for months. He'd never sensed anything beneath the Vampire's façade. Anger at the ancients, a disdain and especially that last meeting at Gia's House, but he'd simply believed the man a hothead.

Rowan appeared and walked unhindered through the doors. "They are dead. All of them. He repeats history here."

"What do you mean?" Bryson asked, catching up to Rowan as he gained the stairs.

Bodies lay everywhere, their throats ripped out or their heads feet from their bodies.

"When Gideon attacked that village, he did so with a purpose." Rowan shouldered through a door barricaded by two broken bodies.

"To take my brother's wife," Isobel whispered, sorrow coloring her tone.

"What?" Bryson caught her arm and kept her outside the room with him while Rowan went inside.

"He took her and raped her in the street of the village. It was there Jorge found him, and his...wife. Tessa had...died during his... While—"

Bryson searched her face, realizing with a shock that she was crying. He didn't think she knew she was. The tears were freely falling from her eyes, finally, after so long. What she had endured—in silence and on her own—staggered him. He clutched her to him and tenderly stroked her hair. His worry grew a hundred times worse than before. She had faced such a horrible reality, alone and for so long, when he had been there, but unable to see through all the lies. "I am sorry, Isobel, If I had known, if we had—"

"I know...now. Now I know." She gripped his shirt tightly, as if he might leave her. After allowing him to soothe her for a few moments, she stiffened and released him. He didn't like it but let her go. She ducked her head then stepped away on her own. "There was nothing you could have done then. They made certain of it."

They had. But no one would ever be able to cloud his judgment of her again. If it came down to her life or his, it would always be his. But until it came to that, if there was a sign of danger, he was taking her away and if he had to, hiding her for centuries.

He sensed she knew some of his thoughts. It wouldn't matter. "I will not let him near you, Isobel."

"I know." She turned as Rowan walked back out of the room.

"Nothing there. I believe most of the damage will be upstairs."

"Do you think he has taken Agatha and will be unable to resist repeating history?" she asked quietly.

Rowan nodded once then motioned for them to follow. "My brother is vain and selfish. He has a plan but he is secure in his belief he is unstoppable."

Bryson snorted. "It is always the case with such evil. They feel above everything, and that is when they are the most dangerous, and at times, the easiest to kill." He ushered Isobel up the stairs, making sure she was on the inside, close to the wall, as they continued.

As they prowled through the long halls and endless rooms, they found not one Vampire alive. Some would rise again, but it would be only the strongest and eldest who did.

At an inner chamber, Rowan pushed a door partway open and stepped inside. A woman and several guards lay dead on the floor. Blood splattered the walls, matted the white carpet and stained the statue of the Thinker. There was even scarlet in a long line on the domed ceiling.

"He found her here." Bryson walked to the woman, a servant, he thought. Her neck had been broken. She would rise again, but he feared she would do so without her mistress.

"He took her. She was still alive." Bryson cocked his head to the side and studied the way the couch was the only piece of furniture still in one piece. "She sat there and watched."

Isobel stayed by his side, closely surveying the scene. "Yes. He killed them as a show of force."

"Agatha did nothing to stop him," Bryson observed.

"There wouldn't have been much she could do." Rowan grimaced. "She was always a coward. No doubt she thought it wiser to stay silent and not interfere with his fury."

"This was Gideon?" Bryson asked.

"Yes. It was him, as himself. The other is there, though, still inside him." She bent and gracefully closed the servant's eyes.

"I agree." Rowan crossed his arms. "This means he will try to regain his own body. He is far from here. It is now day and he..." Rowan's frown deepened the lines around his eyes.

"He what?" Bryson demanded.

"He rests. She lives, but...barely."

At Rowan's warning, Isobel tensed.

"We should go there, now, and end this," Bryson urged. "He will not expect us. We can overwhelm him and —"

Isobel hissed and spun to face the doorway. Bryson drew his sword.

Rowan turned as well and swept in front of them. "Ah, this must be Jaxon and his lovely bonded, Joey."

Jaxon drew up so fast his trench coat snapped around his long legs. Immediately he threw an arm across Joey's chest. "What the fuck is —?" He shook his head, glancing at Bryson, then down at Isobel and back at Bryson with a curse. "Oh, fuck. Is that —?"

Joey covered Jaxon's mouth. "Seeing as how my husband has lost the ability to form sentences, Bryson, I should warn you, that is Isobel next to you, uh, right?" Joey wrinkled her nose. "So that means she's good?"

Jaxon got her hand off his mouth. "Shit, Joey, get the hell —"

"Jaxon, if she meant me harm, I assume I'd already be on the floor with, er, uh, these...people." Joey stepped around Jaxon, then the fallen dead. "Bryson, you pick odd places to visit. Hello, I'm Joey, Jaxon's better half." She held out her hand. After a prolonged silence, Isobel bowed low, hand over her heart.

"It is my pleasure to make your acquaintance, Joey, mate to Jaxon. I am, in fact, Isobel, but you are also correct, I did not cause this harm. Gideon did."

"Uh…" Jaxon swung his head from Bryson to Rowan—who was nodding and smiling as if that would reassure Jaxon—to Isobel and finally to Bryson "You and," he nodded to Isobel with a questioning glance, "her are…you've got to be kidding me."

Bryson stared him down.

"Aidan will kill me for this, after he kills you," Jaxon grumbled. "Shit, so much is not making sense, but at the same time is becoming crystal fucking clear. And not in a good way." Jaxon pointed at him. "This is why the fun trip down opium lane. This is also why the reluctance to share when she busted in on the IC. And for you *not* showing up to the VC."

IC? VC? Bryson belatedly caught the acronyms. Immortal Council and…Vampire Council. "It is."

"It is?" Jaxon repeated with another snap. "That's all you—?"

Joey had her eyes glued on Jaxon's and his arm in a death grip. Bryson was thankful that, at least, someone could talk sense to him. After resisting until he must have realized how stupid that was, Jaxon covered his eyes with his hand, anchoring the other on his hip with a hell of a heavy sigh and nodded.

"Is he ill?" Isobel whispered, wrinkling her nose.

"I believe his…wife may be speaking with him," Rowan replied. "It is common among our kind. In fact, I believe most—"

"Rowan, not now," Bryson snapped.

The elder glanced at the still fuming Jaxon and back at Bryson. "I see. Yes, perhaps later."

"So." Jaxon dropped his hand and Joey took it, hopefully still giving Jaxon hell. "You are Isobel. And you are?" He zeroed in on Rowan like a lifeline.

"Rowan. It is a pleasure to meet you." Rowan bowed.

"Rowan." Jaxon cocked an eyebrow.

"I am the son of Gregory. Gideon is my brother."

"And he did this?" Jaxon asked, somewhat more politely.

Rowan nodded. "Sadly, yes."

"Where is Aidan, Jaxon? Why did he send you?" Bryson demanded.

Jaxon squinted at him to see if he was kidding. He couldn't blame the Vampire. There wasn't time to explain every single detail. Even if they had ten years, it would still be a mind fuck.

"There's word of Rhys and Bridget. He's gone with Allie..." Jaxon hung his head. "This is bad, Bryson. This is fucked up, no matter how you spell it out."

"Jaxon, really, it's not that bad. Obviously we have mistaken Isobel for the bad guy, or girl, in this story." Joey glanced to Rowan when all Jaxon did was shake his head. "And you would be Aidan's brother? You don't look like him. He is so stern and...well, bossy." She offered her hand to Rowan.

Rowan bowed over it, yet not touching her as he did. No doubt Jaxon looming at her left shoulder had a lot to do with that.

"I am Rowan, son of Gregory, and uncle to Aidan, but I am not bossy, I hope not at least, if this means I order people around? But we really should be moving along. Besides the awful scenery, there is the matter of my brother to deal with."

"Oh, fuck, it keeps getting better and better. And no, I think swearing is perfect right now hotshot, because that woman," Jaxon pointed a finger like a gun at Isobel even as he drew Joey back under his arm, "is going to make this one hell of a long night."

Joey laughed and hugged him. "He's always grumpy when he has to come to someone's rescue, but he really does like it. So, what's our plan? Shall we go find Gideon before he does more of this? Will it suddenly free some trapped spirit and release Isobel from a curse?"

Beside him Isobel stiffened.

Rowan drew back and slowly grinned. "Amazing."

"What?" Joey studied her mate and slowly smiled. "Cool, so I wasn't too far off?"

"No, my dear, you were close. Have you been taught anything at all about the Dragon creed?" Rowan asked, taking her hand delicately in his and guiding her to the door.

Jaxon gave Rowan an odd half-smile when the elder checked for permission to speak to his mate. Rowan grinned and moved Joey farther ahead.

"He's going to fill her head with ideas, isn't he?" Jaxon sounded as if didn't like that idea, but Bryson could see the male was proud of his mate.

"Oh, yes, he will have her swearing oaths with you by her side in no time." Isobel's casual words left Jaxon standing dumbfounded behind her.

Bryson grinned and smacked Jaxon on the shoulder. "Come on before Rowan convinces Joey to jump before you can check out what into."

Jaxon grumbled but shot him an assessing frown. "Damn, you owe me for this."

True. More than Jaxon would ever know.

Isobel turned from her study of the ancient ruins of what had once been the seat of power for Vampires, and nearly ran into Joey. The small redhead's mate was watching from his position by the rocks, but he seemed to have come to terms with Isobel not being the enemy he'd believed.

"Oh, my God, this is Count Dracula's castle."

Jaxon walked over and hugged her, for some reason not correcting her.

"No," Isobel corrected. "This is not that count's home. This was the seat of our power. The king reigned here, and in his time, anyone coming upon his home would have done so without fear in their hearts — if they meant our kind no harm."

Joey widened her large eyes and smiled. "Oh, that is amazing. Much better than how you tell it, Jaxon."

Jaxon laughed harder and curled Joey into his arms. Joey didn't seem to mind. Isobel found her pleasing. Even her quick smile and even quicker laugh were pure and unhindered by anything other than the joy she felt. She was the complete opposite of her tall, dark-haired warrior — except when he looked at her. Then, the similarities between them were apparent, or perhaps not the similarities, but the reason for their deep love and commitment. Joey was Jaxon's other half, the light to his darkness.

"We will need a witch, perhaps more than one." Rowan stroked his chin then nodded. "Yes, a few witches should do the trick."

Bryson was in the process of rising from his hunched position and paused to stare at the ancient. "Rowan, just how do you propose we go about doing that?"

"I supposed we would use your phone. Mine is no longer working, if you recall."

"I recall a lot, but not you mentioning a witch or two would be necessary."

"Bryson, we cannot enter his home without breaking his spells. We will need a witch to set a wider net, so if he does run, he is caught." Isobel crouched near the rocks they were hiding behind. "He is under the castle, deep within the darkest levels. But he will sense us entering and it is then he will kill Agatha."

"What if only one of us were to go? Would he be threatened by one?" Joey asked, sharing a look with Jaxon.

"True, if say, Rowan were to go." Jaxon unwrapped a piece of gum. "Then, while you distract him, we could enter, as well."

Rowan watched Jaxon pop his gum in his mouth. "Such a plan might work."

"It would *not* work." Isobel stood and faced her mentor.

Bryson nodded. "He would recognize you, Rowan. He will attack—"

"True." Rowan threw his shoulders back. "Are you suggesting I cannot defeat him?"

"No, of course they aren't," Joey said quickly. "But." She winced. "Bryson does have a point. He would know you, and he's disguised as Warren, who, by the way, I never liked."

Jaxon nodded. "He made her skin crawl."

Rowan shook his hair from his eyes. "He would not expect me. Nor would he—"

"Not going to happen," Bryson argued. "That thing in there is dangerous. He was able to share Warren's body, hide so we couldn't recognize what he was. I should go. He won't expect trouble from me."

Jaxon shook his head. "That thing in there is Rowan's bro. He has powers we don't understand. Rowan is the better bet."

Isobel moved nearer to Bryson. "No, he is not. Bryson is correct." Isobel didn't like it. She worried even more when she saw no other angles they could play. "I do not care for this plan either, Jaxon. But Bryson is strong enough to challenge Gideon—if it comes to that. It should not come to that." She stressed her words, hoping Bryson understood. "If you merely say you are looking for something, and are surprised by him, he might believe you. He trusts you, yes?"

Bryson's handsome face grew harder, but he nodded ever so slightly.

"You simply need to go in, breaking his barriers just enough," she stressed.

Bryson glanced over her head to the stronghold barely visible against the dark stone of the mountain. His gaze met hers again and she experienced a sharp pain in her chest. "For you to sneak in, just as you did with my dogs."

"Yes. Exactly." Even as she agreed, her stomach tightened to a knot of anxiety.

"The idea has merit." Rowan took a piece of gum Jaxon offered.

"Enter. When you do, we'll come storming in." Jaxon snapped his gum. "It's simple, but simple plans suck as far as details go."

"I tend to think the simpler the plan, the less chance of it unraveling." Rowan seemed to test the flavor of the minty gum because, after a few chews, he smiled.

Isobel sensed, even in the tension of the moment, Bryson found her mentor amusing. He didn't smile, but there was something in his tough expression that said he, too, experienced fondness for the elder.

"I agree with Bryson and Isobel. This is the better way, but perhaps…" Rowan studied Bryson as if he'd just opened a fascinating book. "You should be wounded. Just enough to make him think you came here for refuge, and found him by accident."

"I thought he liked simple plans," Jaxon muttered to Joey. "Bryson being wounded enough to be believed is not going to help him defend himself."

Isobel's heart experienced a pain that didn't go away. "I do not like this plan, Rowan. If he is wounded—"

"I will be believed. I will say you tried to kill me when I attempted to save Christian. He will know I was there, he will assume I went after you. If he believes more, then so much the better."

This doesn't feel right. He needs to stay. The urge to beg was hard to stifle.

"It was a good plan, now it is excellent." Rowan grinned.

Jaxon cursed but sounded happy. "Fuck, it might work, but as soon as you breach the bastard's walls, we will be there, so be prepared."

Bryson's hand was firm and solid when he took hers. She still felt this was wrong. But in Bryson's eyes she could see he had decided. *He allowed us to talk, all the while knowing this is what he wanted — to go alone. He even tricked me into agreeing.*

"If this will get us in there, then we will end this, here, tonight," Bryson said confidently.

A shiver raced up her spine. *Does he do this for us?* He glanced at the sky and back down at her. His eyes were bright. *With hope?* She wanted to warn him not to. Hope hurt when ripped away. "It is just now dark. He will rise soon, and when he does—"

"I know. We have no time." She still hesitated.

221

Bryson didn't. He called forth his massive sword. It shimmered brightly under the moonlight. He was so handsome to her in that moment she had to tug at her hair to keep from pleading him not to go.

I never begged for anything. Not since you, Jorge. Not during all the tortures they put me through before walling me up. But for him, I would go to my knees. What does this mean?

"I'll need to be injured or he will have doubts." He turned from her to face Jaxon. "You do it. She will not make it look real enough."

The thud of her heart turned to panicky racing.

Jaxon nodded tightly. A muscle in Bryson's jaw throbbed. Before she could stop this madness, Jaxon drew his sword. With a two-handed grip he brought it down across Bryson's body, then crossed the wound to land another along his ribs.

Bryson grunted. The muscle on his jaw jumped, but he didn't fall. Blood immediately scented the air. His blood. *Exquisite. But wrong. Injured.* The need to *go* to him, to *ease* him, to *heal* him was astronomically intense.

"Go. Now, while you are still strong," Jaxon ordered.

She caught his arm before he could. "I will be looking for you," she managed. She tightened her hand on the firmness of his arm. "I will share my blood so you can heal."

He didn't reply but he narrowed his eyes. Then he was gone.

Joey let out a shuddering breath. "I don't like this plan."

Neither did Isobel. She opened her path to Bryson and felt him shift directly to the crumbling entrance. It was harder to stand still, knowing he was walking into danger than it had been to leave her brother, knowing he would be taken from her.

Please, please, please, do not take him from me.

Bryson held in the groan as he landed on the grassy hill where once had stood the stable yard to the king's court. It had been over six centuries since last he'd set foot inside this place he'd once called home.

Blood ran freely from his chest, diagonally across his stomach and on to his hip. Jaxon, the bastard, had hit him true. The last time he'd been here, he'd been bloodied as well. Fresh from battle, he'd learned his king was gone from this world and Aidan was missing.

Back then, he had also suffered the blow of knowing his bonded had been the one to kill their king. Now, he knew better.

Isobel.

Never once had he thought to question whether or not she had killed the king. Not once had he thought to dig into what he'd been told, to find out the truth for himself.

And I lecture on listening, when in fact it wasn't listening at all, or seeing beyond what I was told.

He knew never again would he trust so explicitly — outside of Isobel. She cared. She did. It was there, in the desperate, fearful brightness of her eyes. She was more than he deserved. *I will never let her go. So now, I will kill any who stand in my way.*

Two steps inside the broken remains of the building and Bryson sensed the presence of Warren — or the other. He pretended much more weakness than he actually felt and stumbled on the uneven ground to one knee and used his sword to lean on. He breathed shallowly, more because of the wounds than he wanted to admit.

"Bryson, what the hell happened to you, man?"

Warren.

Bryson lifted his head as if startled, and grimaced. "Warren. How did you find this place?"

"I was going to ask you the same thing." Warren carried the scent of blood and, under it, sex. The kind you couldn't wash off. The kind that came with taking what wasn't offered.

"You've been wounded. Has there been more trouble?"

Gideon—or Warren—had fooled him once. He wasn't allowing that again. He forced out a laugh, as if amused by the understatement. He also rose to his feet. *Never let an enemy gain your back.*

"You could say that. Never try to help a woman when she's insane."

Warren stepped from the shadows, grinning. "Ah, women can be tricky. They are always more trouble than they are worth. But what are we to do? We need them. At least once a day." He laughed and cupped his hand over his groin with a leer. "Best to keep that in mind, and try for nothing more."

No offer to aid him, no welcome, nothing but a joke. Bryson forced a painful laugh. "True. I seemed to have forgotten that."

Another coarse laugh was his only response. The man was baiting him.

"How did you find this place? I have not been here in years." Bryson leaned against the wall then stood as if thinking of something. "This was our ancient home. Have you searched inside?"

"No, I found this place empty, gutted and as you see it." A hint of suspicion finally tinged his tone. *So, is this Gideon?* "Why do you ask?"

Bryson groaned and shook his head. "It is nothing. I...thought to come here to try to get my head straight, but now that I see this place..." He paused and studied the ruins. "So many memories but little else. I am certain nothing would remain, least of all anything to aid us against Isobel."

Silence, then Warren walked closer. "Aid us against her? She's but one woman. Ah, my, you are wounded, aren't you?"

"A scratch, nothing more," Bryson muttered, straightening. His sword was still in his hand, but Warren didn't back out of range. Bryson sheathed it, not wanting to draw the man's attention. "This was the seat of the king, and at one time, our world. Such things of wonder once resided within these sacred halls that nothing we have now compares."

He walked to the stables, touching a wall, then another, feeling the barrier still firmly in place. "This was the stable, that the blacksmith's, and over there, I believe, there stood a long hall where the king held court. Beyond that was a library hidden in our safest chamber. We once stored books with the knowledge that would foretell her doom."

"Sounds impressive. Now it's little more than rubble." The sneer in Warren's voice made it clear he thought little of such things.

"Ah, but you don't understand. If we could but find the *Book of Ages*, then we could not only defeat Isobel but send out enemies to their deaths, as well." He forced a laugh. "Permanently."

"The *Book of Ages* is a myth." *Is it Gideon I'm speaking to now? Or is it Warren more than Gideon? Warren wouldn't know of the book.* "Such a book does not exist." Gideon then. The sneer made sense now.

"Ah, but it does." Bryson steadied himself again on the wall. "I have seen it. If it were here."

"Why do you think it is here?"

"Because I once hid it away, keeping it safe, when she destroyed our world." A lie, but then Warren wouldn't know. And Gideon had been dead, wandering and without body. By the tension in the Vampire's shoulders, Bryson knew he had him. "I had thought it might be here, but if what you say is true and there is nothing left, then someone had to have found it."

Warren squinted at him. Bryson held his tongue. It would do no good. Saying more would only make the man—

"What if there was one place, deep below, where spells hold it locked?"

Bryson faked a groan and stifled it as if just hearing him. "Are you...? Warren, this is not something to jest over."

Warren barked a laugh. "I'm serious!"

"Then show me," he grated. His chance was now. He held down his excitement.

Warren was still leery.

He waited, willing him to fall for it. "Well?"

"It's through here. I set up a barrier. I'm surprised you didn't notice it."

"Well, if I hadn't lost half my blood supply on these rocks, I might have." He kept the grumble in his tone as he limped after Warren.

As soon as he felt the whisper of the spells allowing him entrance, he drew his sword. The ring of metal was loud, but he had never attacked a man's unguarded back in his life.

Warren spun, eyes narrowed. "Fucking lying bastard!"

He didn't waste time acknowledging that only part of that was actually accurate. He attacked. They impacted like sledgehammers. Warren tried to grab him by the throat. Bryson threw the Vampire off. Quickly, he followed with a volley of sword strokes. *Kill him.* The clash of metal rang loud in the night. *Where's Jaxon? Where's Isobel?*

Blood loss made him slow, but he still managed to dig in a few good slices. Above the clashing of their blades he heard Isobel cry his name. For some reason, her sweet voice rang in his head. To be certain, he turned with his next stroke, forcing Warren back from where he suddenly sensed Isobel. Warren lunged right for her. Bryson caught the Vampire around his waist and pulled his knife, stabbing him deeply. Even as he did, he knew that the shocked gasp wasn't from Warren — but from Isobel.

Time froze, imparting on him every detail with razor-sharp clarity. The wind had blown a dark wisp of her hair across her face, into her dark eyes and along her ivory cheek. But it wasn't her face that burned into his brain. It was the sword rammed into her stomach.

Warren shouted something as if from a distance. Jaxon's muffled curses followed.

All he could understand was that across from him, Isobel collapsed to her knees, holding a hand to her middle as Warren slid his sword free.

He knew, some part of him understood, that nothing would keep her from him again. Not in death or in life. Yet that was as distant as the sound of his labored breath or the fact that his heart beat in time with hers.

In that moment, clarity snapped down. It drilled into him that this woman was his, for all eternity.

The world sped back up. He sprang into action, feeling as if she had shoved every ounce of her strength at him instead of letting it spill from the wound in her stomach. He hit Warren hard from the side at the same time as Rowan attacked him from the front and Jaxon from his other side. He knew, on one level, that Joey was cradling Isobel's head in her lap and already gave her blood, but it was a distant thing. Inside he felt Isobel holding on, to him, just as firmly as he held on to her.

His blade hit Warren in the side, adding to the first deep cut. He maximized the impact by shoving him into Jaxon. Not willing to lose the moment, he twisted, turning Warren so Rowan slammed into him with his blade.

Suddenly through the night a scream rent the air — and a second later Warren vanished into a hundred bats. Jaxon burst into the same, diving and attacking. Rowan surged into a hawk even as his brother copied him and Jaxon followed suit.

Bryson let them. He dropped his sword to the cobblestones, and within seconds had Isobel's hand in his. She was just sitting up, wincing, but alive when he locked eyes with her.

He helped her to her feet with an arm around her shoulders. "You survived."

"So did you." She winced and would have pulled away, but he shook his head.

Joey laughed. "Yeah, it was messy, but she's... Oh, you two need a moment, don't you?" Joey would have walked away, but he knew suddenly that Isobel didn't want her to.

"No. Stay. It's not safe yet," he warned.

Isobel touched his cheek. Her eyes were darker than the night sky. "Here." She bit her wrist and, before he could deny her, knelt before him and offered her arm, head bowed. It was an ancient sign of respect that one showed to those above them. He pulled her to her feet and kissed her fingers, eyes locked with hers.

"You are my life."

Her eyes grew rounded then glistened. "You are mine, as well. Take what is ours," she whispered against his cheek. "A life for a life."

"Always." He kissed her forehead. As gently as possible he held her offered wrist. Her skin was cool. He tried his best to keep it tame. But the first rich taste of her and his shaft swelled. If not for Joey and impending danger, they would have needed a room. The delicate flavor of her blood burst along his taste buds. Her pulse hammered his lips and fangs. She warmed and her womanly body softened for him. Her heart rate quickened — to match his. Another draw and the scent of her arousal tinted the air.

His body roared to life. His wounds closed. Deep inside he felt the bridge between them blossom. She moaned lightly, signaling her growing excitement. He wanted her. Needed her. *Take her, make her mine.*

Instead, he shuddered out a breath, gained control, and closed her wound with a gentle lick. When he knew he had passed the test, he pressed a kiss to the ivory skin.

"You did not take enough," she admonished. "You need your strength, I fear—"

A scream ripped through the air. Joey started. He steadied her and urged Isobel to his side.

"What... What was that?" Joey whispered.

"I think it's...Agatha." Isobel leaned into him as if for support.

Through the link she had allowed he sensed fear, along with painful memories that tried to claim her attention.

He rested her cheek against his chest. "It *is* Agatha. We will go together. I will not leave your side. Joey, you will stay with us, as well."

"Jaxon is pretty clear on that," she agreed. "But, really, I am not thrilled with going down there." She pointed to a broken stairwell leading to the lower level. "If that's the down you're talking about."

"It is safe—for now." Bryson sent Isobel more reassurances through their bond. "Centuries ago, this was the seat of our power. It was built to last but abandoned."

Isobel stood away from him, drawing her shoulders back and standing straight. She had called her own sword and wore it at her hip, a smaller blade than his but no less deadly.

"There was once a throne room that dazzled the eyes. Diamonds were embedded in the walls so that candlelight filled the room with such a glow it looked as if the sun had risen." Isobel waved to the mountains behind what was left of the crumbling ruins. "The mountains were once filled with such treasures. Now"—she surveyed the destruction and sighed—"All is gone. But Bryson is right. The foundation is still strong. Below ground will possibly have survived better than up here, where time took its toll."

"It sounds beautiful. Will Aidan rebuild it, do you think?"

Bryson shook his head. "This place has memories he would rather forget. Be on your guard. Joey, if you have a weapon, draw it. Otherwise, stay close between us. It might not be pretty." Isobel feared it would be like her sister-in-law all over again. "I will go first. If she is not well, then we will take her from this place."

Both women nodded, but it was Isobel he watched. Her eyes were too big, the darkness of them too bright.

"Wait," Joey called suddenly. "Jaxon returns. He wishes us to wait."

Bryson shared his humor with Isobel through their link and felt her worry begin to lessen slightly. *'Most likely Jaxon had much more to say than to wait.'*

'He is protective.'

'Of course.' He moved closer to Isobel. *'As am I.'* To Joey he said, "Is that what he said? Have you considered running the Vampire Council, because you must possess a great deal of tact."

"He's not so bad, Bryson. Besides, someone has to stay level-headed," Joey responded with a sassy smile.

The next instant, Jaxon appeared and she cried out in surprise.

Jaxon laughed and surrounded her with his arms so he could whisper loudly to her, "I have other qualities." As soon as he lifted his head, his expression hardened. "That bastard is good. Rowan is chasing him down. He suggested I come back here in case that *something more* we find here is dangerous."

Bryson let that go. He knew if something dangerous was within a foot of Joey, and his friend wasn't around to protect her, Jaxon would never forgive himself. Neither would he. Isobel's wellbeing was now at his center. All the times he'd wondered at the bondings between couples, and now he knew. *My life for hers.* He took Isobel's hand. It was small, but warmer now. *'Still reacting to the blood share?'*

'No. Simply you.'

"That's really not making this easier," Joey grumbled to Jaxon. "Let's get it over with."

"Yes, I agree. Agatha is...unwell." Isobel looked to him, trusting him to lead. *'I fear she is near death, Bryson.'*

'We will do what we can.' He took a deep breath and wiped his forehead with his sleeve. "Come."

Chapter Twenty-Two

Isobel followed Bryson down the stairs. Every inch of her body tightened with tension. It was more than the worry of what awaited them. It was the descent into the ruins. Long ago, this place had been a wonder to behold. Now it was ancient and decayed. Wind whipped through the gaps in the mortar, making it treacherous. As they reached the lowest level, she heard sobbing.

"Is that...?" Joey's face paled and she took hold of her warrior's hand.

"Fuck, Bryson, what are we heading into?" Jaxon growled.

"Hell," Isobel whispered. "Gideon is beyond mad, he is cunning and cruel. He values little beyond himself."

Bryson radiated anger like a fire gave off heat. He stopped them at the bottom of the stairs and motioned to Jaxon with a sharp nod. "Jaxon, you and Joey guard the door. Isobel, stay —"

"No. I will come with you. At least until we find her," she added when he would have argued.

Another low moan reached them. Bryson's expression turned cold. He tightened his lips but didn't deny her. He also didn't share his thoughts, beyond a sense of growing fury. Instead of mind-speaking to him, she waited. Finally, his sharp gaze met hers and he exhaled.

"Come."

She followed, understanding more than he realized how difficult this was for him. Bryson was ancient, and as such, she knew he was loath to put her in a situation where she could be hurt. Now that he had claimed her, his behavior had completely turned. Gone was the man who had judged her so harshly, and in his place was a warrior who knew where he stood.

The difference in him took her breath away.

The long, dark corridor had once been the most guarded section of the keep. Down here was where the king would have met with his council, where he would have lived and where he would have raised his children. She had been here but once before.

"Here." Bryson stopped at a well-preserved door of ancient wood and iron. The massive thing was shut, but Bryson opened it, only enough for the passage of his broad shoulders and stopped.

She didn't need to enter. She could smell the scent of blood and sex on the air. Tears, too, tinted the breeze, as well as fear. Massive amounts of horror so deep, she worried Agatha would never again find sanity.

"Bryson." Isobel shoved lightly at his shoulder when he didn't move his larger body from blocking her view. "Can we save her?"

Bryson's shoulders hardened under his shirt, but he pushed the door the rest of the way open. Agatha was across from them, in a cabinet, much like Isobel had survived in for six hundred and seventy-five years. But she'd been walled in, never touched again, forgotten most likely. Agatha had not. There were tools, brutal, barbaric instruments of torture colored with her blood, and, she thought with a sickening dread, her flesh and blood. She centered her focus off the table and blood-splattered floor to the cabinet. Blood pooled beneath it, a lake that no doubt was from Agatha.

"What—?" She paused and swallowed. "What did he do to her?"

Bryson made a retching sound, wrist to his lips. "I think he…gutted her."

Isobel turned her face away. Bryson was there. He cradled her head to his chest. The once tough, threatening warrior was gone, replaced by a caring man who sought to ease even this from her. *'It will be worse when we open the doors.'* She knew his warning was meant to make her turn around and leave, but she couldn't.

'I know. We need to save her.'

"Then come, we will see if we can save her, but she might not want saved."

She clung to his gaze. "She might not be able to be saved, Bryson. She…lives. She was alive when he… When he—"

"Yes." By the harshness of his response she knew if he had the chance, Gideon would no longer be part of this world. "I would have you outside for this."

"She might need…me. A woman."

He winced and dropped his gaze, then with a deep breath made her proud by nodding and turning away.

Once again, he took the lead. She waited and steeled herself as he opened the door to the cabinet. It was worse than she had imagined. Agatha was…not herself. The degree of humiliation Warren or Gideon had brought down on her was sickening. She heard Joey gasp in distress. Jaxon cursed. She hadn't heard them walk up. Bryson touched his head to hers, soothing her more than he could ever know. Or perhaps he did know. As gently as he could, he quickly untied the comatose woman and laid her on the floor. A second later he covered her mangled, tortured body with a white blanket he called to him with his mind. It floated over Agatha, immediately turning red with blood, but covered most of the damage. She didn't rise or move. Her eyes were open but unseeing. Her head slowly fell to the side, but her chest still rose and fell, even though a long, bloody cord of her intestines hung from her stomach and out past the protection of her blanket.

"Why... Why would anyone do this?" she whispered.

"Insanity," Bryson snarled, crouching to turn Agatha's face to the side. She didn't respond, not even when he shook her. "She's beyond him now," he whispered so low she barely heard him.

"We will have to take her to the..." Jaxon shook his head and glanced to where Joey stood with her back to them, huddled in the doorway. "We have to take her somewhere," he finished, walking quickly to Joey's side. Over his shoulder, he called, "I'll be right back. Gonna call someone to help."

She grew alarmed. "Bryson —"

"He won't call anyone who can hurt you."

"It's not *me* I'm worried about." She pulled away to meet his light eyes. "It is you."

A flash of his bright smile was more a snarl than a sign of humor. "They can try, but I won't be leaving your side, Isobel." He walked her farther from Agatha, scanning the room as he did. The horrors weren't limited to the one area, but she turned her face away. Now she had to focus on Bryson and his safety.

She caught Bryson's arm and stopped him. "Aidan will have learned that you sided with me. You are not safe with any other Vampires."

Bryson's eyes filled with bemusement. "You worry for me?" He made that sound beyond ridiculous.

"It had occurred to me."

"Woman, I can take care of myself *and* you."

Instead of amusing her, his boast was mere fact. "I know this. But I do not wish to chance you. We can leave. Jaxon can see that she is taken care of. I wish to go. Rowan will contact us if he finds him. Jaxon can contact you if he needs you. I want to leave, Bryson. Is this possible?" She needed to leave. The stench of such evil covered her so much that she couldn't bear it. She wanted Bryson—his warm body and arms holding her so that nothing could ever take him away from her.

"Yes."

At his simple answer, she sighed in relief. Her lips curled in a smile. "Then take me from this place so that we may have time to prepare for the next step."

He took her hand in his larger one and tipped her chin so she gazed up at him while he stared down at her. "The first step will be our words, for I can't protect you as I should. Not with this undone. It distracts me when I should be focused, Isobel. I know you wish to wait and I know that you deserve courting, but—"

"We shall bond this night, Bryson. If you still—"

"Isobel, nothing will ever change the fact that you are mine." His unblinking stare made it clear as did his firm hold on her, that what he spoke was truth. *'You will be mine to protect for an eternity, Isobel. In that time, I will win your forgiveness. Tonight, I hope to move forward in this, my heart.'*

'Then take me away, Bryson.'

The roguish smile she earned for her bold words made her knees weak. But she knew, if she did fall, Bryson would be there, with his strong body and hard muscles, to catch her.

Without looking away, Bryson called out, "Joey, tell Jaxon I will call him."

"Uh, will do. Nice to meet you, Isobel."

Isobel had time to glance at Joey once before Bryson shifted them. Joey's bright green eyes glowed with mischief and no little knowledge of what awaited her.

Bryson.

* * * *

Bryson paced the hall outside of the bedroom he would soon share with his bonded. For centuries he'd never let himself imagine this moment. There had been too many barriers. Now the only barrier that remained was the thick oak door between them and the virginity of the woman he knew he would love for an eternity.

Sweet Jesus, has a man ever been so frightened of having sex before?

The door opened, eliminating one of those barriers. His mind blanked. Isobel stood before him, but an Isobel with her hair flowing around her, dressed in nothing but one of his button-down shirts. Even her small toes were beautiful.

"Bryson? You are making me more nervous rather than less," Isobel whispered. She ducked her head and her long black hair tumbled forward. "If you are fearful, I think I should be, as well."

He reached out and parted that sweet silk to tip her head and gaze down at her perfection. Eyes wide, face pale, she wore a worried frown that suddenly eased the fear he had battled moments before. He smoothed his thumb over her lips and dipped his head so he could kiss her on the brow. "I am only worried that I might disappoint you. I want you more than anything in this world, but I also want this to be good for you. *Enjoyable*," he stressed.

She smiled suddenly and reached up with both hands and opened his robe. "It will be." The feel of her warm hands on his bare chest sent a shock of lust to his aching groin. He'd kept his boxer briefs on because he'd known that the first touch from her would be disaster if he were naked. "I want to see you. All of your magnificent *muscles*."

He laughed at her clear enjoyment of his body. "You can do whatever you wish to me, Isobel." All his life he had battled, from the time he was young because he'd been bigger, stronger than others his age. He'd always secretly worried that women didn't want him because of his size. Through their link, he knew Isobel found him strong and the best of all warriors. It made him throw his shoulders back as she slid the robe over them and let it fall from him.

"Oh, Bryson. You are truly beautiful."

He crossed his arms. "I am a man. Men are not beautiful."

She laughed and covered her mouth, smiling all the same as her eyes widened and she took him in. "You are wrong. You are stunning, so beautiful. And mine."

She was happy, he realized. The impact was as strong as the first touch from her.

"I want to touch you, put these down." She pulled his arms and softly caressed him from his chest, over his pectorals and on to his ribs and back up to his shoulders. She'd done the same through his shirt last evening, but now, her warm skin was bare against his. A shiver raced from the top of his head to his toes. He worried what she'd think of his jutting arousal, but she paid it no mind.

Slowly she walked in a circle around him, touching and caressing him into such a state he feared that he'd haul her to the bed and mount her at that moment. The need was there. The desire to mark her with his fangs and cock pounded at him like a warrior's battle drum. Instead he clenched his hands. *Let her grow comfortable. Ease her into this. Us.*

"So amazing." She kissed his shoulder blade, then began to trail more kisses down his spine.

"Isobel," he grated. "I cannot allow this much longer."

"No, but later, I will want to see you again."

"You can see me all night," he assured her and turned to gather her against him. "For eternity, yes?"

She blinked then smiled, cozying up to him so that her skin brushed his with such intimacy he feared how much more he could take.

"Yes. Now, will you make love to me?"

Is that eagerness in her tone? He groaned. *It is.* "God, I want to. First, we must make you ready."

"For this," she asked. She squeezed him possessively and stroked right through the thin material of his briefs downward to cup his sac.

"Jesus!" He nearly shoved her to the floor. Instead he caught her busy hand and brought it up away from his raging hard-on. "I'll come if you do that. I need to mount you and sink my fangs in so badly it's a battle."

Her eyes widened.

"I won't, not yet. But, angel, I will need to."

Her gaze turned slumberous as if she desired just that. His cock jerked, leaking more pre-cum. He held on, controlling himself.

"I will be demanding," he warned. "I will want you often."

"Good, now, take me to bed, or do we make love standing?" She tilted her head as if she wondered, and again he was slapped in the face by her innocence.

"In bed." He shifted her to the bed, under him. "First, I want to see you."

But when he lifted up to part his shirt from her body, she halted him with a hand on his. Worry clouded her eyes. He recalled how she had been treated by Christian and what the man had said to her. It was unfathomable to him, but he sensed she feared this.

"Isobel," he said gently, feeling a warmth so deep he knew from this moment on he would never be without it. *Love. I love her.* "You are more beautiful to me than anything on this earth. You were then, when I first realized you were mine, and you are now. I waited then, thinking you too young, but I cannot wait now. Angel, I need you. I *need* to see you. To know I am the only man to ever see you and the only man who will *ever* see you."

At his rough words her fear eased and she slowly smiled. Reaching up, she then caressed his face. Cupping his jaw, she gently pulled on him until he lowered his head. "I was made for you. A bonded pair is made for the other. I am yours, Bryson."

"As I am yours," he assured her.

Gently, as to not scare her, he pressed his lips to hers and kissed her with all the love he felt building in his heart. *'You are my love, my life, Isobel. I will be careful.'*

'I know. I want you, oh how I hope I do not disappoint you, though.'

At her words he drew up surprised and sat back on his haunches She watched him, her eyes bright with excitement he hoped, more than fear. Slowly, he slipped the shirt she wore open and down her slender shoulders, revealing her little by little. She took his breath away, then returned it with such force words spilled from him. "Isobel, my heart, you stun me. You are beauty. Not I, not this warrior's body."

He gestured to his scarred chest then touched her delicate shoulder and dared to caress his fingers down between her breasts. The pinkness of her nipples was magnificent, the round areoles large and begging to be sucked, licked, kissed. The womanly curves of her body made his mouth water, the soft but firm line of her stomach enchanted him, while the lush mound of her sex shocked his senses triggering a full body recognition that this—woman—this person was his other half. His cock was made for her pussy. His masculine body the opposite fit to her feminine one.

"You are mine."

At his growl, his cheeks grew warm, but Isobel laughed merrily and hugged him around the neck which drew her smaller body flush with his. Relieved he'd not insulted her, instead made her happy again, he held her body as tightly as he dared.

"I am yours. And you are mine. Perhaps we are the perfect fit, one half of each other," she said, mirroring his thoughts. "I want you. Now, please."

He choked on a laugh and took her hands off his boxers. "These stay on. Let me prepare you."

"What does this mean, prepare me?"

Wincing, he settled her back on the bed and lay next to her, resting his hand on his head so he could admire every inch of her. "You need to be ready for me," he whispered, feeling such a deep emotion for her he could barely get the words out.

"You are not small," she agreed, eyeing the bulging erection pushing against his boxers.

"True, but I believe you will enjoy that."

Her gaze floated up his body to his face. She smiled and sighed. "I believe so too."

His smile grew and he bent to kiss her on the rise of her breast at the same time he settled his hand on her stomach and caressed upward then back down to her sex. "You have such soft skin here, Isobel."

"I do?" She sounded breathless, and, from her, he could scent her growing need. He felt it too. The ache to give and take. For the exchange of blood and sex, and hot, pumping thrusts of his cock in her hot, tight pussy.

"Yes, you're silky soft."

"I am? Is that...good?" She gasped when he dipped a finger along her clit.

"It is *very* good," he growled, slipping his fingers deeper over her sex and cupping her there possessively.

"Oh!" She clenched her legs on his hand, but he allowed it, massaging her as tenderly as possible.

"If you open your thighs, I can show you more of how good it is. Do you like this?"

She was kissing his shoulder and arm but when he asked her she drew his head up and kissed him passionately. *'I love it. Do not stop.'*

'Open your thighs, then, my heart, let me touch you deeper.'

She relaxed her legs a little. He sent her warmth and praise through their bond. Her mouth was eager, following his and learning as he deepened the kiss to something wild and wet. Each stroke of his tongue he matched with the slide of his finger over her sex until her heat was liquid and she was lifting her hips for more. Only then did he slip one finger past her entrance and hold it there.

"Oh!"

At her gasp, he growled into her neck. She was tight. More, she was soft and wet. He could just imagine her around his cock, sucking him in and holding his aching erection. He delved deeper, then back out, taking her mouth again to imitate his fingers. She grabbed handfuls of his hair and lifted her hips with little moans into his mouth. Her fangs sharpened. His did as well. With a shudder, she nicked his lip and they shared a blood kiss. His cock pulsed so hard he worried he'd be unable to keep from tossing her down and entering her. He held back, but just barely. His balls protested, aching as if he'd taken a direct hit there. Isobel didn't seem to care, she pulled his erection free and stroked him perfectly. He increased his pace, rolling his palm over her mound as he slipped another finger in, easier this time than the first.

"I want you. Take me, Bryson."

Had anything ever been sweeter? The look in her eyes, the trust there, and the desire did odd things to him. He slowed down and, swallowing sharply, rose above her. Carefully, he aligned his cock to her sex, easing the head forward until the tip was encased in her sheath. Watching her face, he fed her more, waiting for a sign of discomfort. His cock was so hard he didn't have to guide it but kept his hand on the shaft to stop from bucking forward. He could sense her wanting him, not just his cock, but his blood.

"Wait, wait until I am inside you, then we will share our blood." He fed her more of his shaft, taking his time so his girth didn't tear her but sank in slowly so she stretched around him.

"More, oh, Bryson, please, I can't take it much longer. I need you!"

Even in the midst of such passion, he could barely think, she ordered him around. He kissed her lips, sucking on her bottom one and soothed her with a deeper thrust.

"Trust me, I need you too. But we have to go slow." He took measure of how far they'd gotten and swallowed. Only the head had made it inside, but he didn't dare go faster. Sweat poured from him, his arms trembled, but she had such a tight clamp on him he was forced to ease out and back in, working slowly to let her grow familiar with him. *Gotta go slow. Gotta stay focused. Think on her. Want to have sex for the rest of the night. That means going slow now, then once I'm in, stay in.*

The plan was brilliant. It would have worked, too, he thought, until she began moaning and thrashing her head, clearly growing close to an orgasm. *She's going to come on my cock. Can't come. Cannot join her. Cannot move a muscle.* Almost immediately, as he reminded himself of the rules, she cried out his name and began climaxing. When she did, she sank her fangs into his pectoral.

His mind went blank. Sweat poured from him. His balls drew up hard, tingling in preparation for ejaculating. *Can't move. Cannot thrust. Cannot move.* She broke her bite and cried out his name, bursting into another climax as he fought to hold on to his control. Each tightening of her pussy cinched on his sensitive head. Every gasp and shudder rippled up his body and circled back down to his balls.

"Isobel!" He pulled free, frantic not to hurt her, and angled the head along her sex to rub over her clit. The friction was all he needed. He caught his breath. Her skin was so soft there, so smooth, and she gyrated under him, so clearly lost in her passion, he knew he was seconds behind. *Just thrust, just sink in, end this agony and fill her with my seed.*

No! Can't harm her.

"Bite me. Take from me." His voice sounded rough, too harsh. "Isobel, I need you."

She whimpered but licked along his chest.

The buildup was painful. His body tensed like a bowstring ready to let lose a volley of arrows. "Now, Now!" he shouted, fisting his hands in the sheets instead of around her shapely hips.

She bit down. Her fangs pierced deep. The moment they did, his orgasm ignited. He shouted her name. Head back, body tense, he pulsed jet after jet of hot semen onto her stomach until he was rutting over her, head by her shoulder and pressing his cock as tightly to her heat as he could get. It continued until his toes curled, and he had to fall on her as the last of his strength vanished. Only then did he lower his head and turn it, to lick along her neck. His fangs dropped, her light moan and shift of her thigh up along his was invitation enough. He bit her. Rich, exquisite blood exploded along his taste buds.

Isobel sobbed his name and scored his back with her nails, demanding more. "Bryson, oh, please! I need you, now. Oh, please!"

'No, not yet. Not now. Need to slow.' His body tensed, tightened, and with a rush of pleasure he pulled up, only to seek out her soft breast and bite down on it. Again she sobbed his name in pleasure. Again, her taste exploded in his mouth.

'Yes, oh, Bryson, it's so good, it's so good.'

He couldn't respond, could only feel the rush to climax again and the punch of his release as he pinned her down and savored her body and blood. *Mine. She's mine at last.*

Chapter Twenty-Three

Isobel drew a labored breath even as Bryson twisted and turned them, moving her on top of him. He was sweaty and slick with exertion, hot with the wild things he'd been doing to her. It was stunning, more so because he wrapped his hands around her waist, splayed his fingers wide on her bottom and began pumping upward. He still refused to take her, to claim her.

"Bryson, you will not harm me. We were meant to share our bodies. I want you inside me," she urged.

"We have eternity—"

"Bryson!" She stared at him in amazement. He gave her a roguish grin. She blinked. A sudden thought surfaced. "You are teasing me?"

"Yes." The answer was coupled with him nuzzling her breasts and flicked each with his fangs. Bursts of pleasure tingled up and down her body. "Isobel, my love, come for me again." He spoke to her in languages long since forgotten. Her heart grew full, even as he began driving her to another release. He was relentless. And she loved it. "Once more, come for me."

She sobbed into his shoulder as her body clenched, and within heartbeats she flew again.

Bryson shouted her name, tensing under her, then with a curse he began shaking and coming, heating her stomach again with his seed as he gritted his teeth and groaned repeatedly. Exhausted, but never feeling more alive, she kissed his jaw and chest, his neck and temple, then his mouth as he opened it to catch his breath, still lost to his pleasurable moans.

"You are mine, all of you," she whispered into his ear, feeling him shudder harder. His shaft still flexed and heated her skin with his seed. "I will never let you go."

"Isobel," he grated, pressing his head into the crook of her neck and holding her tighter. He trembled for a long while but the aftershocks were gratifying to him, she knew. It made her feel strong and powerful.

"You have pleased me beyond my wildest dreams."

She peered down at him. He wore such a well-sated male smile of satisfaction she felt another blossom of contentment fill her heart. He looked so different. Happy, she decided.

"I did nothing. You were the one," she reminded him, kissing his jaw. "Why did you not claim me?"

He laughed, which made her gasp because she perched on top of him. "I claimed you, Isobel. I simply want to go slow."

"Ah, I see. But you have not made love to me."

"I have, I have just not taken your virginity completely."

"Ah, I see. So now you will?"

"No, now we will sleep."

"We will sleep?" She could sleep now, she realized. But his behavior baffled her. She surveyed the warm tones of the room. It was rustic, little more than a cabin hidden away deep in a pine forest. But she liked it. Even the colors soothed her. It would be a safe place, a warm, secluded home for them. "We will sleep in here?"

"Yes." He rolled her to the side and kissed her quickly then lifted away to get up.

Nervous suddenly, she sat up but was only in time to get another kiss from him as he took a seat next to her. The bulge of his arm and chest muscles tantalized her, but she refused to be distracted and caught his hand. "What are you doing?"

He brushed a warm, wet cloth over her stomach but stopped when she caught his wrist. He quirked an eyebrow. "Would you rather a shower?"

"I thought… I thought we would sleep then perhaps make love. For *real* this time."

He bent his head until he was a breath away. "We made love for real," he murmured against her lips. She couldn't help how her body responded or how she wrapped her arms around his neck. His skin was so smooth, so toned and rippling with power she sighed.

Bryson pulled up all too soon. "But I think I like the way your mind works. After we shower and rest." She would have argued, but he covered her lips with his finger, a smile twinkling in his eyes. "Rowan might need us, Isobel. I want to be bonded to you so I can always find you."

For some reason, his words hit her wrong. Instead of holding her thoughts, she asked, "Is that the only reason?"

"No." He shrugged. "I will love you forever, Isobel. I want you in my heart, where I can keep you safe. We don't know what tomorrow will bring. I would know what it is like to join our bodies, and our minds."

She didn't disagree but for some reason she hesitated. It wasn't him. She knew she'd never choose another over him. She also knew he would always hold her above all others. But…

If something happens to me, he can move on. If we bond…he will be unable to.

"Do you doubt me? Still?" he asked.

Not wanting him to think such a thing she opened her mouth, but his alarms vibrated between them. Instantly Bryson turned from sexy lover to warrior. His gaze turned cold and a chill rose from his skin. She moved to rise, but Bryson caught her hand to still her. "That could be Jaxon. He is the only person that knows of this home."

"Or Faolan." She sent her mind out but encountered no one. "I cannot tell. Can you?"

His gaze grew distant then clouded as he focused back on her. "It is not Jaxon." He cupped her nape, drawing her close. "It is Aidan."

At his words, a chill raced along her skin. She pulled away. He let her, but with such reluctance she worried he had planned to try to flee. She dressed herself, cleaning her body with a thought and quickly braided her hair as well while he sat across from her, watching her with an unfathomable expression. Within seconds she was presentable, as was Bryson, but her heart raced all the same.

Will Aidan believe me innocent? Does Bryson?

"Steady." Bryson caught her arm. "Aidan will not harm you."

She held her tongue, not willing to voice her opinion.

A moment passed before Bryson, expression grave, led her from the room and out to meet the man who had already ordered her death once.

Bryson had known fear in his life. In some battles to survive he had to have fear spurring him on when anger died out. The fear of survival. Now, as he walked ahead of the woman who held his heart, he experienced a rush of it so deep he paused at the door, suddenly unwilling to open his home to his king.

"Bryson, I will be fine. He will listen to you." Isobel had shut him out. He could still sense her feelings — sadness mixed with worry — but he couldn't mind-speak her.

He reached for the door and opened it. Aidan stood waiting, his bonded missing from his side. *Not a good sign*. Neither was the scowl lining his face. At six-four, Aidan was solid, packed muscle, and the strongest and fastest swordsman Bryson had ever faced.

"Aidan."

Eyes the color of glacier ice, and just as merciless, locked onto his. "So it's true."

"It is. Isobel is my bonded. She is innocent of the charges —"

Aidan held up a hand. "Enough. How do you know she is yours?"

Bryson fought back the rage building in his chest. "I know as you know Allie is yours."

"How long have you known?"

"Over six hundred and eighty centuries, before she was accused of —"

"Why did you never speak of it?"

Bryson clenched his fists. This was Aidan at his worst. Never a man to hold back his thoughts, nor his anger, Aidan was difficult. If not impossible to move on from something he thought. Allie had worked on soothing those sharp edges, but Aidan never let anyone betray him — twice.

"She is my bonded. I have read Christian's mind. He was one of the members of the council who found her guilty. He killed your father, Aidan. *They* killed your father, not Isobel. Think about it. How could one young Vampire kill Aaron?"

Aidan's silver eyes darkened to mercury. Never a good sign. "Invite me in, Bryson."

"Not until you give your word you will not harm her, or order another to do so."

"Bryson." Isobel stepped out from his shadow.

"No," he growled. "He stays out until he gives me his oath," he told her. Turning to Aidan, he crossed his arms. They were of the same height. If it came to a fight, he knew they would both be bloodied. "If you are here to listen, you will have no issue with such a request."

"A request?" Aidan said silkily. "To me it sounds like a demand. Why would my captain make demands of me?"

"Because your captain also believed for centuries that this woman was evil, that she had not only committed regicide, but she had trapped and held you away from saving your father. Have you ever met Isobel, Aidan?"

Aidan twisted his lips and finally flickered a glance over Isobel. "Come here."

Bryson went to grab her but she obeyed Aidan, walking across his threshold and up to Aidan on her own. "If you harm her—"

"Bryson, I can speak for myself," she said in a soothing tone. "If he will listen."

"I am here, am I not? Speak."

Isobel bowed then startled him, as well as Aidan, by going to one knee, left arm over her chest with her head lowered in supplication. "I swear on my honor as a Dragon Guard that I have never, nor will I ever, raise my sword to harm a member of the blood. I did no harm to my king, nor would I ever do so to his son. I will swear my oath to you, if it will please you, Aidan, but I did not kill Aaron, this I swear easily."

Aidan stared down at her bent head for so long, Bryson grew concerned. From Isobel all he could sense was her calm acceptance.

"If you did not, then who did?" Aidan finally asked, his voice skeptical but no longer sharp and harsh with anger.

"Those that I killed when I rose, along with Agatha, who is alive, and Gideon, posing as the young Vampire Warren."

If the impact of that surprised Aidan, he didn't show it. "And you are a Dragon Guard?"

"Yes."

"And my uncle is alive?"

"Rowan is alive, as is Gideon, in another's body."

Aidan's gaze darkened ominously. "And you were going to tell me this when, Bryson?"

Bryson threw his arms up. "Are you going to let my bonded up off her knees, Aidan?" Bryson hauled her up himself with a gentle hand under her arm. He checked she was safe then faced Aidan to see the man hiding a grin. "Come in, but don't make a habit of showing up uninvited. I have very few houses that don't seem to be overrun with unwanted guests."

"Well, I can see why this one is still unknown. Do you even have electricity? Now, Isobel, what of your brother? I thought he was the reason you killed my father."

"Just cut right to it, Aidan, don't give her a moment to adjust to you not wanting to kill her." Bryson walked her to the larger of the two sofas. She gave him a reassuring smile then motioned to where he had a wet bar.

"Drinks?" he guessed.

"Yes, that would be nice." Her lips curled, but he wasn't in the mood for her humor, not yet. The next time – if there was one – she wasn't going to step away from his protection.

"A brandy, yes, or if you have more of the French 1648 hoarded away here, I will have that."

Bryson grumbled but fetched a bottle of the red Aidan had referred to. It was a good year, the best, but sharing it with Aidan wasn't what he'd had in mind for one of the few bottles he had left.

Isobel was waiting when he returned, Aidan sitting across from her, looking cool and calm. Bryson handed her a glass of wine first, then Aidan. The man smiled but took the insult with only a lifted brow. Isobel pulled him down next to her.

"You appear to have survived your torture." Aidan sipped his wine. "Did you kill Aquinas?"

"Yes."

Aidan paused with his wine to his lips, but Isobel didn't continue.

Bryson took her hand. *'Stop blocking me.'*

She didn't respond but softened against him. "Aquinas was one of the members that entombed me."

"Why did they entomb you and not kill you?" Aidan asked.

Isobel hesitated before saying, "I believe they feared me and thought that entombing me would secure their success."

"What success?" Bryson hadn't given much thought to why they had entombed her, rather than killed her. *Why? Why didn't I ask this?*

"The throne. They wished for someone else on the throne so they could be members of the ruling class, unhindered by Aaron's ideas for unification."

"Unification?" Aidan repeated in a dazed tone. "What do you mean?"

Isobel tilted her head. "Your father was to begin a new era amongst us, to stop those that used their gifts to harm others. It was his wish that Vampires would not drink from the flesh until death, nor drink from the flesh of humans at all. He wished for us to begin using cattle for such."

"Cattle?" Aidan spluttered.

Bryson agreed. He had never used an animal for sustenance. Now he used blood banks and butchers, but to hunt and bite a cow?

"My father wished for us to stop hunting?"

"No. He wanted us to hunt, but not to kill and never to drink from humans again. He wanted to forbid it but knew such a thing would cause unrest, so he planned on slowly introducing the concept through firmer leadership in the Houses."

Bryson was stunned. By Aidan's slack-jawed expression, so was he.

"But...how did the members of his council learn of this? And, if they learned of it, what did it have to do with your brother?"

"Nothing, other than Jorge was their chance. He did not kill those villagers. Gideon did. To hide that fact, the council agreed to protect Gideon if he aided them in killing Aaron. They accused Jorge, Aaron believed them, and had them kill Jorge. But instead of simply doing this, since Jorge and I both knew who had really killed the villagers, they sent his soul into the mist. He is able to neither move on, nor return. The council used Gideon to end Aaron's ideas on unification and to hide Gideon's crimes. As soon as Gideon aided them, they killed him. They were greedy, you see, and in their haste to win power, they did not send *his* soul into the abyss. He lingered, and now has a body, a Vampire, whom he controls."

"And now he wants to kill Agatha," Bryson added.

Aidan swirled his wine. Next to him, Isobel sipped hers. By outward appearances, she was calm, but he could sense the tension radiating from her. She believed Aidan still wanted her dead. He wasn't allowing Aidan to touch her.

"Ah, yes. Agatha. Why should I let her live? She was one of the ones who killed my father, and your brother."

Isobel shifted uneasily.

"If you kill Agatha, Gideon may be able to use a spell that would allow him to claim his body again." Bryson held up a hand when Aidan immediately sat forward. "On the other hand, in order to save Isobel's brother and allow him to move on, if we kill her, we have only to kill Warren, who is Gideon."

"And this will free your brother?" Aidan asked sharply.

Isobel nodded. "Yes."

"I take it your brother allowed his death?"

Bryson frowned and turned to see Isobel nod again. "He forbade me to save him. It was his only chance to be with his bride."

There were tears in her tone, ones he knew she fought and ones he knew she had shed centuries before. *Alone. She suffered all this alone, without me, when I was there and could have aided her.* He brought her closer, warning Aidan with a look that if he didn't turn the questions around, he would. There was much he had to do to make amends to Isobel for misjudging her. Beating Aidan to a pulp if he pushed her too hard would be one he'd gladly do. Even now having Aidan here, near her, his woman, set his teeth on edge.

"So, it is now our job to find Warren, who is my uncle. Where is Rowan?"

Bryson loosened up enough to answer. "He is searching for Gideon."

"Ah, and he has been where?"

"I think he has been alone," Isobel said. "He was…harmed. Then I believe he slept, perhaps too lost without us. The Dragons were few, but we were loyal, and to him and to Aaron, we were family."

"Now you have a bonded, he will be your family. Will you let this vendetta go if we decide not to kill Agatha?"

Bryson sighed. It was a question she'd already answered by saving Agatha's life, but Aidan wanted more, always more from them. He'd been betrayed too young, too many times, for him to trust easily.

"She has already allowed Agatha to live, Aidan."

"I see, so by allowing her to live, you have given up on your brother?"

Isobel tensed. "No. There are other means to send his soul onward," she finally responded. "It is not as easy — "

"Killing six ancients is easy, is it?"

"Yes. Corruption and evil weaken a soul, not strengthen it. Gideon will have to be destroyed, Aidan. There is no other way. Agatha, for all her greed and selfishness, is not truly evil for she fears to put herself forward too deeply into such things."

Aidan's gaze turned fierce. "And you can sense this? Evil and good?"

"Yes. We all can. It is part of why God created us, not to kill or be killers, but to cull from his flock those that are. As a Dragon I was taught this, and I still believe that as stronger, more powerful beings we are given a job no human can accomplish."

"Judge, jury and executioner?"

"I did not say it was simple. I can judge easily the thought of humans, and be the jury to decide their fate, just as I can for other immortals, such as Vampires."

"This was the intention of the Dragons, was it not? To be the police of our people." Bryson tipped her head to look into her dark eyes again.

Isobel gave him a slow smile and nodded. "I suppose so."

"Perhaps Rowan could be convinced to train once again," Aidan muttered. He stood abruptly. "I have to go. Allie needs me. Her sister is still risen to the surface. Nor can I locate Rhys."

Bryson helped Isobel to her feet. "Rhys will protect Bridget. He has no choice."

"He will, if he can." Aidan anchored his hands on his hips, head down and sighed. "But I worry. This long with no word from them is not good. Their quest is not easy and because of Bridget's sacrifice I have my bonded. I would not have her suffer for our happiness."

Bryson gripped Aidan's shoulder. "She did so freely. It is Rhys I worry over. His temper is worse than yours, and if he's put into a position where she might be harmed —"

"He will lose his cool. Yes, er, he didn't manage his bonding well. See that you two exchange bonds before you leave this place. You've lost enough, Isobel. I would have you training alongside Bryson and Rowan, but not without bonding to Bryson first. You will not sacrifice yourself for another that you love. See that it is done, Bryson."

Bryson tensed his shoulders at the warning in Aidan's tone but also at what he was saying. Then his king was gone.

"Isobel, explain to me what Aidan meant."

She gave him another slow smile and caught him by surprise by sliding her hands under his shirt and up onto his bare chest. If she did this often, his ability to think might become impaired permanently. Leaning on him she whispered, "I suppose he was referring to my fearing to bond with you, for fear of losing you. Or to my fear of dying and leaving you to suffer alone."

Of all the things she could have said, this shocked him the most. He had wronged her. He had never thought to seek her out and question her. Nor had he given her the benefit of the doubt, but accused her of vile things without knowing her at all. And she would sacrifice herself for him?

"Woman..."

Isobel made him catch his breath with a caress down the front of his trousers to grip his shaft.

"But I think we should obey our king, don't you? We should see that this is done."

The air left him on a groan. *Mine*. This was his woman. His *hungry* and *aroused* woman.

"It will be this night, my heart, this I swear. You will never have to face this world alone again, Isobel. Never alone."

Chapter Twenty-Four

Things had changed. Bryson had changed. Gone was the barely in control, but firmly resolved to wait lover from earlier this eve. In his place, her bonded was focused on her with a single-mindedness that equally thrilled and frightened her.

"What are you doing, Bryson?"

He hovered above her on stiff arms, his face inches from hers, too far to kiss but close enough that she could see the way the firelight played on the shadows of his fathomless expression. His wide set eyes were pinned on her so intently she worried what was going on in that mind of his. She'd undressed then sought out and found another one of his long button-down shirts and covered herself with it before he'd entered their bedroom.

"I am memorizing every inch of your beauty. You are mine, Isobel. As I am yours. Forever we will be one. Do you understand?"

"Yes, I understand," she whispered, suddenly caught in the magic of this moment. This man was her bonded. Only once before had she wondered if she would find happiness. Then her brother's death had ripped all of those fleeting hopes aside.

She reached up and framed Bryson's face between her hands. The whiskers on his jaw were thicker now. He needed to shave. The idea of such knowledge struck her as momentous. From now until forever, she would be able to touch him just so. Feel him. Know with a glance that when his eyes turned such a light shade he was aroused — for her.

"You are beautiful," he murmured, resting on top of her so his weight pressed her down. The heat of his body was incredible. So was the full, long length of his erection pressing against her through the material of his slacks. He leaned on his elbows and gazed down at her. "You take my breath away. Your eyes are captivating. Your lips" — he pressed a kiss to her mouth — "kissable. And your neck…" He trailed his mouth along her throat, nicking her once and sucking the spot. Her body clenched for him. He had the shirt she'd borrowed unbuttoned before she knew what he was about. Only the cooler air on her bare chest alerted her.

"Your breasts…" He rose and cupped one in his hand, kissing the nipple until it hardened and ached. Her stomach felt as if it had dropped to her toes.

"Bryson."

At her cry, he took the bud in his mouth and sucked gently. Her toes curled and she clasped his rounded bottom. The muscles there were so hard she dug her nails in, testing them. His shaft jerked, but otherwise he kept up his slow seduction. He placed kisses under her aching nipples, so gently she wanted to demand more from him. Instead, she fisted her hands in the sheets to hold on for more of what he was doing. Only the longer she held her breath the more he seemed to savor her until finally he began sucking and kissing both of her breasts, one right after the other. She was certain she couldn't take much more.

"Bryson, please," she begged.

He spread the shirt. She shivered as his warm breath heated her skin. Nothing in her life had ever felt so good. *So exciting. And it will only get better?*

"Ah, yes, and your ribs, and stomach, I can't forget how beautiful both are to me." He left a hot path everywhere his mouth grazed her skin, making her frantic and achy all at once. By the time he reached her mound, she was pressing his head down shamelessly, wanting that devilish mouth on her like nothing she'd ever wanted before.

He hovered, staring between her open thighs as if mesmerized.

Embarrassed, she tried to cover herself, but Bryson halted her by grabbing her hand. Eyes on her, he placed a warm kiss to her palm. His eyes were hypnotic.

"No, don't be shy. You are beautiful, Isobel. Show me what you like."

She couldn't. She also couldn't ask him to give her relief because she wanted his mouth on her. *Right there.* Instead, he left feather-light kisses on her inner thighs and harder stinging kisses along her legs down to her toes. Once there, he gave each digit his full attention along with her feet and ankles until she was brazenly touching herself.

"Yes. Show me." His voice sounded rough and only added to the excitement.

Holding her breath, she let her legs fall open and lightly traced her fingers along her clit, shivering from the small touch. It still wasn't enough. "Bryson, please."

He startled her by pushing her hand away and, thankfully, brought his mouth down on her.

Perfect!

Fire seemed to explode in her veins. Electricity zipped along her flesh. Her body took off on its own as she rose to the heavens. Her toes curled. Her fingers dug into the sheets. Her neck arched and she was held there, as if by invisible strings. Bryson growled her name then pressed two fingers past her entrance. At the same time, he rubbed his hot tongue over her clit.

Without meaning to, she clenched her hands in his hair and held him there. The orgasm exploded, catching her by surprise. She wrapped her legs around his head and cried out as stars burst along her vision. Bliss carried her away, higher and higher than ever before, but she knew he held her and would never, ever let her go.

"Do you know what a bond means, Bryson?" Isobel whispered. Her voice was rough from the screams he'd dragged from her. She was tousled, sated, and watching him with contentment. "What it really means?"

Bryson nodded, for words were merely bizarre sounds that couldn't ever say more. He could taste and scent her sweet essence and knew such pride at giving her pleasure he could barely think straight. Now she wanted to talk? His body ached — he needed to drink from her as desperately as he needed to empty his seed in her body. Less than hours before he'd emptied himself on her repeatedly but that seemed like centuries ago *Need her.* Sweat soaked his body, making his clothing unbearable. Under his pants, he felt strangled. But her voice, her mesmerizing eyes held him in place.

"Tell me," she whispered. "Tell me what it means."

The idea that he could take what he felt for this woman and compact it into syllables was an impossible task. But for her, he would move mountains. "It means that for the rest of my existence, I will put your life before mine. As long as there is strength left in my body then I will not stop, will not rest, until I know you are safe."

Her eyebrows lifted delicately. "Does this mean you will love me?"

"Love you? Such a word doesn't describe adequately the depth of my devotion to you, Isobel. If you were gone from this earth, I would follow. I would not rest until you were once again in my arms. I will *be yours* for the rest of eternity. So, yes," he whispered in her ear, "this means I love you."

She suddenly threw her arms around his neck and buried her face in his chest.

"This pleases you?"

"I thought perhaps you would always think me a monster, and so, thought I might never be able to feel this, your arms around me again," she whispered against his pectorals.

He stroked her hair, feelings so tender racing through him they even diminished the urges to bed and mate her. "I never thought you a monster." He felt shamed once again that he had thought such things of her. "I have wronged you—"

"No, do not think such things. For a while, I *was* a monster," she admitted, pulling back to gaze at him with something he hoped was love in her eyes. "I nearly died trying to draw Warren away from you."

At the memory of her wound, he stiffened. "I never want you do to such a—"

She covered his mouth with her hand. He froze, caught by how enchanting she was.

"Ah, yes, your threats." Her smile grew then faded. "I did not say this to rouse your threats, my love. Yet, even after I risked my life for yours, I feel as if you need me to say the words. Since I enjoyed them when you uttered them, I will do the same." Staring deeply into his eyes, she slipped her hand from his mouth to stroke the side of his face and held her palm there. "I love you, Bryson MacAfee. And yes, if you were to die, I would first seek out and burn anyone that would do this to you, *then* I would follow you to death."

He crushed her tightly to his chest. "You had better. I also think you should ensure they do not rise again." When he could finally release his arms, she leaned away from him but she wasn't smiling. There was excitement and anticipation there, though, and he realized something more. *Trust. Love. Happiness.*

"Will you make me yours now?"

Of all the scenarios, this was one he hadn't imagined. She looked eager. Her face was still flushed from her orgasm, but he could see the way her breathing was already speeding up at the thought of them making love. Her breasts quivered with each rise and fall of her chest. Every breath brought a glow to her skin along with the scent of her arousal. *She wants me.* She'd been demanding before, ordering him to take her, and he could only imagine what she would be like once they got through this. *I have to get through this, then we can really see what we can do.*

"Bryson? Why are you staring at me?"

He swallowed, thrown once again by her. He studied her eyes and saw truth there, and more, complete trust. "I will go slowly."

"Yes, you keep saying that, but...perhaps a little quicker than this."

There wasn't an answer for that. "We will be bonded."

"Yes."

"I will want you as my wife, as well."

"I believe it is the same thing, is it not?" She stroked her hand over his shoulder as she spoke. Everywhere she touched him he felt more alive than he ever had in his life. "The bonding words are even more powerful than the vows Christians take."

He considered that as he tried to tame his immediate reaction to her touching him. "Yes, but I want to wed you all the same."

"Then we will do this, but later." She pushed him gently on the chest. "I want to touch you until you know pleasure."

The idea had his cock stiffening painfully. Deliberately, he rose to his knees as she did the same. His shaft was bent down, the heavy flesh hanging out and away from his hips under the confining material.

"Oh, Bryson, my poor man," she whispered. She settled his hands to his sides. "I want to please you. Will you let me? Touch you anywhere I wish?"

He nodded, unable to speak. He could allow this. She was new to him, wanted to learn his body so she wasn't afraid, he thought. *I can do this for her to be at ease with me.* He waited for the torture. She was dressed in little more than his button-down shirt, while he was clothed. The first thing she did was smooth her hand over his erection. The telltale spot under his balls shivered and pre-cum wet the tip. Even under his pants, she had to feel it.

"You are ready."

"I am."

"Good." She watched him as she explored the length then as she sat taller she began unbuttoning his shirt. He swallowed and watched the way the moonlight reflected on her glowing skin. The material of his shirt slid down with an appreciative sound from her. His heart swelled.

"You are all muscle, Bryson. So many muscles. And so hard."

He could attest to that and, after a small gasp from her, knew she could as well. His pants had been much easier for her to unfasten and, since he was achingly hard, his cock sprang free, angling up and straight out in an attempt to reach her.

"You are so long and big. I will enjoy this?" She squinted at him to see what he would say. At this rate neither of them might enjoy it. He needed her. Not because she was his and he'd not had a woman under him in centuries, but because she was his other half. The pressure to fill her, to mount her, and drink from her was enormous. *But for her I would suffer this for as long as it takes to ensure she is not in pain. No pain, only pleasure. I have come already, climaxed so hard we dented the headboard.* "Bryson?"

"Yes, yes, you will." He gritted his teeth and fisted his hands at the first feel of her warm palms on his cock. She watched his flesh as she stroked along the shaft, cupping the sensitive head, then worked both hands back down. His eyes crossed when she explored his sac then stroked upward again. "It's so heavy and warm.

So hard, too. The skin here is like velvet, warm, tempered steel, except here." She rolled her fingers along the head. "Here I think you are sensitive, and here," she whispered, rubbing her thumb along the slit.

His eyes rolled back in his head. He groaned like an animal.

"You like this." She rubbed harder, right where he was the most sensitive.

"I do, but…" He grabbed her hand and stilled her, panicked he'd come right then and there. He breathed in and out, tempering his response.

"You are close?"

He eyed her curious, eager expression. "I am. If you do not stop, I will come."

She appeared pleased by that. "I do not think that will matter in the least," she whispered, pulling free and slipping from her clothing.

He'd seen every inch of her, but as she slid the shirt free for him, he held his breath. Her pink nipples and the curvy expanse of her rounded breasts hit hard. He moved back and exhaled as his gaze pinned on the mound of flesh between her slender thighs. His muscles jerked at the sight. He could still taste her on his tongue. Knew the sounds of pleasure she made. Could close his eyes and picture her pretty sex opening around the head of his erection.

"You do like the way I look."

He laughed, but it was a painful one. "Like? I will never want you to wear clothing."

She smoothed her hand down his stomach then reached out and took hold of his heavy cock again. "I want you this way all the time, too."

"Isobel," he warned, halfway to begging her to handle him.

"With this, I believe you will...come several times this night."

He shuddered as she kissed his chest, licking him after. "Isobel, I will come so much we will both be covered in release." He bit his tongue, not believing he'd said something so coarse to her.

She glanced up at him, then laughed merrily as if what he'd said pleased her immensely. "Oh, that sounds...very naughty, but pleasurable."

"Isobel."

With a firm grip on him, she pressed so close he could feel the tight points of her nipples on his chest. "Bryson, I am aching. I want you this badly. Stop teasing me."

"Isobel." He didn't know what to say, how to begin.

"Now, take me now. Show me now."

"Gods, yes, I will show you. I will make love to you until you beg me to stop." He took her mouth and tried for slow but ended up still in his trousers and boots, crawling up the bed and pressing her back so he could settle between her thighs. *I'm going to fuck my bride in my boots.* For some reason that thrilled him, and if Isobel's frantic kisses meant anything, she liked the idea too.

His body was boiling, his cock throbbed. She was wet and ready. Just the scent of how ready made him insane. Instincts raged at him to take her, pin her, make her his.

"Widen your thighs, Isobel."

She did as he instructed and stroked his back. At the same time, she lifted her hips with a hungry moan.

"I'm going to make love to you for the rest of the night, but this first time." He caught her arms over her head, "I will be as careful as I can."

He nudged his body against hers, finding her entrance by the heated wetness against his sensitive cockhead. Her body tensed then she moaned again in growing excitement. Her fangs had sharpened, her irises darkened and she looked sexier to him than ever.

The bonding had begun.

"You will be mine."

She watched his face as he thrust inside. It was beyond good. It was beyond anything he'd ever dreamed. Her eyes widened then grew slumberous and sexy. Biting her lip, she angled her hips, giving him permission to take more. Just like earlier, he carefully pulled his body back, but this time, he thrust again, working deeper. He gave her a harder, firmer press but froze as he felt something brush the head.

"Isobel," he managed in a strangled tone.

She peeked her head up, worrying her lip. "It doesn't hurt."

"Are you certain?" His arm muscles tensed. He could just make out the thin skin of her virginity against the tip of his cock, separating them. The sensation had his balls drawing up tightly. He had known, but not known. *A virgin. Mine.*

Her eyes shimmered with passion and acceptance. "I am certain."

"You will be mine from this moment on, Isobel. Mine to love, mine to cherish."

"And you will be mine, Bryson. To love. To cherish. Now. *Now.*"

At her urging, he took her mouth. This time he gently demonstrated how much he adored her with every stroke of his tongue. He drew his hand up her thigh and caressed her dewy sex with his thumb, lingering stroke after stroke on her until she writhed under him.

Between his gnashed teeth, he commanded her, "Don't move."

He spread her legs wider with a nudge from his hips and took both her hands. She tightened her fingers through his but watched him, trusting him as he pulled almost free then with a harder, more powerful flex of his hips, he penetrated her. The whisper of the barrier broke under his evasion, then they experienced a deeper, hotter position as he sank in, not stopping until with a rush, his balls rested tight to her flesh.

"Drink! Drink from me!"

She cried out, locked her legs around his waist and pierced his chest, drinking deeply. His muscles pulled bowstring-taut even as he felt the delicate squeeze on his cock that indicated her climax. At her orgasm, he couldn't help himself from biting her, as well. Or from pumping in and out of her soft, warm pussy. He tried for slow, but she tightened around him so rhythmically, his pace increased. Until, with each frenzied thrust, he claimed what was his at last.

He broke his bite and roared her name. His seed erupted in searing jets deep in her womb. It went on for so long he felt dizzy. When he could see straight, he tugged her hair gently until she rolled her head to peer up at him. She still clenched ever so lightly around his cock.

"You are my one true mate, Isobel. I want you as my female, for now and always. I freely bond myself to you for all time. With this breath," he whispered against her mouth, "with this body…" He gave her one firm thrust until he was sheathed completely and held his ground.

"With this love, I freely bond myself to you for all time."

Stunned. Tears threatened Isobel. The emotion in Bryson's voice whispered through her mind, burying itself deep and wiping away the sorrow and loneliness she had known for so long. This man would never let her struggle alone. Never leave her nor harm her.

Isobel blinked, but his handsome face still registered such love and devotion that mist clouded her eyes. The need to taste him grew impossible to ignore. With it came a need to satisfy him. She locked her legs around his waist and her arms as far around his broad shoulders as they would go. His shaft hardened and filled her until she knew she would always feel every thick inch of his body taking hers.

Never want to lose him.

"You are my one true mate, Bryson MacAfee. I want you as my male, for now and always. With this breath." She tugged his face down to hers and kissed him passionately. "With this body." She ground her hips, riding his cock with strong pulls of her muscles until his body grew rigid in that way she thought meant he was close to climaxing. Only then did she release his mouth to stare up at him. His irises sparkled, his handsome face tense with need. She rubbed her nipples against his sweaty chest and surged upward as she caressed his damp hair. "With this love, I freely bond myself to you for all time. Drink, Bryson, and in return, share your blood with me."

His eyes were mesmerizing as they caught and held hers. "Aye, my heart."

He bent his head. Anticipation had her squirming. She knew his bite, craved it, always would. She felt his fangs lengthen along her neck. He pressed his hot mouth to her throat.

"Take my blood, Isobel, as I take yours," he ordered heatedly.

The urge was there, a pressure like nothing else she'd ever known. *Addictive.*

"From me, only me," he growled and bit her.

Her body squeezed down on his thick shaft, propelling her into orgasm. She sank her fangs into his heavy pectoral. Warm, tangy blood filled her mouth.

Bryson growled and the delicious stimulation made her lock her legs around his waist tight and move up and down on his cock. He thrashed between her legs, giving her powerful thrusts again and again until she was delirious with passion. He broke his bite, threw his head back and roared. His seed heated her womb in long, luscious streams. It went on for so long, she thought she might pass out from the pleasure, but held on, never wanting it to end. *My strong, powerful mate climaxing because of me.* With a louder grunt, he gave two more firm, solid thrusts and surged between her legs as hard as he could, holding himself there as he shuddered and groaned into the bed.

It was perfect. She lost her bite. Another orgasm overtook her. His brawny arms surrounded her, his hard body weighed hers down, and his flesh filled her perfectly. She never wanted it to end. Then he pierced her shoulder with his fangs. The ability to think disappeared, only pleasure remained, taking her far afield but still anchored to her mate's hot embrace.

By the time they had exhausted themselves, she knew she would never have enough of him, or of sex. *My wild, sweet, warrior.* She eased into sleep, but felt him curl himself protectively around her.

"Rest, Isobel."

She sighed and wiggled her body so she could shift one of her legs between his big thighs.

"Yes," she whispered. "Then we will make love again?"

He shook against her with his laughter. "Yes. On the morrow, I will show you how you can ride me, how is that?"

"Oh, I like this idea," she said, but was already half asleep. "It will be my goal to exhaust you each night, Bryson."

More laughter met her promise, but it was good. So were his arms holding her.

She nestled closer and drifted, for the first time in her existence, into something wonderful.

Chapter Twenty-Five

Rowan stared from Isobel to Bryson, then back to Isobel. She glowed. Bryson's lips curled. She looked happy.

"Well, I am surprised you are finished," Rowan said in an irritated mutter.

"Rowan," Bryson cautioned. Rowan sniffed and muttered something Bryson didn't bother to make out. "Where is Gideon?"

"I do not know at the moment. But Warren is in Seattle. I have spoken with Aidan. He has grown into his power, but I fear is distracted by this hunt for his bonded's sister."

"Bridget sacrificed a great deal to ensure her sister's happiness, and Aidan's. He owes her a debt but he will be ready. Will we need him?"

"Most assuredly. He is the king."

"You are older."

'As king, Aidan has power an elder does not possess.' Her thoughts slid into his mind, comforting him from the

inside out. She took his hand, threading her fingers through his with a delicate firmness.

'So this is why Rowan looks worried?'

'Perhaps.' "Do you feel uncertain that you, I and Bryson can defeat him, Rowan?" she asked aloud.

In their link, he could feel her anxiety returning. Their night and their rising had been more wondrous than anything he'd ever dreamed. She fit him. Each time he'd made love to her, the ties binding them had grown, like spider webs, drawing them closer to being one. They had done more than shared their bodies, they had shared their minds. It felt as if he'd never *not* known her. As if she were a part of him he'd been unable to see until she'd shed light on all he'd missed out on. He'd sensed from her that she'd done the same. She had much to learn but had much to teach him as well.

Rowan sighed wearily and shook his head. He looked exhausted. His eyes were dull and his complexion gray. He'd not cleaned himself and there was dirt and grime on his neck and his scarlet shirt was torn at the cuff. His library was barely lit, and from the stairway, Bryson sensed cold air coming down from what must be the upper story of his home. No doubt he'd not lit the fires anywhere and that cold was filling every room.

"Did you find him?" Bryson asked, intrigued by how off the elder appeared.

"I found him. But we did not battle, if that is what you are concerned with. He locked himself away before I could reach him." He waved his hand and a few candles burst to light, and from above the sound of a door slamming shut punctuated his sentence.

"Where is he?" Bryson asked.

"He is gone by now, no doubt. But I believe he will go after Agatha again."

"She is safely hidden —"

"No one is safely hidden." Isobel took his hand and leading him to one of the couches. She sat and pulled him down next to her.

He was too restless to relax but sank down near her, then leaned forward with his elbows on his knees. "Are you saying he knows where Agatha is?"

"I don't even know where Jaxon and Joey took her, but it is possible he does. If so, then no, she is not safe. It is her he needs to kill. He is somewhat limited by the body he possesses."

"Not too limited," Bryson grumbled. "Not if you couldn't catch him, eh?"

Rowan inclined his head at that. "He still possesses great power."

"Well then, we need a means to *negate* that power. You mentioned spells, Isobel. What if we were to use a spell to *stop* him, rather than wait for him to show up and kill again?" Bryson stood and paced to the book shelves. Something tantalized him, something that would aid them he believed, but what it was he couldn't bring to the surface. "If we could somehow trap him in this body and take away his powers... Then couldn't we remove him? I don't know, exorcise him?"

"He's not an evil spirit," Rowan protested.

"That depends on your point of view," Bryson muttered. He earned a stern look from Rowan, but the man also frowned thoughtfully.

"If we could remove Gideon from Warren..."

'What do you think, my love?' He watched Isobel's eyes widen.

'I think you are amazing.' She sent him something that felt like a warm, intense ray of sunlight—but not harmful. "It would work. We only need a witch, or...two?"

"Six would be better. If not six, then three." Rowan stood and ran his hands through his hair. "In my time, we had dealings with a few of the covens. Not many, mind you, for witches are unpredictable and can hold a grudge if wronged, but there were a few covens I worked with. I have no idea now."

"Bryson does." Isobel walked to him and encircled his waist with her arms, pleasing him beyond measure.

"I do. And they happen to owe me a few favors. But something else is troubling me, Isobel."

She scanned his face and frowned at his thoughts. "The boy? Why does your mind turn to Faolan?"

"He is a part of this." Bryson worried. "Somehow."

"The boy who visited me, yes. He is a piece of this puzzle, but how I am not certain," Rowan added.

'Do you think Faolan is safe?'

'Jamie watches him closely.'

'He came to me, alone. He visited you, alone.'

"Jamie and Elsa are newly coupled, Isobel. I am sure if I warn them, they will keep the boy in." *'Newly bonded can be...busy.'*

'Ah, I see.' Humor and a rush of arousal flooded their bond. *'As we will be.'*

'Gods, yes, angel, as we will be. Once this is over, you are never stepping foot outside our bedroom again.'

'That sounds...wonderful.'

'I love you, Isobel.'

"If you two would stop, I could in fact be of some help, if I knew what you were speaking of," Rowan said, sounding offended.

Isobel turned her face to his chest, laughing through their bond. Her blush heated him.

"If Faolan is in danger, Jamie needs to know," Bryson responded, not about to inform Isobel's mentor he'd been thinking dirty thoughts to his protégée.

"If he is in danger," she muttered, again focusing on the issue of the boy.

"I think Bryson is correct in his worry. It is too much to believe that the boy shows up here, and only recently in your lifetime, Bryson. He was found, was he not? And while I agree he is part Lykae, it is not that part of him that is strongest, but other powers."

"Vampire?" Bryson asked.

"Yes, there is that I sense—deep, but there. But something else is hidden, and that is what worries me."

"You think he is possessed?" Worry clouded Isobel's tone.

Bryson held his tongue. Isobel knew his thoughts and drew closer to him.

"No. He is not possessed," Rowan said. "At least there is no part of him that does not *belong*."

Isobel relaxed against him.

'We will keep him safe, my heart. You must trust that.'

'I know. I do. I trust you.'

He gathered her closer and rubbed his jaw to her hair. "I know you trust me, but believe me, nothing will happen to the little rascal."

"It might be wise to speak to his family," Rowan said quietly.

"And say what? We fear he is somehow involved with an ancient, insane Vampire?" Bryson laughed at Rowan's offended snort. "He is no longer your brother, old man, best you remember that."

"He is and always will be my brother. But it shames me to admit it. I will do my part to see him pay for his crimes." Rowan stood taller. "But the more I think on it, the more I wish to meet this boy's family. I assume they did not birth him?"

"Elsa and Jamie. They found him. He was being held by something evil. Jamie is a bitten Lykae. Elsa was born a Lykae but raised by humans. She was bitten by Samuel, nearly ten years ago now."

Rowan paused in the midst of adjusting his sword belt. "Samuel?"

"Yes, Samuel. You knew him?" Bryson asked.

"Yes." Rowan made a distasteful expression.

"We killed him just two months ago." Bryson rubbed his chin, still feeling that sensation that he was missing something.

"He was evil, Rowan. The things he had done were...horrifying. They reminded me of the past. I sensed this Vampire, Warren, there, in the midst of it all."

Rowan sat on the edge of the desk and crossed his arms. "Yes. I see. More is becoming clear."

Bryson opened his mouth to ask what, but Isobel stopped him with a hand on his arm.

'It is his way. His mind is brilliant, Bryson.'

'As is yours, but his ways are...'

'Sweet.'

He curled his arm around her shoulders and nodded.

"Yes, more is unfolding, eh? Samuel was always with Gideon, there at the end, and after he would have found and aided my brother. Gideon can be charismatic when he tries. Worse, he knows *when* to try." Rowan paused again and seemed to grow more despondent than earlier. A heavy weariness colored the man's tone. It must have been horrible for him to have a brother like Gideon. Bryson knew what it felt like to know that someone you loved — even potentially *could* love — was evil. He'd once thought that Isobel had been such. But Rowan *knew* his brother was evil.

"There is a reason my brother is as evil as he is, or not a reason." Rowan flicked his wrist. "But there is a history to his madness. Not that it discounts or relieves him of his guilt." After a long pause, Rowan sighed heavily. "He was once bonded, you see, and his bonded took her life. Afterwards, well, afterwards, Gideon was not the same. Or else he was more open with his madness that until then, he had hidden."

Bryson froze from stroking Isobel's long hair. "Is that even possible? Suicide?"

"Yes. If a Vampire is determined enough." Rowan studied the intricately designed floor with a heavy frown. "She threw herself from Gideon's tallest tower to the rocky shore. The ocean dragged her body out to sea before Gideon knew she'd gone."

Bryson stared from the eccentric ancient to Isobel. She was as shocked as he felt. To be bonded should have removed even the *option* of suicide — unless one of the pair died first. Then suicide was common, but never when a couple both lived."

"She killed herself? *After* he bonded her?" Isobel asked.

Rowan turned and regarded them both solemnly. "On their bonding night."

"Jesus," Bryson muttered.

"I doubt Christ had much to do with it. My brother has always been a selfish man. Always seeking pleasure and gain above all else. With his bonded, he gained much. She was beautiful and came with wealth and prestige. All qualities my brother held dear," he added on a sigh. "But like too many of our females, she was sheltered and innocent of the ways of the world. Not that she threw herself upon the rocky shore because he didn't help her from her chair after their meal." He grimaced and glanced at both of them. "What she must have endured to do such a thing..." He bowed his head, arms crossed as he added, "I was aware, even then, how sick Gideon had become. I believed she would bring him back from that."

Silence descended on them. Bryson took Isobel's hand and stroked his thumb over her knuckles. Sorrow filled her for Rowan. Through their bond he could see that to her, a child without parents, this man had been her comfort outside of her brother. Rowan had given her the nurturing she'd been denied. Bryson owed the man more than he could ever repay. But he couldn't see a way to allowing Gideon to live. They would have to kill him and do it right this time. The thought of all those that had suffered from his sickness made Bryson's stomach churn. *Just how many has the man killed?*

"Rowan." Bryson tensed, suddenly seeing more to what was laid out before them. *Samuel was ancient enough to have aided Gideon. Does that mean that Gideon was the 'one' behind the killings in France and Seattle?* "Does *forever* mean anything to you?"

Rowan looked up at him quizzically. "Forever?"

"A pendant, with just that word, sometimes in French, but just that one word scrolled on a golden locket."

Rowan nodded. "Forever. Yes, Gideon used to say it as a joke. Nothing was forever, yes? You've heard this surely."

"I have."

"Why do you ask? I have no knowledge of a pendent with *forever* written on it."

"What are you thinking, Bryson?" Isobel asked then frowned at him, seeking the answers through their links. She started and stood. "But... But that would mean Faolan *is* involved. Elsa, as well."

"Slow down, Isobel," Bryson cautioned. "We killed Samuel, and the one we thought was his master. They'd been kidnapping and torturing men and women, children too, then killing them, for centuries. Elsa was taken. Faolan was found when she was freed by Jamie. Witches were involved," he added. "But we thought we had killed the master..."

"And now you think *Gideon* is this master?" Rowan asked.

"I am leaning toward it, yes." Bryson paced the room, away from Rowan and his skepticism. "Is it possible? Do you believe he's been taking over bodies before this? *Before* Warren?"

"Of course. Samuel would have aided him as soon as he could."

"There was this link, something I overlooked because the master wasn't immortal, merely a sick, perverted creature."

"What did you overlook?" Isobel asked, caressing his arm.

"The tattoo on Samuel's wrist. The Fleur. It was odd, even Jamie noted it. I had thought, well..." Bryson ran a hand through his hair nervously. "There was a man... Gilles de Rais." Bryson laughed. "Insane, but I think Gideon... I think Gideon possessed the man."

"A mortal?" Rowan asked, frowning, not laughing at him.

"Yes, he was human. A hero even, until he turned rabid. He was accused of killing hundreds of children—not merely *killing*, but maiming and... abusing them. The same signature we found in Seattle and in the witch's basement in France. I thought it an odd repeat of history, but now... If Gideon has been possessing one body after another all this time..."

"He will be more powerful than we imagined. And it explains how he has evaded detection. If he took to mortals then he would have changed his body multiple times. Perhaps Warren, this young Vampire, was him realizing the end was drawing near." Rowan studied first him then Isobel, who'd remained quiet.

"If this is true, if he has moved his soul from body to body, he will be well-used to the experience and harder for us to trap," Isobel warned.

Bryson agreed. So did Rowan, if his deeper frown meant anything. "We will need a coven, or several, to aid us."

"If Gideon wanted someone, did he ever give up on getting them?" Isobel asked.

"No, child, you know he did not. Tessa was an example of that," he added. "He will finish Agatha if he can, then he will go after Elsa, perhaps not now, but he will as soon as he has his body back."

"Then we need to stop him. I will contact Jamie." He held up his hand at Rowan's protest. "Jamie is a protective Lykae. It's best I tell him. He will want to ward Elsa and Faolan. Worse, if Gideon is this master, he is familiar with covens, as well. Even now, he could be working with one, trying to hide until he can kill Agatha."

"True, we should contact whomever you can trust, Bryson," Isobel said.

"I agree," Rowan said firmly, his doubts vanished. "We must be prepared. Gideon, free, in his own body, with the power he has gained through the ages. We cannot let this happen."

He gripped the older Vampire's arm and felt the strength there. "He is not your flesh and blood any longer, Rowan. That man has long since passed." Rowan met his eyes squarely and nodded once. It was enough for now. He would ensure Rowan recovered from this. Isobel, and he hoped Faolan, would see to it that the man was not alone to brood over such matters.

'I love you so much, Bryson.'

Isobel's words caught him by surprise, as did the rush of painful emotions she sent to him, but he accepted both and caught her hand in his. "I love you too, Isobel. We will find him, and we will end this. First, I will need to call Circerran. She is probably going to put up a fight, especially since she was the one that laid the spells you broke at the council. When you killed Gia?"

Isobel nodded. "I recall. Spells cannot bind us nor keep us from entering."

"She knows this now. We don't reveal our powers, my heart. She will be…touchy."

"Ah." Isobel lifted an eyebrow. "I will remain calm, then."

"It is probably best." He could recall Isobel losing her temper quite easily. Circerran and Isobel both doing it… Throw Elsa in and he wanted to miss the meeting. "We should all remain calm."

Rowan drew himself up. "I always remain calm. I shall ensure the house is adequately warmed for our guests." He walked away, back straight, clearly offended.

Bryson was too busy to worry over it.

"I feel we are still missing something. Gideon would not chance his plans falling to ruins because we have discovered him." Isobel tucked her long hair behind her ears, appearing much too young.

"If there is something we will catch it, Isobel. Or our friends will." He took her hands again and smoothed his thumb over her small knuckles.

"Your friends."

"Soon, I think they will be yours." *'Just give them time.'*

'We may not have time.'

He worried the same but made the call. Circerran picked up on the fourth ring.

"By four you're supposed to give up. Three is the max, four is ridiculous."

"I need your help to remove a soul from a Vampire who is possessed."

Silence. Then she cleared her throat. "I take it that you're not the one possessed?"

"No. Warren. By an ancient soul. Can you remove an ancient?"

He thought he heard Jack in the background, but Circerran started speaking. "It depends. How long has he taken up residency? And this is *way* bigger than what you did for me."

"Lives and souls depend on it. Can you come to us, where I am now?"

"If I open my link, but I'm not sure I'm signing up for this. Rumors are running wild, via the Jaxon-Joey show, that you are hooking up with the drop dead gorgeous and deadly Isobel. Do I need to remind you that she broke my spell? And if she can, what's to stop this ancient possessing Warren? And on that note, you know, I never liked Warren anyway."

Isobel raised both of her eyebrows and slowly smiled. *'Drop dead gorgeous and deadly Isobel?'*

'You are drop dead gorgeous.'

'And deadly.'

"You owe me a debt, Circerran. I believe this would even our ledger."

"Oh boy, would it ever. So, you are hooked up with—"

"Circerran, need I remind you that you were once hysterical and crying for me to come and save your bonded? That I not only did this but aided him in—"

"Got it, got it. So, we need a few minutes and I'll have to call... Oh, hell, I guess Aubrey and...Sorcha. Thrilling. My sister will not like this, and if she doesn't, then you know Alex won't."

"Alex is not coming within a mile of my bonded," he said icily.

"Oh my, then we have a problem. I need three, but hold on before you go Darth Vader on me again. I have someone. We'll be with you in a few hours. Possibly sooner, so hold your angst, okay?"

"I'm holding my breath."

"Good. Although you don't have to breathe, so that doesn't really—"

"Circerran—"

"Got it. Look, glad you found someone, not so sure on the someone, but anyway, wanted to say that. Opening link, don't pry and got you. Seamless and you are... Hell, what is it with Vampires and icy freaking cold locations? I'll be there when I get there." She hung up before he could respond.

"She's on her way."

"Is she?" Isobel asked in a surprised tone. "That didn't sound as if she was willing."

"She's like that, and more, but she's a…friend."

'Truly?' Isobel sent him a laugh through their bond at his thoughts. The closeness warmed him. *'You sound doubtful.'*

He brushed his cheek to her sweet smelling hair. *'Not doubtful, yet sometimes we take for granted those we know. She is a friend.'*

'You have helped her and many others, Bryson. You are a good man.'

'I am a man, neither good nor bad, simply a man.'

'You are insane, but I still love you.'

Chapter Twenty-Six

Isobel was impressed with the three witches. She had only met a few witches in her time, before being entombed. Tessa had been alone, her mother and father both dead from a sickness. The Dragon Guard had been a secluded order, set away from almost everyone. From her interactions with Tessa, though, she had assumed witches were soft spoken and avoided notice.

Circerran was a vibrant, scarlet-haired woman who was at once a powerful presence. Her mate, a tall, odd man with a duality to him that worried Isobel, stood solidly by Circerran's side, dwarfing her in size but not power. Aubrey was a silent, courteous dark-haired witch and mild compared to Circerran, but her power was also deep, like an ancient loch. The fourth member was neither as silent as Aubrey, nor as outspoken as Circerran. Emerald intrigued Isobel. She'd arrived with Circerran but was clearly not one of Circerran's coven. It wasn't the way they spoke, but rather how the lighter red-haired girl held herself away, quiet until spoken to.

She reminded Isobel of Tessa, but a Tessa who'd been hurt by all the world had shown her. Jorge had once told her that Tessa had seen much hardship and survived. That she was stronger than she appeared. Isobel sensed the same from Emerald.

"Circerran, are you certain three of you are enough? What if Gideon has his own witches, like the coven we fought in Alaska?" Bryson asked.

Circerran raised her crimson eyebrows and tilted her head to the side. "That would be Emerald's coven. And yes, she's safe, if that's your next question. But what if he does have a coven of witches? What is it you think he will do? Possess his body once he kills Agatha?"

"Exactly. If he kills Agatha —"

"How will he find her?" Aubrey asked, stepping forward and setting down a small book she had been studying. "She is hidden, aye?"

"She is, but there are no —"

"Guarantees in this world, got the memo." Circerran pinned her clover-green gaze on Isobel and she breathed out through her nose. "So, Isobel. What do you think? Is Gideon going to find Agatha? Or should I say, can *you* find Agatha?"

"Why would she —"

"Bryson." Isobel tightened her hold on his sleeve. Since the arrival of the four he had been anxious. "I know where she is, or in what direction."

Rowan nodded. "Because you were given the task of freeing your brother, I see. So you believe Gideon, because his task is the same, can also sense her." Rowan sounded impressed.

Aubrey nodded. "Aye. Gideon is a wee bit more hard pressed. He wants this woman dead, and when he does this, then he is free, eh?"

"Not exactly." Rowan stepped forward politely. Bryson had already introduced everyone but Rowan still bowed his head. "Aubrey. If my brother kills Agatha, then he will have to kill Warren. Only then can he can claim his body. Since Samuel is no longer here to aid him, I assume he will have another appointed to this task."

"Someone he can trust to do as he asks," Emerald said when there was a pause. "It could be the coven in France. They are connected to the Scarlet."

"But the Scarlet has been disbanded," Bryson commented. "Are you saying that some of them are free to roam?"

"I am. Not everyone has been brought before the Coven Congress." Emerald ducked her head nervously and her side braid slipped down her shoulder. "Many are still to be found."

"And these witches could be the ones that aid Gideon," Circerran confirmed. "They will aid him in bringing his body back and help him possess it once more with his spirit. But to do this, a sacrifice will have to be made. It will not be enough to kill the members of this council who killed him. He will need to appease the…darker forces, shall I say? Then, if he succeeds, his body will again be his own."

"Is this what your brother wished?" Aubrey asked Isobel.

Bryson held in a curse. Isobel's claws in his arm had a great deal to do with that.

"No. My brother wanted his soul free to move on, with his bonded, to the next existence. He did not want to lose Tessa, nor chance never seeing her again and being lost without her."

"Ah." Aubrey drummed her fingers on the table.

No one spoke until Circerran kicked the chair next to Aubrey. "Well?"

Aubrey sniffed but folded her arms over her chest. She was dressed in pale blue jeans, soft-looking and comfortable, with a long cable-knit sweater of deepest blue. A white blouse peeked out at the bottom and collar and she wore brown, scuffed but well-loved boots on her feet. She was beautiful, with her hair loosely held away from her face and flowing down her back. Even her creamy complexion was beautiful. All three witches were.

'And? You are more so.'

'You pry into my thoughts?'

Bryson laughed through their link. *'Not pry. But I cannot stand the distance.'*

"I think," Aubrey stressed the word *think* for some reason, "our worry should no' be whether Gideon kills Agatha or no', but when she will die."

"I agree. She has suffered much," Rowan answered. "If she ends her life, as we worry she will, then can Gideon still use her death to satisfy his conditions?"

"Only if he spreads her ashes and throws her spirit to the wind," Isobel cautioned. "He must do this in order for her to be truly dead."

"I fear he will do this, Isobel. What will stop him?" Rowan asked. "Only if we reach her, stop her and wait, will we be able to prevent it."

"Then that is what we will do." Jack stood away from the desk he'd been leaning on. Isobel had almost forgotten the once-human now half-Vampire half-Lykae was there. "We will move her, secure the location, and wait. If Gideon comes, then that is just as well. We end him there, if that serves?" He turned to Rowan, showing no fear of the elder as he held his gaze.

Rowan studied him in turn. She could tell that Rowan wasn't certain what to think of the man, both because he was bonded to a witch and because of his mixed blood. But to Rowan's credit, her mentor weighed the facts. "If we can save Agatha, it would be well. If Gideon is killed, it will be better. At the least we can attempt to force him from Warren, but if the chance arises to end his existence then we should take it."

Jack nodded, once, sharply as if Rowan had done the right thing. For some reason, her mentor stood straighter after.

'His guilt is heavy.'

'He has nothing to be guilty over.'

'But he believes he does, my love.'

'Just as you felt over me?'

Bryson sent her warmth and love so deep she felt tears sting her throat. *'All I know is that he is a good man and his brother is not. We will help him survive this. Or perhaps he will survive on his own.'*

'He is strong.'

Circerran rubbed her hands together. "Fine, then we have a plan. I suggest we find a location that is easy to fortify. Jack, you can deal with that. And we'd better call in Jamie. He's going to flip his lid."

Jack grinned. "No doubt. He thought we'd ended this craziness, but he needs to know, Bryson. ASAP."

"That means *now*," Circerran said to Isobel "In case you don't get the lingo yet. So," Circerran added, walking over, "you can break spells, huh? How long will it take Gid to break one if we make it really, really complicated?"

"It depends on how complicated." Isobel started when Circerran dropped her arm around her shoulders and steered her toward the central table. "What are you doing?"

"We thought we'd figure this out with you, while they contact, then deal with Jamie and Elsa freaking out over their pup."

'Their pup?'

"Circerran means over Faolan. The boy is dear to them," Aubrey supplied. "He will come, as well. Unless he is sent to stay with Samantha and Derrick."

Isobel blinked.

'Are you okay?'

'I am not certain.'

'They mean you no harm.'

'Are you...laughing at me?'

Complete silence from Bryson was her answer. She narrowed her eyes at him, but oddly enough, he wouldn't glance over.

"Who are Samantha and Derrick?" Emerald asked, taking a seat in one of the chairs and drawing her legs up to her chest. "I've never heard of either of them."

"Samantha is part-Jade. She is married to Derrick, brother to the Lykae king, Alrick. They have a son, around Faolan's age." Circerran dropped her arm and sat down as well, gesturing for Isobel to join her. "Sit down. So, what I'm thinking is we—"

Sirens, the scream of them so loud Isobel covered her ears, was their only warning before thick black smoke filled the room. Shrieks rent the air. Through her bond with Bryson she felt something like a blow, then complete silence and the absence of him entirely, as if he had never been there. But now there was nothing, a huge nothingness that brought her to her knees, where for a brief, shining moment in her life there had been warmth and love. A rush of panic had her gaining her feet and with a shout of her own, she flung the table out of her way to face the enemy. Only all there was to face was billowing swirls of black smoke.

"Show yourselves!"

She thought she heard Circerran shout and a green light blasted on her left. To her right, a steady blue glow appeared, closer to her, warming her side, but nowhere did she see Bryson or Rowan. Her panic deepened. Out of the smoke a woman dressed in a flowing scarlet gown appeared. Whiter than snow with long black hair that hung silkily down to her thighs, she strode forward as if walking on air. Flames flashed in her eyes, circling where her irises should have been.

"What have you done to Bryson?" Isobel drew her sword from the air. The hilt reassured her when mist and shadows swirled all around her. She could sense the witches battling, knew by the cries and curses that they were, but she couldn't see them. Help them. *Don't lose focus. Bryson! Rowan! Where are you?*

The witch stopped scant feet from her. The temptation to strike her down was enormous. She knew this woman. Could feel the spells seep into her pores from centuries before when she had been trapped by her, or another like her.

"You want him, don't you?"

"If you wish to live you will answer me." Isobel drew a deep breath and steadied herself. *Never again. Can't be taken. Never again.*

"Is that so? Well, my dear, you have grown bold. But you see, you have it all wrong. If you want *him* to live, you will come with *me. Now.*" Fire rose in her eyes and with it, heat blossomed all along Isobel's front.

There was no other choice.

I can't lose him. Jorge, help me now. Help me save you and my heart, Bryson.

She took the witch's hand. Scorching pain exploded from where they touched to encompass her entire being. Heat that should have melted her skin from her bones caused such agony she couldn't even scream it was so intense. But with it, something else struck her so that the pain diminished and a soothing, calming presence crept over her.

Chapter Twenty-Seven

Darkness surrounded Bryson, a black so thick he couldn't penetrate it. After a moment he realized why. He was hooded. A cloth smelling of old gym socks covered his face, brushing against his chin as if it fluttered in the wind. It wasn't a breeze, more like a typhoon, wet and strong, gusting over his entire body.

Have they hung me up like a mermaid on a ship?

Over the wind, he heard something clanking then thudding softly near him. The horrible cloth prevented him from inhaling too deeply. His senses were limited but worse, his link with Isobel was gone. *Severed or merely muffled? Does it matter?* He was tied tightly. There was more rope around him then there were places without rope. So whoever held him was frightened of him. Not Gideon, then.

Witches.

It had to be, but until they revealed themselves, there was little he could do — yet. They'd used spells as well as the rope. He tested the intricate magic, finding little give in the complicated knots. The patterns shone bright scarlet, like spilled blood, and at his push, a painful ache began in his skull.

There were no voices. For that, he was grateful.

The wind hit harder, blasting him with freezing cold water. Ocean. *I'm either on a boat or on the shore, or an island.*

The reasoning didn't help. At the next blustery wash of wind, he shook his head and felt the hood lift with the breeze. It fell back down, but he got a glimpse of something that made him realize how little time he had.

Sunrise.

Fuck! Think. Think. Icy wind. Tied down. Spells. Think! He pushed against the spells, forcing more pain to rebound through his head. It felt as if someone was hammering nails through his skull. He expected warm blood to flow from his forehead. Another gust and he tried to toss the hood off again. The material fucked with him. Shouting—since they'd not bound his mouth—he cursed the situation and the gods.

"Dude! I thought Jamie swore!"

Bryson sagged in relief for a second—that was all he was given. Shouts, Jamie, Elsa, someone he didn't know, sounded around him. He thought he heard a woman screaming, then for certain, he did, along with others in unison. Pain rushed his flesh as if he were being flayed alive. Suddenly, the ropes were cut and he fell, still caught in the pain, to his side.

The hood was ripped off. *Elsa.* Her big gray eyes were narrowed and her face paler than normal, but he'd never been so happy to see anyone in his life. The wind whipped her long blonde hair around them both, partially blocking his view, but all around him the ocean blasted into what looked like an iceberg.

"Bryson, come on, we have to go. Faolan is here. Jamie is holding them!" She turned and slid her hand through a woman coming at her from behind, ripping the witch's heart out and flinging it to the ground before he could manage to move. It skidded, bright crimson and wet, along the icy snow, leaving a trail of gore behind before it fell out of sight and into the ocean. Elsa grabbed his shirtsleeve and shook the material. "Bryson! Get up!"

He held in the curses and concentrated on gaining his feet.

"Bryson, what's wrong?"

He shoved to his knees, saw Faolan half-hiding half-peering out from behind a concrete shed, then Jamie came into view. The big wolf took the head off a witch who'd been staring at Bryson. When the woman collapsed forward, the pain surging along Bryson's back and shoulders disappeared slowly. He managed to rise to his feet with Elsa pulling on his arm. "Where are we?"

"We have no idea. Faolan was upset. He dragged us here. It looks like the middle of the Arctic to me." Elsa tossed her hair off her eyes and squinted at him. "It's a good thing we listened to him, too. Come on, unless you want to fry with the dawn."

The wind brought another salty spray at them, drenching him and soaking Elsa, too. She was already wet, but the wave left her hair plastered to her skull and down her back. She shook her arms and hands, looking even more pissed off, if possible. "Seriously?"

Faolan raced to him, hugging him hard around the middle. He didn't have the energy to do more than groan at the tight embrace. Jamie walked up, taking off his jacket as he did and wrapping Elsa in it. The frigid air had a bite to it that dug under Bryson's skin.

"Bryson," Jamie growled by way of greeting. "What's this all about? Who are these witches?"

He used both hands to shove the water off his face before answering. Faolan was still holding on tightly. "Hey, Faolan, you wanna let up on the squeeze." The boy did but only a little. For some reason, the child's need for reassurance reassured Bryson, as well. "We'd better talk somewhere warmer. It's the mess we were in before, though, with Samuel."

Elsa paused from where she'd been giving Jamie back his coat. "What? What do you mean?"

Jamie caught her hand and put the coat right back on her shoulders. "Bryson?"

"You did good, Bryson."

"Faolan?" Jamie said. "Did you know about this?"

He shook his head. "Not about the connection, no."

"Connection to Samuel? But you knew Bryson was in trouble. And Isobel is the friend you made, the woman we've heard so much about?" Elsa asked.

"We have to go somewhere warmer and not so bright," Jamie reminded them. "Where?"

Right now safety was relative. He wanted to go check on Rowan, but that would be suicide. "Do you remember where you first were bound, Elsa? The witch's?"

"How could I forget?"

"Then we go there."

Jamie nodded and curled Elsa up close to his chest. "Now. Faolan, go with Bryson. I want you there when we land. Got it?"

"Okay, Jamie. I will be." Faolan sounded worried, so Bryson took his hand, trying to steady himself. Isobel was nowhere. *Is she gone?* The thought made his throat clench and his heart thud painfully.

"Don't worry, Bryson. She is still here, with us." Faolan rubbed his small hand over Bryson's heart, soothing him.

"Let's go." Bryson accessed the nearing dawn. Elsa was gone when he looked back and Faolan was silent.

He traced them to the ruins of the witch's house. Jamie was already standing with his hands on his hips, face tight with tension.

Elsa took Faolan's hand and brought him closer to her, but she wore an identical frown to her mate. "What's going on? You said Samuel —"

"He might not have been the one running the show, Elsa. We think another is behind it, and if he is, then he will still want to get his hands on you."

"We. Define 'we' for me, Bryson." Jamie put a growl to his name Bryson was familiar with from other dealings with the man. Any hint at danger to Elsa, and the wolf was unreasonably protective. Now, with Isobel missing, Bryson could see why. *Have to get to her. Have to find her.*

Elsa took Jamie's hand. "Jamie, please, this is all moving fast, let him explain."

"Now would be good, since we haven't heard any of this before," Jamie snapped, but Elsa must have communicated something to him through their link because he exhaled heavily and brought her close to his chest. His shoulders relaxed. "All right, Bryson, explain this so we can find out what's going on."

Bryson nodded. He considered asking that Faolan go somewhere else, but one look at the boy in the protective circle of Elsa's and Jamie's arms, and he knew they'd never let him out of their sight. *I had Isobel in mine and she is still missing. Think. Think.*

He paced a few feet away then back. "I was meeting with Circerran and two witches. We were with Rowan, uncle to Aidan. He is the one who realized that one of our young Vampires, Warren, is his brother, Gideon. Gideon is the one that murdered an enter village. That crime was thought to be committed by Isobel's brother, thus his execution and later what we thought was Isobel's revenge, the killing of Aidan's father." He paused for breath and to check that they were following. Jamie nodded and Elsa did, as well. Faolan watched him solemnly. "We now know that Isobel made a promise to her brother not to interfere with his death. He had lost his bonded to Gideon in that village. To be with her again, a non-vampire, he had to join her in the next life. So," he paused again, this time thinking it through. "Now, we have found Rowan, the head of an ancient sect, one Isobel was part of. He is the one aiding us. But, this is where I am lost. We were attacked. This is not only uncommon, since we were in Rowan's home," he ticked off the point with his finger, "but nearly impossible. It would have to be done by witches who not only knew where his home was, and it is well hidden, but how to breach his barrier. So…that means…" He paced away and back.

"Gideon aided them?" Jamie offered.

"Yes, I think so, too. Where are they? Did you all get taken at one time?" Elsa asked.

"I'm not sure where they are. I bonded to Isobel but I can't sense her. She's…" He glanced down at Faolan and the boy nodded.

"She lives."

"How — no, scratch that — Faolan, what is going on? Why do you know these things?" Elsa demanded, turning to him.

Faolan hung his head, but when he looked up Bryson saw the worry on his face. "Will you still be my family if I tell you?" he whispered to Elsa.

"We will *always* be your family," Elsa said fiercely, tears shining in her eyes.

"Faolan, no one will ever change that. Not even you, buddy," Jamie added.

Faolan swallowed and ducked his head, hiding his face with his long hair. "I am not only Faolan, Jamie. I am also more. *Him*. I am him, too."

Elsa met his eyes and mouthed 'him' with a worried wide-eyed look.

"Faolan, who is…? Who is this…*him*?" Jamie asked more gently than Bryson had ever heard the big man speak.

The boy looked up and tossed his hair away from his eyes. "Jorge was his father. Tessa his mother. His soul left and wandered until it found mine. Now, together, we are strong."

"Oh, my God," Elsa whispered, clinging to both Faolan and Jamie.

Bryson nodded to Elsa's whispered words. "We need to find Isobel, Faolan. Can you find Isobel for us?"

"Yes. I can always find her." Faolan touched his chest then turned to stare into the distance. "She is being protected by Aubrey, but they will break the protections soon. We should hurry."

"Then take us there. Who else is with her?" Jamie pulled out his phone.

"Jack, Circerran, Emerald, Aubrey and Rowan were all gathered at Rowan's home." Bryson had no phone, but he waited, anxious for Jamie to call one of them.

"I haven't heard from Cir or Jack. I don't know Emerald and only know Aubrey by name. But I doubt Cir is taking calls…" Jamie listened for a while but got nothing. He frowned and punched in another number. "Calling Derrick. Samantha would know…" He waited again.

"No one is answering or you have no service?" Elsa asked.

Jamie frowned. "No one is answering. We can't wait. Faolan, we do it my way. You lead then hide. Got it?"

"Yes, Jamie." Faolan smiled big. "I am good at hiding."

"Elsa, shift or hide if this goes south. We could be walking into a trap."

"Only if you come with me."

Jamie grimaced.

"You should go with her. Never lose her, Jamie," Bryson said, taking Jamie's shoulder. "Never."

Jamie winced and nodded. "If shit goes south, we all do."

Elsa leaned her head on his shoulder while Faolan did the same, but to Elsa.

"No, I will ensure it's not a trap. Faolan can show me where, you two should stay here."

"You are not going alone, man," Jamie snapped, surprising him.

Elsa laughed. "He really doesn't like you scaring him, but he's not going to let you face the stampede alone. Besides, we are your friends, Bryson. Just what do you think friends are for?"

"Friends don't let friends go it alone," Faolan told him.

Jamie met his eyes steadily. "Let's get this over with. Shit hits the fan—"

"—all go south," Elsa and Faolan said in unison.

Bryson snorted. "I have a hard time believing her."

Jamie cracked a grin. "I don't even try to believe her but I trust her not to get hurt."

Elsa didn't deny it, and she had a pretty satisfied smile for her mate.

Isobel, hold on for me. Wait for me.

'Isobel? Isobel, you need to wake up. You're late. We'll miss the ceremony.'

Isobel turned over, burying her head in the warm softness of her blankets. Tonight was a distant dream. It couldn't be here—not yet.

'Isobel, if you do not wake, I will wake you!'

The threat in Jorge's voice was real, but tinted with his colorful humor. She grumbled a denial, but the warmth of her furs was suddenly gone. Along with the loss of warmth came freezing cold.

'Jorge!' She tossed her hair off her face and glared as hard as she could, but her brother, she could tell, would not quell his humor or his excitement so easily.

'You can't be in a foul mood tonight. Come now, it's our blooding night.'

True. Today they would both be full members of the Dragon Guard.

"Isobel! Isobel, you must wake!"

The urgent whisper in her ear snapped Isobel from her dream. Events came back to her, along with the memories and worse, her fear that she'd lost Bryson.

"Isobel, I cannae keep you this way much longer! You must rise and *fight*."

She blinked, narrowing her eyes as the images before her face took shape. *Aubrey*. The witch from Rowan's home hovered over her. As she concentrated on her, Aubrey nodded tightly.

"Good. Now, you must break free."

Break free. She must break free. *From what?* Aubrey grew shadowy as if she were no longer a witch but a ghost.

"Don't leave." Isobel's voice came out in a whisper, cracked and dry.

"I am no' even here. Rise. Fight. I will repair the link. Bryson will come for you." With her words, the witch floated away into nothing. Nothing happened for a space of time. Silently, not moving, Isobel tested her surroundings. *Heat and rock. The hint of salt on the air.* Heat she saw in the distance, from an enormous central hearth. *Salt. Salt from the air?*

I am near the sea. Metal, ancient and heavy, hung from the towering ceiling. Cages, like the one she was in, hung down, each with bones in them — *Except mine.* Torture devices, antique and covered in centuries of suffering, hung from walls and racks. *A tower. I'm in a tower.* The circular staircase trailed around the inside of the room, reaching up out of the pit she was in.

Magic surrounded her. More protected her, but she sensed that unraveling at the same time as she became aware of murmuring — chanting. Witches and warlocks dressed in black and scarlet hooded capes moved in a pattern around the central hearth, bowing and twisting to a heavy drumbeat. Somewhere someone was screaming. Elsewhere, she could hear singing in a language long since dead. The words were dark, darker than even the most ancient civilization's devils.

Inside the circle of magic users stood a man she knew only from Christian's thoughts. Sandy blond-haired, handsome, but in a cruel, arrogant way that warned he was not to be trusted. At his feet two women dressed in little more than sheer gauze knelt, their bodies clearly outlined from the glow of the fire. Between them lay another woman — Agatha. Her head was drawn back with a noose someone had tied between her teeth like a bit for a horse — only her back was bent until her head nearly touched her bare feet where the rope circled her ankles. The gruesome display was only made worse by the way the women fondled the trapped ancient.

Isobel shut her eyes and assessed the bindings around her. They were many. Each spell was covered and wrapped with another and another and another without end. *No! Do not follow that path. Tricks. Look deeper.*

She sought the power, the telltale heat of the spell a witch leaves behind, and through that she pried and shoved. Each spell was a layer of painful webbing she needed to destroy. From a distance she heard her name. Then closer, closer, until with a shout, Bryson in all his power and glory was there. Relief made her weak even as she struggled to break completely free.

'Show me what you are fighting! Show me where you are!'

'You are unharmed!' She sucked back the need to break into tears and clung to her sanity by reaching through their bond toward him. He was there. *Strong. Brave. Solid.*

*'I am here. Show me. Ah, gods, what is this? They have…
Look again, they have Rowan, too, and you are… You are
harmed!'*

At his panic, she felt pain surge along her arms. Two
long slices on the inside of each wrist upward to her
forearm. Her blood dripped down, spilling on the cage
flooring and taking her strength with it.

Bryson's rage roared between them in bright reds.
She couldn't stop him or warn him not to come.
Already she was too weak, already she was bound by
ropes. Just like before.

'Bryson! Be careful!'

But this time, she was not alone.

This time, with a shout, Bryson was there, and more
warriors were at his back. But all she saw was Bryson —
her warrior bursting into being and destroying the
circle of magic. He beheaded two witches with a
mighty cry. With another savage yell he turned to the
man in the middle. They battled fiercely but Bryson
was methodical and deadly. He forced the battle
against a wall then followed as his opponent dove low
and behind a pillar. When they were lost to her sight,
panic rose up from the lethargy stealing over her.
Blinking, she tried to find them. Instead, another man,
and along with him a woman with long flowing blonde
hair struggled through the remaining magic users. The
warrior beheaded a big warlock and both he and the
blonde spun to face Isobel. He shouted something and
the woman nodded, then she disappeared and
reappeared by the cage.

"I'm Elsa. Faolan told us you were in trouble. Hold
on. This might hurt!"

The cage crashed to the stone floor, tossing her
against the heavy bars. It didn't matter. She sobbed out

a breath, impatient for her release. The door was difficult. Elsa had to go and find something and returned with a heavy bar which she struck to the lock repeatedly until with a loud snap, the lock and chain fell to the floor.

"Now, come here, Bryson—he needs you. Wait, you're hurt!" Elsa dragged her to the side of the fighting, sliced her bonds, and crouched beside her breathlessly. "How bad?"

"Bad. I need—blood."

Elsa nodded. "Does it matter who from?"

"I would form a bond with you if you—"

"Not me. Jamie would freak. How about him?"

She pointed to a warlock fighting off Jaxon, she realized with a start. Joey shocked her by appearing behind a man and attacking him. The small woman fought well, keeping herself far from the other's blade and downing him easily. She also moved closer to Jaxon with each step so they flowed together. *How many have come?*

'As many as I could call. Drink, quickly!'

"Yes, he will do, but—"

"Hold the phone on that." Elsa disappeared and reappeared behind the warlock and hit him with her large metal bar. He crumpled to the ground. She spoke to Jaxon who, after exchanging words, took on another man in a sword fight. Seconds later, Elsa dropped the warlock at her side. "Here. Drink."

'Yes. Drink! Faolan is your nephew, he is here. Hurry, you are weak!'

Isobel blinked then bent and pierced his neck, drinking until he was nearly gone. Only then did she stop. Her wounds began to close. The loss of blood was still great, but now she could see clearer, hear the sharp sounds of combat better, and best of all, rise to her feet. "Faolan is here?"

"Yes. You are his...aunt, but he is ours, you know? Jamie and I are his parents, if you understand?" Elsa squinted at her, but her words weren't meant to be cruel or unfriendly. "He means a lot to us."

Isobel understood that. He meant a great deal to her. And she knew through her bond with Bryson that Faolan was important to him, as well. "You love him. I understand. Where is he?"

Elsa grinned quickly but said, "Hiding. Look for nothingness and that is him, but right now we had better aid Rowan and Bryson."

Isobel agreed. She took a second to grip Elsa's hand. The touch startled the young woman. "Thank you. I will be in your debt if we live through this."

"*I'm* living through this. I recommend you do the same." Elsa squeezed her hand and smiled. She glowed when she did that, as if her soul shone through. "We've survived worse. Aidan is here," she whispered. "Is that okay? Should you leave?"

"No, he has pardoned me." Isobel sensed Aidan above them, but Elsa had felt him first. It intrigued her, but she lost her focus as her king's presence intensified.

A door slammed open at the top of the circular staircase. With a blast of cold the room grew silent — even the last remaining fights stilled and the combatants stepped away from each other to gaze upward.

Aidan swept down the stairs, a blonde woman a few steps after him. He waved his hand, just that and Warren was plastered to the floor, his head pressed so tightly that he gritted his teeth.

Rowan went to one knee, arm over his chest. Every Vampire in the room followed, except Joey and Elsa. The big Lykae warrior walked over to Elsa and stood by her side. Jaxon grinned from where he had taken a knee, but Joey crossed her arms.

Bryson was bloody, his hair sweat drenched and his shirt ripped in several places, but he never looked more handsome to her. *'You are harmed?'*

'No. It is not my blood.'

The woman behind Aidan, a Vampire, but also more, a witch, Isobel guessed, touched his shoulder. Aidan must have loosened his grip slightly on Warren, for he was allowed to move his head a fraction. *'Aidan's bride, Allie.'*

'She is stunning.'

Bryson sent her a denial. *'She is pale compared to you.'*

She smiled but inside shook her head at Bryson's silliness. *'She is our queen. It is right for her to be the best.'*

'She is not the best, but we will discuss this later. Aidan will need our support now.'

"So, it is true." Aidan paused at the last step, his head held high, silver eyes flashing. He was a true king. A warrior of strength and courage she was proud to call her king. "Rowan, it has been long. I would not have my uncle kneel before me. Nor anyone. Rise please, this is not required." He pulled Rowan up with a firm handhold and gripped his shoulder. Everyone else rose slowly. Jaxon winked at his Joey, and Elsa lifted a brow, as if she didn't agree with Aidan.

'Elsa and Joey have not seen Aidan at his best.'

'Ah...and they judge him?'

'It is a different age. They are independent.'

She tipped her head to regard his steady expression. He was laughing inside, but there was no evidence of it on his handsome face other than his flashing eyes. *'You enjoy their disrespect.'*

'They are refreshing, don't you agree?'

'Yes.' He laughed through their bond, warming her.

Aidan had moved to stand, speaking quietly to Rowan. "Come, counsel me on this tragedy, for it is a long unhealed wound that has been laid bare again."

"Perhaps, now that it is, we can finally find healing." Rowan bowed his head once and accepted the honor Aidan bestowed on him by gripping his arm in turn. The similarities between the two men were stunning. It was clear that here stood two men of close heritage and power. "You have grown into a potent king, Aidan. I would honor you even if you had not taken the throne, for it is your grandfather, my father, I see in your eyes."

Aidan flashed a smile, but it was gone quickly. "Rowan, Alexandria, and I are pleased you are once again here." Aidan gestured to his bonded.

"Aidan speaks highly of you, Rowan. I have many questions about these Dragon Guards…"

Her words brought a true smile to the old warrior's face. "I would be honored to answer any of your questions, my lady." He bowed over her hand. "After we have dealt with sadder things, I can share with you all you wish to know."

"Rowan," Aidan drew his uncle closer. "I think that you wish to share the blame of your brother's guilt. I will not allow this. Gideon has acted on his own, made his own decisions, and, in fact, has laid down the road he has traveled by himself. It is not from lack of your trying that he did not turn back. Every darkness has a light, Rowan. Gideon perhaps is our darkness."

"It's true, Rowan. Aidan doesn't hold you accountable for your brother's actions. How could he?

You have suffered because of him, too," Allie said softly.

Rowan bowed his head again then straightened. Isobel thought he stood taller, taking his place next to Aidan's side.

"Gideon," Aidan called. "Come to me."

Gideon — Warren — stood woodenly, and just as stiffly, walked to where Aidan waited at the foot of the stairs.

'Will he kill him now?'

'He will die, but I believe Aidan wishes to free the boy, Warren, of him.'

She considered that. *'Warren may not thank him for it. He is a passenger to all Gideon has done.'*

'We shall see. If it is possible, we should try to save him.'

Aidan raised his hand and stopped Gideon a foot from him. "Gideon, I wish you to leave this body."

"I *own* this body." Tension flowed from every inch of him. His shoulders were hunched, his hands fisted at his sides, and clearly Isobel could see sweat dripping along his jaw. "This is mine. My right!"

"You do not own this body. Nor do you deserve it. Release it. Show yourself to me as you are now."

The body Gideon possessed trembled as Gideon fought Aidan. From behind his clenched jaw, he cursed Aidan. But Aidan held firm. Without speaking again his eyes flared molten silver.

From the side, a bright light appeared suddenly where a dark wall of stone stood. Out of the shimmering glow a room became clear, then Circerran, Aubrey and Emerald. Jack towered behind his mate, appearing fierce and protective.

"You know I'm not exactly sure I want you mind-speaking me, Allie, but it seems like you've calmed things down a bit. Come on, let's see what the Vampires are up to now."

Joey covered a laugh with a cough, but Elsa didn't. She tipped her head up and her mate kissed her on the lips.

'They do not like…us?'

'They are both new to being Vampires, and Jamie, Elsa's mate, enjoys rubbing it in that she was a wolf first, then a Vampire.'

'Ah… And where is Faolan?'

'He hides until it is safe. Is that okay?'

'Yes, of course.' Bryson held her hand, brushing her fingers with his larger, stronger ones. *'I would not want him here, but with this much power, he is protected.'*

Emerald, the strawberry-blonde witch, hung back until Circerran called her name. "Emerald, I think these few are yours, are they not?"

Circerran had stopped by the kneeling and captive magic users. Emerald glanced at one upturned face then another. "This one and this one are Scarlet, but that does not make them mine."

"Right," Circerran muttered.

"They are the same ones we ran into before," Jack said, glancing at Bryson, who nodded. "Maybe we've collected the last of them?"

"We can hope," Bryson replied.

"So, soul removal." Circerran came to stand by Aidan and Allie, staring from them to the still tension-filled Vampire. "It *can* be done. You know that, Allie."

"Yes, but we need help doing it. One witch is not enough. Even Aidan would have to harm the body to release the hold Gideon has on him."

"It is true. Gideon has forced Warren into a small, very small space in his own mind. He cannot answer my call, and Gideon is fighting me."

Aubrey stepped closer but not within touching distance of them, Isobel noticed. "We need to ensure the host doesn't suffer."

"That is what we are worried over," Allie explained.

"It's more than that, though." Circerran shared a look with Jack, who stiffened and moved closer to her. Without speaking, the couple appeared to form a solid front. "When we remove Gideon, Warren will be… Well, let's just say it will be a shock. We don't want him to lose his cool and strike out like you would if you were having a nightmare and someone woke you."

"Ah," Aidan said. "Respond with instinct?"

"Yes. He's been a captive, too, right?" Circerran said when Aidan frowned.

"He has suffered but he will survive." Aidan folded his arms. "Can this be done?"

Circerran and Aubrey both glanced at Emerald. The witch walked up and hesitantly touched the Vampire Warren on the forehead.

"Don't move!" Aidan's command slashed through the air like a whip.

Isobel jumped at the order, but Emerald didn't even blink. "He is in there, still, the man, Warren, fighting Gideon. That will help…" She closed her eyes, tipping her head down slightly. "Gideon is strong. Where will you have him go, once he leaves this body?"

"We will create a casting," Aubrey said, walking up closer to Emerald. She held up a small silver box lined with intricate carvings on all six sides. It was the size of her palm. "You pull him free, I will drive him in and

Circerran will close him inside. Then it is up to you, Aidan, to do what you will with him."

"This casting will hold him?" Aidan appeared doubtful.

"For as long as you wish, but I would not test that. I would ditch him as soon as possible." As Circerran spoke, Gideon trembled harder. His eyes rounded, showing the whites even as his square jaw bulged and his head tipped back on his broad shoulders, as if he struggled to carry a heavy weight.

"We must proceed." Emerald touched Gideon on the middle of his chest and whispered something musical. His tension dissipated. "If you wish him to pay for his crimes, it is now you should do so, for Warren has suffered enough. I will need to barricade him, or else I fear he will never recover."

"Barricade him?" Aidan repeated.

"Yes, he has suffered much trauma. Imagine the things he has had to see and how his body was used to do them."

Everyone near Warren stiffened, but Allie winced. "It would be terrible. He is young, too, Aidan. Let her help him. Emerald, you can do this, I know you can."

"Yes." Emerald waited, though watched Aidan for permission.

"Rowan?" Aidan turned to her mentor.

"I agree this must be done, but perhaps we might outline his crimes?" Rowan gestured to the people present. "These people should at least hear. They are enough to decide his fate."

Aidan seemed to consider Rowan's words good counsel for he nodded. "Yes. From this point on, let no one think that justice has not been served. If Agatha's death and torture were not enough." He gestured to where someone had covered Agatha's body with a white linen cloth. "Then what was done centuries before, to an entire village, as well as Isobel's brother, Jorge, should suffice. Jorge *and* his bride were tortured, their souls left to wander. Tonight we will repair that wrong, as well as sentence this man, Gideon, to eternal imprisonment. All those who wish to speak for him, may."

No one, not even the few magic users that remained in custody, offered a word in his defense. Gideon, in Warren's body, couldn't move, but hatred shone in his eyes, hatred and malice. If he could break free, he would have smote them all. Isobel's worry for the man, Warren, increased.

Aidan bowed his head regally. "Then so be it. Circerran, this man has been found guilty of crimes against his people, as well as others. I, his king and rightful ruler, sentence him to eternal imprisonment or until such a time as I deem his soul has suffered enough and set it to the four winds to never again take shape."

Images of Tessa and her babe filled Isobel's mind. Their deaths had been brutal, their suffering horrible, and yet, even with this sentence, she felt Gideon had not eased the ache for revenge.

'Nothing will, my love. Only living a long, happy life will ease this pain. Jorge will be free soon, as well.'

'Do you think so?'

'I know he will.'

"Circerran, be prepared. He is strong. Aubrey," Emerald said quietly, "he will fight you and he is ready."

"Aye, I know," Aubrey whispered in her soft brogue. "You see to Warren. His mind willnae be able to withstand the loss after fighting him so long."

"I will take care of Warren," Emerald said quietly.

Isobel drew a nervous breath. So much had gone wrong. This was too close to being over for her to trust that it would be easy. The witches gathered round Warren and, as one, linked hands. From palm to palm light spilled, green, blue and red, then grew too bright to behold. They began to chant in lilting, sweet voices that grew as they continued.

From Aubrey came swirls of blue circles seeping from her exposed hands and temples and out from her body to mist around Warren. Circerran's magic was brighter, sharper like a jewel as it hung green and dark over his body. Emerald's was a hazy red smoke that billowed up and circled him like a snake, growing denser as it reached his head. Their chants crested on a shout, which they repeated louder and louder until, with the third call, Warren fell to his knees. Circerran and Aubrey linked hands while Emerald cupped Warren's skull between her hands, her head bowed, almost touching his as she continued to chant.

"What the hell...?" Jaxon muttered.

"What is she doing?" Jamie asked quietly.

"Emerald is binding Warren so he can recover," Allie said. "It is almost over. Circerran has Gideon now. He is fighting still, but Aubrey is stronger."

"They are all wicked cool," Joey whispered, winking at her. "Almost as cool as we are."

"Not even close." Jaxon grunted when Joey jabbed him with an elbow. "But they can hold their own."

Circerran gasped and stumbled back. Jack caught her and bent his head to speak to her. She shook her head and answered. Aubrey sighed heavily and brushed her hand over the silver box. Green eyes flashing, Circerran seemed to lose focus, then with another shake of her head she closed her eyes. "He's in there."

Aubrey nodded and appeared exhausted. Emerald sank to the steps, eyes wide as she nodded to something Aubrey had said. Warren had fallen against the witch, but Emerald held his head to her knees, brushing his light blond hair from his forehead. There was such tenderness there, in her gesture, Isobel wondered at it.

'I know only a little of her. She was at one time a Scarlet witch, like the ones we have here, but Cir has been aiding her in some way or another for years. She is young.'

'Where is her family?'

'She escaped them.'

'Escaped?'

'Aye, not all of her story is clear to me, only bits and pieces from what has happened recently. I know that she, too, will face charges by the Coven Congress. She should suffer no punishment, though, since she has long been out of the Scarlet's reach.'

Isobel was amazed. There was so much she didn't know and understand, but one thing she did know was that the woman holding the man's head on her lap wasn't evil. She was filled with sadness, that was clear, but she was not evil. Nor was she guilty of any crimes that would taint her soul.

"Circerran, are you all right?" Joey asked, breaking Isobel from her thoughts.

Circerran waved her hand, dismissing the concern, but the witch's pallid complexion spoke of exhaustion.

'We owe them much.'

'Aye, we do.'

"She's exhausted, but Gideon is bound. The casting is holding," Jack explained. "We need to leave, this was draining—"

"I'm okay, just a little dizzy, but man, am I done here, people. If it's not ancient, disgusting, evil Vampires, its changelings running amuck, or Lucifer fucking with us. I need a vacation."

"I second that," Jack said, smiling when Circerran laughed.

Everyone except Aidan and Rowan joined her. Even Bryson chuckled.

Aidan stepped forward. "Circerran, you have our—"

"Allie, how do you stand him always being so stoic? Really, seriously, Aidan," Circerran said, handing him the silver box. "Would it kill you to smile? You just defeated a gruesome creature, with our help, and made things right, almost, with one of yours. I'd say it's Miller time."

"Almost?" Jack muttered, anchoring his arm over her shoulders.

Aidan laughed, but it was a short one. "I am not stoic, merely serious when the occasion warrants."

"You *are* stoic when surrounded by your people, but we are grateful, Cir, we all are," Allie said with a glance to Isobel.

"Well, we still need to free Jorge, but I think we need a little rascal to aid us with that, right? Faolan! Come on, hasn't anyone told you hiding is for girls?" Circerran called.

Elsa sucked in a scandalized breath and muttered about whipping some witch butt if Cir didn't stop.

Jamie laughed but shouted, "Faolan, we need you here now—"

"And don't listen to her, she's nuts." Elsa laughed when Faolan appeared in front of her. She brushed his long hair back from his eyes with a fond smile. "She's so wrong. Hiding is difficult and someone famous once said, only fools rush in."

Circerran snorted. Jack laughed.

This time, Aidan did as well, and his grin remained. "Faolan, listen to Elsa, it is more difficult to hang back and watch than it is to go in guns blazing."

"True," Allie said, smiling up at Aidan.

Aidan returned the look, and for a brief moment, Isobel saw the man, not the king she'd feared would hate her.

'Their bond is strong.'

'Yes, Allie makes him a better man.'

"I do not own a gun." Faolan grinned, showing his bright smile, minus one tooth in front. It made him even more enchanting. It also gave his words a slight lisp. "Jamie says they are dangerous."

"Really? Did he say that?" Circerran asked, licking her thumb and brushing it along his forehead, where there had been a long, brown streak. "You're covered in dirt from hiding."

Elsa pulled him away from Circerran. "Ew! Don't do that!" She rubbed his head with her sweater sleeve. "Your mouth is not sanitary."

"I assure you, it's better than whatever he's been rolling around in." Circerran sniffed. "And I smell like cinnamon, he cannot claim the same."

Faolan's smile grew and he laughed merrily. "*Claim the same...* That rhymes. But I bathed this morning, Circerran. I am clean."

"Oy, I do not know about that, pup."

"Cir —"

"She is teasing me, Elsa," Faolan explained. "Or perhaps you," he added with a frown.

"Are they always like this?" Aidan asked.

"Yes." Jamie grinned.

"Everyone loves the boy," Allie supplied. "Including you."

"He is one of ours. He holds the soul of your nephew, Isobel," Rowan explained. "Along with a great deal of wisdom for one so young."

At his words, Faolan stared up at him, then her. She smiled at the worry in his eyes. "He is much more than the soul of my nephew. He is Faolan, which means *little wolf*. But to me, this also means *friend*." For some reason, her throat burned as she spoke, so the words came out roughly. She had to blink, unsure why the room had grown quiet or why her vision was blurred.

'Isobel, are you all right?'

At Bryson's worry, she sniffed back the emotions threatening to spill over. *'Yes. I think so.'*

Faolan hugged her tightly and smiled up at her after a moment of that.

"I knew you would like Elsa. Jamie is fun too. Even Bryson likes him even though he pretends he does not," he whispered so loudly that even Jaxon, over by the hearth, chuckled.

"I like her very much. I am sure Bryson will try harder not to pretend, if you wish it."

"Nah, it's okay. It's a man thing, Jamie says."

Jamie coughed into his fist and Elsa grinned and dabbed at her eyes with her sweater sleeve.

"I am going to free my mother and father, aren't I?" Faolan peered up at her with such trust and something like hope in his eyes she couldn't respond at first.

"Do you recall them?" she asked.

He scrunched his nose and mouth up with an adorable frown of concentration. "I remember sensations. Warmth and love," he said quietly. "It was like a warm blanket. It covered me." Brown eyes bright, he caught and held her gaze. "I remember you, or your voice, your happiness, then your sorrow and pain. Then your fear before you disappeared." His expression grew solemn. "Then you were back and you were *you*. I was with Faolan and we were hiding, too. Like you." He finished with a bright smile, as if that answered everything. In a way it did.

"So you knew, always knew you were more?" Elsa asked from his left.

He shook his head. "Not more. I am still Faolan. I am *me*, but this…" He touched his head then his heart. "This is also there. A part of me. He keeps me safe, Elsa. When they hurt me." He added in a whisper, "He kept me safe."

Jamie reached out and pulled the boy into his arms. Elsa hugged him, too, so the three were a unit, a small family of three. "Then we will aid him, won't we? In freeing his father and mother."

"My father and mother, too. Just like you are."

The wolf's eyes shimmered. "I can be your father, Faolan, even if that means sharing you with this…with Isobel's brother." Elsa gazed at him as if he'd just said the most amazing thing. Isobel had to agree. Faolan hugged the man harder for it. "I will give it a try, at least," he muttered, seeming embarrassed by the attention.

Elsa wiped at her eyes and laughed. "You always do. Now," she said, clearly trying to keep from crying. "How do we help?"

Everyone seemed to shake off the experience slowly. Isobel waited but when no one answered Elsa, she stepped forward, Bryson by her side. "Agatha has passed on, but her soul lingers. We must burn her body and release her to the wind. I believe this will be enough."

"I thought we needed Gideon dead, as well. *All* the members of the council," Bryson stressed.

"What? What do you mean?" Aidan asked.

"The council has to be destroyed to take off the curse they placed on Jorge," Isobel clarified.

Aidan shook his head. "Gideon was not on the council. There were only five. Not six. It was the king's choice. My father thought it would be more secret with five." He smiled and shrugged. "The council is gone as soon as Agatha is burned. Then your brother will come here, not where he was murdered?"

"He will come to the place where the last body leaves this plane," Aubrey answered. "If this was a curse put down by witches."

"I believe it was," Isobel said. "It was a witch that aided them in capturing me then entombing me."

"The same with me, my dear," Rowan offered. "We can only find out if we try this, am I right? Agatha is gone. Her spirit is too damaged."

"I agree. After what she endured, this last escape will be a relief." Aidan walked over. Fire bloomed on his palm, white, powerful and strong. He tossed his hand down and the flames erupted along Agatha's body. Within minutes, it was done. He flung the ashes to the winds, whispering the required words to send her soul outward.

Everyone, including Bryson, waited, breath held. Within seconds a cold breeze scented with the sea, blew along Isobel's face. Tears rushed her eyes. The shadowy form of her brother appeared. His tall warrior body was ghost like and without substance but more dear to her than life. His eyes, though, his eyes were as bright and dark as she remembered. On his left his bride, her hair flowing down her back, a smile on her lips, stepped from the gloom. They took one another's hands and walked forward, growing more solid as they did.

"Sister. I knew you would not fail us." Jorge's dear voice sounded far away, but, like him, brought her such joy that tears fell from her eyes unheeded. "And this, you bring us this." His gaze fastened on Faolan. Tessa clung to Jorge's arm, her own tears falling free as she beheld her son.

"Father. Mother," Faolan said, sounding different, older perhaps, but still the child who enchanted so many of the immortals present.

Jorge blinked past his own shimmering tears and grinned. The boy went to him and they hugged for a brief moment. Her brother gazed down at Faolan with wonder on his face. He brushed the boy's hair from his eyes. "You have done well. So strong and big, so brave you have been."

Tessa crouched in front of Faolan and took his hands in hers. Her blue eyes overflowed with unchecked tears. "My son." She shook his hands and gave him a fierce smile. "I knew you would not leave this earth. I knew you would survive. I willed it with all my hope."

"I felt it, Mother. I tried to do well."

"You have done well," Tessa said, hugging him hard before setting him in front of her again as if she couldn't lose a moment of seeing him.

"And you are happy, son. That is all we wanted for you." Jorge helped Tessa to her feet and, arm around his bonded, he took Faolan's hand.

"I am happy." Faolan nodded eagerly. "I have a family now, see?"

"Yes, yes, and we thank you, all of you," Tessa said, nodding to the group of immortals witnessing their private moment.

"My king, you would have been a king I would have followed anywhere," Jorge said and took to his knee, arm crossed over his chest.

"Rise, Jorge, it is I who have wronged you and yours. I will see that your son is treated much better, as is your sister." Aidan shook his head. "I will do all I can to ensure Faolan has all he needs, if ever he is in want. Jamie and Elsa are strong and will guide him right."

Tessa smiled warmly at Elsa and Jamie, hugging Faolan again and whispering to him. But Isobel could see that their time was short.

'Can they not stay?'

'You know they cannot. If they could, they would.' Bryson fortified her with his love and strength, something that helped ease the panic at the thought of missing Jorge and Tessa all over again. *'You will always have them, here, in your heart.'*

'And you.'

'And me. You saved me, Isobel. You gave me a heart.'

'I love you.'

'As I love you.'

Jorge rose to his feet and gave Aidan a grin she'd not seen for far too long. "Thank you, Aidan. We can go in peace now, knowing our son is well cared for. Faolan." Jorge drew his shoulders back. Faolan copied him. "A good name, a solid name, thank you," Jorge said to Jamie, then to Bryson he said, "Love her well for you will never have long enough."

Isobel's panic rose. He was leaving now.

"*Sister*. Our love for you is without end. Because of you, we have this," Jorge said, growing dimmer as he spoke. "Do not think of me being gone from this world and no longer me. Think instead of me going ahead to another plane, so that when you do decide to leave this one, I have paved the way for you."

The old tease was there, in his voice, the cajoling bigger brother who could get her out of bed or push her to make her mark in this world.

"Or else I will come and carve my own path, with my bonded, beside me."

His grin returned and he bowed his head slightly. "It will be so, then. Until we share the same path again, sister, we both have much to do."

Tessa smiled up at Jorge then to her. "Sister, you always had much to do and you always did it well. I have tried to be with you this long time. Through the centuries I was able to come and go but never for long. But when I did, I hope my love was felt and aided you in your darkness."

"It was." And it had been. Only Isobel hadn't understood until now what had led her on dreams of better times. Now she recognized the presence of Tessa, the light, sunshine and happiness that was so much a part of the woman. *The dreams. The times I had drifted in the sun, that was Tessa, aiding me when I was at my most desperate.*

'Then I have much to be thankful to her for.'

Tessa seemed to grow brighter and Jorge hugged her tightly with both arms. "We must go now. Faolan shall do great things, Rowan, wait and see."

"Jorge. Tessa, my blessings," Rowan whispered, sounding as choked up as she was.

Too soon, their shadows were gone and in their place only the scent of the sea, the one place her brother had found happiness with Tessa, and for a short while, with her, remained.

No one spoke after, but through their link, Bryson filled her with warmth and shared with her his love until she felt ready to burst with it.

Faolan sighed, breaking the spell. "They are gone. But I think they are happy. I never remembered how tall my father was, Jamie. Or how much my mother looks like you, Elsa. Beautiful."

"Oh, Faolan." Elsa hugged him tightly, but over his head she met Isobel's gaze and she smiled. There were tears in her eyes, but most of the immortals were silent, the couples closer she noted, at the witness of such a connection.

Even Circerran seemed touched. She ruffled the boy's hair and said, "You are such a sweet talker, pup. How about something to eat? Bryson probably has chocolate, or Aubrey probably has some candy..."

The tension dissipated at her words, and with it, the sadness. But the love Bryson held for her remained, a steady warm glow that filled her where once there had been only emptiness and sorrow.

'You've saved my heart.'

'No, I did not save your heart, Bryson. You gave me yours.'

'And you will keep it safe, I know.'

'Forever.'

Epilogue

"I am unsure what this ceremony means, Bryson." Rowan picked up a long stick that Bryson had put different sizes of meats and vegetables on. "My need to eat food has much diminished."

"It is not a ceremony. It is a barbecue. It's something to do when we have company over on this day. Isobel likes it," he added with a glance at his happy bonded. She sent him a quick smile and a burst of love through their link.

"And this is your wedding celebration?" Rowan set down the stick and regarded the yard, where Faolan, Jamie and Elsa were setting out a picnic table and chairs for their company.

"Yes. We wanted something simple."

Today Aidan would come and with him Allie. They'd had word from Allie's sister, Bridget, and had cause to relax in their worry for the couple. Bridget had not killed Rhys yet, at least, but they had not come any closer to freeing her of her curse.

"Bryson? Where should we put this?" Jamie held the banquet-style table over one shoulder.

"Isobel?" Bryson turned and she was there, wrapping her arms around his waist. "Ah, there you are."

"I am always here. Now, I think that table should go over there, under those willow trees. Elsa said it would look pretty."

"Then I'll put it there. She's gone to get a tablecloth and I'm sure anything else she can find to make it look pretty." Jamie grinned and headed off to situate the table.

"Rowan, this will be good for you. You are spending too much time alone again. Even Faolan is tired of always visiting you in your aerie."

"Aerie? There was once a school named thus —"

"It is not because of the school but because your place is so high up, like an aerie." Faolan handed Rowan a piece of cheese and stuffed two into his mouth.

Rowan regarded the aged Cheddar as if it might bite him. Faolan assisted by lifting it to the man's lips. "You eat it. Like this." Faolan swallowed quickly and took another bite of his cheese, chewing with exaggeration. Bryson almost laughed aloud.

'Do not! He is nervous around us now.'

'I will not, but Isobel, admit it, Rowan needs to learn more about this century.'

'Perhaps.'

"See?" Faolan prompted. "It's good."

"Ah, I do realize how to masticate food, young sir." Rowan took a bite, slowly, and with a studied expression of patience, chewed. After a moment he lifted his dark eyebrows and hummed. Regarding the

Cheddar again, he turned it this way and that. "Not bad. I suppose with wine this would be enjoyable."

"Jamie says wine makes everything more enjoyable, especially with Elsa."

"Boy!"

Faolan jumped at Jamie's shout and raced off before Jamie could catch him. Bryson busted up, wiping at his eyes when Jamie nearly slipped on the wet grass trying to reach Faolan. It was funnier when Elsa arrived and Faolan ducked under her protection. Jamie stopped short and towering over her, nose to nose, though he must have gotten a lecture because he grimaced.

"He is adorable," Isobel said at his elbow.

"The boy? Of course."

"No, Jamie. He loves the boy but enjoys teasing him, as he does Elsa." At her words, Jamie scooped both up in his arms and threatened to throw them into the small fountain. Both of his victims broke into giggles.

"You should not think another man cute," he teased.

Isobel blinked up at him, all innocence. *'Why is this? You are not cute. You are handsome and strong.'*

'I am not cute?'

She smiled and memories of their night before eased between them, each one so erotic he grew aroused within seconds. *'You are this, not...cute.'*

He hugged her tightly and growled into her ear. "You are more than I ever deserved, but I will love you forever."

"All right, enough of that, didn't you two have a full month to carry on like that?" Circerran called from the gate. The back yard to Bryson's Seattle home was built with twenty foot shrubs around the entire property, except where he had cut out a gate. This far from town, hidden with spells and surrounded by his hounds, they were safe. Even from witches. He turned with Isobel under his arm and grinned.

"We will never have enough of that," he stressed, earning a shocked gasp from Isobel.

"True, man, true." Jack sauntered over, giving him a firm hands clasp. Circerran smiled and Bryson noticed the stress and exhaustion was missing from her gaze. "Rest has done you good."

Bryson accepted the silver and white wrapped gift Jack held out, touched by their thoughtfulness. "Thank you."

"We had a mini vacation, too." Circerran let Jack drape his arm over her shoulder.

"We thought it best before more shit hits the fan," Jack added darkly.

"And there will be?" Bryson asked.

Jack shrugged. "Never know, right?"

"Come, no talk of these things now," Isobel insisted. "Circerran, would you like something to drink? We have some wine that Rowan supplied. I believe it is considered very old."

"As old as Rowan? I'm in, if so." Jaxon walked up to smack Rowan on the back like a long-lost friend. "Old man, how's it hanging?"

"Jaxon," Rowan said stiffly then warmed to bow politely to Joey. "Joey, you look as enchanting as ever."

"Rowan, you are always so sweet. How do you tolerate Jaxon teasing you? I would advise you remind him how much stronger you are than he is," Joey said in a loud whisper.

Jaxon grinned and raised his eyebrows.

"I would never shame your mate with a display of how easily I can make him kneel."

Bryson sputtered on his sip of wine. Joey made an 'oh' and turned to mouth *'easily'* to Jaxon then hugged him with a giggle.

"Dude, that was beyond excellent," Jaxon said, not offended at all. "You're getting the hang of this age. See, I told you, Bryson. He'd come along. Now, where's the food?"

Isobel laughed lightly at his side, happiness radiating from her. *'He is a good man.'*

'He has always been a good man, but Joey completes him, complements him, I would say.'

'I agree. Rowan needs the same.'

'We are not matchmakers, my heart.'

She hugged him tighter. "Perhaps not. Will Aubrey come? And Emerald?"

"Aubrey and Tabbie will be here. Aeros had some things to take care of first. Emerald, though..." Circerran grimaced. "She has been called in for charges placed on her coven. They are being disbanded, some of them imprisoned."

"But not her." Isobel's worry grew when Circerran shrugged uneasily.

"I am not certain. I will go tomorrow, then I'll know more."

"But she aided us and helped Warren. We were told she even has been aiding him still." Isobel stared from him to Circerran, who winced.

"I know. She's a good healer, a good listener. But I'll know more and when I do. Trust me, I'll call you if she's in a bind."

"But for now, we need to relax and celebrate your wedding," Jack said, raising his wine glass.

Jamie and Elsa joined them, along with the others until in a circle their guests raised their glasses, toasting to a happy union. Bryson felt his heart grow too big, as if his chest had no room for all the joy he felt. Isobel hugged her arm around him tighter and reached up to kiss his jaw. It was good. It was beyond good. It was more than he had ever dreamed.

Hours later, he still believed so, especially sitting with his bonded on his lap, her hand toying with the buttons of his shirt as they talked to their friends.

"You two are going to be happy," Elsa said suddenly.

Everyone was gathered around, talking quietly or watching the fire dying down in the fire pit. They had all sampled Rowan's excellent wine, except Faolan who had toasted them with his cup of soda. Most of the food had been eaten, then more had been brought out until everyone was content.

"Do you think so?" Isobel asked.

Bryson heard the contentment in her voice and kissed her hair. The night was perfect.

Jamie had manned the grill, with Elsa beside him, helping him keep the meat and vegetables from falling between the bars. The couple had laughed and carried on with Jaxon and Joey for most of the night. Bryson thought Joey and Elsa would soon become close friends, along with Isobel. They had already planned a shopping trip with Star, a fashion diva if ever there was one. She had been invited, but Ranger and Star were aiding Alrick with something he wasn't sure he wanted to know about. The wolf pack was in trouble. Jamie had shared some of it with him, but Jamie was a lone wolf and the pack was far removed from where he and Elsa lived in France.

Jack and Circerran had been pleasant company, and when Aeros the Spartan and Circerran's niece Tabithia had arrived, Isobel had immediately been pulled into a discussion with the witches on the heritage of Tessa, Jorge's wife. It seemed she might have been a Jade witch. Bryson had watched more than joined in the talks, not even getting involved in the discussion Jack, Aidan, Rowan and Aeros had on matters concerning the changelings.

"Oh, yes, you two will be *very* happy together." Elsa laughed, calling him back to the discussion.

"I think we will be, but why do you say this?" Isobel asked softly, sounding tired.

It had been a long night, and before their guests had arrived, they had not slept, but prepared food and satisfied other more heated hungers. He found himself unable to go more than a few hours without her, and thankfully, she was as needy. Just that waking he'd risen to her mouth sliding hot and wet down his raging erection. She was in all ways a fast learner.

'I am, aren't I?'

He shifted her so she could feel the effects of how well she learned. She boldly caressed him, knowing exactly how to keep him on edge now for hours.

"Oh," Elsa sighed, unaware of their byplay.

'Behave, soon enough I want you to do that thing you do with your tongue.'

'My tongue?' He sent her an image of her licking a line down the underside of his cock. *'What of your tongue?'*

'Bryson!'

"It's in your eyes. You match. Like Jamie and I. I knew way before he did, but now, everyone sees it. I think Bryson saw it," Joey said dreamily, resting back on Jamie who looked as content as she appeared.

Bryson had a sudden suspicion the two had snuck off.

Through their bond, Isobel giggled.

"Didn't you?" Elsa asked.

Bryson nodded but sent Isobel a warning to behave. This time she listened, content to merely lean into him. "I saw it. Jamie was a little slower, but there is no harm in taking time to earn what will make your life complete."

"Yes," Faolan agreed, surprising him into hiding a laugh with a cough. "Even if Jamie made a few mistakes along the way, now he knows Elsa is his, just like Bryson. He made mistakes but now he is yours forever. The *real* forever." Faolan sipped his Coke and smiled when everyone simply stared. "What? It is not what Gideon wanted, *his* forever was forced. Forever is when you love someone and know, no matter how long you are given, it will never be enough time to love them. My father said this, remember?"

Bryson curled his arm around Isobel to hold her closer.

"Faolan is correct," Rowan said. "My brother did not understand love. When his bonded took her life, he thought that he could bind her to him with his...actions."

"This was the reason for the token with *forever* scrolled upon it." Circerran sat up from where she had been quietly regarding the dying embers of their fire. "I could never make that connection. I mean I got it, *forever*," she stressed. "But why *forever* when he killed every victim? Then when you told us this murderer was Gideon... I started to look back to records Sorcha had kept and before her other witches. Gideon first popped up in ancient times. His signature was always this, a token, cursed to trap a spirit. A witch spelled each, not only to call him in when it was placed on the chosen victim's neck, but to bind his bonded to him through their evil. But such things cannot force someone to you if they do not love you."

"Does this mean that somewhere, out there, his...bonded is bound to him? Trapped?" Elsa asked.

Bryson frowned over at Rowan, who shook his head. "No, she has passed on," he said sadly. "She has long since been out of Gideon's reach. These charms, the spells, were meant to bring her back. But he couldn't force her, Circerran is correct. She would not come, and so he kept on, refusing to give up and, when he did, he grew more and more mad, perhaps. Certainly more and more evil."

"But you and Bryson, you will have it—forever, I mean." Faolan nodded. He sat on a big chair, his legs swinging as he slumped forward. But in his eyes the reflection wasn't a child, but someone far, far older. Wiser. "You both give freely, that is what he didn't understand. You can't take it or force it, you have to give it."

"And hope it is returned," Rowan added, winking at the boy.

Faolan grinned and nodded. The gathering of immortals all laughed and Elsa tousled Faolan's hair. Each one of the men and woman around them were comrades, ones he could lose on the next campaign, and yet, he would not have his life any other way. Isobel was just as content and happy.

'We will have forever. I can feel it, Isobel.'

'I feel it too.'

'If I could give you anything right now, anything at all, what would it be?'

He had given her jewelry, clothing, and trips to see the world, but with each gift he only wanted to give her more. Tonight they had friends around them, even Aidan and Allie were here, all of them talking and enjoying themselves. For the time being, everyone was happy. He wanted it to always be this way but knew they would face challenges in their world. He'd face them all knowing his bonded would be by his side. Always. *'You mean more to me than anything else in this world. If I could give you something, anything at all, what would it be?'*

'This. Happiness, Bryson. A family, friends, and someday a child of our own. Perhaps more than one.' His heart sped up, an image of her rounded with their child filling his mind. *'But you and me together is all I will ever want, my love. I am not alone. I am with you. This is worth more to me than anything else you could ever give me.'*

He hugged her closer and took her lips, kissing her deeply as he could without needing to take her to the house. The memory of their first time, him so impatient for her he hadn't even taken his pants or boots off, rose in his mind. Isobel giggled through their bond, joining him in the memory.

'I wouldn't have changed a thing. I will forever know you needed me so badly you couldn't wait to disrobe.'

'I always need you this badly.'

'And I you. This, you, is all I need or will ever want.'

'I will give you a lifetime of this and beyond.'

'Then I am content.' His heart swelled again, making him bury his face in her luxurious hair.

"I will love you forever, Bryson."

"And I will love you as long, Isobel."

Want to see more from this author?
Here's a taster for you to enjoy!

Sisterhood of Jade: In Her Dreams
Billi Jean

Excerpt

Warren stepped out from the shelter of the awning he'd been waiting under for half an hour. Across the street, the witch he'd been following almost every night for the last six months startled. Emerald. An odd name for a witch from the Scarlet Coven. She had helped free him from an ancient Vampire's possession. Since that night, he'd been unable to resist tracking her all over the globe. She stared at him with her hand up, clutching her delicate throat. Afraid? If anyone would be safe around him, it would be her. He owed her.

The street lights flickered on, then off, then burned brighter than ever. He didn't need them to see it was her, yet under their shimmering glow, her freckles were highlighted as if the clouds had moved aside to reveal the beauty of the starry sky. He had memorized each and every one. It hadn't been by choice. Since she'd saved him, he'd been unable to get the witch out of his mind. She'd set up a barrier to hold back the memories of his possession, helping him get his shit together after being a silent bystander to Gideon's carnage. For that, he was grateful. But ever since he'd woken, himself once again, he felt connected to her. During the night, and sometimes waking him from his day sleep, he could feel her, or, rather, her emotions. Tendrils of them, like hints of something more he craved. Fear radiated from her now, either from him being here, or from seeing him. It extinguished suddenly, as if she'd shut off the light.

He met her halfway across the street, confused by the loss of contact. She avoided his eyes by adjusting her jacket, so he wasn't sure what to say. Finally, he cleared his throat so he could speak. "Emerald."

"Hey, Warren."

"I've been looking for you." He'd been trying to find her alone—without her constant witch friends—since he'd come to terms with the fact that he had to talk to her. He didn't want to, he *needed* to. Now, standing so close to her, he worried that what he needed might be something more than talking. The tension, a constant strain on him, eased.

"Oh?" She tucked something deeper in her jacket pocket, then hunched her shoulders and stared at him. Curiosity sparked, he tried to see whatever it was she'd stowed away, but whatever it was, she had it too hidden. "Why?"

Focusing back on her face, he noticed she again avoided eye contact. "It's wet. You're cold. Let's go over there and talk." He pointed to a coffee shop on the corner.

She glanced from him to the coffee shop, then back in confusion. Her eyes were bluer than gray. The color reminded him of jeans that had been washed until they were a slice of heaven to wear.

"Coffee. You drink it. We can go in there and out of this." He motioned to the drizzle.

"You want to go have coffee?" She made that sound crazy. He had the uncomfortable sensation that he'd just asked her out and she was amazed he thought she'd want to go out with him. "Do you *drink* coffee?"

Relieved that his first thought was bullshit, he shrugged. "I drink coffee. I eat food, too." He flashed a smile and her focus landed on his fangs. Interesting, especially when her cheeks flushed a pretty pink under the wash of freckles. She brushed her hair off her face. He couldn't pick up anything from her. Either she wasn't feeling anything or...she was blocking him.

Can she do that?

"I know that." She had slender, small fingers and pretty nails with a thin strip of glitter on the rounded tips, as if she'd dipped them in a bowl of stars. "I mean, of course you eat." He had a feeling her knowledge of Vampires was limited to what she'd seen in movies. It was odd, especially since her coven had a history of dealing with Vampires. "But... I was... I mean, *I am* busy."

He considered that perhaps she *was* frightened of him. She was keeping a distance, and the lack of eye contact had to mean something. Possibly fear. He tried to sense her, but got nothing. Frustrated and more than a little embarrassed, he admitted, "I wasn't myself when I woke, that last time you saw me." The disorientation he'd experienced returned. Chaos. Fear. Anger. Panic. All those things he'd suffered rose to suffocate him. His palms grew moist. His heart raced. The choking sensation of losing control of his own body pulled him under its heavy weight.

"No, of course you weren't," she said, saving him. The memories vanished, replaced by the sweet warmth of the concern he could hear in her tone. "Warren? Are you okay?"

Her worry stabilized him. "Of course." He could only remember scattered bits of waking without

Gideon there, ruling his body. One thing always came to him in crystal clear detail—her sweet face. Only, when he'd fully come to, he'd feared that, once again, Gideon had called him to finish his grisly work. He had shoved her away so hard she'd hit a wall and hurt her head. "I hurt you—"

She dismissed that with a wave of her hand. "You were confused. Don't worry about it. You didn't hurt me. We were glad you were alive, I mean, really, truly alive. It wasn't easy, and for a while, we thought it impossible to get you back."

He took a deep breath, the first one he could clearly remember since waking up free of Gideon's possession. He tried to think of what to say to explain. *She's beautiful, so alive. How did I miss how vibrant she is?* "I thought I'd been called up to hurt you, or finish hurting you. That's why I shoved you away. I know I hurt you. Your head hit that post." She winced, but when she seemed ready to speak, he did instead. "He did that, just to make me pay for trying to get him out of my body." For some reason, once he started explaining to Emerald, he couldn't seem to stop. "I was afraid you were another victim. Sick that I'd hurt you, like that."

"So, you *are* remembering," she said in a musing tone. "That's good."

He blinked, unsure he'd heard her correctly. "Excuse me?"

"You remembering is good. You need to remember in order to heal. So, remembering things that happened is a good thing."

Outraged, he stepped closer to her so she could be clear on this. "It sucks. It's not good. It's as far from *good* as you can fucking get. I want it fixed, better, erase all of it."

"Oh. I see."

At her faint reply, he froze. *I just shouted at her.*

She didn't appear offended as much as drained. With a worried frown, she stared up the street. He wanted her attention back on him so badly his palms itched from keeping them off her.

"Well, I can't do that, and really, if you stopped for a minute, you'd know messing with your mind isn't a smart idea."

His fear that he'd insulted her vanished. Since waking, the anger was always simmering, waiting for him to tap into it. With one sarcastic snip from the witch, all that melted away. He watched her, fascinated to the point where even he recognized it was an obsession. She continued to survey the street with a great deal more interest than the deserted road deserved. It gave him the time to take stock of the situation. *I shout at her. She's offended. I have to be calm. Stay calm.*

"It's been a long night." It was kind of an apology, but she didn't meet his eyes. *Shit, have I blown this? Fuck! Think.* "Let's go inside. I need to explain."

His suggestion clearly didn't please her. But she stepped back, tilting her head to gaze up at him, at last. The shock of her gaze hit, an exciting, oh, so sweet tingle he felt shiver down his chest and angle straight down to his groin. Her cheeks were flushing an amazing pink to match her lips. He couldn't glance away. She had so many freckles, there was even one delicate dot near her full bottom lip, like a droplet of something decadent he needed to clean off for her — with his tongue. He took a deep breath and forced his eyes off, in the pretense of scanning the street. It wouldn't help his cause if he showed her a rampant erection. That would run her off more than his shouting.

"I can't."

He whipped around to face her at the two softly spoken words.

There was a tremor in her voice, a catch. "I mean I can't have coffee." She licked her lips, going near that enticing freckle. All the while she stood, staring at him.

Do I affect her as much as she blows my mind? The thought made an ache of longing burn his throat.

"Sorry, I mean... I'm really busy."

Even as she spoke, he sensed her drawing away. He pushed desperately to feel her emotions, got nothing, then a sliver of fear. His hard-on waned, growing soft so fast he had to bite back a shudder. She *did* fear him.

"I really do have things I need to do. Things that *can't* wait."

Home of Erotic Romance

Sign up for our newsletter and find out about all our romance book releases, eBook sales and promotions, sneak peeks and FREE romance books!

About the Author

Billi Jean was born in California but didn't stay put for long. She's lived in New York, Indiana, Missouri, Arizona, Colorado, Florida, Massachusetts and Vermont. She's lived in and worked from ranches to beach-side coffee shops to the woods in western Massachusetts. Now living and working in China, she continues to write for Totally Bound Publishing.

Billi Jean has been writing since high school when she couldn't wait for Robert Jordon to write his Wheel of Time series faster. As an adult, she still finds herself drawn to fantasy-adventure stories, but with an erotic romance flair. Her books are extremely hot, with a focus on strong characters that are shoved into fast-paced adventures. Her unique style of incredible journeys infused with hot passion leave her fans hoping for more.

Billi Jean loves to hear from readers. You can find her contact information, website details and author profile page at https://www.totallybound.com

www.ingramcontent.com/pod-product-compliance
Lightning Source LLC
Chambersburg PA
CBHW022026260626

47156CB00017B/348